M000235453

SHADES OF BRILLIANCE

THE MASTER'S PROTÉGÉ TRILOGY BOOK I

ELEANOR CHANCE

Darlington Publishing

Published by Darlington Publishing

eBook ISBN: 978-1-951870-06-5
Paperback ISBN: 978-1-951870-05-8
Hardcover ISBN: 978-1-951870-04-1

Cover Design by Dissect Designs, London

✾ Created with Vellum

SHADES OF BRILLIANCE

ALSO BY ELEANOR CHANCE

(Arms of Grace Series)

ARMS OF GRACE

LITTLE LOST THINGS

GRACE'S FAVORITE ITALIAN DISHES

THE COMPLETE ARMS OF GRACE SERIES

(The Master's Protege Trilogy)

DELICATE BRUSHSTROKES: BOOK II

THE LAST MASTERPIECE: BOOK III

(Eleanor also writes as E.A. Chance)

CONTENTS

ACKNOWLEDGMENTS

As always, I must thank Joseph Nassise, my mentor/editor/*Sensei* and NYT bestselling author in his own right, for his invaluable guidance, patience, and encouragement.

I'd also like to thank my talented award-winning cover designer, Tim Barber, for creating this incredible cover in the midst of a pandemic with his first child on the way. You never cease to amaze.

Thank you to my family and friends, who continue to cheer me on to *The End*. I feed off your energy, and you strengthen me in times of doubt.

I must thank my husband of thirty-six years who offered insightful advice for this project. Thank you for always believing in me. I love you and couldn't do it without you.

Lastly, thank you to my readers. None of this would have matter without you. I appreciate your kind and enthusiastic support.

To Jill, my sister, champion, and friend

FROM THE AUTHOR

When I read *The Agony and the Ecstasy*, by Irving Stone, as a young adult, it sparked a life-long fascination with the art and history of the Renaissance. From that time on, I planned to write a novel based in that time period. When I read Tracy Chevalier's *The Girl with a Pearl Earring* years later, a tale formed in my mind. *Shades of Brilliance*, Book I in my *Master's Protégé* trilogy is the result. I hope you enjoy reading it as much I enjoyed writing it.

Historical Information:

Naming Conventions: Italian women during the Renaissance did not take their husband's surname when they married. The father's surname was passed on to his children. This continues to be the convention in Italy today.

The Guilds: The majority of artists during the Renaissance belonged to the merchant class, and in the fifteenth century, were considered more craftsmen than inspired artisans. Master artists owned workshops and operated as businessmen as well as creators. They usually employed several people, including apprentices. Just as other merchants and craftsmen, these artists were required to belong to one of a number of guilds in order to secure commissions and sell their artwork. These guilds were powerful and had their own system of laws and regulations. They governed all aspects of merchant business and also religious aspects of artists lives.

CAST OF CHARACTERS

Celeste Gabriele: (17) Impoverished nanny from disgraced prominent shipping family

Luciano Vicente, Duca: (28) Florentine duca living in Venice, revered master artist, married to Isabella Niccolo

Livia: (19) Beloved handmaid and friend to Celeste Gabriele

Giovani Gabriele: (43) Celeste Gabriele's father, disgraced head of Gabriele ship building empire

Portia Gabriele: (38) Beloved Aunt of Celeste Gabriele (Father's sister)

Cesare Gabriele : (41) Celeste's Uncle – Portia's brother

Marco Gabriele: (13) Brother to Celeste Gabriele

Jacopo Gabriele: (9) Brother of Celeste Gabriele

Veronica Gabriele: (8) Sister of Celeste Gabriele

Bianca Gabriele: (4) Sister of Celeste Gabriele

Sandro Gabriele: (2) Brother of Celeste Gabriele

Maria Foscari: (38) Celeste's Mistress, Pietro Benetto's Wife, Luciano Vicente's cousin

Pietro Benetto: (45) Maria Foscari's Husband

Francesca Niccolo: (46) Luciano's mother-in-law

Isabella Niccolo: (23) Luciano's first wife

Marsilia Niccolo: (19) Isabella Niccolo's sister

Teresa Niccolo: (17) Isabella Niccolo's sister

Sofia Viari : (24) Francesca Niccolo's cousin and Celeste's employer

Signore Rosselli: (33) Sofia Viari's husband

Marcello Viari: (23) Sofia's brother

Elisabetta Vicente: (21) Sister to Luciano Vicente

Giulio Ferretti: (28) Husband of Elisabetta Vicente

Angelica Vicente: (19) Sister to Luciano Vicente

Silvio de Santis: (27) Husband to Angelica Vicente

Diana Vicente: (16) Sister to Luciano Vicente

Umberto Donato: (23) Husband to Diana Vicente

Paolo Fonte: (43) Aunt Portia's second husband

Stefano de Calvio: (18) Luciano Vicente's apprentice

Filippo: (28) Trusted Valet to Luciano Vicente

Luigi : (19) Maria Foscari's gondolier and spy

Carlo Riva: (23) Luciano Vicente's gondolier

Pia: (35) Maria Foscari's housekeeper

Cristina: (17) Maria Foscari's maid

Fiora   : (40) Sofia's housekeeper

Tessa: (16) Maria Foscari's housemaid

Lapa: (21) Sofia's wet-nurse

Adamo: (25) Lucca Farmer

Masina: (21) Lucca Farmer's wife

PART I

VENICE 1473-1476

CHAPTER ONE

VENICE 1473

*C*eleste Gabriele stood on the dusty street, envying the fortunate souls boarding the ferry from Venice to the mainland. Her greatest desire was to join them and escape her wretched life. Fingering the weight of coins sewn into her skirt told her she had just enough for passage to freedom, but that was a hopeless dream. Her five brothers and sisters waiting inside the hovel they called home wouldn't survive a week without her. As the ferry drifted out of sight, she turned to face the door but couldn't persuade her hand to lift the latch.

"What are you doing there, girl?" a voice called from behind her.

Celeste turned to find her aunt glaring at her over the basket she carried. She wore a plum-colored cap with feathers and a gown embossed with preening birds. *How fitting*, Celeste thought as Aunt Portia pushed past her into the house without waiting for an answer. Her lady's maid and gondolier eyed Celeste arrogantly before joining their mistress inside. With all hope of escape gone, Celeste reluctantly followed them.

Just as Portia thrust the basket at Celeste, her brother, Jacopo, knocked two-year-old Sandro down near the fireplace. Sandro landed only inches from the flames and let out a wail. Celeste dropped the basket and rushed to his aid. She dusted the soot from Sandro's legs and carried him to Mamma's rocking chair as four pairs of frightened eyes followed her.

"Jacopo, you'll kill poor Sandro one day," she scolded. "He could have tumbled into the fire."

Jacopo bowed his head and clasped his hands in front of his dirty tunic. "I'm sorry, sister."

Celeste frowned at him. "Are you? Mamma died bringing our precious Sandro into this world. We must honor her sacrifice by cherishing him."

Portia cleared her throat. "Very touching, but I'm not accustomed to being ignored. Celeste, I'm waiting for an answer."

Four-year-old Bianca glanced at Aunt Portia in terror, then ran to Celeste and buried her face in her skirts.

Still ignoring her aunt, Celeste wrapped an arm around Bianca and said, "Jacopo, fetch a bucket of water from the well. Veronica, help Bianca clean up this mess, and Marco, go scrounge more wood for the fire."

As the children scattered to carry out Celeste's orders, she turned to Portia and said, "To answer your question, I was contemplating how much food I could buy with our last handful of coins." Portia raised an eyebrow but didn't question Celeste's lie. "What are you doing here, Aunt? Do you bring news of Papa? We haven't seen him for days."

"I know nothing of my worthless brother's whereabouts. Nor do I care." Portia took Sandro from Celeste and squeezed him so tightly Celeste feared he would suffocate. "Shush you," Portia said when Sandro took up his wailing. "He's a perfect little miniature of your mother. It's a shame he'll never know her."

"Yes, a shame," Celeste said without emotion.

"There's enough food in that basket to last three or four days. It was all my brother Cesare would allow."

When Sandro reached for Celeste, she took him from Portia and fished a chunk of cheese from the basket. He grabbed it and hungrily stuffed it into his mouth.

4

"We haven't seen you once in the five years since Papa's downfall, not even when Mamma died. I feared you'd forgotten us."

Portia blushed and turned away as she dabbed her forehead with a scented handkerchief. "That couldn't be helped. I'm here to take you to work for my friend, Maria Foscari. You're to be her new nanny. Prepare a pot of soup. We'll go as soon as you've eaten. I can't have you fainting from hunger at Maria's feet."

Celeste was tempted to drop her brother and run for the door before Portia changed her mind, but Sandro fidgeted in her lap and looked up with a slobbery grin.

She smiled and kissed his cheek. "How can I go? Yes, the wages I'd earn would buy food to fill our bellies, but the children are too young to fend for themselves. Mamma's dying wish was that I care for them no matter what. I refuse to abandon them."

Portia raised her hand to silence Celeste's protests. "Do you imagine me to be a monster? I've arranged for another to take your place. Maria's last nanny got herself with child from the gondolier. She'll tend to your brothers and sisters for a roof, a bed, and food. You'll take her place as nanny at the Benetto palazzo. Maria is desperate for help."

Portia leaned out of the doorway and said, "Come in, Lorena. Meet your new charges."

A young woman of Celeste's age with long black braids and dark eyes walked in with her head bowed. The bump where her baby grew was visible beneath her apron.

"Thank you for giving me this chance, madam. I don't know what would have become of me." She dropped to her knees and sobbed into her hands.

"Enough of that, girl," Portia said. "Get up. There's work to do."

Celeste helped Lorena to her feet and called for the children to meet their newest surrogate mother. They were shy with her at first, but Lorena soon had them crowded around, all talking at once. Celeste left them to get acquainted while she prepared the soup. She hadn't seen meat in months, and her stomach growled at the sight of the chicken and fish.

Portia brushed crumbs off a bench with her handkerchief and spread her voluminous skirts to sit. She was as out of place in the shabby room as a glorious peacock amongst dull gray gulls.

"It tears my heart to see your potential being wasted in this place. You were born a Gabriele, daughter of the greatest shipbuilding empire in Venice. Your mother and I had such hopes for you. Your father had nearly completed the marriage contract negotiations with Signore Bernardo when Cesare discovered your father's betrayal. Signore Bernardo was old for you, but you would have had a luxurious life. He had no need for an heir, so he would have left you alone in that regard. Then, my worthless brother, Giovanni, destroyed all our plans. When God called your sainted mother home, I blamed Giovanni for that, too. Five children were already more than he could afford. What did he need with one more?"

"Shame killed Mamma, not birthing Sandro, but why dig up memories of our long-dead hopes?"

"To remind you of your noble bloodline. Fortunes change. Futures change. Never forget who you are."

Celeste shrugged and continued chopping vegetables. The Gabriele name meant nothing to her. That life was as dead as her saintly mother. Her only concern was what awaited her at the Benetto palazzo.

"How many children will be in my care? Will my mistress allow me to return home for visits? What kind of mistress is Signora Foscari?"

"So many questions," Portia said and gave a backhanded wave. "Federigo will be your only responsibility. He's in his seventh year and is Maria's youngest. Her other children have outgrown the nursery. Their palazzo equals your Uncle Cesare's, and Maria is proud but fair. She'll be a good mistress if you're obedient and don't disappoint her. Don't expect visits home. Maria has many responsibilities and doesn't expect to concern herself with Federigo."

"We can't expect the grand lady to care for her own child, now, can we?" Celeste said as she slammed her knife down on the chicken's neck.

Portia thumped her palm on the table. "Watch your tongue, girl.

You won't last long with that attitude. The Benetto family is one of the most powerful in Venice. You'll do well not to cross Maria."

Celeste curtsied and said, "Forgive me. I'm grateful, Aunt, and I promise not to bring more shame upon the Gabriele name."

"I wouldn't be here otherwise. Gather your belongings while the soup boils."

Celeste did as she was told, then ate quickly before leaving Lorena instructions for the care of her siblings. She said a tearful goodbye to her brothers and sisters, promising to visit as soon as she could. God alone knew when that would be.

CELESTE FOLLOWED Portia to the waiting gondola and settled into the fur-trimmed cushions. She relished the feel of the sea breeze caressing her face, and the sight of the ships bobbing in the harbor. Only the guilt of leaving her brothers and sisters spoiled the blissful moment. Her quality of life would be far grander than theirs, but at fourteen, Marco was the only one who remembered their former existence. The rest wouldn't know to envy the luxuries she'd enjoy.

Turning to Portia, she said. "What will happen when Papa returns to find me gone? He'll take it out on Lorena. That poor girl has suffered enough."

"You mean if your father returns, but don't fret, dear. I'll see to it Cesare deals with him. That poor girl, as you call her, brought this misfortune upon herself. I'm willing to help her, but don't follow in her ways. I won't be so forgiving of you."

Portia's words offended Celeste. She raised her chin and said, "Lorena has committed a grave sin, but I would never behave that way. I promised Mamma to be a virtuous, obedient girl, and I have honored that promise. She watches from heaven, and I wouldn't do anything to sadden her."

Portia squeezed her hand. "Yes, she was a virtuous woman, Celeste, especially for enduring marriage with my ruinous brother. This, I understand. Forgive me for doubting you."

Celeste nodded but remained quiet for the rest of the trip until Portia tapped her arm and said, "Here we are."

The gondolier eased the boat to the landing and offered his hand to help them out. Celeste stopped at the foot of the stairs leading to the grand entryway, unsure what to do.

Portia hooked her arm in Celeste's. "You may enter through this door today, but from then on, you'll use the servants' entrance. Do you understand me?"

"Yes, Aunt," she said, humbled by the reminder of her place and why she was there.

A maid greeted them and led the way to Signora Foscari in the sala. Celeste glanced at the glistening tile floors that mocked the dust on her tattered shoes. She tucked her trembling hands into her apron and waited for her new mistress to speak.

The signora leaned back in her chair and rested her hands on the intricately carved wooden arms. Her smugness permeated the room, and Celeste silently cursed her father for forcing her to grovel before this woman. If not for his ruin, she would have been visiting Signora Foscari as an equal, not a groveling servant.

Signora Foscari gestured for Portia to take the chair next to her, but Celeste remained standing. Turning to Portia, she said, "The girl is small and seems frail. Is she strong enough to handle the work?"

Celeste was incensed that the signora had called her frail. If she had glimpsed the drudgery and toil of Celeste's life, she wouldn't have needed to ask.

"She's more than capable, Maria," Portia said. "She's been a gem since Angela's death. Heaven knows what would have happened to those children without her."

"True. Such a tragedy." Signora Foscari crossed herself and bowed her head in a show of what Celeste judged as false piety. "She's too pretty," the signora continued. "I was hoping for a plain girl after the scandalous behavior of my last nanny. We'll need to hide those unruly curls, and where does that shameful auburn coloring come from? Those pale eyes of hers will mean trouble, too. They're too bewitching. The houseboys won't be able to resist her."

Celeste felt the blood rise in her cheeks. She couldn't help the color of her hair or eyes, but that didn't mean she was evil, as Papa often accused her of being.

"Don't concern yourself on that account. Celeste is a shy and pious girl. She understands her family's survival is at stake," Portia said. "I wouldn't have recommended her otherwise. Trust me, Maria, my niece will be an asset to you."

Signora Foscari turned her gaze back to Celeste. "You're here on a trial basis only. I'm considering you as a favor to your aunt and to honor the memory of your mother, who was once my dear friend,"

"Yes, madam," Celeste said without raising her eyes. She wondered why, if Mamma had been such a dear friend, Signora Foscari had deserted her in a time of need?

"Just because your father nearly destroyed the Gabriele name doesn't mean you should suffer. I trust you will make the most of this invaluable opportunity."

Celeste choked back her humiliation. "We are deeply indebted to you, madam. My family would be destitute without your kindness. It comforts me to know my brothers and sisters will have full bellies instead of going to bed hungry."

"Yes, very well," she said. "My housekeeper, Pia, will show you to your room and introduce you to my dearest Federigo."

As if by magic, Pia appeared out of the shadows and motioned for Celeste to follow. Celeste made a quick curtsy and nodded to her aunt, wishing she could hug her and thank her. Pia led her down a long hallway to the nursery, then through a small door to a room no bigger than a closet. Nannies usually shared the nursery with their charges, so Celeste was grateful to have private quarters, no matter how small.

"Stow your belongings and wait in the nursery for me to bring Federigo from the garden," Pia said. "I'll explain your duties then."

Celeste nodded and smiled. Pia looked to be roughly thirty, with red, doughy cheeks and a plump belly. Celeste wouldn't have called her jolly, but she didn't appear stern or unfriendly. As head housekeeper, Pia had significant responsibilities in such a large household, but Celeste hoped for her friendship and guidance

Once Pia had left her alone to get settled, Celeste went to the small window overlooking the canal. Venice and the sea were in Gabriele blood. As long as she was within sight of the water, she'd be content.

She turned from her window and surveyed the rest of her room. There was a straw mattress on a wooden platform and two shelves holding covered baskets. She dropped her bundle on the bed and unwrapped her few belongings before placing them in the baskets. With that finished, she spread the blanket on the mattress and laid down to reflect on her unforgettable day. Her head spun from the transformation her life had taken in a matter of hours. Moments later, she heard sounds in the nursery and left her precious new sanctuary to meet Federigo and begin her new adventure.

CHAPTER TWO

$\mathcal{M}$orning sunlight brushed over Celeste's face and roused her from sleep. She threw off her blanket and rushed to the small window in her room. Merchants and workers bustled about on the congested waterways below. The familiar sight comforted her as it had every morning in the months since becoming Federigo's nanny. She may have left her family behind, but she was always home within sight of her beloved canals of Venice.

Turning from the window, she crossed herself and thanked God for freeing her from a life of drudgery and deprivation, then asked for the same blessing for her brothers and sisters. In the first weeks after leaving home, she'd requested permission from Signora Foscari several times to visit her siblings, but she always refused. Her mistress insisted that Celeste's only concern was Federigo and ordered her to cut the ties with the past.

Celeste had bristled at her mistress' command, thinking it cruel to ask her to forget her family. She pleaded for permission to write Portia and ask after their welfare, but her mistress again said no. She offered to inquire about them when she dined with Portia, but weeks passed with no word, so Celeste let the matter drop.

While she imagined her brothers and sisters sitting by the fire with

Lorena, she heard a faint rustling and turned to find Federigo framed in the doorway. Though she had the small room to herself, it was anything but private. Members of the household barged in at will without bothering to knock.

She took Federigo's hand and led him to the bed. "What are you doing up, little master? I was planning to let you sleep for another hour."

He dropped onto the rumpled blanket and pointed to the window. "It's noisy today. I waited in my room until I heard your footsteps."

Celeste sat next to him and pulled him into her arms. Federigo was a pleasant and sensitive boy who craved affection. His mother was a stern, ill-tempered woman who withheld her love to toughen him up for the future he faced. As a third son and fifth child, Federigo wouldn't have many prospects even if the Benettos were one of the most prominent families in Venice. Celeste made it her mission to assure him of a happy, carefree childhood.

"It is noisy, but don't you love waking to sounds from the canals?" When Federigo shrugged, she said, "Let's get you dressed and have our breakfast. After that, you must work on your painting for Maestro Vicente. Your art lesson is in two days."

A cloud passed over Federigo's face at the mention of his maestro. The boy would much rather chase insects in the garden than paint, but his mother insisted on the weekly art lessons. Maestro Luciano Vicente was Signora Foscari's cousin and one of the most revered artists in Venice, as well as being heir to a Florentine Duca. The signora shamelessly boasted to her endless stream of guests that Federigo was receiving lessons from her renowned cousin.

Escorting Federigo to his lessons was the highlight of Celeste's life. The maestro was stunningly handsome, and Celeste's gaze often wandered to his face while she embroidered on a bench outside his studio. He once removed his cap and ran paint-stained fingers through his dark curls. The sight left her breathless, and visions of him soon invaded her dreams. She told no one of her infatuation except the priest during weekly confession.

The other gift of Federigo's lesson was that for two hours each week, Celeste glimpsed a world that few women would ever see. She was secretly learning the techniques of painting from a skilled master. She didn't dare enter the studio, but his voice carried well enough for her to hear his lessons from her bench on the landing.

In the beginning, she just listened and gleaned what she could, but it wasn't enough to satisfy her after a time. She longed to paint like Federigo but had to content herself with snatching discarded scraps of paper and nubs of charcoal from the nursery. No one would view her drawings but sketching by the light of her oil-lamp after Federigo went to sleep gave her immense pleasure. She couldn't understand why the boy didn't share her passion.

Federigo fidgeted beside her on the bed, drawing her out of her musings. "If you work hard and paint for one hour today, I'll take you to watch the ships in the harbor as a reward," she said to encourage him.

Federigo's eyes brightened at the mention of the ships, which were his passion. He jumped up and tugged on her arm, pulling her toward the nursery. She congratulated herself that her ploy had worked as she dressed him for the day.

NOTHING but the murmur of the maestro's voice and the colors splashed across his canvas existed for Celeste. Curling wisps of hair clung to the perspiration on her forehead. Breathing was a distraction. Ignoring the pain in her cramped fingers, she guided the charcoal over the paper. Only moments remained to draw a copy of the painting before Federigo's lesson ended. Celeste worked feverishly until she heard the maestro say, "What is this, Federigo?"

She peeked into the studio and froze when she recognized the scrap of paper in the maestro's hand.

"Celeste drew it," the boy said.

"Who is Celeste?" the maestro asked.

Federigo pointed at Celeste. "My nanny."

The maestro frowned. "Your nanny drew this?"

13

Federigo nodded and stifled a yawn. The maestro brushed past Federigo and walked toward the landing. She trembled as his shadow crept up her arms as he approached.

"This is your work?"

She gave a quick nod, too terrified to speak. The maestro lifted the drawing to light streaming in the window and studied it as Federigo fidgeted behind him.

"Go play in the courtyard," he ordered.

"Stay away from the canal," Celeste called as Federigo bounded down the steps.

"I asked you a question," the maestro said without turning to face her.

His voice was soft and controlled, but Celeste felt the command in his words. She dreaded revealing her secret but dared not disobey.

"I draw to pass the time in the nursery and during Federigo's lessons. Please forgive me, sir, I beg of you. I'll not do it again. You may destroy the sketch if you wish." Her words tumbled out in a rush, and she felt the color rise in her cheeks.

He stepped in front of her and crossed his arms. "You misunderstand. I'm not angry. Please look at me." She slowly raised her eyes to meet his. "How long did it take you to draw this?"

"Two days. I'm getting faster with each attempt."

"Each attempt? You have other sketches?"

His interest in the rough scribblings of a nanny baffled her, but she said, "Yes, sir, many."

He leaned closer to her. "Do you have them with you?"

"No, sir. I hide them in my room."

He studied Celeste for several moments as if seeing her for the first time. "Bring the others with you next week," he said abruptly and strode away with her drawing clenched in his fist.

LUCIANO WATCHED from the window as Celeste helped Federigo into the gondola. A gust of wind caught a loose curl of her hair, and she reached up to tuck it under her cap. Such a commonplace reflex, but the sight mesmerized Luciano. How had he not noticed her in the months she'd been bringing Federigo to his lessons? He prided himself on his keen artist's eye, and few details escaped his notice, but that exquisite creature had somehow managed it. More astonishing, she seemed to possess innate artistic abilities.

He stayed at the window until the gondola floated from sight before turning to the sketch of his latest work. He recalled those early days when his talent had been as untrained as Celeste's. He developed a passion for art when he was very young. By the time he was ten years old, he was begging his father to let him apprentice to one of the master painters in Florence. His father refused. As the only son of a Duca, he would inherit the title and management of their family estate upon his father's death. He needed preparation for such a tremendous responsibility, and being an artist was below his elevated station.

Luciano had no desire to inherit and wished the title could pass to one of his younger sisters, but that was unthinkable. His mother had died giving birth to his youngest sister, and his father had never remarried, so there would be no more sons to take the title.

He continued to pester his father to let him apprentice until he relented when Luciano was twelve, but only on the condition that he promise to take up his title when the time came. Luciano readily agreed to his father's terms.

To avoid scorn from his contemporaries, Luciano's father sent him to Venice, his mother's ancestral home. He arranged for him to apprentice in the Scuola Grande di San Marco under Lazzaro Bastiani. Luciano's father hoped his son's desire to be a painter was a passing phase, but the more he learned, the greater his passion grew.

Luciano had been a young man when he arrived in Venice, and other pursuits had fueled his passions besides painting. While he worked hard in the workshop, he squandered much of his free time in public houses and in the company of courtesans. His two spinster aunts did their best to rein in his behavior, but there was little they could do to stop him.

When Luciano's father received reports of his son's antics, he hurried to Venice to get him back into line and seek a wife for him. That wife turned out to be Isabella Visconti, the daughter of a wealthy merchant.

Luciano's father saw the match as beneficial to both families. Luciano would bring Visconti the Florentine title he craved for his daughter, and she would contribute a substantial dowry. Luciano had no desire to marry but didn't dare oppose his powerful father. Isabella was young and beautiful, if not too sensible. He found her flirtatious manner intriguing after the processional of virginal maidens he'd had to endure while his father searched for his bride. If only he'd known what lurked behind those dark, fiery eyes of hers.

After their marriage, Luciano set up a workshop with quarters for his apprentices on the lowest level of his palazzo that fronted the Grand Canal. On the next level, he created a private studio for himself. He put Stefano de Calvio, an apprentice who had recently reached the level of Journeyman, in charge of supervising the younger apprentices, which freed time for his own commissions.

In time, Luciano started spending most nights on a cot in his studio. Isabella complained that he had abandoned her for his art. When Isabella's father died a year later, her mother, Francesca Nicollo, and her two younger sisters moved into their palazzo. Luciano was glad for the distraction it provided his wife until his mother-in-law began asking why they had yet to produce an heir. Isabella assured her mother that she and Luciano were doing their best. Francesca saw through her daughter's deception and noticed Isabella didn't seem disappointed that she was not yet carrying Luciano's child.

Luciano earned commissions as fast as he could paint them, and soon, his workshop was one of the busiest in Venice. Isabella only grumbled more and squandered his money on extravagant clothes to parade at the constant social functions she attended. Luciano soon began hearing rumors of her increasingly outrageous behavior. What shocked him most was how little he cared. He should have been incensed but was secretly relieved because it meant Isabella left him in peace.

He poured himself into his work to compensate and began seeking new talent to add to his workshop. On that day, he cursed the fact that Celeste Gabriele wasn't a boy he could bring in as an apprentice. He began devising ways to train her in secret if her talent proved to be as promising as he hoped.

~

CELESTE'S EMOTIONS swung from elation to dread as the gondola floated closer to home. She was pleased her sketch had impressed Maestro Vicente, but she had committed the cardinal sin by attracting his attention. Servants existed as voiceless shadows to fulfill the whims of their masters. They were expected to avoid notice, never encourage it, but it seemed no matter how Celeste tried to be a shadow, she was still noticed, especially by men.

She feared Signora Foscari would hear of the encounter at the studio and dismiss her. Her anxiety increased as the afternoon dragged on until she bumped into Pia and dropped Federigo's dinner tray at her feet.

"What's wrong, child? You're so jumpy this evening. Confess your crime and rid us all of your guilt."

Celeste hesitated for only an instant before blurting out the story of what happened at Federigo's lesson. Pia blinked several times, then burst into laughter.

"That's the cause of your nerves? The mistress doesn't care if her cousin caught you drawing on discarded scraps of paper, and I guarantee the maestro has forgotten you exist by now. Clean up this mess and get Federigo a fresh tray."

Pia laughed all the way to their mistress' chambers as Celeste knelt to pick up the spilled food. She was grateful Pia had made light of her transgression. Celeste tried to follow her example and put the incident out of her mind.

When four days passed without incident, Celeste relaxed and forgot the maestro until the mistress called her to her chamber that afternoon. Celeste curtsied and awaited her punishment in terrified silence. Signora Foscari studied her for several seconds before ordering her to come closer. She squeezed Celeste's chin between her fingers and turned her head from side to side.

"How pale you are, girl. Are you ill?" she asked and released her chin.

"No, madam. I ate some overripe fruit in the market and have been off my food," Celeste said and waited for God to strike her for lying. She'd have a new sin to confess at mass that week.

Signora Foscari eyed her before nodding in satisfaction. "Pay more attention to what you put in your mouth. I can't afford to have you sick. Who would look after Federigo?"

"Yes, madam," she said, wondering what would be so terrible if her mistress had to care for her own son for a day or two.

The signora gave Celeste orders to prepare Federigo for a visit from her sister's family the following day. Celeste curtsied but stopped before turning to go and summoned the courage to ask permission to visit her family that afternoon.

"Since Federigo is with his father today, I was hoping you would allow me time to visit my brothers and sisters. I've had no word of them for five months."

The signora scowled and shook her head. "You are part of the Benetto family now, and Federigo is your only concern. I've told you to forget your family and worry about the welfare of my son. You try my patience by nagging me on this matter. Do not ask again."

The mistress waved her off when she nodded. She hurried to her room and dropped onto the bed, heartbroken. She did her best to shake off thoughts of home and focused on preparing her drawings for the maestro. She pulled them from their hiding place beneath the mattress and tucked them into the bottom of her embroidery bag, thrilled at the prospect of showing him her work. She only hoped not to disappoint him.

～

MAESTRO VICENTE KEPT a busy workshop filled with apprentices and only used his private studio to paint in solitude or give instruction to elect clients. She'd never stepped through the studio doorway, but the maestro waved her inside when she arrived with Federigo for his lesson. She sat in a shadowed corner like a statue, hardly daring to breathe. It was a relief when the maestro finally sent Federigo to play in the courtyard.

"You have the drawings?" he asked once they were alone.

He'd never spoken in such a warm and inviting tone to Federigo as he had with her. He usually barked at the boy out of frustration with his inability to focus. Federigo was only eight, and Celeste pitied him but was glad the maestro spoke kindly to her.

When she nodded in answer to his question, he pulled a chair out from the small, rough-hewn table and gestured for her to sit, but she remained standing.

"I cannot, sir. It would be improper to sit in your presence," she said.

"I'll not tell anyone." When she still didn't move, he said, "I command you to sit."

She saw by the glint in his eye that he was teasing her, so she only hesitated an instant before sinking into the chair. She'd never been alone with any man except her father, and especially not with a nobleman.

Maestro Vicente took the chair opposite her and said, "Please place your samples on the table."

Celeste withdrew the sketches and smoothed each one for him to view them clearly. His face was emotionless as he studied her work.

"Have you ever painted?" he asked after several minutes.

She let out her breath and said, "Never, sir. Women don't paint, especially not servants like me."

"Who told you that?" he asked with a grin.

Celeste shrugged. "No one needed to tell me. Everyone knows this."

He stared into her eyes as if trying to penetrate her thoughts. She squirmed and bowed her head.

"Your drawings are extraordinary for someone with no training. Few could have done better, me included."

"Please, do not mock me, sir. The drawings are pitiful. I could never equal your mastery."

"I am not mocking you." He stood and paced the studio, occasionally pausing to examine one of his own paintings, which lined the walls. He pointed to the sketches that weren't copies of his work. "Why did you choose these subjects to draw?"

She was unsure of how to answer. The images appeared in her head without thought or effort. "I merely draw what I see in my mind."

He stopped pacing, and without turning, said, "I want you to paint for me."

She jumped up and sent the chair clattering to the floor. When the maestro turned toward the sound, she righted the chair but remained standing.

"That is impossible, sir. My mistress would send me away if she discovered me wasting time painting. My family relies on my wages, and poor Federigo needs me."

"Federigo," he said and rubbed his forehead. "That child has no talent and little desire to be here. I only give him lessons as a favor to my cousin."

A giggle escaped her lips before she could stop it. Hearing him speak in such a way would have shocked her mistress, but even Celeste recognized that Federigo had no talent.

"The boy is young. His abilities will improve under your expert tutelage as he matures," she said.

"No, you're wrong. Anyone can learn to paint. A genuine artist is born with a talent that no maestro can teach. Listen to my proposal before you dismiss the idea. Start with a small canvas. I'll furnish the materials. How much of my instruction to Federigo have you overheard?"

"Much, maestro, but I cannot do what you ask. Aside from worries of being discovered, my day is full of tending to Federigo and performing other duties as my mistress requires. I arise at sunrise and go to bed long after dark. When would I paint?"

"You found time to draw these," he said and pointed to the sketches scattered on the table.

"Only in small, stolen moments," she said. "I would have to devote hours to painting. Hours I don't have."

"What do you do while Federigo makes his feeble attempts to paint?"

"I remind him of your instructions and encourage him, but my mistress often comes to observe his progress. She would disapprove of me painting alongside her son."

"Then get up earlier and go to bed later. When you return the finished painting, I'll judge your abilities. We can decide on a future course then."

Agreeing to the maestro's plan would mean defying her mistress, family, and everything she'd learned about her place in the world. She was a nothing, a shadow. Even if she possessed the talent he imagined, Venetian society would never accept her into their tight-knit community of artists. Would taking such a risk be worth the consequences? Maestro Vicente thought so, but he had little to lose from the venture.

She was curious to learn how it would feel to hold a brush and put paint to canvas. Would she be a fool to pass on such a rare opportunity? She had to admit that the thought of painting for him in secret was tantalizing. The threat of being discovered made it more so.

Deciding that one small painting wouldn't upset the whole balance of Venetian society, she said, "I have a small window that overlooks the canal. I could paint in the mornings when the sun rises and before I must begin my duties." She glanced at him to gauge his reaction. He held her gaze, and she felt the color rise in her cheeks.

"Your progress will be slow with so little time to paint, but I'll have to be patient." He moved a step closer and lowered his voice. "Don't rush and don't paint for me. Create what you see and feel as if no one will ever see the finished work. I want this to be authentic."

"I'll do as you wish, maestro, but now I must go. My mistress will wonder where we are."

He hesitated a moment before going to collect the materials she needed and handing them over to her. She concealed them in her embroidery bag with the sketches and felt the maestro's eyes watching her as she did. She curtsied and started for the door, but he caught her wrist as she brushed past him.

"Sit behind that changing screen during Federigo's lessons. I'll angle it so you can see and hear me clearly."

Celeste nodded, then glanced at his hand on her arm. He released her and gave a small, backhanded wave. She nodded and rushed out to collect Federigo in the courtyard.

CHAPTER THREE

$\mathcal{C}$eleste stroked the smooth wood of the brush handle before cradling it in her hand. She had been reborn since Maestro Vicente had granted her entrance into his secret and fascinating world. She longed to spend every minute of the day in that world but only had thirty stolen minutes each morning and night. She trained herself to rise before the first rays of light trickled in the window, so she'd have enough time to paint before beginning her chores.

She'd chosen her view of the Grand Canal and the magnificent palazzi that towered over the water as her first subject to paint. Recreating the scene on canvas was a revelation. She discovered subtle variations in color as the sun rose and the light shifted across the rippling canal. The water changed from gray to green to blue as the shadows moved and reflected the varied colors of the surrounding buildings. The shades on the stones also transformed in the shifting sunlight.

She forgot Federigo and her responsibilities that lay beyond the door as she painted. She forgot Signora Foscari and even Maestro Vicente. All that mattered was the brush's feel in her fingers and the image emerging on the canvas. She delighted in guiding the pigments to recreate what her mind envisioned.

Soon she was getting up earlier and going to bed later, sometimes working by the light of her oil lamp. She was only sleeping three or four hours each night. Occasionally, she painted through the night without bothering to sleep. Her work and health suffered, but driven by her passion, she ignored her exhaustion and continued to create.

Signora Foscari discovered her asleep on a bench in the courtyard one afternoon and clapped her hands to wake her. Celeste jumped to her feet and curtsied.

"What's the matter with you, girl? You are as pale as a sheet. Have you caught the fever that's infecting the city? Or are you sneaking out at night for some carnal reason?" She put her hands on her hips and glared at Celeste, waiting for an answer.

Celeste shook her head to clear the fog of sleep. "No, madam. I would never do that. I have been unwell, but it's only a cold. Don't concern yourself with me."

"Are you sure it's only a cold? Need I call the physician?"

Celeste backed away and held up her hands. Signora Foscari's physician killed more patients than he cured. "No, madam. All I need is rest."

"Very well. I'll have Cristina care for Federigo until you are well. Don't go near him in case you have a fever. Keep to your room. I'll have food brought to you. If you're not better in three days, I'll send you home to recover."

She panicked at the mention of being sent home. As much as she wanted to see her family, Papa would punish her and accuse her of starving them with her laziness.

"That's not necessary, madam. Three days will be enough time to recover and resume my duties."

Signora Foscari pulled a scented handkerchief from her sleeve to cover her nose and dismissed Celeste like a diseased rat. For once, Celeste didn't mind her mistress' disdain. She curtsied and hid her elation, forcing herself to keep her natural pace until she was out of sight.

Signora Foscari had unwittingly granted Celeste three days to do nothing but paint. She allowed enough time for sleep and meals so she would look recovered when her quarantine ended. She only had to care for her own needs and not cater to anyone else. Her only contact with the household was when Cristina brought her meals. Long-buried memories of her early luxurious life surfaced, but she wasn't bitter. She was overjoyed at having time to finish her painting before Federigo's next lesson.

She woke on the fourth morning, prepared to return to her life as a servant. Her mistress had insisted that she report to her first thing. When Celeste entered the mistress' chambers and curtsied, the signora studied her intently.

"You appear recovered. In fact, you look stronger than you have in some time. Maybe you believe I work you too hard."

"No, madam. The illness kept me from sleeping well," she said in a rush. "You are a fair and kind mistress. I could not ask for a better one." She would again need to confess for lying.

"Return to your duties then. Next time tell me sooner if you become ill. I'll not have you spreading disease here."

"Yes, madam," Celeste said and hurried out, relieved to leave her mistress to her needlepoint.

CELESTE HANDED Maestro Vicente the rolled canvas without a word two days later. He ended Federigo's lesson early and sent him to the courtyard. When they were alone, the maestro anchored the painting to an easel with wooden clips and studied it for several minutes. Celeste waited in anguish for his impression of her work.

"You did this on your own without help?" he asked.

"Who could I ask for help, Maestro? I paint in secret."

"My most experienced apprentices could not have done such excellent work. Your perspective is accurate, and you've masterfully used shading and color. The brushwork is astonishing. The strokes blend into a continuous movement of color." He tenderly ran his fingers over the fine ridges and valleys in the paint. "It's difficult to tell where one stroke ends, and another begins. Many experienced artists have not mastered such techniques. I've never witnessed such raw artistic genius. I insist you allow me to train you. Leave Maria's employ and grant me the honor of molding your brilliance."

Celeste let the passion of his words wash over her. "How can this be true, sir?" she asked with tears glistening in her eyes.

He moved closer and held her gaze. "God has blessed you with a remarkable gift."

She wiped her eyes and dropped into a chair. "How can I leave my position as nanny? My family will starve without my wages, and where would I live? I can't stay with the apprentices in your workshop."

The maestro stroked his beard. "No, I suppose not. Is your family's situation as desperate as that? I'm acquainted with your Uncle Cesare. His shipbuilding business does well."

"Uncle Cesare is my father's younger brother, but the rest of the Gabrieles ostracized my family. You must know of my father's reputation."

"I've heard rumors. I believed they were exaggerated."

"The Gabrieles have long been revered as the best shipbuilders in Venice. My father betrayed our family by trading with our enemies and squandering his fortune on women and wine. The business passed to my uncle after he banished my father. It has taken Uncle Cesare years to restore our family's good name."

"But surely, the rest of your family bears no responsibility for your father's sins."

She raised her chin and squared her shoulders. "The family turned their backs on my father, as was right, but we ceased to exist to them as well. My Aunt Portia defied my uncle to secure a position for me in your cousin's household. I can't betray the trust she placed in me. For now, we must be content with me painting behind the screen during Federigo's lessons and in stolen moments in my room."

He stared at the painting for a moment in silence. "If we must, but I'm determined to arrange a way to train you. For years I've dreamed of discovering a painter who I could guide to greatness. Who could have known I'd find that artist in a poor serving girl? A girl!" He chuckled and shook his head. "Take more supplies and start again. Attempt a human figure this time. Take as long as you need." He glanced at her face as he handed her a fresh roll of canvas. "You look well. Painting has put color in your cheeks."

She giggled and told him what happened with Signora Foscari. "I cherished that time while I was free to paint, but I must be more careful. I cannot lose my position."

"Then, we will continue as before until I find a better solution."

When he waved her away, she raced downstairs to find Federigo. He was trying to capture a lizard sunning itself on a wall. He looked up when he heard her footsteps.

"Why are your cheeks red, Celeste? Are you ill again?"

She smiled to reassure him. "It was hot in the studio, and I raced down the stairs too quickly, nothing more."

He nodded and dropped the lizard into a small bag before skipping to the gondola. Celeste followed him and settled into the cushions. Her thoughts whirled as they floated home. She could scarcely comprehend what Maestro Vicente had said of her little painting. How could this miracle be happening to her? She closed her eyes with a sigh and dreamed of her next creation.

LUCIANO WAS weary and pensive as he climbed the stairs from his workshop to the family's quarters that night. The echo of his footsteps on the sala tiles was the only sound in the house. He'd stayed in his studio long after Celeste had gone but lost interest in his own commission. He kept returning to stare in wonder at her painting.

He hadn't known what to expect of her abilities. The works of his novice apprentices were usually amateurish messes, as expected. Celeste's abilities had astounded him. She had the skills of a painter with years of training. He was determined to mentor her despite the risk to either of them. He longed to ask his wife's opinion but knew she'd have no interest in a talented servant girl. All she cared for was gowns and jewels.

27

He quietly opened her bedchamber door to see if she was awake, but the bed was empty and undisturbed. He slammed the door in disgust. She was out late as usual. He went to his own chamber but was too agitated to sleep. He lit a lamp and laid on the bed without bothering to undress.

Encouraging Celeste to paint had been rash. How could he expect her to abandon the world she knew and step into an unknown and possibly dangerous future? But how could he ignore her extraordinary gift? Artists like her emerged once in a generation. He couldn't let such a precious gem escape his grasp.

As he lay in the silent room, he admitted that his attraction to Celeste had to do with more than her artistic abilities. In the short time since he'd discovered her talent, he'd also come to recognize a depth in her that Isabella would never possess. He wondered if that resulted from the difference in their social classes or merely their natures. Luciano suspected the latter and hoped to get the chance to find out.

He pictured her face as she had gazed up at him in hopeful innocence. Her skin was as flawless as that of countless paintings of the Blessed Virgin he'd seen. Her speckled, hazel eyes had an alluring brilliance to them, and he was fond of how her auburn curls had a way of escaping her cap. He imagined her hair cascading freely across her bare shoulders and longed to push her locks aside and caress her neck. He would never act on his urges. He valued his marriage vows even if his wife did not but fantasizing about Celeste gave him a thrill he hadn't felt in years.

He closed his mind to thoughts of Celeste and blew out the candle, praying for sleep to come.

HE MANAGED a few restless hours of sleep before giving up and going down to breakfast. He found his mother-in-law eating alone in the dining room, not surprised that Isabella and her sisters were absent, assuming they had not returned home until early morning.

Francesca had informed Luciano the previous day that she was tired of escorting her daughters to endless social gatherings and had persuaded a cousin to be their chaperon. Francesca said she preferred Luciano accompany them but understood his reluctance. He'd made it clear he had no intention of being his wife's nanny.

He went to the sideboard and piled fish with eggs and black bread onto his plate. He sat opposite Francesca and felt her eyeing him.

"You came up late from the workshop last night," she said. Luciano huffed at her without looking up from his food. "It's not a criticism, just an observation. It's nice to see you at home instead of on that cot in your studio."

She leaned back in the chair and gracefully rested her hands on its arms. Luciano studied her face as he ate but found little of Isabella there. His wife took more after her father. Francesca was fair and graceful, where Isabella was dark, fiery, and proud.

"I was working," he finally said. "How else can I keep up with all those commissions you arrange for me?"

She chuckled when he smiled at her. "It keeps that meat on your plate, does it not?"

"And the gowns on your daughters," he said, turning back to his food.

"You know full well that nothing for Teresa or Marsilia comes from household funds. I use the money their father left for their needs."

"True, but Isabella costs more than all of us together. Have you spoken to her as I asked?"

"I have, but it would be better coming from you. My daughter never listens to me."

"And she listens to me? Do your best to convince her she has more than enough gowns to clothe all of Venice." He took a bite of bread and chewed it slowly. "I would like your opinion on another matter. I was speaking with a fellow Guild member yesterday who has a dilemma. It's out of my area of expertise, but I thought you might be of some help."

Francesca stared at him before saying, "May I know who this friend is?"

"No, and when I explain, you will understand why he wishes to remain anonymous." When Francesca nodded, he said, "This friend has discovered rare artistic talent in a serving girl. She comes from a family that once had social standing, but an ancestor squandered their fortune. My friend wants to give her lessons but sees no way to do this without jeopardizing her position and setting all the tongues in town wagging. I said I would ask if you think it's possible or worth the risk for either of them."

She eyed him suspiciously. "And how did he discover her talent?"

Luciano grinned. "He assures me it's nothing like what you imagine. He says this girl has potential, and he wants to train her. Maybe he only sees the growing piles of coins in his coffers from exploiting her abilities."

"Your friend must be mad, but if he insists on training her, she will have to leave her employer, and he would have to provide room and board for her. That would most definitely start tongues wagging. Either that or he would need to find someone to take her in. Few would be willing or able to do that. It's an immense risk to take for the girl. Pity she isn't a boy. Your friend would do well to give up the idea."

"I told him the same, but he says he's never seen a novice with such innate abilities," Luciano studied Francesca for her reaction.

"Then, for his sake, I hope she holds as much promise as he believes she does to make the gamble worth it."

Luciano stood, and Francesca followed. "I must go so I can keep my wife in dresses and shoes." He kissed the top of his mother-in-law's head. "Tell Isabella I expect her here tonight when I return."

Francesca curtsied, then left Luciano alone. Her advice brought him no closer to a solution for Celeste. He grabbed his smock and went to the studio, hoping for inspiration to strike as he worked.

CELESTE TOOK her painting to the nursery one afternoon while Federigo slept and placed it on a spare easel next to his latest disastrous attempt. She'd grown frustrated with having so little time to paint, and since no one in the household paid much attention to what happened behind the nursery door, she felt bold enough to take the chance. Signora Foscari's visits were infrequent, so Celeste knew there was little chance of getting caught.

After she'd worked for an hour, she reluctantly made her last few strokes to finish before Federigo stirred. She was about to lay her brush aside when the door swung open, and the maestro stepped in dressed in a silver tunic under a royal blue, fur-lined cape. Celeste gasped at seeing him dressed in such finery instead of his usual paint-stained smock.

She sprang to her feet and lowered into a curtsy. "I was not expecting this honor, Maestro."

He gently took the paintbrush from her and laid it on the palette. "Get up, Celeste," he whispered. She slowly straightened but avoided his eyes. He cocked his head toward Federigo, lying on the bed behind him. "I'm visiting my cousins and thought I'd see how the boy is doing. I didn't expect to find my true protégé at the easel. What would my cousin think if she found you painting instead of her son?"

"I'm sorry, sir. It was reckless of me to take advantage of my mistress."

He winked and gave a half-grin. "Don't apologize. I'm pleased to see you taking advantage of Maria. Your talents are wasted here. The offer stands for you to leave my cousin's service and answer your true calling."

Federigo sat up and rubbed his eyes. When he saw the maestro, he scampered to his feet and bowed. Luciano laughed, and Celeste couldn't remember a more exquisite sound.

"I'm not your Maestro here, just your cousin. Come, show me your work."

Celeste stepped back and watched them. Maestro Vicente pretended to listen to Federigo, but his eyes were on her painting. After studying it for several minutes, he gave her a look she didn't understand.

"Well done," the maestro said when Federigo finished explaining his work. "As a reward, you may go play in the garden."

Federigo looked at Celeste for permission. When she gave a slight nod, he was out of the room as fast as his legs could carry him. Celeste went to the easel to retrieve her painting and return it to its hiding place in her room. She felt the maestro's gaze on her as she did.

When she returned to the nursery, he said, "What is your vision for the finished work?"

Celeste shook her head. "It's too early, Maestro. I'm not yet sure what I want it to be. I hadn't planned for you to see it at this stage."

"You can't move forward without knowing where you're headed."

Celeste looked away as she thought of how to answer. She had the exact image of her finished composition in her mind but wasn't ready to reveal it to him.

"May I have more time to tell you?"

He studied her for a moment. "I can give you guidance that could save you from making mistakes costing precious time."

"Making mistakes helps us learn. Isn't that what you tell Federigo?"

"I'm pleased to see you're paying attention. I'll grant you more time, but only because you're my favorite apprentice. Let me know as soon as you're ready for me to see it."

Celeste gave a shy smile but said nothing.

He stepped toward her and said, "Please, come with..." but stopped when Federigo shrieked in the garden.

Celeste ran to the window, but it was merely Federigo's brother chasing him with a stick. She laughed and turned to the maestro, but she was alone. If not for his smell lingering in the room, she would have wondered if he had indeed been there or had just been a vision. She dropped into a chair and propped her chin in her hands. What had he been about to say? To ask her to leave with him? She would never know, and that was probably for the best.

CHAPTER FOUR

THREE MONTHS LATER

*L*uciano woke in a foul mood after attending a lavish dinner party with Isabella's uncle the previous night. The evening had been a disaster. Pisani kept pushing food and drink on Luciano until he felt he would burst, but he hadn't wanted to offend his host by refusing.

To make matters worse, Isabella flirted shamelessly with Pisani's nephew, Antonio. Luciano warned her to behave several times, but she simply drank more wine and ignored him. When Luciano finally escaped Pisani, he went in search of his wife. After hunting through the grounds for what seemed like hours, he stumbled upon her in a dark corner, snuggled up in Antonio's arms. They were both clothed, but Luciano wondered what would have happened if he hadn't discovered them when he did.

He dragged his wayward wife home, and they had an ugly argument that disturbed the entire household. They shouted horrible things at each other until Isabella fled to her chambers in tears. Luciano slept little afterward and woke with a pounding headache. He went to the dining room for breakfast to calm his sick stomach and again found Francesca alone.

"You look terrible," she said.

"With good reason. Have you spoken to your daughter? Her behavior last night was appalling." He closed his eyes and rubbed his temples to stop the pounding in his head.

"I heard it was nothing more than a harmless flirtation. My Bella's still a young woman, and she's lonely, Luciano."

He stepped toward Francesca and glared at her. "What she is, Francesca, is my wife. Are you blaming this on me or making excuses for her? It was far more than harmless flirting. If this is how she behaves when I'm present, what does she do when I'm not?"

Francesca leaned away at the force of his words. He regretted losing his temper, but he'd reached the end of his patience with Isabella.

"People are talking, and I'll not have my family disgraced. Don't you care about her reputation and that of your other daughters? Please rein her in, Francesca, or I'll be forced to take drastic action."

He left Francesca staring after him. He would never toss his wife and her family into the street as other men might, but he couldn't stand by and let her make a fool of him. He had neglected Isabella, but countless other men had done the same, and their wives didn't go out making public spectacles of themselves. Isabella had a wild spirit, and he was at a loss of how to tame her.

His mood worsened with each passing hour. He snapped and barked at his apprentices until his frustration reached its peak in the hour before Federigo was to arrive for his lesson. Luciano didn't know how he'd survive the tedious hour with his cousin. Only the anticipation of seeing Celeste kept him from canceling.

WHEN CELESTE and Federigo entered the studio, the maestro ordered the boy to place his canvas on the easel while Celeste went behind the screen.

When the maestro saw how little Federigo had accomplished during the week, he said, "Have you spent one moment working on this all week? You're not practicing. In fact, I believe you're getting worse. I've never seen such a terrible effort. If you don't show improvement soon, I shall speak with your mother about discontinuing your lessons."

Celeste peeked around the screen and found Federigo cowering under the maestro's harsh words. She was about to comfort him when Maestro Vicente gently laid his hand on the boy's shoulder.

"I'm sorry, cousin. I just want you to try harder. Celeste, come here, please."

Celeste's cheeks flushed as she came out from behind the screen. The maestro had never spoken to her in front of the child.

"Federigo, put your canvas away. There will be no painting today. Go play while I speak to your nanny about how we can help you."

Federigo ran out so quickly that Celeste giggled. "You've made that boy very happy by setting him free today."

He turned to face her with a stern look. Instead of cowering as Federigo had done, she raised her chin and held his gaze. He relaxed his shoulders and stroked his beard. She recognized the red-rimmed eyes she'd seen many times in her father and wondered if he'd been out drinking. The thought made her realize how little she knew of his life beyond the studio. Her servant's existence must have been equally alien to him.

"I'm not myself today," he said. "Are you ready to show me your progress?"

He'd been asking to see her work since their encounter in the nursery, but Celeste hoped to be further along before showing him.

"I've made little progress. My mistress watches me and keeps making greater demands. She's growing suspicious. I'm afraid she'll dismiss me."

"Forget about Maria. I'll deal with her if she causes trouble. Please, Celeste, show me your painting."

As always, her heart raced at the sound of her name on his lips. She was defenseless to deny him whatever he asked. She retrieved her painting and placed it in the center of the studio.

"Is this Our Blessed Virgin?" he asked after studying it for several moments.

When she nodded, he stepped behind Celeste and looked at the painting over her shoulder. She described her vision for the completed work. He was quiet when she finished.

She turned toward him and said, "Have I also displeased you today, sir?"

His eyes glistened as he shook his head. "Your talent continues to astound me. You're an extraordinary artist." He leaned closer to the easel and stroked his beard. "Are you copying this from something else you've seen?"

"No, sir. It's my original creation." She was close enough to smell the paint on his stained frock, and her breath quickened to match her pounding heart. "This is how I imagine her." She wondered if she'd disappointed him, so she lowered her head and clasped her hands in front of her apron. He put his finger under her chin and gently raised it until her eyes met his.

"Never be ashamed of your work, Celeste."

The warmth of his finger traveled down her neck and into her chest. She suppressed a shiver and took a small step away from him.

The maestro cleared his throat and turned to the easel. "This is comparable to the style of Lazzaro Bastiani but softened by your female interpretation. I would suggest minor changes in shading where the shadow falls across her face. See, here and here."

He pointed out a few other areas where Celeste could improve, but she heard little of his words as she concentrated on remembering to breathe. He finished and told her to go. She gave him a lingering look and left without bothering to curtsy. She caressed the spot where he'd touched her as she slowly descended the stairs. She could no longer deny what she'd seen in his eyes. It frightened and thrilled her, but only danger lay down that road. She vowed to pour her feelings for him into her art and stay beyond the maestro's reach in the future.

LUCIANO STRUGGLED to lock Celeste out of his mind for the rest of that day by throwing himself into his work, but his effort was futile. He left his studio earlier than usual and went upstairs, hoping to find Isabella there to greet him, but the house was silent and empty.

After an evening meal, Luciano settled down to wait for his wife. He used the time to make notes on his new commissions and his apprentices' progress, but his irritation increased with each passing hour. By the time he heard the women returning, he was livid. As they came into the sala, he asked Francesca and her other daughters to leave them alone. Francesca glanced at him, then closed the door on her way out.

When they were alone, Isabella brushed close to Luciano and eyed him seductively. He ignored her vain attempts to distract him, and calmly ordered her to sit. He pulled a chair around to face her, and Isabella watched him with her chin raised, showing no sign of humility or remorse. Her arrogance angered Luciano further.

"Where have you been?" he asked, struggling to keep his voice even.

"We received an invitation to dine with Cousin Rinaldo tonight, my love. Had you forgotten?" She gave him her most alluring smile before lowering her head.

"I wanted you home when I returned. Didn't your mother tell you?"

Isabella hesitated before answering. Luciano could see her concocting an answer that would pacify him. She couldn't lie since he could easily verify her story with Francesca.

"Yes, my dear, Mamma told me, but we'd already accepted the invitation and we were obliged to go." She seemed relieved at having a legitimate excuse.

"That doesn't explain why you remained for five hours after dinner. If you knew I was waiting at home, you could have politely fulfilled your obligations and slipped away without giving offense."

"We tried to leave, my love, but Rinaldo refused to let us go. Your absence had already offended him. He questioned me about it more than once. I'm tired of making excuses for you, and he has the ear of the Doge, you know. People are talking and wondering why you rarely accompany the family into society anymore."

Luciano stood and glared at her. "I do go into society, but you refuse to accompany me."

"I'm not talking about the time you spend with artists as if they are the only people that exist." Isabella crossed her arms and crinkled her nose. "They're dirty, and they smell. Why can't you just frequent the courtesans like other men?"

"Don't turn this on me. If there's talk of our family in Venice, it's not about me. If the accounts of your behavior that have reached me are true, you have much to answer for."

Isabella dropped her shoulders and lowered her eyes. It was the first time she'd ever backed down from him. Luciano wasn't a man given to angry outbursts, but he didn't regret his words. He'd given Isabella a loose rein in their marriage, but she'd abused the privilege. Though little intimacy remained in their relationship, that didn't give her license to ignore the boundaries of decency.

Without looking up, Isabella said, "What rumors, my love? You know how the hens will cluck. They're bored and need to gossip."

"The reports are coming from other sources. Reliable sources." He raised her chin with the tip of his finger as he'd done with Celeste, but his touch wasn't gentle. "My patience is wearing thin. You bear the Vicente title. Don't disgrace us. You wouldn't want word to get back to my father and bring down his wrath, would you? Curb your behavior before it's too late."

The fear was visible in Isabella's eyes. He took her hand and pulled her to her feet. "Come, wife, sleep with your husband tonight. I don't wish to be alone."

Isabella obeyed without protest and followed Luciano to his room. As he watched her undress, he realized that she had become little more than a stranger to him. She shivered when he pulled her into his arms, but he knew it wasn't from the cold. As he kissed her, he tried to imagine her as his young and eager bride, but the only face he saw was Celeste's.

CHAPTER FIVE

he maestro was aloof and withdrawn in the weeks that followed their intimate exchange in the studio. He didn't speak to her directly or ask about her painting. The only sign that he was aware of her was his instructions to Federigo became increasingly difficult. She sensed that the maestro's lessons were meant for her and not the boy.

Their routine continued this way until the maestro ordered Celeste to sit on her old bench one day instead of entering the studio. When she eyed him in confusion, he said, "Don't fret. I have a purpose for this. I have a visitor coming. Give me your canvas and pay close attention to what he says."

She shrugged and settled into her former place while the maestro began the lesson as usual. Celeste heard voices in the front hall twenty minutes later, and a footman appeared to announce that Maestro Lazzaro Bastiani had arrived. Maestro Bastiani pushed past the footman, then hugged Maestro Vicente and pounded him on the back. The maestro pulled back and gripped his friend's forearms before kissing each cheek.

"Welcome, old friend. Thank you for taking time away from your work to come," he said.

"How could I not come? You piqued my curiosity with talk of this new genius apprentice. When are you going to reveal who it is? It's not this child, is it?" Bastiani asked and cocked his thumb at Federigo.

Maestro Vicente chuckled. "No, he's one of my private pupils, my cousin Maria Foscari's son, Federigo." He turned to the boy. "This is the greatest artist you'll ever meet. Welcome him."

Federigo bowed low and said, "It is an honor, Maestro Bastiani."

"Flattery will take you far in this world, boy," Maestro Bastiani. said and laughed. "Show me what you're working on." When Federigo pointed out his painting, the artist looked at Maestro Vicente and rolled his eyes. "Work harder, young man. That's the only way to succeed." He patted the boy on the head and turned to the maestro. "Now, where's the work of the new apprentice?"

Celeste's paintings of the canal and the Virgin were on easels in the center of the studio. Bastiani studied each one carefully for several minutes.

When he stood back with his hands on his hips, Maestro Vicente said, "Am I right? Doesn't this pupil show promise?"

He gestured toward the canal painting. "Promise? Need you ask? You say this is the boy's first attempt?" When the maestro nodded, he said, "Remarkable. I see shades of our maestro, Bellini, and something more. Are you honest, friend? Are these truly his first works?"

"Indeed. I need your opinion to prove to myself that I didn't see more than is there."

"If this student is starting with such abilities, there's no limit to the heights he can attain. Don't be coy. Who is he? Bring him into my workshop so he can learn under a true master."

The maestro laughed and shook his finger at him. "No, sir. I discovered this pupil. I will be the maestro. My pupil has much to learn."

"That's very selfish of you, but I respect it. It's an exciting prospect. If the student lives up to his potential, it will do much for the reputation of the Venetian school."

"My hope, exactly. When is the unveiling of your latest work, though I don't know how you can outdo the last one," the maestro said?

"Soon, my friend. Soon."

They chatted for several minutes until Maestro Bastiani said he needed to go.

"I don't want to interrupt Federigo's lesson any longer. He needs all the training he can get." He winked at the maestro and headed for the door.

Maestro Vicente told Federigo to get back to work and escorted his friend to the street before rushing back to Celeste.

"Did you hear what he said?" he asked, unable to contain his excitement.

"Yes, maestro, but I am no one and a woman."

"I hoped that hearing another master's confirmation would convince you of your talent. Stop doubting yourself."

"But why has God blessed me with a talent I can never share with the world? Is He punishing me? That would be cruel," Celeste said and looked to him for answers.

"Who knows the mind of God? But don't despair. I'll discover a way to share your extraordinary talent with the world."

She smiled as she fought back her tears. "How can I repay your kindness, sir?"

Federigo dropped a brush, and they turned toward the sound. The boy watched them with wide eyes.

"I'd forgotten he was here, which isn't hard to do," he said and winked at her. "You can repay me by remembering what you heard today. Burn Maestro Bastiani's words into your heart and begin living up to your potential. Forget that you're a woman and a servant. Become the artist I envision you to be."

He went into the studio and left her standing in a daze on the landing.

"That's enough for today, Federigo," the maestro said. "Clean up your materials and go."

Celeste waited for Federigo but wished nothing more than to remain and paint in the studio or even the workshop. As she turned to leave, an apprentice brushed past her on his way into the studio. She had envied no one more in her life.

THE LIGHT FADED from Luciano as he watched Celeste descend the stairs. Bastiani's confirmation of her talent had validated his impressions but got him no closer to a solution of how to make her his pupil. Why couldn't she have been born a boy?

He returned to his easel and tried to work but was too distracted. He went to the workshop and told the workers to go. The apprentices couldn't conceal their joy at being set free early. An open afternoon was rare for them, and Luciano knew they would make the most of it. He remembered what it was like to be full of energy and optimism at that age.

He dragged himself up the stairs to join his family. Unbidden images of Celeste invaded his thoughts as he did. He wished he had known her before being forced into marriage with Isabella, even though his father never would have approved of the daughter of a disgraced shipbuilder with no dowry. He wondered if he would have had the courage to defy his father in the hope of a life with Celeste but speculating about what could have been was futile.

He opened the door of the family chambers to find the women of his household quietly embroidering. Isabella was polite and remorseful, and Luciano was grateful. He didn't have the strength or desire to quarrel with her. He settled in with them and even laughed at Marsilia's imitation of Doge Loredan from Carnevale. It was the first quiet evening his family had spent together in months.

The serenity helped Luciano forget Celeste and focus on his obligations to them. He bore some responsibility for Isabella's behavior and recommitted himself to be the husband she deserved. He relaxed and enjoyed the evening, hoping it would be the first of many to come.

MAESTRO BASTIANI'S reaction to Celeste's paintings spawned a change in her. She let go of doubts that had plagued her and threw herself into her art with renewed vigor and confidence. The brush became an extension of her body. She only felt whole when cradling it in her hand.

She often rushed through her chores until her responsibilities once again suffered. The mistress admonished her more than once for neglecting Federigo, but Celeste had trouble making herself care about her mistress' wishes. Nothing mattered but painting. Some days, she fantasized about accepting the maestro's offer to abandon her position and become his full-time protégé. It was a hopeless dream, but it gave her delicious pleasure to contemplate.

The mistress summoned Celeste to her apartments one day just as she was leaving to take Federigo to his lesson. She went to the signora, fearing that she'd finally worn out her patience. Signora Foscari lounged on her bed, acting as if speaking to Celeste was exhausting.

"I've been extraordinarily tolerant of your failings, have I not?"

"Yes, madam. You are most patient," Celeste said, hoping to appease her mistress.

"Then why is it you continue to take advantage of my kindness? You neglect Federigo and your other responsibilities. This isn't like you. Have you taken up with a young man like your predecessor?"

Celeste understood why her mistress would make that assumption. It wouldn't have occurred to her that Celeste's desire was for painting, not for a man.

"No, madam. I would never behave in such a sinful way," Celeste said and prayed that her protests were convincing.

"Then what is it, girl? If this continues, I'll demote you to housemaid. If that doesn't work, I'll send you in disgrace back to your father. Is that what you want?"

The mention of being sent home frightened her, but it also gave her an idea.

"I'm sorry I've disappointed you, but my distraction is out of worry for my family. I know you told me to forget them, but I can't. I fear my earnings aren't enough to support them. This isn't a complaint. I just don't know how they'll survive."

She felt a pang of guilt for using her family as an excuse to cover her selfish desire to paint, but her worry for her family was real. Her papa had earned his punishment, but her brothers and sisters didn't deserve to suffer along with him. For all Celeste knew, he was spending the wages she sent home on drink and women.

Her mistress sat forward, and Celeste saw genuine concern in her eyes.

"Why haven't you told me this before? Our families have been friends and allies for generations. I don't want them to suffer, even if it's brought on by your waste of a father. Have you spoken to your Aunt Portia?"

"No, madam. You forbade me to contact her," Celeste said and wrung her hands for effect.

"Let me tend to this. Focus on your responsibilities. Don't worry about your family any longer."

Celeste curtsied and thanked her, but the mistress waved her away and chewed her nail, deep in thought. It took all of Celeste's strength to not skip away in joy. Not only had she kept her job and deflected Signora Foscari's suspicions, but she'd tricked her into helping her brothers and sisters as well.

Celeste enjoyed the freedom from Signora Foscari's ever watching eye after their talk, but the threat of losing her position had scared her into rededicating herself to her responsibilities. Artistic creation was her passion, but it wouldn't put bread in the mouths of her family. She couldn't afford the luxury of an artist's life.

She was sure her mistress would forget her promise to help her family, but Federigo needed her. His moods improved drastically when Celeste returned to giving him the attention he craved. She packed up her dream of becoming an artist along with her brushes and only painted during Federigo's lessons.

CHAPTER SIX

One day as Celeste worked behind the screen during Federigo's lesson, the maestro said, "Celeste, come here, please. I must speak with you."

He hadn't spoken to her for weeks, and her breath quickened as she left her hiding place. He hadn't sent Federigo away, so she feared his cousin had discovered their secret and he was using the boy as a witness to their conversation.

"How may I serve you, Maestro?" Celeste asked and curtsied, trying to hide her trembling hands.

He gestured for her to come closer. "I don't wish certain ears to overhear," he said and glanced at Federigo.

When she stepped toward him, she heard his breath quicken to match hers.

"You are so beautiful," he whispered. Celeste wasn't sure she'd heard correctly until he said, "I've never seen eyes that capture light the way yours do, and your skin is like porcelain. I'll paint your portrait one day."

She glanced at Federigo, shocked that the maestro had spoken to her in such a way in front of him, but he was stacking wood scraps into a pile and paid them no mind. Maestro Vicente raised his hand as if to caress her face but stopped with his fingertips inches from her skin. She felt his warmth even though he hadn't touched her. She knew she should back away, but her feet refused to move.

"Maestro, Messer Gabriele is here to see you," a voice said behind them.

They spun in unison to find an apprentice watching them from the studio doorway. Before Celeste could recover from her shame at the boy catching them in such an intimate moment, her papa stepped into the studio.

Narrowing his eyes at Celeste, he said, "What's going on here?"

"Papa!" she cried and ran to him with outstretched arms but stopped when she saw Marco standing behind her father. "What are you doing here, brother?" She was even more shocked to see him than her father.

Giovanni Gabriele pushed Celeste's arms away and said, "I should ask you that question. You, alone here with Signore Vicente? Why aren't you at the Benettos'? Has Signora Foscari dismissed you?"

"Please, let me explain, Papa," Celeste said, not knowing how much her father had seen of what passed with the maestro.

Maestro Vicente brushed past her and called for Federigo before she could speak.

"It's my place to explain, Messer Gabriele. This is Federigo Benetto, my cousin's son. Your daughter brings him to me each week for lessons. I was instructing her on what I'd like Federigo to accomplish this week. You must be Marco," the maestro said before turning to Celeste. "I was about to tell you that Signora Foscari and I have arranged for Marco to become my apprentice. He's joining my workshop today. Wasn't that generous of my cousin?"

All Celeste could do was stare, gaping at her maestro. Marco apprenticing in the workshop would make it impossible for her to paint during Federigo's lessons. Signora Foscari's actions may have been a boon to her family, but they destroyed Celeste's hope of becoming an artist.

"Yes, Maestro, Signora Foscari is very kind," she finally managed to say. "I must thank her. My family owes her, and you, a great debt."

Maestro Vicente nodded and turned to Giovanni. "Thank you for bringing Marco to me. I pledge to do my best to train your son."

"The Gabriele family is truly honored, sir. Marco is a bright boy and a hard worker. I hope he won't disappoint you," he said with pride showing in his eyes.

"I'm sure he won't," the maestro said and gestured for them to follow him to the workshop. "Come, Marco, I'll introduce you."

Celeste had often heard sounds coming from the workshop but could never enter. She hesitated at the doorway, uncertain of what to do.

The maestro turned and gave her a look loaded with meaning. "Join us, Celeste. Come see where Marco will live and work. This may be your only chance to enter my workshop."

Her papa raised his eyebrows but didn't dare question the maestro. She pushed past him with her head high and forgot her papa's disapproval the instant she entered the workshop. The reality far exceeded her imagination.

Three young boys stood at a workbench grinding minerals into powders mixed with oils to create the pigments for paints. Other boys were cutting wood for panels. The smell of sawdust overpowered even the pungent odors of the oils and varnishes. Several older boys and young men stood before easels working on paintings and drawings at differing stages of completion. Celeste wanted to cry for joy and sadness at the glorious world that lay beyond her reach. She would have sacrificed anything to change places with Marco.

Maestro Vicente called to Stefano, his master-apprentice. Celeste had seen him frequently coming and going through the studio. He was about her age and handsome. The maestro had told her that Stefano showed promise. He smiled at Celeste as he passed her.

"Stefano, this is Marco. Take him to his bed in the loft and have him stow his belongings. I'm relying on you to show him what I expect from him. I'll begin his training in the morning."

Celeste gave Marco a quick hug, not knowing when or if she would see him again. Her father patted Marco's back. Marco looked terrified as Stefano led him away from the only life and family he'd ever known. Workshop life would be entirely foreign to him.

Leaving home to work for Signora Foscari had been a hard adjustment for Celeste, but it would be worse for Marco, even if it turned out to be the best thing to happen for him. He gave Celeste a last forlorn look as he mounted the stairs to the loft. She longed to reassure him that Maestro Vicente was the best of men who would treat him well, but it would have been inappropriate for her to speak.

The maestro left them to speak with one of his apprentices working on a painting, so Celeste took her father and Federigo back to the studio. She was about to send Federigo to the courtyard so she could have a moment alone with her papa, but the maestro returned before she could.

"Federigo, make sure you practice what I taught you today," he said.

Federigo nodded, and Maestro Vicente glanced at Celeste, confirming that his comment was meant for her. She'd have to wait until Federigo's next lesson to speak with him about how Marco's arrival would change their arrangement.

"Thank you again, Signore Vicente. I know I'm leaving my son in excellent care." Giovanni said and bowed.

"Yes, well, I must get back to work. Signorina, Federigo, I'll see you next week."

Celeste took Federigo's hand and followed the maestro out of the studio. When they reached the courtyard, her father said, "I must speak with you alone, girl." He glanced at Federigo, who was tossing pebbles at a trail of ants.

"I must take Master Benetto home and finish my duties. I'll ask permission to meet with you after Federigo's supper," she said and withdrew a coin from her bag and pressed it into his palm. "For a gondola. Not drink. Wait for me outside the servants' entrance after sundown."

He examined the coin and nodded. "Don't make me wait, child."

"I'll do my best, but my responsibilities must come before all else.

Isn't that true, Papa?" she asked as she helped Federigo into the gondola.

His mouth fell open, and his eyes widened as Celeste dropped onto the cushions with her back to her father. She'd never dared to challenge him and felt their battle of wills take a subtle shift in her favor.

~

CELESTE GOT Federigo settled in later that night and hurried through the rest of her chores before rushing to the mistress' chamber.

"I must thank you for the great honor you have arranged for our family," she said. "My father arrived at Signore Vicente's studio with Marco just as Federigo and I were leaving. There's no way to show the depth of my gratitude, madam."

Signora Foscari gave her an arrogant smile. "I'm always happy to help those less fortunate than myself. I hope you thanked my cousin."

"I did, madam. He is also most kind. We don't deserve such generosity," she said with her head bowed.

"Make sure your brother understands. This arrangement was mostly my cousin's doing. He came to me with the idea, and I instantly saw it as an answer to your family's circumstances. It won't provide for them for some time, but it could raise all of you up in time. Having a maestro of my cousin's reputation is a tremendous honor."

"True, madam. You are truly wise." When the mistress turned to her needlepoint, Celeste said, "I have one more favor to ask. My father wishes to speak to me before he returns home. May I have your permission to see him?"

She swallowed hard, and half hoped Signora Foscari would say no. She wasn't sure why Papa wanted to talk but assumed it was to ask for money. He'd never pay her the least attention otherwise.

"Yes, go. A daughter must obey if her father demands it, even a father like yours. Just don't stay out too long. I expect you up early and ready to work in the morning as usual."

"Yes, madam. Thank you."

Celeste rushed to the servants' entrance and grabbed her cloak. She stepped out, expecting to find Papa waiting, but the canal was empty. *He has drunk the money I gave him*, she thought and dropped onto the stoop. She was frustrated but also relieved to have a few spare moments alone. She leaned against the warm stone wall and looked out over the water. She hadn't been out of doors at dusk in months. The changes in colors of the canal and buildings in the light of the setting sun fascinated her. She imagined painting the scene and began picking pigments in her mind. Lost in her thoughts, Celeste failed to see the gondola pull up to the landing.

"Stop daydreaming and get in the boat, girl," her father said.

She jumped and climbed in beside him. "Sorry, Papa. You're late. I'll not have much time before Signora Foscari expects me. Where are we going?"

"To the basilica. I wish to light a candle for your poor mother."

She raised her eyebrows but said, "I would like that, too."

Giovanni had never been a devout man but took part in family devotions when he was at home and sober, which wasn't often. Celeste was glad they were going to the basilica. The Benetto family worshiped in their private chapel except on Holy Days, so she rarely got to attend mass at Basilica San Marco. She was in awe of the beautiful artwork and soaring ceilings and felt the view drew her closer to God.

She was also pleased that her father chose to take her to the basilica because it meant he was sober. He'd probably stopped drinking to be presentable for Maestro Vicente, but she was grateful whatever the reason. She wished the sobriety would be permanent but knew from painful experience not to expect it.

They arrived in time for vespers and found an open pew at the rear of the chapel. Though the service was moving and the music beautiful, Celeste was so absorbed in admiring the exquisite artwork that she looked up when she should have bowed her head. Her father elbowed her and scowled. She dropped to her knees and was about to scold herself until she realized that art was from God, too. She smiled and dreamed of the day when one of her paintings would adorn such a sacred place.

They strolled around the piazza after the service until her papa found an empty bench away from the crowds.

He turned to her and said, "I'm concerned by what I saw when I came upon you in Signore Vicente's studio."

It was the last thing she expected. She stared at him in feigned confusion and said, "I don't understand, Papa," hoping he believed her.

"You're a naïve, inexperienced girl. You understand nothing of men. I didn't like what I saw in the maestro's eyes. He is a wealthy and powerful man. Men like him think nothing of taking advantage of maidens like you."

It sickened her to think his words came from personal experience. She pushed the thought aside and gave her most convincing smile. "You worry for nothing. The maestro was merely explaining how I may assist Federigo in his painting, nothing more. Maestro Vicente would never take an interest in a girl like me. He hardly notices me." She placed her hand on his arm. "I've rarely been alone with him for more than a few moments, so don't concern yourself. I'd never disgrace our family name, not even for a powerful Duca."

He searched her eyes for several moments. "Very well but stay on your guard. There's too much at stake for you and the family. And address him as Signore. He's not your maestro."

Celeste nodded, disappointed that he hadn't caught her insinuation. What right did he have to speak of what was at stake for her family? If not for his disgraceful betrayal, she would have been on equal status with Maestro Vicente and possibly free to take lessons from him.

Giovanni stood and gave her his hand. As they walked, he wrapped her hand around his arm and patted it. "Did you have a part in arranging Marco's apprenticeship? Did you ask Signora Foscari for help?" he asked.

"No, Papa. My mistress knew of my family's concerns, but I didn't know she was arranging for Marco to apprentice to Maestro Vicente. I mean, Signore Vicente. He is a good man. I'm delighted for Marco and what it could mean for all of us."

"I am as well. Let's hope Marco has the required talent. If he falls short, maybe the maestro can find some other work for him."

He patted her hand again and directed her to the gondola. It was the first time her father had conversed with her as an adult. She wondered if he'd been that way with her mamma when they were young. It gave her a small hope.

Once in the gondola, she said, "Signore Vicente is an excellent teacher. I know little of art, but even Federigo has improved under his tutelage. If he can learn, Marco will excel."

"I hope you are right," he said and grew quiet.

When they reached the Benetto's palazzo, she kissed her father's cheeks and climbed onto the landing, waving as the boat pulled out of sight. She didn't know when she would see him again but was grateful for the pleasant memory, nonetheless.

Signora Foscari sent for Celeste the following afternoon. She left Federigo with Cristina and went to her mistress.

"You wish to see me, madam?" Celeste said as she entered her chamber.

"Yes. Federigo's father believes his son has reached an age where he should begin training with the tutor we engaged for his brothers. You'll be staying as a housekeeper to assist Pia. Report to her tomorrow morning so she can explain your duties."

Celeste was too shocked to respond. She'd expected the day when Federigo would be too old for a nanny but didn't expect it for at least two more years. She'd also hoped for some warning but shouldn't have. She was nothing more than a piece of property to her master and mistress. To her mistress, Celeste was no different from the horses that pulled their carriages when they traveled abroad.

"You have nothing to say to this news?" Signora Foscari asked.

Celeste had plenty she wished to say but wouldn't dare. "No, madam. Signore Benetto knows what is best for his son. I'll report to Pia in the morning."

She curtsied and went to her room before returning to the nursery. Her emotions were already in chaos from what had happened the previous day. Her mistress' pronouncement only made matters worse. She should have been grateful that the mistress was keeping her on as a maid, but her only thought was that she'd never see the maestro again. Her life as an artist ended before it began. Why had God opened a world of promise and wonder only to tear it away?

Celeste reluctantly packed her art supplies into an old bag and kicked it into a corner. Tears spilled onto her cheeks as she rolled the painting of the Blessed Virgin and tied it with string. She'd spent countless hours lovingly painting her Lady, but no one would ever know. She somehow hoped to return the canvas to the maestro so he could use it with another pupil.

Wiping her cheeks with her apron, she squared her shoulders and raised her chin. Celeste's only purpose was to keep her position until her brother could assume the place at Maestro Vicente's side that should have been hers. Her family's hopes now rested with Marco.

LUCIANO WAS ABSORBED in his latest commission when he looked up to find his cousin Maria standing in the studio doorway. Her visit surprised him since she'd never come to his studio. He put his brush down and wiped paint-covered hands on a rag before kissing her cheeks.

"What are you doing here? Where is Pietro? Is Federigo with you?"

"So many questions," Maria said. She waved him off with the back of her hand and entered the studio with a swish of her skirts. "Pietro is in your workshop, checking on Marco. He wants to make sure the money he's paying to support him is going to good use. Federigo isn't with us, but my visit concerns him." She stepped back and looked Luciano up and down. "Your tunic is in tatters, and when was the last time you bought a new cloak? You disgrace the Vicente name. What would your father say?"

"Nothing he could repeat in your presence, but I'm working, not attending court at the Doge's Palace. I ask again, what brings you here?"

"Pietro has decided it's time for Federigo to train with the tutor and no longer wants him to come for lessons. He appreciates the time you've spent with our son but being an artist won't help Federigo in the family business."

Luciano was glad to be relieved of the obligation to teach Federigo, but Maria's words meant Celeste was lost to him. The news devastated him, but he hid his emotions.

Maria waited for a response, so he said, "Pietro is right, but I'm sad to lose Federigo as a pupil. He's a pleasant boy."

"He may be pleasant, but I don't believe you're sad to lose him as a pupil. You and I both know he lacks talent or desire to paint. I believe his abilities lie in mathematics."

Luciano laughed and patted her shoulder. "You are also right, but honestly, I'll miss him."

Maria went to the easel and studied his painting. With her back to him, she said, "How is Marco Gabriele doing? Federigo's former nanny asked about him the other day."

Luciano's heart beat a little faster at the mention of Celeste, and he wondered what would become of her. "The boy works hard and follows instructions. It's too early to know if he has talent. What will become of his sister now that you no longer require a nanny?"

She turned to face him. "What interest do you have in the girl?"

"Only that I took Marco in hoping he'll one day improve his family's fortunes, but he has many years in my workshop before that can happen. If you dismiss his sister, the family will be destitute. I'd be sorry to see that happen."

Maria smiled. "As would I, which is why I'm keeping the girl on to assist the housekeeper. If she continues to work hard, Celeste may one day replace Pia in running my household. She is a bright girl, even if she is distracted at times."

The news that Maria hadn't dismissed Celeste was a relief, but Luciano hated to think of her artistic genius being wasted on a life of servitude. He gave Maria a half-hearted smile. "You are a kind-hearted soul."

"I must go, but I also wanted to invite you to a family gala in three weeks. I don't want to waste sending a written invitation if you'll just refuse again." She put her hands on her hips and scowled at him.

He swept his arm across his body in an exaggerated bow. "I'm a busy man, but I would be honored to attend. What are we celebrating this time?"

"Pietro's brother has been elevated to the Senate. Bring Isabella and her mother. I haven't seen them in ages."

Luciano agreed to do as she asked and escorted her to the workshop. While she waited outside, he went in search of Pietro. After assuring him that Marco was doing well, he walked Pietro and Maria to their gondola. As soon as the boat drifted out of sight, he returned to his studio and slammed the door.

Pietro had unwittingly thwarted his plans for Celeste. Even worse, Luciano had lost the only light in his life and felt drained of hope. He was being denied the chance to mold Celeste into the artistic genius he knew she could become, and he'd miss seeing her angelic face in the studio.

He sat at the table where Celeste had first displayed her sketches. How would he survive without her weekly visits? Nothing but Celeste had mattered to him since she came into his life. His effort to be a better husband had failed, and Isabella's behavior was increasingly shameful. They rarely spoke or even saw each other.

Only one thought made escorting Isabella to the Benetto's celebration bearable; he might catch a glimpse of Celeste. He sat up and grabbed a scrap of paper. Furiously dipping his quill, he scratched out the words he hoped would set his plans back on course. No matter the risk, he refused to let Celeste disappear from his life.

CHAPTER SEVEN

*C*eleste's life as a maid was little different from the one she left at home, except there were no children under her care. She buffed and scrubbed until her knees ached, and her hands cracked and bled. The only blessing was that the mistress allowed her to keep the small nursery room because there was no other bed for her. Federigo came to her the first few mornings after the change and begged her to return to the nursery. She told him to be brave and sent him off to join his brothers. She cared for the boy but was jealous because he might still have lessons with the maestro.

Three weeks after her demotion, Pia announced that their master was throwing a gala to honor his brother's promotion. Signora Foscari had ordered them to scrub and polish every inch of the palazzo. Celeste pined for her leisurely days as Federigo's nanny. She felt guilty for not treating the other maids better before she became one of them.

The hours she'd spent painting felt like memories from another lifetime. Occasionally, her bag of art supplies beckoned from the corner, but she was always too exhausted to paint by day's end.

She drifted off to sleep at the end of the first week, remembering those glorious days in the maestro's presence, and wondered if he ever thought of her. The only bright spot in her life was receiving the dress she was to wear for serving at the gala. She had owned nothing so lovely in years and laughed at herself for being so pleased since it was only a dress meant for a servant.

One afternoon when her mistress was away, Celeste put the dress on and sneaked to her mistress' chamber to view herself in the glass. What she saw pleased her. The pale blue fabric highlighted her fair skin and auburn hair. Swaying slightly, she watched the light glide over the folds of the skirt and imagined painting the image of her reflection. When she opened her eyes and saw her raw and calloused hands that would never again cradle a paintbrush or piece of charcoal. It felt as if a part of her body had been severed. She left her mistress' chamber and went to her room to return the dress to its peg.

On the afternoon of the party, the mistress sent all but the kitchen staff to take a short rest in preparation for their long night of work. Celeste dropped onto the bed, too weary to feel excitement at the prospect of wearing the new dress. She just wanted the party to be over so she could return to her usual workload. Signore Benetto had promised the staff a full day off as a reward for their hard work. Celeste planned to sleep it away.

She rose after a fitful nap and dressed before going to find Pia in the servant's wing. Pia's dress pulled across her plump belly, and Celeste wondered how she maintained her girth despite long hours of hard work. Celeste's gown was already loose on her.

Pia gave out assignments but pulled Celeste aside and said she needed her as a right hand during the event. Celeste was flattered but knew that meant she would work harder than the others and would likely have to stay long after they'd returned to their rooms. She hoped if she performed well, the mistress would promote her to the assistant housekeeper. It was the most she could expect in her new life.

LUCIANO'S MANSERVANT laced his doublet and pulled leather boots over his scarlet leggings. Maria's words about his clothing had left an impression, so he'd ordered a new cloak and hat for the gala.

He didn't believe in parading around in finery to show off his wealth like most Venetian aristocrats, but his peers expected a certain level of dress. When he was ready, he called Isabella and Francesca, telling them it was time to leave. Isabella stepped from her room, only half-dressed.

Luciano huffed and said, "I told you an hour ago that it was time to leave. Wishing to make an entrance is one thing. Being rude is another."

Isabella glared at him. "When have you ever been in a hurry to get to a social event? I usually have to drag you along."

Luciano shrugged. "True, but I promised Maria we'd be there. I don't want to disappoint her."

"Fine, just a bit longer," she said and ran back to her chamber.

Luciano strode to the front hall and paced while he waited for Isabella to emerge. Waiting for the day of the gala had been agonizing enough, but Isabella delaying him further was torture. Francesca joined him in the hall and placed her gloved hand on his arm.

"Calm down. Bella will join us shortly," she said.

Luciano eyed Francesca's new gown and winked. "You look lovely for a woman your age. I should be searching for a new husband for you."

Francesca smiled and curtsied. "I don't want to be competition for my daughters. You have a new costume as well, I see. It's about time."

Luciano and Francesca chatted comfortably until Isabella finally descended the stairs wearing an extravagant red satin gown. Luciano helped the women into the gondola and arranged their pillows and blankets before taking his seat. He wanted to order the gondolier to row faster but didn't wish to arouse suspicion. The gondolier fought his way through the tangle of boats and finally pulled up to the Benetto's palazzo. Luciano had to restrain himself from running up the front stairs.

Maria greeted them warmly and led the women to introduce them to the Doge's son. The crowd was so thick, it spilled into the courtyard. Luciano had expected an intimate family gathering, but every patrician in Venice seemed to be present. The throng reminded him of a pride of squawking peacocks. He smiled and ducked behind a column just in time to avoid Amando Pisani. His plans for the evening didn't involve stuffing his face and drinking too much. He made his way to the courtyard and found an empty corner. He breathed in the scented air to clear his head and help him summon the courage to follow through with his plan.

He waited for a quarter of an hour before he saw Celeste retreat into the kitchen carrying a tray piled with dirty dishes. He crossed the courtyard and leaned against a wall near the kitchen entrance to wait. His patience was rewarded when she emerged half an hour later. He stepped into her path to prevent her from passing. She would have run into him if he hadn't placed his hands on her shoulders.

Celeste stopped and made a deep curtsy when she recognized him.

"Please forgive me, Signore. I didn't see you there."

Seeing her left him breathless. Her cheeks were flushed with exertion, and perspiration glistened on her forehead, but she was still the most beautiful woman present.

"Don't apologize, Celeste. It was my fault. I needed to give you this."

He pressed a folded note into her hand. She glanced at it and raised her eyebrows.

"What is it, sir?" she asked.

"Read it as soon as you can without being seen. You'll understand."

He glanced at her one last time and strode up the stairs to the sala without looking back.

CELESTE STARTED at the folded parchment for only an instant before shoving it into her pocket. She felt the burning weight of it against her thigh while rushing about tending to her duties. More than an hour passed before she could sneak away to read the note. She found a quiet corner near the master's chambers and unfolded the parchment.

"I must speak with you. Come to the alcove on the western side of the courtyard. Wait until my family and guests have had too much wine to notice your absence. I'll meet you there."

It was signed with his initials. The thought of doing what he asked frightened and thrilled her, but the enticement of being alone with him won out. She raised the note to her nose and inhaled. It didn't smell of exotic fragrances she expected but of oils, varnish, and minerals from his workshop. The aroma reawakened her desire for him and for the studio. She tenderly folded the note and returned it to her pocket. She should have tossed it into the kitchen fires but couldn't bring herself to let it go.

The celebration roared on into the early hours of the morning. Waiting to meet the maestro was agonizing, but Celeste forced herself to continue working until no one would notice her gone. She stole across the courtyard, making sure not to disturb the guests sprawled on benches or on the ground in the garden.

The closer Celeste got to the meeting place, the more her courage wavered. If Signora Foscari were to find her with Maestro Vicente, she wouldn't hesitate to toss her into the street. She didn't know if she could count on the maestro to protect her.

She glimpsed his scarlet tunic in the shadows and paused before ordering her feet to keep going. He was asleep on a bench. She hesitated to wake him so she could watch him unobserved, longing to stroke his cheek or feel his lips on hers. She had to be content with caressing him with her eyes.

He must have sensed her and sat up facing her.

"We must hurry before I'm missed, sir," she said in a rush. "What do you wish to tell me?"

"I doubt anyone will miss you for hours or maybe even days," he said and smiled to ease the tension.

"Pia will. She is not as young as I am, and the exertion may be too much for her. I can't abandon her."

"Come here, then."

He patted the bench for her to sit. Celeste hesitated, just as she had the day she first showed him her sketches.

"You may sit. I'll not tell anyone," the maestro said and winked.

She relaxed at his joke and sat next to him. "As you command, sir."

"Maria told me you're no longer Federigo's nanny. Did you know he's no longer taking lessons from me? His father thought he needed more time studying maps and numbers. He's probably right. I admit I'm relieved. Teaching that boy was becoming intolerable."

Celeste giggled and said, "I'm sure he's as relieved as you are."

He smiled before growing serious. "I refuse to abandon my quest to mentor you, Celeste. You need to keep painting. I've thought of nothing else since Maria came to see me."

She didn't lower her eyes but held his gaze. "It's my desire, too, but it's impossible. I have even less free time now. I shouldn't even be here with you."

He grew silent, and Celeste worried that she'd offended him.

"What are you willing to sacrifice to continue painting?" he finally asked.

"Sacrifice? What do I have to sacrifice? My position here supports my family. Without that, they would starve. I have nothing else. I am nothing else."

The maestro cringed. "Can you still not see your extraordinary gift and potential? This drove me to risk speaking with you tonight. I have a new proposal. I'm going to request that Maria allow you to visit Marco one evening each week. I'll prepare an excuse to allay her suspicions. We won't begin your lessons until the third or fourth visit. I'll do all in my power to protect you and ensure we're not discovered."

"You would do this for me?" she asked in a whisper.

"I would do anything for you." He watched her quietly for a moment. "I'll make the arrangements. Wait for word from Maria. Your journey as an artist is about to begin."

He reached up and gently caressed her cheek with the back of his hand. She trembled under his touch and desired more but forced herself to stand.

He lowered his eyes and said, "Go before Pia misses you."

WEEKS PASSED without a word from her mistress or the maestro about his plan for visits to Marco. Celeste had been foolish to hope that Signora Foscari would agree. She tried to content herself with being a maid but couldn't resist the bundle of materials in the corner of her room.

One Sunday afternoon, she relented when the master and his family were away from home for the evening. She unrolled the canvas and gingerly picked up the paintbrush. As she worked, thoughts of the maestro in the garden washed over her. The memory of his touch still burned on her cheek. It was the only ray of light in her otherwise dreary life.

She arose early the following morning and painted again, and again the day after that. Resuming her artistic creation buoyed her spirits and provided an outlet for her frustrations. Chores became more tolerable, and Celeste was more pleasant with the other staff.

Pia stopped her in the hall one day and said, "What right do you have to be grinning? Have you found yourself a man?"

They both laughed at the joke, knowing Celeste had no time for romance.

"No, I've just adjusted to my life as a housekeeper instead of a nanny. It's not so terrible once you get used to it."

"Keep telling yourself that if it works. I came to tell you that the mistress wants to see you. Try not to look so cheerful. She'll think she's too easy on us."

Celeste's heart pounded as she climbed the stairs to the sala. She was afraid her mistress would notice it beating through her gown. She took three slow, even breaths to calm herself and went to face her fate.

"I've received an unusual request from Signore Vicente," she said when Celeste entered her chamber. "He wishes you to visit your brother Marco for a short time each week. Apparently, the boy is pining for home, and it's interfering with his work. Maestro Vicente feels that seeing you will calm him so he can focus. I was reluctant to comply because your absence will be a burden to Pia and me, but my cousin convinced me that your brother shows talent, and Signore Benetto expects the funds we're providing for his support to go to good use. You will finish your chores early each Monday and leave while we're at our evening meal. My husband's manservant, Luigi, will accompany you since you cannot go out alone. Do you understand?"

Celeste bowed her head and said, "Yes, madam. I'll do my best to help my brother since you've been so generous to my family. I'll also work harder, so my time away won't burden you."

"Yes, yes," she said and waved her hand. "You will go on Monday but don't stay too long. I hope these trips will be temporary. You must encourage your brother to be strong."

"I'll do my best, madam," she said and curtsied.

Signora Foscari shooed her away, and Celeste's feet hardly touched the tiles as she danced to her room. The maestro had done it! She was going to see him in four days and become his pupil. It was a miracle and more than she deserved.

LUCIANO ENTERED the workshop on Monday morning and ordered Marco to carry a stack of framing wood to his studio. After the boy dropped the wood in a corner, Luciano said he needed to speak with him.

"Have I done something wrong, Maestro?" Marco asked.

"Not at all," Luciano said to reassure him. "Signora Foscari has informed me that your family is concerned about how you are doing here. She has arranged for your sister Celeste to visit each Monday. She'll be here this afternoon. I assured my cousin you're doing well, but she wants Celeste to report to her herself. You may visit with your sister after you finish your chores. Don't tell the other boys. We don't want them to become jealous," Luciano said and winked.

Marco looked confused but said, "Yes, Maestro. Thank you."

Luciano returned to the workshop with Marco but couldn't focus on his work. All he could think of was that Celeste would be downstairs in a few hours. He'd planned to stay away from the workshop on her first visit but later decided it would be better to make sure it went according to plan.

He worked on an altarpiece with two of his more experienced apprentices until he heard Pietro's manservant asking for Marco. Luciano went to Luigi and pointed the boy out to him. He watched longingly as Luigi led Marco to meet Celeste. He would have to be patient and wait until it was safe to begin her lessons.

CELESTE'S ANXIETY had grown with each push of the gondolier's pole, pushing them closer to Maestro Vicente's palazzo. Why had she been so foolish to take such a risk? She'd convinced herself that she would sacrifice anything to become the maestro's apprentice, but so many lives depended on her, and the Gabrieles wouldn't survive another scandal. It was too late for second thoughts as Luigi helped her onto the landing. There was no turning back.

Waiting for Marco to come out of the workshop was torture. She let out her breath when he emerged behind Luigi, but her heart sank that the maestro wasn't with them. She should have known he wouldn't show himself to a lowly servant visiting an apprenticed brother. Great men like the maestro didn't bother with such insignificant matters.

Luigi left them and went to nap in the gondola, so Celeste led Marco to a courtyard bench. He'd grown several inches in the months since they'd been apart and was an exact replica of their father. She prayed the resemblance was merely physical.

Marco was awkward and fidgety at first, but Celeste did her best to set him at ease. She unwrapped bread and cheese from the basket and broke pieces off for him. He relaxed once he started eating and chatted away about life in the workshop. It was clear he was content in his new life.

While Celeste returned their leftover food to the basket, Marco said, "Why are you here? Maestro says the family is worried about me."

"Don't be concerned. I just wanted to make sure the master is treating you well. Our brothers and sisters must miss you as I do," she said.

"Have you seen them? I miss them, too, but life is better here. Maestro says I'm a good apprentice." He puffed out his chest, obviously pleased with himself.

She smiled. "I've not seen the family. Maybe we'll see them at the festivals. Until then, Signora Foscari says I may visit each week. I'm glad. I get lonely for family."

"Me, too," Marco said and kicked at a pebble. "I better get back. The boys will wonder where I am."

Celeste walked with him as far as the workshop entrance and kissed his cheeks before he waved and disappeared into the workshop. She stood before the door, longing to follow him.

Luigi was still sleeping when she climbed into the gondola, so she settled in and thought of her visit with Marco without waking him. She hadn't meant to tell Marco she'd return the following week, but it had been so pleasant to see her brother. She'd allow herself two or three more visits before putting a stop to them. There wouldn't be harm in sharing a few evenings with her brother.

Celeste poked Luigi to wake him when the gondolier guided the boat to the landing. He leaped up and offered Celeste his hand. She turned at the top of the servant's entrance steps and gazed over the canal for a moment before closing the door behind her and returning to her servant's life.

CELESTE'S next visit with Marco was just like the first, except Marco was more relaxed. Without having to worry about seeing the maestro, Celeste was calmer as well.

She'd planned on the fourth visit being the last, but since no one seemed bothered by the arrangement, she took advantage of the privilege and continued to visit her brother. Those hours of freedom each Monday were an unexpected pleasure.

The maestro had not tried to communicate with her. Celeste feared he'd changed his mind about training her. She'd run out of paint and missed painting. She'd put her panel of the Madonna aside, wondering if, once again, the prospect of becoming an artist had been ripped from her grasp.

CELESTE'S MIND wandered during her eighth visit with Marco. She shook off thoughts of the maestro and focused on a story Marco was telling about another apprentice. Moments later, she spotted the maestro coming toward them across the courtyard. They jumped to their feet as he approached.

"We're just finishing, Maestro," Marco said. "Do you need me?"

"No. You may return to the workshop," the maestro said. "I have a message for your sister to deliver to Signora Foscari."

Marco kissed her cheeks and ran off without another word. She watched him go and smiled. "He is a good boy."

"He is, and he shows promise, but not as much as his sister. Come to my studio, please," he said and headed for the stairs.

His brusqueness startled Celeste, but she obeyed and rushed after him. He moved aside to let her enter the studio and motioned to a chair, but he remained standing. Celeste folded her hands in her lap and tried to slow her breathing. She hadn't seen him since the night of the gala. Watching him in his tattered and stained work clothes made her heart pound. She glanced up and waited for him to speak.

"I must apologize for my behavior when we last met. Don't worry. It won't be repeated." He crossed his arms and leaned against the cabinet with the slightest grin. "The moonlight and wine seduced me."

Celeste was both relieved and disappointed. His caress had been the most meaningful thing to happen in her life, but he was right that they couldn't repeat how they'd behaved in the garden. He was a married man.

"Don't apologize, Maestro. I'm equally at fault for allowing it."

"Then, let's put it behind us. I'm sorry for taking so long to contact you. God has seen fit to shower me with commissions. I pray that you'll be blessed with equal favor one day, but for now, we must start at the beginning. Your lessons will begin next week. You will not meet with Marco then and only occasionally after that to divert suspicion. Bring your canvas and supplies each time."

She stood and faced him. "I'm frightened, Maestro. What will become of my family and me if we're discovered?"

" I promise to protect you. Trust me. This is as much for my benefit as yours. I'll not abandon you."

He spoke with such conviction and had always been true to his word, so Celeste had no reason to doubt him.

She gave a deep curtsy. "Then, I place myself in your hands, Maestro."

He rubbed his hands together in excitement. "Excellent! Do you need supplies?"

Celeste told him what supplies she lacked and placed the materials under the food in her basket when he handed them to her.

"You must go now." He reached into his cloak and withdrew a piece of folded parchment sealed with his mark. "Deliver this to Maria in case anyone questions you about why you came to my studio. I'll see you in one week."

She curtsied and started to go but turned before she reached the door. "A question, Maestro. You gave me a note on the night of the party. How did you know I could read it? I don't remember telling you."

"Marco told me. I've queried him about your family at length. He said your mother was a well-educated woman and taught her children to read and write in Latin and Venetian. It's a skill that will serve you well."

"I'm glad to hear you're pleased," she said and nodded before rushing to the waiting gondola. Luigi was awake for once and helped her into the boat.

"Where have you been?" he asked. "I was about to go searching for you."

"Maestro Vicente needed to give me a letter for my mistress. I'm surprised by your complaints. You're never in a hurry to get back to your chores."

"I'm never in a hurry for anything, Celeste. You were just gone longer than usual," he said and shrugged. He leaned against the cushion and covered his eyes with his cap. "Wake me when we arrive."

Celeste followed Luigi's lead and settled into the cushions with her eyes closed. Her anxiety faded as they floated home. She had the maestro's promise of protection. What did she have to fear with one of the most powerful men in Venice on her side?

LUCIANO'S QUILL scratched over the paper as he constructed his training plan for Celeste. He couldn't treat her like his other apprentices when they first arrived at his workshop. Her skills were far beyond what they brought as novices, but there were gaps in her learning. She had to learn how to grind and wash pigments, make brushes, and mix plaster. The list seemed endless, and though she'd been born with artistic genius, she had to understand art fundamentals and history, as well as the mediums of creation available.

Once he had a workable plan, he put his quill aside and relaxed in his chair. He'd spoken the truth with Celeste about not making advances on her, but it would take all his strength to resist. He stroked his beard as he recalled the pleasure on her face when she saw him approaching across the courtyard. What would he have given to see that look in Isabella's eyes?

He felt an almost mystic connection to Celeste and ached to make her more than his student, but he had to content himself with guiding her artistic journey. He couldn't do anything to jeopardize Celeste's future that he held in his hands.

CHAPTER EIGHT

aestro Vicente handed Celeste a paint-stained smock and ordered her to put it over her dress when she entered the studio the following week. While she did, he dropped a large wooden box on an extra worktable he'd moved into the room.

"You've had the luxury of skipping the fundamentals of art education and gone directly to painting. That ends today, and your true apprenticeship begins. Your training will start as it does for all novices. You will construct your frames and panels and learn to prepare glues and plasters. In time, I'll teach you the basics of sculpting, wood carving, and mosaics. It's too damp in Venice for frescoes, but I will instruct you in the basics in case you ever work in Florence."

"Florence, Maestro? How would I ever go to Florence? It might as well be China."

"To reach your full artistic potential, you must spend time in Florence. It's the crucible of art for our age. We'll figure out how that is to happen when the time comes."

Celeste shrugged and shook her head. It was a struggle to travel the short distance from the Benetto's palazzo to the maestro's studio. She couldn't imagine a future where she would go to Florence.

"Are you listening?" the maestro asked, interrupting her thoughts. When she nodded, he said, "After you have a working knowledge of those skills, I'll teach you to paint. You have a good beginning, but my instructions to Federigo were rudimentary. With my guidance, you'll emerge as a master artist one day."

Celeste followed the maestro with her eyes while he paced the studio. He spoke with his mouth as well as his hands, and her excitement matched his. He would initiate her into a world that few women would ever know. The opportunity was a precious treasure, and she trembled in anticipation.

He began her lesson by taking items from the box one-by-one and stating their names and purposes. He rattled off information so quickly that it was a struggle to commit it to memory, and her first lesson ended all too quickly. As Celeste removed the smock and returned the materials to the box, the maestro told her to leave the canvas and paint jars.

"You won't need those for many months. I'll keep your painting safe." He handed her a small leather pouch filled with the materials she'd need to practice making brushes. "Bring them with you next week. If they are satisfactory, I'll begin teaching you about pigments. Now you must hurry. We've taken longer than I intended."

Celeste slipped the pouch into her bag and left without a word. She'd expected the maestro to teach her as he had Federigo, but he'd seemed like a different man during the lesson. Her head swam with terms and the methods he'd demonstrated.

She wondered if Marco had felt the same when he entered the workshop. Celeste climbed into the gondola beside the sleeping Luigi and covered her legs with a blanket. Her quest would be more challenging than she'd imagined, but she looked forward to it with restless hunger.

∼

CELESTE MEASURED her life in hours spent with the maestro and days away from him. Working as a maid became nothing more than mindless drudgery. She couldn't remember why she had taken pride in her work before becoming an apprentice.

The maestro taught her more than just art. While she worked at the table in his studio, he educated her on government functions and the mechanisms of trade. He shared experiences from his life in Florence and the history of his family. The more she learned, the gloomier she felt for her sex. Men had relegated women to lives of tedious service or endless hours of boredom spent in needlepoint or sewing. While many women excelled at those tasks, their lives would be nothing more. Celeste longed to be a force in improving the lives of women one day.

In the meantime, she focused on color, shading, perspective, and plaster consistency. The maestro taught her of the old masters and what it took to create a masterpiece. She was proud to learn of the great Venetian masters and their contributions to art. Celeste had no doubt that Maestro Vicente would be among their ranks one day.

She had no illusions about her own prospects. The maestro confessed his plan one day to sell her work under one of his apprentices' names, maybe even Marco. He had a budding talent, but the maestro said it was nothing compared to hers.

She'd worried enough about getting caught going to her lessons. The idea of the Guilds discovering the maestro passing off her work as Marco's terrified her. She doubted Marco would even agree to take part in the fraud. Her only comfort was that it would be years before she'd have to face that prospect. She drove thoughts of the future from her mind and worked hard to please the maestro and improve her skills.

Her anxiety lessened as the weeks passed until she became complacent. Marco was there to meet her on some visits. That was the maestro's way of alerting her that there would be no lesson that day. If Marco wasn't there, Celeste went through the courtyard to a back entrance that led to the studio. At times, the maestro got her started and left her alone to work. No one ever entered the studio while she was there, and the room became a sanctuary. In time, she stopped checking to see if anyone noticed or followed her and laughed at her earlier fears.

CELESTE ARRIVED for her lesson one bleak winter day to find Maestro Vicente waiting at the studio door. Materials were not out on the table as usual. Without explaining, he motioned for her to sit. She obeyed and waited for him to speak. She'd been his apprentice for six months and no longer lowered her eyes when he spoke to her or hesitated to sit in his presence.

The maestro crossed his arms and leaned against the worktable. "I have another obligation today and must go out, so there will be no lesson, but I need to speak with you before I go."

Celeste felt a twinge of worry at the seriousness of his tone. "Of course, Maestro," she said.

"An hour a week is not enough time for your lessons. Your training is taking too long. You'll start coming two nights a week in addition to your Monday lessons."

She stood and backed away from him. She'd become accustomed to their weekly lessons and didn't want that to change. What he suggested was too dangerous.

"We've discussed this, sir. How can I go out alone at night? What if I'm caught, and how will I get here? We can't trust Luigi to bring me."

He smiled and said, "I've made arrangements that answer your concerns. Please sit and listen."

Celeste doubted his answers would placate her fear, but she sat just as he asked.

"My gondolier, named Carlo, is going to help us. I trust him, and he's in my debt for an unrelated matter. He'll arrive each Tuesday and Thursday night at ten to bring you here. We'll work until midnight. No one will miss you that late."

"Is this worth the risk? Can't I just work harder during the week?"

"Hard work isn't our problem. It's about the knowledge I need to impart. My apprentices work ten hours per day or more and begin their training at a much younger age. It still takes them years to progress. I don't want us to run out of time," he said and rubbed his chin.

"I'm not going anywhere, Maestro," she said to reassure him.

"But I may be. My father is gravely ill. If he should die, I will be forced to return to Florence and take my place as head of our ancestral estate." He walked to the window that overlooked the canal. "That's not your concern, but when it happens, it will mean the end of our endeavor. I've considered taking you on to my staff in Florence, but I'd have no way to explain to Maria. It's not possible."

Celeste walked up behind him but stopped just out of his reach. She longed to caress him and relieve his distress. "I'm sorry that your father is ill. Do you not want to be at his side?"

The maestro faced her and smiled sadly. "My father never wants me at his side. He hasn't forgiven me for insisting on becoming an artist. He says such a vocation is beneath our rank in society. He softened after I married Isabella and opened my workshop, but he's still disappointed despite my success. He also expects me to produce an heir, but that's unlikely to happen."

He'd never spoken of Isabella. Just the mention of her name made Celeste uneasy. She liked to pretend the maestro wasn't married. She pushed thoughts of Isabella aside and said, "I'm sure you are wrong. You're revered as one of the greatest artists of our day. It's well earned."

"But not for a Florentine Duca, and not for a Vicente. My life will be far different when I return home. I hope to open a workshop but don't know if that will be possible." He stopped and studied his paint-stained boots. Without looking up, he said, "I must go. Please do as I ask, Celeste." He raised his head. "You still have my promise of protection. Look for Carlo tomorrow night. He'll remain until you come, so don't leave him waiting in the cold."

He strode out of the studio before Celeste could protest. She'd trusted him, and he hadn't betrayed that trust. She would have to summon that courage to place her fate in his hands once more.

She pulled her hood up and left through the back door. The weather had worsened, so she ran across the courtyard to the gondola. Luigi wasn't there. She searched for him, but he was nowhere to be found, so she ducked into a shallow alcove to wait and felt a tap on her shoulder fifteen minutes later. She turned to see Marco scowling.

"What are you doing here? Maestro told me you weren't coming today because of the rain. Did you not get word?"

"No, I didn't and didn't know where to find you," she said, hating having to lie to him, but he'd caught her off guard.

He lifted the small piece of wood he carried over his head as protection against the rain. "Why are you still here? I've had my supper, and Maestro gave me extra work today. I need to get back to the workshop."

"I can't find Luigi. He must be sheltering from the rain somewhere. Did he go to the workshop?" When Marco shook his head, she said, "Go back to work. I'm sure Luigi will turn up soon."

Celeste smiled to encourage him. He kissed her cheeks before darting off into the rain. She pulled her cloak closer and leaned back to wait for Luigi. She considered going back to the studio but didn't want to risk being spotted since Marco knew she was there. When she was about to give up and find another way home, Luigi came from behind the small wall that led to the garden.

"Where have you been?" Celeste asked as she followed him into the gondola.

"Did you expect me to wait in this rain while you were off on your escapades?" he asked.

The harshness of his response startled her. He'd never shown any interest in her "escapades," as he called them. He usually seemed grateful for the time away from his usual duties, so she put his mood down to the foul weather.

"I'm sorry for leaving you waiting out here. I should have stayed home today," Celeste said and covered Luigi with a blanket.

He gave her an odd look before settling in for the ride home. His behavior reminded her she needed to be on her guard around him. Luigi worked for Signore Benetto, not Maestro Vicente. She couldn't give him a reason for suspicion, especially in light of the more dangerous risk that she was about to take.

~

CELESTE DIDN'T SLEEP for agonizing over how to get out of the house unnoticed the following night. As the first rays of dawn crept into her room, she decided to send word with Carlo to the maestro she'd changed her mind about the nighttime lessons. She dressed, secure in knowing she'd made the right choice. She didn't want to defy her maestro, but what he was asking was too big a risk. She found a scrap of paper in the empty nursery and scribbled a quick note to pass to Carlo.

With no sleep, Celeste was exhausted when she dropped onto the bed that night. She had to make a show of going to bed before sneaking out to deliver her message to Carlo. An hour passed before the house was quiet. She crept from her room in the dark, not daring to light a candle, and tiptoed down the stairs.

After passing the houseboys sleeping on their mats by the kitchen fireplace, she grabbed her cloak from the hook by the servants' entrance and cringed when she pulled the door latch. Miraculously, it didn't squeak for once. She stepped to the landing in the dark and chilly air and was just able to make out Carlo's gondola.

"I'm not going with you," she said as she held the note out to him. "Please give my apologies to the maestro. I'll see him Monday as usual."

Carlo climbed out of the gondola, but instead of taking the note, he grabbed Celeste around the waist and lifted her over his shoulder.

"What do you think you're doing?" she hissed as she pounded on his back with her fists.

He tossed her onto the cushions like a sack of flour and straightened his cloak with a huff.

"The maestro warned me you might refuse to come. He ordered me to bring you to him, so that's what I'm doing. You might as well get comfortable."

Carlo was twice her size, so it was futile to escape. She didn't dare scream because how could she explain what she was doing outside if someone came to her rescue? No one would take her word over his. She took the blanket Carlo offered but glared at him for the entire trip.

When they reached Maestro Vicente's palazzo, Celeste pulled her cloak closer and tiptoed up the back stairs to the studio on bare feet. Flames from oil lamps and candles flickered on every surface. The maestro looked as relieved as she felt to have arrived safely.

"I'm not staying," she said and handed him the note. "Carlo brought me here against my will, and quite rudely, I might add."

The maestro raised an eyebrow and glanced at her bare feet but read the note without a word.

"Now that you're here, you might as well stay. I was afraid you'd lose your nerve at the last moment. Give me your cloak and put on this smock. I'll find you some slippers."

Celeste removed her cloak and handed it to the maestro. His eyes widened as he watched her. She was dressed only in a nightdress. With the candles illuminating the space behind her, he was able to see through the thin fabric.

He cleared his throat and grinned. "I suggest you dress in your day clothes next time."

She snatched the smock from him and stepped behind the screen to change. The maestro handed her some worn slippers when she came out and immediately began firing instructions at her. She held up her hands to stop him.

"Please, wait, sir. I'll cooperate tonight since I'm here, but this is the last time. My hands are shaking so hard that I'll not be able to hold a brush. We have to find another way." She dropped into a chair and covered her face with her hands.

He gave her a wry look and crossed his arms. "Were you spotted? Did you run into any trouble?"

"No, I had no trouble this time," she mumbled. "That doesn't mean I'll get away so easily in the future. I'm bound to get caught. They may have noticed my absence already."

He took the chair facing her. "I'm sorry for putting you through this ordeal. It was selfish of me, but now that you know what to do, won't it be easier next time? Please continue coming until I find a better way."

He looked so hopeful that she didn't have the heart to say no, but she was tiring of his schemes. He was so desperate to train her, but she was the one shouldering the risk.

"I may try once more, but I won't promise beyond that."

"Done," he said and patted her shoulder. "You don't have to paint tonight. I have a painting of my mother from upstairs that I'd like you to study. It's Paolo di Dono or Paolo Uccello, as he is known for his fascination with birds and animals. My father commissioned it years ago and allowed me to bring it here to remember her."

Celeste watched as the maestro placed the painting on the mantelpiece, then stepped back to admire it. It was a masterful work and seeing the image of his mother moved her. She felt closer to him somehow. Celeste listened intently while he described the aspects of perspective, which, according to the maestro, was another of Uccello's obsessions.

"I met Uccello once before his death. I would have loved to learn at his feet." He grew quiet again, then said, "I want you to replicate this work. It will help you master perspective and the use of bright color."

She was elated and flattered at the prospect of imitating such a skilled master. The work she'd been doing was rudimentary. The new project was a significant step forward.

"I'd be honored, sir."

He turned to face her and said, "You'll begin Thursday. You may go now. Tell Carlo to come to see me when he returns."

Celeste curtsied and went to change back into her nightdress. She thought of him while she dressed and realized that she'd only been alone with him one other time at night. Memories of their encounter in the garden washed over her. She imagined him stepping behind the changing screen and pulling her into his arms.

When he cleared his throat, she shook her head to chase away the carnal thoughts. She wrapped her cloak tightly around her shoulders and went to him. It was clear the maestro had shared her memory of the garden. She held his gaze for a moment, then left the studio without a word.

~

CELESTE'S COURAGE grew with each nighttime lesson until she faced her nocturnal escapes without worry. She and the maestro were careful to avoid a repeat of what happened that first night. Her training had to be their sole focus.

With the increased lessons, her skills progressed at a rapid pace, and she couldn't get enough of the knowledge her maestro poured into her. Her longing to enter the workshop grew each day, but it was a desire that would go forever unfulfilled. Celeste did her best to be content with the rare opportunity for private lessons that Maestro Vicente had given her but feared that one day that wouldn't be enough to satisfy her.

She was fantasizing about her artwork gracing the Basilica San Marco walls one night as Carlo guided the gondola to the Benetto's palazzo. When they arrived, she thanked him as he helped her out of the boat and smiled in contentment as he floated away into the darkness. She congratulated herself for once more getting away with the subterfuge when she heard the faint splash of an oar only feet from where she stood. It was too dark to see more than an arm's length ahead, but Celeste sensed she wasn't alone.

She raced up the steps to the servant's entrance and grabbed for the latch, but the door swung open before she reached it. Signora Foscari stood in the doorway, blocking her way. Not knowing what else to do, Celeste prostrated herself at her mistress' feet.

"Get up, girl," she ordered.

Celeste obeyed but kept her head bowed. Her heart pounded so hard she feared she would faint and topple into the canal. "Please, Signora, you must let me explain," she cried.

"I must do nothing. There's no need to explain. I know where you've been and what you have been doing. Luigi has been my faithful spy for many weeks."

Luigi stepped out of a gondola onto the landing and snickered. Celeste again dropped to her knees.

"If you know where I have been going and why then go to Maestro Vicente. He will explain. He's been giving me art lessons. Nothing more. I'm under his protection."

Signora Foscari stepped toward her. "How dare you speak my cousin's name? What he does is his business. But why would a future Duca of Florence care about a nothing girl from a worthless family like yours?"

Signora Foscari raised her arm to strike, but Pia knelt at her feet to stop her.

"Forgive me, Mistress, but what will Signore Vicente think if what Celeste says is true and you harm her? You wouldn't want to anger him. It may be best to just send her away."

Signora Foscari took three deep breaths and glared at Pia. "Since you were not aware of her deceit, I'll forgive your defiance this once," Pia mumbled her thanks and moved out of the way. Signora Foscari stabbed her finger at Celeste. "Get your things and go. Don't show your face to me again. You've betrayed the faith your Aunt Portia placed in you. You disgust me."

She stomped into the house, leaving Celeste sobbing on the landing. Luigi kicked her leg before racing up the stairs behind his mistress. She tried to stand, but her legs wouldn't move. She'd destroyed her life and that of her family. By morning, Portia and the rest of the Gabriele clan would know what she'd done. She had no choice but to return home in shame.

Celeste heard footsteps and raised her head as Pia came toward her. She recognized the cloth bag Pia carried. She placed it on the ground and squatted next to Celeste.

"I don't know what you have done to anger our mistress, but I can guess. You are not the first maid to get herself into trouble, and you will not be the last, though I thought you had more sense than most. I'm sorry there's nothing I can do to help. Is the Signore you've taken up with willing to take you in?"

Celeste looked at her in confusion. "I've not taken up with any man. It's just as I told the mistress. Maestro Vicente has been giving me art lessons, nothing more. He discovered my unique talent and wanted to train me. He promised to protect me. Pia, I beg you to please get word to him."

"That's impossible. I shouldn't even be talking to you. If my mistress were to hear that I'm helping you, I'd be joining you on the street. Why would you take such a risk to make paintings? A woman like you has no hope of becoming an artist. You've ruined your life and that of your brothers and sisters who depend on you."

Celeste had no answer. She'd fooled herself into believing she was safe, but she should have known better. She'd learned from bitter experience how quickly the world can turn its back. She covered her face and wept softly into her hands.

Pia took pity on her and said, "Signore Vicente may hear of what has happened and come to your rescue but do not count on it. Powerful men are full of promises they never keep." She stood and withdrew a small pouch from her pocket. "Here are your wages for the week. My mistress didn't want to pay you, but I convinced her she could not throw you out with no money to get home. She may be furious, but I don't believe she wants to be responsible for your death."

After dropping the pouch in Celeste's lap, Pia rushed up the steps and went inside, leaving Celeste alone on the dark landing. It was pointless to go after her and beg for help. Celeste had ruined enough lives through her selfish behavior and didn't want to add Pia to the list.

She climbed to her feet and wiped her face on her sleeve. At least Signora Foscari had not demanded that she return the cloak. It was too dangerous to start for home in the dark, so she dragged her bag to an alley four blocks away and chased a rat out of the cleanest corner, then curled up on the cold stones to wait for dawn.

❧

THE FIRST RAYS of light trickled into the alley and brought Celeste out of fitful sleep. The rat had returned and was gnawing on her bag. She kicked it away and opened the bag to find dried fish, cheese, and brown bread Pia had wrapped in a cloth. Not knowing how long it would be before she had another meal, she ate just enough food to satisfy her hunger and covered the rest with the cloth.

Pia had also left her a small cup. Celeste carried it to the well in the square and hid in the shadows until the women who might recognize her had gone. While waiting, she recalled the many times she'd gone to draw water and gossip with servants from nearby palazzi. Now, she didn't dare show her face.

Once the square was quiet, she went to the well and drank until her stomach was full. With her strength renewed, she gathered her meager belongings and started for home. She left the clean, well-organized streets of the grand palazzi and made her way to the chaos of the old quarter where her family lived.

She dared not spend her precious few coins on a public gondola since Papa would demand that she turn over every bit of the money Signora Foscari had given her. She swallowed her bitterness at knowing her current troubles all led back to her father's failings. Her fiery resentment toward Giovanni Gabriele grew with each step Celeste took toward home. The pleasant evening she'd spent with him in Piazza San Marco was forgotten.

She accepted responsibility for her choice to study with Maestro Vicente, but the consequences would have been far less if she had still been a member of the Gabriele clan. The worst Papa would have done for punishment was to lock her in her room. What awaited her would be far worse.

The neighborhoods became shabbier as Celeste got closer to home. After her time with the Benettos, she felt like she was entering a discarded and forgotten world. She took a breath when she reached her house and thought of the day Portia had rescued her and again fought the urge to flee to the mainland.

She pushed the door open without knocking and found her brothers and sisters on the floor surrounding the cold fireplace. The room was in shambles. Bianca noticed her standing in the doorway and squealed with delight. Celeste ran to her and gathered her youngest sister up in her arms, feeling Bianca's ribs through her dress. Jacopo and Veronica ran to their sister, too, but Sandro stayed back, eyeing her suspiciously. Her heart ached at the realization that he didn't remember her.

"What are you doing here, Celeste?" Jacopo asked.

She studied him before answering. His face was drawn, and his eyes were sunken and rimmed with dark circles.

She held him at arm's length and said, "I'll explain later. Where is Papa? Where is Lorena?"

Jacopo's eyes darkened, and he shook his head. "We haven't seen Papa for a week, but he'll be here at any moment for your wages. Go before he returns."

Celeste put her hands on her hips. "I'm not leaving. Where's Lorena?"

Her brothers and sisters glanced at each other. Veronica took a deep breath and said, "Papa wouldn't keep his hands off her after she gave birth and got her with another baby. She left many months ago when Papa was away. A servant came to deliver your weekly wages, so Lorena took her baby with the money and left us. We haven't seen her since. Papa only comes home to get the money you send. He leaves us a little for food and goes away again. We don't know where."

"Why are you here, Celeste? What's happened?" Jacopo asked again.

She looked at her famished brothers and sisters as they watched her with wide, hopeful eyes. Her siblings were going to starve because of her selfishness.

"I acted foolishly, and Signora Foscari threw me out, but I'm here to take care of you. I'll make this right. What about Aunt Portia? Does she know what has happened to Lorena?"

"We haven't seen her since the day you left. At first, she sent the occasional basket, but even those have stopped. She's forgotten us," Veronica said.

Celeste sat in the dusty rocking chair and pulled Sandro into her lap. He didn't fight but rested his head on her chest and closed his eyes. She felt the weight of what she'd done pressing down on her. Celeste's siblings had been alone and starving for all those months while she worried about whether she'd be able to paint. It was a wonder God hadn't struck her dead.

"Hand me my bag, Veronica," she said. She withdrew some coins from the pouch and pressed them into her hand. "Go to the market and buy food." She gave a few more coins to Jacopo. "Buy some firewood. Bianca, fetch some water."

Their eyes brightened at the thought of a meal and rushed off to do her bidding. While they were gone, she cradled Sandro and tried to figure a way out of the disaster she'd caused. Jacopo ran in the door before she came up with a single idea.

"Papa's coming. You must go. He'll kill you if he finds there's no money for wine."

"Hide the money I gave you but give him this." Celeste took out the pouch with the rest of the coins. She only kept enough for herself to buy a crust of bread. "I'll go to Aunt Portia. She'll help us. Look for me tomorrow."

She handed him Sandro and was back on the street almost as soon as she'd arrived. Papa would wonder why there was less money that week, but he'd never risk confronting Signora Foscari. Celeste prayed that he wouldn't take his anger out on the children. She ducked around the corner and headed for the Gabriele palazzo and Aunt Portia. All Celeste's hopes rested on her.

CELESTE'S MOOD brightened when she put her old neighborhood behind her and neared Uncle Cesare's palazzo. She'd risked paying for a gondola to reach her aunt before nightfall, but her stomach tightened as the boat rounded a bend, and her destination came into view. She hadn't seen the palazzo since her father's downfall, and her resentment returned. She shoved it down and focused on her objective.

She didn't dare approach the main entrance but walked along a side canal to the servant's door. She wiped her face and smoothed her hair before knocking. A boy of about Marco's age answered.

He narrowed his eyes at her and said, "Who are you? What do you want?"

Celeste squared her shoulders and said, "I'm Celeste Gabriele. I must speak with my aunt, Signora Portia Gabriele."

The boy looked her up and down and sneered. "Wait here," he said, then slammed the door.

She lowered her shoulders and reminded herself to breathe. The door swung open moments later. A woman who she guessed to be the head housekeeper glared at her.

"I know who you are. Word has reached my mistress' ears of what you did. She refuses to see you. No one in this house wants anything to do with you. Leave and never return."

The housekeeper tried to close the door, but Celeste threw herself against it. "What do you mean, my aunt knows what I have done?"

"Carrying on with Signore Vicente like some street wench. You should be ashamed to show your face."

"Maestro Vicente was giving me art lessons. I was not 'carrying on' with him. Signora Foscari knows this. Tell my aunt to go to Maestro Vicente. He promised to protect me. He'll explain or let me explain to my aunt myself."

"Are you saying that Signora Foscari lied? How dare you accuse her?" She gave Celeste the evil eye and slammed the door.

Celeste dropped onto the stoop and let the tears she'd been fighting come. She considered pounding on the front door but knew she'd face the same reception. Her last hope was to go to Maestro Vicente. Pia had warned that powerful men didn't honor their promises, but she trusted the maestro. Done with her tears, she dusted off her skirt and walked toward the canal. She'd committed no sin. It was time to stop being a helpless victim. She was an educated artist on the verge of greatness.

The sun was setting, so Celeste looked for another alley to be her home for the night. She rounded a corner and sensed someone following her. She raised her chin and walked like she was on an errand for her master. The garden gate for the grandest palazzo on the block was open, so she pretended to head there. As she reached for the gate latch, a hand grabbed hers and dragged her to the closest alley before she could struggle free.

A man pushed her to the ground and put his knee on her ear before she could look at him, but she didn't need to see his face to recognize him. The sound of his breathing told her it was her papa. He reeked of wine and swayed as he leaned over her. Celeste swallowed her revulsion and forced herself to speak calmly.

"Papa! How did you find me? Did you come to bring me home?"

He jerked Celeste to her feet and slapped her with the back of his hand in answer. The blow knocked her to her knees.

"Don't act innocent with me. Word of your disgrace is spreading through Venice. I heard the sordid tale from a trusted friend. You've destroyed us. How long before the maestro tosses Marco out after you?"

She rubbed her cheek and glared at him. "I have not destroyed us. You have. It's all your fault. I've been falsely accused and have done nothing more sinful than taking art lessons. He promised to protect me. I'm on my way to him."

"How dare you speak back to me?"

Celeste climbed to her feet to defend herself when he struck her harder. She crumpled to the ground. Not satisfied, he yanked her up by the hair.

"Stop, Papa, please," she cried. "I'm telling the truth. Come with me to Maestro Vicente. He'll explain."

Papa was in a blind rage. He slammed his fist into her jaw, knocking her flat. She tried to rise, but he kicked her harder in the ribs. When she cried out, he kicked her in the jaw before running off into the darkness. When Celeste tried to stand, the world spun and went black.

CHAPTER NINE

$\mathcal{L}$uciano's anxiety mounted while he waited for Celeste to arrive for her lesson. He hadn't worried when she wasn't in the studio when he got there. Situations often arose that prevented her from being on time, but he grew anxious when she was more than an hour late. He tried to paint but couldn't keep his mind on his work. He threw down his brush and ran a hand through his hair, trying to figure out how to discover where she was. He couldn't go storming into Pietro's home in search of her, and it would be hard to explain to his gondolier why he was out scanning the canal for a young woman late at night.

He hadn't slept in his studio since he'd moved into separate chambers upstairs, but he still kept a cot there. He stayed in case Celeste came, praying her absence was because of nothing more than not being able to get away unnoticed. Maria was probably hosting one of her incessant parties that ran late.

He tried to ignore the most likely cause of Celeste's tardiness that Maria had discovered the secret lessons. If that were true, her situation was dire, and she would need him. He'd made a promise to protect her, no matter the cost.

He drifted off before dawn and slept until the sunlight shone blindingly in the studio. He went upstairs for breakfast and was relieved to find the dining room empty. After gulping down some bread and cheese, he went to the workshop and pulled Marco aside after handing out his apprentices' assignments.

"Have you had word from your sister since her last visit?" he asked.

Marco shook his head. "No, Maestro. I haven't seen or heard from her in many weeks. During her last visit, she told me that she would be busier than usual and wouldn't come for a time. She promised to write as soon as she could, but I haven't heard from her."

"I see," Luciano said and stroked his beard. "I have a question for her about something involving Signora Foscari. I'll see her myself. Go back to work."

He left Marco staring after him and went to his studio. He'd hoped that Celeste had sent a letter to Marco but decided to get word to Celeste through Carlo before going directly to Maria. Hopefully, the servants wouldn't be suspicious if a messenger arrived with a note for Celeste.

Luciano did his best to focus on his work until going in search of Carlo at dusk. He sent Carlo off on his mission and went back to the studio to give his cot another try. He'd just fallen asleep when he heard a tap on the door. He sat up and rubbed his face when he saw Carlo through the doorway.

"Back so soon? Do you have a reply from Celeste?"

Carlo fidgeted and kept his eyes lowered. "Signora Foscari dismissed Celeste two nights ago. No one would tell me where she is. The housekeeper slammed the door in my face."

Luciano reached into his pocket and withdrew some coins from a leather pouch. It was twice as much as he owed Carlo, but he hoped the extra money would buy his loyalty and silence. "I appreciate your help, but I'll no longer need your services tonight."

Carlo bowed and rushed away, squeezing the coins in his palm. Luciano slammed the studio door and kicked his cot, sending it flying across the room. It knocked over the easel, and as Luciano watched his latest painting crash to the floor, he felt his life falling with it. He was furious with himself for failing Celeste and putting her in danger.

There was nothing he could do until morning, so he righted his cot and straightened the studio, hoping he hadn't seen the last of Celeste.

CELESTE'S EYES fluttered open just after midnight. Once she got her bearings, she dragged herself to the back of the alley, flinching in pain with every movement. Instinct told her she'd die there if she didn't go for help. She cleaned her wounds as best she could and choked down the last morsels of bread and cheese from the bag. With just enough strength to stand, she set her feet for Maestro Vicente's palazzo.

She numbed her mind to the pain and focused on making her feet continue taking steps. Few people were out at that hour, so she didn't fear getting recognized or attacked. She stopped every few blocks to rest. Only her hope of getting to the maestro kept her moving.

After four agonizing hours, his palazzo finally rose before her. She crawled up the back stairs to his studio. Expecting everyone in the household to have gone to bed long before, seeing candlelight flickering under his door was a miracle. She knocked softly and nearly cried in relief when he answered.

"Maestro," she whispered and collapsed in his arms.

He carried her to a cot in the corner and gently tapped her cheek. "Can you hear me? Celeste, speak to me."

She heard him but was too weak to respond. She roused moments later by the sharp odor of ammonia and coughed. "Maestro?" she whispered through cracked lips.

"Yes, Celeste. You're safe in my studio. I'm going for the physician. I'll lock the door behind me. Rest until I return."

"Yes, Maestro. I'm safe. I can rest now."

She closed her eyes and knew nothing until she again felt the maestro tap her cheek. She opened her eyes and tried to focus on the four people staring down at her. She recognized Marco, and Signora Niccolo stood next to him. Celeste recognized her from her occasional visits to Signora Foscari. A young woman Celeste knew as the signora's lady's maid stood behind her mistress. The maestro stood next to the Signora.

The first to speak was the maid. "What's Celeste doing here? How did she get hurt? Is she alive?"

"I said no questions, Livia," the maestro barked.

Livia bowed her head and curtsied. "Forgive me, sir."

"She needs clean clothes. Go to my wife's chambers and find something plain and comfortable if you can. If not, bring one of your dresses."

"I only have this dress." When he glared at her, she bowed and said, "Yes, sir. I'll find a suitable outfit in the young Signora Niccolo's closet."

The maestro shook his head as she scurried from the room. He took a pitcher from his worktable and poured water into a ceramic bowl. Signora Niccolo gasped when he knelt next to the cot, dipped a clean cloth into the water, and gently scrubbed Celeste's cheek. She pulled away in protest.

"No, Maestro. You mustn't. I can wash my own face."

"Nonsense," he said and kept working.

She was too weak to fight him, so she laid back and watched his face as he tended to her injuries.

"Can you tell me what happened?" he asked softly.

Celeste told him of Luigi's betrayal and her journey home.

"I had to escape before my father returned. I left what little food and money I had with my brothers and sisters and started for my Uncle Cesare's palazzo to beg Portia for help. Word of my disgrace reached the servants before I did. They refused to let me speak with my family and slammed the door in my face. I was on my way here when my father found me."

When she grimaced, the maestro said, "Am I hurting you?"

Forgetting the others in the room, she put her hand over his. "No, it's not you." Her tears dripped onto the cot as she recounted what her Papa had done. "I must have lain in that alley for hours. When I awoke, all I could think of was getting here. I knew you would help me. Pia said you wouldn't keep your promise to protect me. I knew she was wrong."

"I caused this. The fault is mine alone," he said. "I'll do whatever it takes to make up for what has happened to you."

She shook her head. "You didn't force me. It's what I deserve."

The maestro cringed at her words. "You deserve the world and nothing less. I'm more determined than ever to get it for you."

Signora Niccolo cleared her throat and said, "May I ask what's happening here? I have a right to know. This better not be what I think it is. You're my daughter's husband."

Celeste glanced at Signora Niccolo when the maestro pulled away and stood to face her. Livia returned at that moment with a dress draped over her arm. She stopped behind her mistress and cocked her head to listen.

"I owe no explanations after the way Isabella has behaved, but I'll give it for the sake of this girl's reputation and my respect for you. I've been giving Celeste art lessons in secret. She has an extraordinary talent. She was a maid in Maria's household. When Maria discovered what we were doing, she threw Celeste out without coming to me." He clenched his fists at his side. "I hold her responsible for this."

Marco stared at Celeste with wide eyes, but Livia smirked. "Art lessons. A handy excuse."

"Silence, Livia," Signora Niccolo said. Livia bowed her head and stepped closer to Marco. "Livia's right, though. If I don't believe you, no one will."

"No one outside this room will hear of this. Is that understood?"

The maestro was so fierce that even the signora bowed.

Celeste pushed herself up to her elbows and said, "He speaks the truth. I would never do what you're implying, Signora. Please, Maestro, show her my paintings."

The maestro pulled Celeste's painting of the canal from behind a stack of wooden panels. Her Madonna was still on an easel in the opposite corner. He carried them to the signora and held them up for her to examine. She studied them, looked at Celeste, then back at the paintings.

"This is truly your work?" she asked Celeste.

"Yes, madam, I swear it. The maestro has been giving me lessons for a year. There is nothing improper or sinful between us."

Marco stepped to her side and took her hand. "These are incredible, Celeste. Why didn't you tell me? Is this the real reason for your visits?"

Tears dripped onto her cheeks at his praise. "I'm so pleased you approve. It was the reason for my visits at first, but I've treasured my time with you."

A knock at the back entrance interrupted them.

"That will be the physician," the maestro said.

He ordered Livia to help Celeste undress. Livia eyed him suspiciously but obeyed when he scowled at her. He dragged the dressing screen in front of the cot for privacy and went to answer the door. Stefano came in, followed by the physician. The maestro thanked Stefano and sent him off to bed. Celeste heard Maestro Vicente explain the situation to the physician while Livia helped her change. He stopped when he heard Livia gasp.

"What is it?" he asked.

"Her body, sir. These wounds are serious. What happened to you, Celeste?"

The physician rushed behind the screen and began firing questions at Celeste. Livia's face was as white as bone.

"Thank you for your help, Livia," the maestro said. "You may go, and please, not a word of this to anyone. Your future here depends on your silence. Do you understand?"

She made a deep curtsy. "You have my word, sir."

The physician tended to Celeste's wounds as best he could and offered her wine to help her rest before he rejoined the maestro.

"Her condition is grave, but she is young and may survive. She'll need several weeks of care, at least. Take her to the hospital, Luciano."

"That's impossible. We can provide the care she needs here. Can I count on you to be discreet? The situation isn't what it appears."

"Of course, Signore," the physician said and bowed. "I'll come daily to check on her."

He left the maestro with herbs and instructions. Celeste heard the door lock after he had gone, and the maestro left the room for several minutes. He returned carrying some blankets, which he used to fashion a makeshift bed on the floor next to the cot. She waited to hear his even breathing before closing her eyes. Despite her injuries, she slept more soundly than she had in weeks.

LUCIANO HURRIED from his studio to Francesca's chamber as soon as he woke and pounded on her door.

Francesca opened the door a crack. "What's the emergency? Is there a fire?" she asked.

"No emergency. We must discuss the girl."

"Very well but keep your voice down. I don't want Bella to overhear."

"Bella had enough wine after dinner to knock out a bear. She'll hear nothing. Open the door." Francesca stepped aside and let him pass. Luciano noticed that Francesca still wore the gown she'd had on earlier. "Going somewhere?"

"To check on the girl until you came pounding on my door like an insane person," she said.

"Spy on her, don't you mean?" Luciano asked.

"Don't accuse me, Luci. You're the one harboring an unmarried serving girl under your wife's nose. Maybe I'll expose your dirty secret."

"Do that, and you'll all be looking for a new roof to cover your honorable head. I took in you and your daughters after your husband's death, but my patience is wearing thin."

"It's not charity. I earn my keep with the commissions I bring. Or have you forgotten? It keeps meat on your table, does it not?"

"And gowns on your daughter," Luciano went on. "I'd manage fine without you. I've made my own reputation, and the proceeds from my Florentine estates far surpass the earnings on my commissions." Luciano stopped and shook his head. "We don't have to argue this now. I need Livia's help for the next several weeks. She can still serve you, but free up time for her to assist me."

"You have a workshop full of boys that cater to your every whim. Why can't you use one of them? Why should I have to suffer?"

"Don't be ridiculous, and it's my money that pays Livia, too. I don't need your permission."

"All true, Signore, but you've never made such demands. Does this girl matter that much to you?"

Luciano nodded. "More than any pupil I've ever taught. If she reaches her potential, I'll never need another commission."

"You're not planning on her staying, are you, Luci? Prodigy or no, you must make other arrangements when she's recovered. Give up this idea of taking her on as an apprentice. It's impossible."

"I'll find somewhere for her to go once she's well. Maybe you can help. Now, please send for Livia."

"Very well," Francesca said and left Luciano alone in her quarters.

He sat near the fire and thought of Francesca's words. She was right. Training Celeste was an insane notion. He'd attempted to teach her for so long and look at what they'd gotten for his efforts.

"You sent for me, sir," Livia said and gave a formal curtsy.

Luciano saw that she was still shaken. The sight of Celeste's wounds must have sobered her.

"Yes, Livia. I need your help to care for Celeste. I don't want you badgering her with questions about what happened. You're here to care for her physical needs only, and I remind you to keep your silence. Don't even discuss it with your mistress or the other servants. If I find you gossiping, you will be dismissed immediately. Is that clear?"

"I gave my word, sir. I stand by that," she said. "I promise to take good care of Celeste."

"I knew I could rely on you."

"Very well," Francesca said and climbed into bed. "Livia, bring my breakfast." The girl curtsied and scurried out of the room. "Poor thing looks scared to death, but I trust her to hold her tongue. I hope you know what you're doing, Luci."

"Me, too," Luciano whispered as he left his mother-in-law to rest.

～

THE STUDIO WAS STILL DARK when Celeste opened her eyes. Her head pounded, and pain shot through her body when she tried to raise herself. She fell back onto the pillow with a groan, and something brushed her hand. She would have screamed if she'd had the strength.

"It's only me, Celeste." The maestro knelt beside the cot and studied her face. "I'm relieved to see you're still alive."

She tried to smile, but her lips were too swollen. "Yes, I have survived. There may be hope for me." She adjusted her position and groaned again. "I heard you speaking with the physician, Maestro. You're not responsible for me. This is my father's doing. Send me to the hospital or a convent. The sisters will tend to me."

"Don't waste your strength on arguing. You're staying here." He stood and stretched before turning to face her. "Please, call me Luciano."

Celeste shook her head. "Are you not still my maestro, then?"

"I'll be your maestro until my dying breath, but you don't have to call me that when we're alone." He took her hand and smiled sadly. "I had such plans for you. I'll make this right."

He walked around the screen, and Celeste heard clattering noises across the room. The journey leading her to his studio had been a nightmare but being with him in the studio felt like coming home. She didn't know what her future held, but for that moment, she was safe.

He returned with the bowl and pitcher, and a chamber pot. "I'll send Livia to help you, and I'll do my best to keep your presence here a secret. My staff will be discreet."

"Why are you doing this? I have no way to repay you."

"Call me Luciano."

"Luciano," she said, savoring the feel of his name on her tongue.

"Repay me by getting well. That's all I need. I must go, but I'll return tonight. Rest now, Celeste."

～

LIVIA POKED her head around the screen and stared at Celeste with wide, frightened eyes. Celeste did her best to smile and put Livia at ease.

"Come here," she said and patted the blanket. Livia hesitated for a moment before lowering herself onto the cot. "I see you're the lucky one who gets to take care of me. I'm grateful."

"Don't be. I'm just following my master's orders. He says I'm not to ask questions, but how can I help you if I don't?"

"I give you permission to ask whatever you wish, but first, please help me up so I can relieve myself," Celeste said.

Livia put her arms around Celeste's waist to lift her, and Celeste screeched in pain. Livia was even smaller than Celeste, so it took several tries for them to negotiate Celeste onto the chamber pot. Getting back into bed afterward was even worse.

"We must find a better way to do that," Celeste whispered through her chattering teeth once she was back on her makeshift bed.

"It will get easier each day. I took care of my mamma once after her mistress beat her, so I know. My master has ordered me to feed you gruel. I'm not to leave until you finish the bowl."

Livia hurried out and returned moments later with a steaming dish. "You must sit up higher to eat."

Celeste pointed to Luciano's blankets scattered on the floor. "Fold those and prop them behind my back."

Livia studied the pile of blankets and glanced knowingly at Celeste before rolling them to slide behind Celeste's back. Celeste wanted to feed herself, but Livia insisted upon doing it.

"There is nothing wrong with my hands," Celeste said

"I don't want you to spill on Signora Niccolo's nightgown. I'm the one who will have to wash it."

She relented and allowed Livia to feed her. It was challenging to eat with her sore and swollen mouth, but the food was comforting and revived her strength. While she ate, Livia peppered her with questions about having lessons with the maestro and how she got injured. Celeste answered honestly.

"You were so smart and brave," Livia said when her curiosity was satisfied.

"No, not brave. Foolish. I've caused my family pain through my selfishness. I imagined myself as an independent woman above my station, like some chaste courtesan. I was deceiving myself. I'm no different from you, Livia. Signore Benetto owned me just as Signore Vicente owns you. There's no shame in that, and I should have been content."

Livia nodded and stood. "And just as Signore Vicente owns Signora Niccolo. My mistress and her daughters have no more freedom than we do. Maybe less. It's the lot of all women. Better to accept it. I'll come back later to check on you. Rest now."

Celeste laid on the cot in her maestro's studio and pondered Livia's words. They made sense in her mind, but her heart wasn't persuaded. She'd never again be the innocent servant who sketched during Federigo's lessons; her dream of becoming an artist was dead. She longed to discover where she belonged in the world and hoped Luciano would be there to guide her.

It was long after dark when Luciano slid his key into the studio door lock. When he walked behind the screen, he was pleased to see the blanket bed waiting for him even though he wouldn't be using it.

"Are you awake, Celeste?" he asked softly.

"Yes," Celeste said and tried to lift herself to a sitting position.

"Don't try to sit." Luciano moved the lamp closer and studied her face. "You're looking stronger. Are you able to walk?"

"I don't believe so, Luciano," she said with a groan.

There was a gasp on the other side of the room.

"Hush, Livia," Luciano said. "You can't stay in the studio, Celeste. I've made space for you in a small storage room down the hall. It's not much bigger than a closet, but it will suffice. You won't be bothered there. I've brought help to move you."

He motioned for the others to join him. Livia stepped aside to make room for Stefano and Marco.

Marco glanced at Luciano before taking Celeste's hand. "I'll kill Papa for what he's done to you!"

Luciano turned away at the reminder he'd caused Celeste's injuries, even if Giovanni Gabriele had been the one who struck the blows.

Celeste put her hand over Marco's. "You'll do no such thing. Continue to work hard and obey the maestro. Forget about me. Do you understand?"

Marco glanced at Luciano, then nodded.

"I've brought someone else to help," Luciano said.

Marco and Stefano bowed and backed away as Signora Niccolo swept behind the screen to join them. Celeste turned her face to the wall.

"Don't turn away, Celeste," Luciano said. "Look her in the eyes."

"Yes, look at me, girl? " the signora asked.

"Her name is Celeste," Luciano growled.

Signora Niccolo dipped her chin to him.

"I'm ashamed to have caused so much trouble, madam," Celeste said.

"Nonsense. My son-in-law takes responsibility for this. He defends you. I hope you appreciate what that means."

"I do, madam," Celeste said and tried to nod. "I'd be dead without his help."

Francesca waved her comment off and said, "My son-in-law says your former mistress bears some responsibility, but I put the blame wholly on your father. What kind of man treats his daughter this way? He nearly killed you. I'm not unaware of his reputation."

"True, but this is my personal trouble. I don't deserve Signore Vicente's kindness or yours."

"I'll decide what you deserve. I'm taking charge of your care. Luciano is far too busy for such unimportant matters." Francesca turned to Stefano. "You and that boy carry her to the storage room. Livia and I will bring her things."

They jumped into action at the mistress' command and lifted the cot as ordered.

"Does this meet with your approval?" Luciano asked Francesca once they were all in the small closet room.

Signora Niccolo inspected the space and nodded. She turned to Celeste. "This will do well. The household staff doesn't come here. To avoid suspicion, Livia won't be able to come often, so you must amuse yourself. You appear strong. I expect your recovery will be short-lived."

"She'll not be idle. I've left materials for her to study," Luciano said and pointed to a small shelf. "You may take a few more days to rest before you begin. When you've recovered enough, I'll test you."

Marco gasped, but Luciano winked at him and grinned. "Afraid your sister will surpass you?"

"It will take time to get used to my sister as an artist, but I'll work harder to keep up with her, Maestro," Marco said and beamed at Celeste.

"No more talk of lessons," Francesca said and shooed Marco and Stefano out of the room. "Livia, help Celeste settle in for the night and come to my chamber when you finish. I'll wait for you in the hall, Luciano."

Livia curtsied, and Signora Niccolo left with a swish of her gown. Luciano asked Livia to return the key to his studio and gave her another.

"There are only two keys to this room. Your mistress has the other. Don't lose it and always lock the door when you leave."

"Yes, sir," Livia said and curtsied.

"Fetch fresh water and wine for Celeste."

Luciano waited for Livia to go before taking Celeste's hand and pressing a key into her palm. He held her gaze for a moment.

"I'll knock once," he whispered and left Celeste staring after him.

CELESTE STARED at the key resting in her palm. Why had Luciano lied to Livia about the number of keys? He could have given her the key and said nothing more. Acting with her heart had gotten Celeste into enough trouble. The logical thing would be to ignore Luciano's knock. She prayed for the strength to do so.

She heard voices in the hall moments later. It was Luciano speaking with the signora.

"I don't like this, Luci," Signora Niccolo said. "You should send that girl to the hospital. She's not a stray dog off the street. The physician said it will take weeks for her to heal. It's not safe for her to stay that long. No matter how much the servants promise to stay quiet, this will reach Isabella's ear."

"If that happens, they'll be on the street," Luciano said. "If we can't trust our servants to keep quiet, they shouldn't be here."

"What are you going to do, replace the entire household?" Francesca asked and snickered.

"If necessary," Luciano said.

There were several moments of silence. Celeste wondered if they had left until the signora said, "And you must give up this obsession of mentoring her. I don't doubt that she's as talented as you say and look at the trouble she's caused. Imagine what will happen if Isabella discovers what you've been doing under her nose. And you can't have failed to notice the way she looks at you. That girl is in love with you."

Their voices faded, so Celeste couldn't hear Luciano's response. Signora Niccolo's comparison was closer than she knew. Celeste felt like little more than a dog off the street, and her future was in the hands of others.

Celeste scolded herself for being such a fool. Luciano was a married man and saw her as nothing more than a talented student. She had to forget her feelings and focus on her future. As soon as she was well, she would rescue her brothers and sisters and find a safe place for the family. They could go to the countryside and work in the fields. Nothing could stand in the way of making it up to them, even if it meant losing Luciano forever.

Luciano didn't knock on her door the next day or the one after that. The storage room was near the studio, and even though she wouldn't see Luciano, it was a comfort to know he was close. She used the time to rest and focus on regaining her strength. The room wasn't much smaller than her quarters at the Benetto palazzo, and Celeste was glad to have a secluded place to herself.

She and Livia became comfortable with each other, and Celeste looked forward to her visits. She tried to give Livia as little to do as possible. The poor girl had enough on her hands, serving the signora. Celeste didn't want to be a burden. Her only other visitor was the physician, but he came less often as Celeste grew stronger.

The time between visits was lonely and silent. As soon as she could walk without help, she turned to the books Luciano had left. Studying invigorated her mind, but her hand still felt naked without a paintbrush, and she missed the soothing voice of her maestro.

LUCIANO WAITED three days before going to see Celeste. Working in his studio had been torture, knowing she was so close. He'd realized long before that Celeste was in love with him. Having her under his roof forced him to admit he loved her, too. They were like lovers in ancient tales, kept apart by destiny. As much as Luciano longed to be with her, he cared more about her potential as an artist. As soon as she was well, he'd secure another position for her and stop her training until a safer and more practical way could be found. He didn't know how he'd bear the separation from her, but he had no other choice.

After tossing in his bed until midnight on the third day, he got up and dressed, leaving his feet bare, and crept to Celeste's room. He hesitated at her door for what felt like hours before he gave one knock. Silence answered him. As he turned to go, he heard the key in the lock and a voice say, "Come in, Luciano."

His hand shook as he grabbed for the latch. "What am I doing?" he whispered to himself before gently opening the door. Celeste was propped in her bed with the blankets pulled tight under her chin. In the light of her oil-lamp, he saw that her cheeks were rosy, which he took as a sign that she was recovering. Livia had been giving him daily reports on her progress, but he was relieved to see for himself.

He knelt next to the cot as he had on the first night. "Did I wake you?"

"No, Maestro. I slept most of the day, and now my eyes refuse to close. I was thinking about you when you knocked. I was going to talk to you tomorrow, but now since you're here..."

When her voice trailed off, Luciano said, "I asked you to call me Luciano."

Celeste shook her head. "No, Maestro. I won't. We need to end our association. I'm deeply indebted to you. I owe you my life, and I can't ever repay you for opening the world up to me. But going on would be futile. We need to let this go. You know it's true."

Luciano knew but hadn't found a way to let her go. He was defenseless against the mystic power she had over him. He took her hand and gently brushed his thumb over her tender skin.

"I do know, Celeste, but it angers me. You're a treasure that I'm forced to discard. I'll never stop searching for a way to help you."

"I know you will, and I'm grateful, but how can I live with my mind always torn between my reality and my dream? How long before we admit defeat?"

The anguish in her eyes tore at his heart. Knowing he was the cause made it worse. How he wished he'd never laid eyes on her sketch that day in his studio.

"The answer will come. I'm certain of it. We'll part for a time, but not without hope that we'll both achieve our dreams." He let her hand drop and stood to go. "Don't give up, Celeste. Continue to be a bright light of hope in this dismal world. Promise me."

Tears rolled down her cheeks, but she smiled and nodded. "You have my word, Maestro."

CELESTE FELT like a caged tiger by the start of the fourth week in her closet room. When she could no longer endure the dark solitude, she took

Luciano's key and escaped to the garden after Livia finished tending to her in the morning. She sneaked down the back stairs and found a bench in a secluded corner. Raising her face to the glorious sun, she savored the respite before it was time to return to the dim and stuffy room.

Her stomach tightened when it was time to head back to her closet, but her reluctance turned to concern as she reached for her door and found it ajar. She was sure she'd locked it before she left. She pushed it open and peeked inside. Signora Niccolo stood in the center of the room with her arms folded.

"Where have you been, girl?" she asked, keeping her voice even.

Celeste curtsied and lowered her eyes. "I needed fresh air, Signora. I felt like I was suffocating. I promise it was the first time I've left this room. No one saw me."

"You'd better hope that's true. Sit down. I have news."

Celeste was uncomfortable sitting in the noble lady's presence, but she obeyed and lowered herself onto the cot.

"I've found work for you. Are you strong enough to handle the duties of a nanny?"

The unexpected question shocked Celeste, but she said, "I believe so, madam."

"I've secured a position for you in the home of my cousin, Sofia Viari. She has three young children. Her previous nanny has become too old and infirm to work, so they had to dismiss her. I told her about you but used your mother's surname, Prioli, so she won't connect you with Maria Foscari. I gave you a glowing recommendation. Don't make me regret risking my reputation on you."

"Is this by Maestro Vicente's order?" Celeste asked.

Signora Niccolo lowered herself into the only chair and arranged her voluminous skirts. "My son-in-law is aware. That's not to say he's pleased with the arrangement. He implored me to hire you for our household, but that would be a mistake. I've persuaded him to give up this folly of training you as an artist. You can't remain here. I'm sure you understand."

She looked directly into Celeste's eyes, who had no doubt of the signora's meaning.

"Gather your belongings as quickly as you can. I'll accompany you to my cousin's palazzo."

Celeste scanned the small room and shrugged. "I don't have any belongings, madam. Even this dress is not mine."

Signora Niccolo pursed her lips and said, "It would be suspicious for you to arrive empty-handed. I'll have Livia gather some items that no one will miss. Stay here until I return."

"Madam," Celeste said before she reached the door. "I'm grateful for your efforts to find me employment, but I'm not going with you. If I must leave, I'll be returning home to rescue my family. They're starving and have no one to care for them. I've worried about them every hour I've been here."

The signora regarded her before nodding. "Your loyalty serves you well, but that matter has been resolved."

She reached into a pouch at her waist and withdrew a folded square of parchment sealed with Luciano's mark.

"I'd planned to give this to you once you were settled with Signora Viari, but since you won't go with me otherwise, read it now."

She handed Celeste the note and hurried from the room before she could protest. Celeste dropped onto the cot and unfolded the letter.

Signorina Gabriele,

I know your mind is troubled by your family's dire circumstances. I have taken the liberty of seeing to their welfare. I first contacted your uncle, Cesare Gabriele, to inform him of your father's deplorable actions. While his brother's actions did not shock your uncle, he assured me he would take the necessary steps to deal with him.

I next wrote to a tenant farmer on one of my estates in Lucca. He and his wife recently lost their three daughters to a fever and have been deeply grieved. I told them of the plight of your siblings and asked if they are willing to take them and raise them as their own. They were overjoyed to accept. Your brothers and sisters are on their way to them now. It won't be an easy life. They'll be expected to work hard, but the farmer and his wife are good people who will treat them well.

I've taken the responsibility to cover the cost of their travel, clothing, and other materials they'll need. With the obstacle of their care removed, I hope your mind and spirit will be at ease. I expect no thanks, and nor will I accept any from you. I deem it my duty to do this after putting you in a vulnerable position out of selfishness.

It's my continued wish that I will discover a way to resume mentoring you, but in the meantime, may God grant you solace and a peaceful heart.

Your devoted maestro,

L.V.

Celeste didn't fight her tears. She was overjoyed for her brothers and sisters but saddened that she'd never see them or Marco again. Though deeply indebted to Luciano, she was dismayed that their time had ended and longed for the chance to say goodbye. She owed him so much, even her life. She slipped his key into the cover of the top book on her shelf, hoping he'd find it one day and know her last thought before leaving had been of him.

PART II

VENICE, LUCCA, AND FLORENCE 1476-1478

CHAPTER TEN

A painting that hung in the hallway near the nursery caught Celeste's eye on her first day as the nanny to Sofia Viari's children. She recognized it at first glance as Maestro Vicente's work. After checking to make sure no one was watching, she lovingly ran her fingers over the paint and longed to touch it with her lips.

Having his painting so near helped her feel less alone, though life in the Rosselli household was far different from the Benetto's. The Rosselli palazzo was just as grand, but the atmosphere was relaxed and welcoming. Signora Viari was a kind, lighthearted mistress. She often came to the nursery to cuddle and play with her children, something Signora Foscari never did.

Celeste enjoyed caring for younger children. Rosalia was a four-year-old angel with blond curls and the cheerful disposition of her mother. Benito was two and had dark hair and eyes like his father. He was a quiet child, but he took to Celeste from the first day. Lapa, the wet nurse, had the primary care of the infant, Tomaso. Their days passed in quiet contentment, and Celeste hoped her mistress would have many children so she could remain with the family forever.

The maestro had always praised Celeste's powers of observation. He encouraged her keen ability to divine the emotions of others and recreate them on the canvas. When Signora Viari introduced her to Lapa, Celeste discerned profound grief in her eyes. Most would have called her jolly with her round face and perpetually rosy cheeks, but Celeste saw that Lapa's smiles never reached her eyes. In time, Lapa told Celeste of how her son had been born too early and struggled to draw his first breath. He lived only three weeks, and the light in her eyes died with him.

Lapa had hired herself out as a wet nurse, hoping that nourishing another baby would ease her grief. Signora Viari took her in just days before Tomaso's birth. Nursing Tomaso had given Lapa a small measure of comfort, but nothing would ever fill the void of losing her precious son. Celeste did her best to console Lapa but would never comprehend the depth of her loss. Celeste's fate was to raise children born to others, but she enjoyed Lapa's companionship and hoped to call her a friend.

SIGNORA VIARI CAME to the nursery one day when Celeste had been with the family for three months. "I have an announcement," she said with a smile. "My brother Marcello is coming to stay. He's been at sea on one of our family's merchant ships, but now he's come ashore to find a wife."

Pride glowed in the signora's eyes as she described her handsome and successful brother. Her sisterly love reminded Celeste of Marco. She often wondered how he'd taken the news of her abrupt departure. She hadn't seen him since the night he helped move her cot into the storage room. She prayed that he was happy and would have a successful life.

The mistress had the household in an uproar as they prepared for her brother's appearance. She came to the nursery earlier than usual to visit the children on the day of his arrival. She snuggled Tomaso and handed him to Lapa before giving Rosalia and Benito each a kiss.

"I won't be able to visit for a few days as I'll be busy with Marcello," she told Celeste and Lapa. "He has no interest in children, at least not yet. Hopefully, he'll be blessed with that joy once he's married."

Celeste smiled and glanced at Lapa. Her lips curved into a weak smile that nearly reached her eyes. Signora Viari gave her darlings one last wave and left to greet her brother. Even though Celeste didn't mind her mistress' visits, she looked forward to the five of them getting their little world to themselves for a few days. Celeste considered asking one of the maids to deliver their meals to the nursery but decided that it wasn't fair to give them extra chores.

Lapa suggested they take turns fetching the trays, but Celeste offered to be the one to get them. Her offer wasn't only out of kindness to Lapa. She was also eager to get a glimpse of the long-awaited Marcello Viari. No one would raise an eyebrow if she came upon him in the courtyard or sala.

She had to wait three days before getting a peek at him. As she wandered the halls near the kitchens, the housekeeper spotted her and said that the master had invited a large party to dinner that night. Since Celeste wouldn't have been allowed near the guests, she volunteered to help serve once the children were asleep.

"Fiora, I have experience serving at the master's table from my former position," she said.

Fiora's relief was evident. "What a blessing. Stefania has been ill all morning, and Tessa turned her ankle on her way back from the well. I was on my way to ask the mistress for extra help. You look to be about Tessa's size. See if her serving dress fits you."

"Yes, Fiora," Celeste said and clapped in delight.

She turned to find Tessa but stopped when she saw a man who looked like a masculine version of Signora Viari coming toward them.

Fiora curtsied and mumbled, "Good morning, Signore Viari," before scurrying off, leaving Celeste alone with him.

Celeste imitated Fiora and made a deep curtsy. "Signore," she whispered.

"What's your name, and where have they been hiding you?" he asked with a grin.

Celeste glanced at him and said, "I'm Celeste Gab..." She paused, remembering that Signora Niccolo had given Signora Viari her mother's surname. "My name is Celeste Prioli."

"Well, Signorina Prioli, what do you do around here?"

He crossed his arms and leaned against the archway, blocking her path. He had dark eyes, but his sister's light coloring. The combination was striking. Celeste envied the woman lucky enough to be chosen as his bride.

She lowered her eyes and clasped her hands beneath her apron. "I'm the nanny, sir, but I help in other ways as needed."

"You help in other ways? What ways?"

His interest in a lowly nanny baffled her, but she said, "I'll be serving at the master's table tonight."

"I look forward to seeing you then, Celeste Prioli," he said and left her staring after him.

She'd satisfied her curiosity, but anxiety took its place. Men other than Luciano had only shown interest in her for one reason, and it was impossible to miss the intent on Signore Viari's face. Celeste hoped that, for once, her powers of observation were mistaken.

CELESTE HESITATED JUST out of sight of the sala and struggled to silence her rattling tray. The guests in their Venetian finery lined the long tables and chatted merrily. Celeste ordinarily would have been elated to tend the guests at such a gathering, but she chided herself for volunteering to serve that night. Not only did she have to avoid Marcello Viari's leering eyes and groping hands, but she had to avoid the attention of Luciano, Isabella, and Signora Niccolo.

She'd been foolish to forget that her mistress was Signora Niccolo's cousin. Of course, her mistress would invite Luciano to dinner. Celeste did her best to serve the guests at the opposite end of the room, but it was impossible to avoid Luciano's family. She kept her head lowered and did her best to survive with a sliver of her dignity intact.

She'd never seen Luciano with Isabella. They were the most

captivating couple in the room, but there could be no doubt of their lack of affection. Celeste had overheard rumors about them from her former mistress but had ignored them because Maria Foscari gossiped about all of Venice. Seeing the stories verified gave Celeste perverse pleasure. She didn't wish Luciano unhappiness, but witnessing him expressing affection to his wife would have been distressing.

Being in his presence stirred up emotions that Celeste had hoped were dead and buried, but they'd only been hibernating. As she poured wine for Isabella, Luciano spoke with the man seated next to him and acted as if she didn't exist. It was what he should have done, but it hurt all the same.

After the last of the guests departed in the early hours of the morning, Celeste gratefully headed to the nursery and bed. She heard footsteps approaching as she reached for the doorknob, and she froze. The footfalls were too heavy to belong to Signora Viari.

"Good morning, Celeste Prioli," the man said.

Celeste recognized the voice without needing to see the owner. "Good morning, Signore Viari," she said, without turning.

He reached around and took the candle she held.

"Come with me," he whispered into her hair.

When Celeste didn't move, he took her hand and pulled her away from the door. Panic welled up as he took her into darker and darker hallways. Marcello was much stronger than Celeste, so she was powerless to resist him. He found an alcove bathed in shadow and blew out the candle, leaving them in total darkness. Celeste heard the candle holder clatter on the floor just as she felt his hands reach up and tug at the laces on her dress.

"You're a beautiful woman," he said between short gasping breaths with his lips mere inches from her face. "I've thought of nothing else since meeting you this morning. I had to restrain myself from taking you in front of everyone at dinner."

He pressed against her so hard that she felt the ridges of the stone wall through her dress. A scream rose in her throat, but she kept her lips clamped to stifle it. No one ever sided with the servants against their masters.

Celeste took a deep breath and said, "Lapa is waiting for me in the nursery. She'll wonder where I am and will come looking for me."

He ignored her and ran his lips down her neck while his hand slid down from the laces and groped at her skirts.

"Signore, please don't. I'm still a virgin," Celeste cried, but he smothered her words with his mouth.

His breath reeked of stale wine and sour meat. Celeste was about to retch when she heard voices at the far end of the hallway. He pulled away and yanked her further into the alcove with his hand pressed against her mouth.

"I don't know where Marcello has gone," Signora Viari said. "He must be in bed. I'm going to kiss my darlings one last time and go to bed myself."

Celeste didn't recognize the voices that wished the mistress goodnight and heard doors opening and closing moments later.

She pried his hand from her mouth. "I must get back to the nursery. Mistress will search for me if I'm not there."

Signore Viari grabbed her hand and took off at a run toward the nursery. He threw the door open and pushed Celeste inside. She had just enough time to throw herself onto the bed before the light from the mistress' candle flooded the room. She was too absorbed in her children to notice Celeste inching the blanket over her body. As soon as Signora Viari closed the door behind her, Celeste sat up and sobbed into her hands. She felt Lapa's arm on her shoulder moments later.

"What's happened, Celeste?" she asked softly.

Celeste told Lapa of Marcello's assault. "If God hadn't sent the signora when he did, I don't know what he would have done to me."

"Don't you?" Lapa asked and raised her eyebrows. "Well, God or fate, I'm glad you're safe. Don't leave the nursery alone after dark for as long as he's here. Men like him don't stop until they get what they want. I'll fetch our meals from now on. He won't look twice at a lump of butter like me." When Celeste hugged her, Lapa smiled and patted her shoulder. "Sleep as late as you'd like tomorrow. The mistress won't be in, and I can care for the children. Put this terrible night behind you."

Celeste thanked her and sent her back to bed. Celeste's hands trembled as she undressed. She left her clothes in a heap on the floor and fell onto her mattress, weary of trouble following wherever she went. It was the curse of her unruly curls and bewitching eyes, just as her Papa never let her forget.

LUCIANO DRANK more wine than usual at dinner, hoping to sleep off the memory of Celeste, but his plan failed. All the wine did was give him a headache and a sick stomach. He'd done his best to keep her out of his thoughts in the months since she left but seeing her at Sofia's made his efforts pointless. She was as captivating as ever, and he was tempted to abandon his life and run away with her. They could find a house in the countryside where they could paint and live together as lovers.

Luciano let the fantasy play out before getting up and going to the studio. He dug Celeste's last painting from where he'd buried it under a stack of canvases and set it on an easel. The unfinished painting was a mocking reminder of his love for Celeste that would forever go unfulfilled. He grabbed some paints to finish the work but stopped before the brush's tip touched the canvas. He had another idea.

He threw the brush into a bag with the paints and rolled the painting before tying it with some twine. Wrapping the bundles in a cloth, he put them in a corner to wait until morning. After one last longing look at the package, he returned to his bed and slept soundly until the sun was high.

CELESTE PLAYED with Rosalia the following day when one of the master's pages came into the nursery carrying a large bundle wrapped in cloth.

"Are you Celeste?" he asked. When she nodded, he dropped the bundle and said, "This is for you."

He left without another word, and Celeste stared at the package for several moments before standing up to get a closer look. Lapa was getting their lunch but would return soon, so Celeste hurried to find out what it was.

She cut the twine and unfolded the cloth to reveal a rolled canvas and a cloth bag she recognized as belonging to the maestro. She pulled the bag open as quickly as she could. It contained jars of paint, brushes, and other painting materials. At the bottom of the bag was a folded note with Luciano's seal.

Celeste put the note in her pocket without reading it and hid the other items under her bed before Lapa returned. She'd never told Lapa about her life before coming to be the nanny for Signora Foscari's children and didn't want to explain the unusual package. She had just enough time to pick Rosalia up and take her chair before Lapa kicked at the door for Celeste to open it. Her note would have to wait until after lunch.

Celeste felt the note pressing against her leg, distracting her from the story Lapa told her about one of the maids.

"Are you listening?" Lapa asked. "Not still thinking about last night, are you? Marcello can't reach you here."

Celeste shook her head. " I'm only tired from being up so late. I'm not used to it. Please continue."

Lapa seemed satisfied with Celeste's answer and finished her story while they ate. Celeste put the two older children down for their naps while Lapa fed Tomaso. Once she had him settled in his cradle, she dozed in her chair as she did every afternoon. As soon as Celeste felt it was safe, she took the note from her pocket and read.

Dear Signora Gabriele,

I was so pleased to see you looking well last night. I've worried about you since you left. I came upon your painting today and thought you should have it. The work belongs to you. Just because I'm no longer your maestro doesn't mean you shouldn't continue to paint. I know it might be difficult, but I hope you'll find a way. I'd love to see your finished work one day.

Your devoted maestro,

L.V.

CELESTE WATCHED her teardrops spread over his words. He had noticed her at dinner and had been thoughtful enough to send the painting. Celeste ached to pick up the brushes again but knew she couldn't. It had been kind of the maestro to think of her, but she had put that life behind her. She put the note in the bag with the art supplies and pushed it under the bed. She'd find a better hiding place for his gifts later, but for the time being, it was a comfort knowing they were close.

CELESTE FOUND ways to distract herself from thoughts of Luciano as she hid from Marcello in the nursery. She only left her sanctuary to take the children for walks or play with them in the garden. She missed wandering the palazzo to visit the other servants or catch a moment for herself, but sacrificing those freedoms was worth it to avoid Marcello.

When she felt safe again, she heard the mistress' voice through the nursery door one evening.

"What are you doing here, Marcello?" Signora Viari asked.

"I'm looking for you, sister. It's time I visit Rosalia and Benito and meet my new nephew," Marcello said. "Don't you agree, sister?"

"I'm so pleased, but we'll only have a moment before our guests arrive."

Celeste glanced at Lapa in panic, but there wasn't time to escape before the mistress and Marcello burst into the room. She and Lapa rose and curtsied. Celeste hoped the mistress wouldn't notice her hands trembling while she and Marcello fawned over the children. Celeste breathed in relief when Signora Viari announced it was time to greet their guests.

"You go ahead. I'd like a few more minutes," Marcello said.

"It's pleasing to see you taking such an interest in the children. You may stay, but please don't keep us waiting."

Marcello kissed his sister's cheek and closed the door behind her. He handed Rosalia a toy and told her to go to Lapa before taking Celeste's hand and leading her to a dark corner of the nursery.

"Think you can hide from me forever? I hear rumors the servants are getting suspicious of your absence. Maybe my sister is, too."

He put his fingers under Celeste's chin and stroked her cheek with his thumb. She cringed at his touch but didn't dare remove his hand.

"Celeste, I need to change Tomaso," Lapa said. "Can you take Rosalia?"

"Coming," Celeste said and slipped past him.

She lifted Rosalia into her lap and distracted her with a cloth doll. Signore Viari glared at her, but she just smiled and kissed the top of Rosalia's head. Marcello stormed out of the nursery, and Lapa ran to lock the door.

Celeste squeezed Rosalia tighter to calm her pounding heart. "Thank you, Lapa. That was quick thinking."

Lapa picked up Tomaso and sat next to her. "He wouldn't have dared try anything in front of the children and me. Rosalia's old enough to tell her mother if she saw anything unusual."

"I'm not convinced of that, but he was right about one thing. I can't hide in here forever. What am I going to do?"

"You could tell Fiora and have her talk to the mistress."

Celeste shook her head. "The signora adores her brother and would never believe Fiora or me."

"Lock the door when I go to the kitchen from now on and make sure you're never alone outside the nursery. If the mistress comes and finds the door locked, tell her Rosalia has learned to open it."

"I will," she said.

Celeste knew locking the door wouldn't be enough to stop Marcello. He wouldn't stop until he got his hands on her. If Celeste resisted too forcefully, he might have her punished, or worse, thrown out. Then where would she go? There'd be no running to Luciano a second time.

CHAPTER ELEVEN

Signora Viari came to the nursery one afternoon, and after settling into a chair with Tomaso, called to Celeste and said, "Your work the last time you helped serve at the master's table impressed Fiora. She'd like you to assist again tonight. My dear brother was impressed, too, although I found it amusing that he noticed you. He tried to persuade me to free you from the nursery, but I convinced him you're far more valuable here. I'm pleased he's paying more attention to domestic matters as he matures."

Celeste nodded but wondered how her mistress could be so oblivious to her brother's true intentions. As much as they were alike in appearance, they were different in temperament.

Lapa took Celeste's hands as soon as they were alone. "I must go to Fiora for you. You'll be at that beast's mercy."

"But the request came from our mistress. Fiora can't go against her wishes," Celeste said. "I'm creative. I'll protect myself." She squeezed Lapa's hands when she saw the concern on her face. "Stop worrying. I'll ask Fiora to escort me to the nursery when I'm finished."

"Make sure you do," Lapa said and shook her head. "I won't be able to think of anything until you're back here safely."

Celeste's anxiety grew as the hour for her to leave the nursery grew closer. Her hands shook as she laced the serving costume her mistress had left for her. Lapa refused to let her go out alone and gathered up the children to march her to the servants' quarters. They encountered no one along the way, so Lapa was satisfied that Celeste would be safe. Fiora found Celeste and put her to work moments after she lovingly ordered Lapa back to the nursery. She was grateful because rushing about serving the guests would allow little time to worry about Marcello.

The first person Celeste saw in the sala was Isabella Visconti. She sat next to Marcello, and they were chatting with their heads together in an intimate conversation. Celeste searched the room for Maestro Vicente or Francesca Niccolo, but neither were present. Another relative must have escorted Isabella to dinner. Luciano never would have allowed her out without a male family member as an escort.

Celeste sighed in relief that Marcello had found another object for his attentions. He was mesmerized by Isabella for the rest of the evening and didn't even acknowledge Celeste when she delivered a full wine bottle to their table. She could have been a ghost. Even so, she kept her eye on them while she worked and wondered if anyone else realized what was happening.

Their chairs were empty when Celeste went to clear the last of the dishes at midnight. She was delighted Marcello had ignored her but felt sorry for the maestro and Signora Viari, who surely couldn't have missed her brother's behavior. The signora had told Lapa and Celeste how the master helped arrange their social engagements, hoping to find Marcello a bride. That would be difficult if he was consorting with married women. Celeste shrugged and cast her worries of Patrician intrigue aside. All that mattered was that she was safe from Marcello.

Once she completed her duties, she went in search of Fiora, but couldn't find her. A houseboy finally told her Fiora had gone to bed an hour earlier. Celeste panicked at having to walk back to the nursery alone until she remembered Marcello was with Isabella. Confident she had nothing to fear, she took the brightest lamp available and headed off to bed. The children would be awake just after dawn, so she would have little time to sleep.

Marcello hissed at her from the shadows as she approached the nursery door, causing her to jump and nearly drop the lamp.

"Stay quiet, or I'll see that you sleep in the canal tonight."

When she froze, he took the lamp and threw an arm around her waist to drag her down the hallway. Celeste prayed that he'd take her to the same alcove, and someone would save her as before, but Marcello turned a corner and headed for the stairs that led to the garden. He dragged her to a secluded corner and shoved her onto the dewy grass. As his hands fumbled with her laces, she frantically searched for a way to escape.

"Signore," she purred into his ear and went limp instead of fighting him. "If you'll not be so violent and give me a moment to catch my breath, I'll assist you with those laces."

He froze and squinted at her in the moonlight. "What?"

"Don't be in such a rush. This will be more enjoyable for both of us that way," she said and lowered her eyes.

He leered at her but lifted his weight off her body. Celeste reached for her laces and slowly began loosening them while he ran his lips over her neck. She shivered in disgust, which he mistook as a sign of pleasure.

While he was distracted, she said, "I thought your interest was in Signora Niccolo, or I wouldn't have left so quickly tonight."

He stopped kissing her neck and pounded his hand on the ground. "That vixen. She aroused my desires and left without allowing me to satisfy them."

"But she's married to Signore Vicente. She made the virtuous choice," she said, attempting to keep the conversation going.

He scoffed and said, "Virtuous is not a word I'd ever use for Isabella, but I know her game. She'll not escape so easily next time. Now, you're going to let me finish what she started."

Celeste nodded and started slowly working on her laces while Marcello went back to working on her neck.

"You're taking too long," Marcello growled.

In desperation, she said, "Don't you want to kiss my lips first? I've never kissed a man."

His breath quickened, and he pushed his mouth hard onto hers. Celeste's teeth cut into her lip, and she let out a squeal of pain. He pressed harder until Celeste tasted blood. Bile rose in her throat from fear and his foul breath. She wondered if he would stop if she vomited.

He reached his hand down her leg and lifted her skirt until her thigh was exposed. She struggled to get free, but he gripped her tighter. He reached under his tunic, and Celeste knew her chance for escape was gone. Her efforts to stall had only aroused him more.

She screamed when he pushed her legs apart, so he clamped his hand over her mouth so hard she could barely breathe. As he was about to enter her, she reached out in desperation and her fingers closed around a rock. She gripped it and slammed it into the back of his head.

His hand loosened, and he fell limp on top of her. When Marcello remained still for several moments, she opened her eyes and saw Lapa staring down at them. Celeste dropped the rock and rolled Marcello off of her.

"How did you know where I was?" Celeste asked as she tried to gather her wits.

Lapa covered Celeste's legs with her skirts and held out a hand to help her to her feet.

"When the house was quiet, and you still hadn't returned, I got worried and came looking for you. The door to the garden was open, so I came here first." Lapa led her to a nearby bench and made her sit. "How did this happen? You promised to stay with Fiora."

She explained about Marcello and Isabella. "They left the sala together. Fiora went to bed before I finished with my work. I thought I was safe, but Isabella spurned him, so he sought me out."

Lapa stood when Marcello groaned. "We'd better get out of here before he wakes." She tossed the rock into the shrubs. "Maybe that lump on his skull will remind him to think twice before taking advantage of defenseless women."

Celeste gave Marcello a kick in the leg as she passed. "Not likely. It takes more than a bump on the head to teach a man like Marcello."

~

MUCH TO CELESTE'S RELIEF, Isabella frequently visited Signora Viari in the days that followed, so Celeste was free from Marcello's attention. The mistress brought Isabella to the nursery twice and consoled her cousin for not yet knowing the blessing of motherhood. Isabella nodded and smiled but didn't seem to mind not having children of her own.

Celeste was also pleased with Isabella's childless state. It meant the maestro would have less of an attachment to her. If Isabella was having an affair with Marcello, there was little chance of producing a child with Luciano.

Celeste noticed a distinct change in her mistress' usual cheerful mood during that time. She seemed less than glad of her cousin's visits. Even though Celeste was sorry to see her mistress unhappy, she was elated to be free of the nursery to wander the grounds.

She passed her mistress' chambers one morning after breakfast and heard angry voices through the door. Though the sounds were muffled, Celeste recognized Marcello's voice and knew the cause for their argument. She'd never heard Signora Viari angry but was relieved she finally saw her brother for what he was.

The mistress came to the nursery that afternoon, cheerful and smiling. It surprised Celeste after what she'd heard earlier.

"My husband has found a suitable bride for my brother. They're negotiating the marriage contracts. Plans for the wedding have begun."

Lapa and Celeste congratulated her but pitied the unfortunate woman chosen as his wife. Celeste wondered how long Marcello would wait after the wedding before preying on their defenseless chambermaids. At least his reign of terror in the Rosselli household would soon end, and that was cause for celebration.

~

CELESTE TOOK advantage of the agreeable air that evening to stroll the garden after putting the children to bed. She savored the warm breeze that carried the comforting smell of the sea. She had dreamed of sailing off on adventures as her uncle, Giorgio, had done. She had often accompanied her mamma to the fish market to watch the massive ships moving out of the harbor and imagined what it was like onboard. She'd hoped to recreate her dreams on canvas one day, but that chance was gone.

The moon was bright enough that Celeste had left her lamp in the nursery. She stopped to admire the roses climbing the trellis and wondered which pigments she'd use to paint them. As she turned to find a bench, she heard sounds in the shadows. She was about to call out when the sound of Isabella's voice reached her.

"What does it matter if you are to marry? I'm married," she said.

"My sister said she'll kick me out and tell Father if I don't end this. He'll disown me. My wife's dowry isn't enough for me to establish my own estate," Marcello said. "I need my inheritance."

"I'll stay away until the deed is done, but once you are your own master, no one can stop us."

Celeste covered her mouth to stifle a gasp and stepped toward the sounds. She knew she should stop eavesdropping and return to the nursery, but her legs wouldn't obey.

"Fate is cruel," Marcello said. "I would have you as my wife instead of that dough-faced donkey Father and my brother-in-law found for me. The woman may be rich, but I loathe having to wake up to her face for the rest of my life. I'm certain she knows nothing about pleasing a man the way you do. Your husband is a fool. I would have you every night if you were mine."

Isabella giggled. "You don't have to wake up next to her. Luciano and I haven't shared a bed in ages. Get a son out of her and then move into your own chambers."

Her words sickened Celeste. How could Isabella not see Luciano for the rare and remarkable man he was? He deserved much better than her.

"Come here and let me practice getting a son on you," Marcello said.

Celeste cringed at the next sounds coming from the darkened corner and ran from the garden. Lapa raised her eyebrows at seeing her out of breath, but Celeste just smiled and went to bed. She lay for hours trying to shut out what she'd overheard and felt an obligation to get word to Luciano. He'd rescued her in a most desperate time. She owed him the same.

She rose early the next morning and scribbled a message before Lapa or the children awoke.

My Dear Maestro,

My apologies, but I must inform you of events that will cause you great pain. I hesitated to write this letter, but you have a right to know. I unintentionally observed your wife in a compromising position with Signore Marcello Viari last night. I overheard them discussing plans to continue their liaison after his marriage. I didn't mean to eavesdrop, but they were unaware I was nearby. I got away as soon as I could without being seen.

It breaks my heart to be the one to make you aware of your wife's affair. You don't deserve such betrayal. I am sure you will know which steps to take.

Your devoted pupil,

C.

She found Signore Rosselli's page, the one who had delivered the maestro's gift, and handed him her carefully folded note.

"Please take this to Signore Luciano Vicente for the mistress. You must hand it directly to Signore Vicente. I believe it's a surprise for the signora's cousin."

The page dipped his head and hurried down the stairs. Celeste doubted that the boy could read, so she wasn't concerned that he'd open the letter. With her obligation fulfilled, she took her breakfast to the nursery and put Marcello and Isabella out of her mind.

LUCIANO'S LIFE had become a tedious cycle of misery since Celeste left. He had argued with Francesca for days about keeping Celeste with them, but she convinced him that her leaving was for the best. Luciano knew she was right, but it didn't make the loss easier to endure.

His hopes and dreams had gone with Celeste, and his future spread before him as a colorless landscape of monotony. He did his best to summon enthusiasm for his work but continued to fall short. Seeing Marco every day didn't help, even though his appearance and temperament were far different from Celeste's. Just the memory of bringing the boy into his workshop was enough to frustrate him. It wasn't the boy's fault. He worked hard and showed some promise, but he would never be the master his sister had the potential to become.

Luciano was trudging through a dull morning when Stefano led a young page into the workshop.

"I'm sorry to disturb you, Maestro, but this boy has a note for you and insisted on delivering it directly into your hand. He says it's from Signora Viari."

Luciano gestured with his head for the boy to give him the note. "Did your mistress instruct you to wait for a reply?" Luciano asked.

"The mistress' nanny gave me the note, sir. She didn't mention a reply."

"You may go," Luciano said and waved him off.

Luciano walked nonchalantly from the workshop but raced up the steps to his studio when he was out of sight. He'd had no communication with Celeste since he sent the painting. He'd been tempted to pass a message to her a few times but was afraid Francesca would find out from her network of spies. He couldn't fathom why Celeste would risk contacting him and feared she was in trouble.

He tore the message open and read it as soon as the studio door closed. Bile rose in his throat as he read. He wasn't sure what sickened him more, that his wife had betrayed him or that Celeste had been forced to witness it. He'd deluded himself into believing that Isabella had been faithful since the night he caught her in the garden with

Antonio Pisani. Celeste's revelation made him wonder how many other affairs he'd been blind to.

He left the studio and rushed upstairs in search of his depraved wife. He found Francesca first.

"What is it, Luci?" she said when he nearly knocked her over in his haste to get to Isabella.

He didn't answer, so she grabbed his wrist to stop him. He thrust Celeste's note at her without a word.

After Francesca read it, he said, "I better not find that you were aware of this, or I will send you and all of your daughters from my house today."

Francesca went pale and began to tremble. "I give you my word, sir. I had no knowledge of Bella's betrayal. Is this from who I think it is?" He gave a slight nod. "Are you sure it's true? She could benefit from causing trouble for Isabella."

Luciano clenched his fists. "Do you doubt that it's true?"

Francesca lowered her gaze and shook her head. "She has been visiting Sofia frequently, but I thought it was because they are friends. I did not suspect this."

Luciano grabbed the note. "Where is your daughter?"

"In her chambers."

Luciano started down the hall with Francesca following close behind and burst into Isabella's chamber just as she vomited into a bowl.

Francesca rushed to her side. "Are you ill, my love?"

The maid handed Isabella a towel to wipe her lips as she turned to Luciano without answering her mother. "What are you doing here?"

"She's not sick. She's carrying Marcello's child," Luciano said and turned to Francesca. "Still wondering if Celeste lied?"

Isabella's eyes widened at the mention of Celeste, but she said, "How could I be pregnant? We both know that's impossible."

As Luciano read the note to her, Isabella stared at him in horror before collapsing into her mother's arms. Luciano shook with rage while Isabella sobbed on Francesca's shoulder.

"I blinded myself to your behavior because I didn't want to believe you were capable of this, but now you can't deny the truth. You're not to set foot out of this house for the rest of your pregnancy. Once the bastard is born, I'm sending all of you to my country estate in Florence. If Marcello refuses to take responsibility for his bastard child, I'll send it to an orphanage."

"Luciano, no!" Francesca cried as Isabella sobbed harder. "I wouldn't send a rat to one of those places. Most of the children die. This isn't this baby's fault."

Luciano threw the note into the fire, then rubbed his face. He knew Francesca was right and was ashamed of himself for thinking it, but the thought of Isabella's illegitimate child living under his roof sickened him.

"I'll take my daughters to live with my family after the baby comes. We'll free you of the burden of supporting us. It's what you've always wanted," Francesca said.

It wasn't true, but Luciano was tempted to accept her offer. Even though he couldn't divorce Isabella, at least she wouldn't be his responsibility. "Where would you go?"

"I have enough family willing to take us, or I could find a husband for one of my other girls before news of this becomes a public scandal."

Luciano stared into the fire and watched the last bits of Celeste's note fall into the ashes. "We have time to decide. Marcello may accept responsibility, even if Isabella will not. Until then, I meant what I said, Isabella. Don't leave this house, and don't contact Marcello or anyone else. See to it, Francesca."

"What will I tell people when they ask where she is? Others will notice her abrupt absence from society," Francesca said.

"Tell them she has a prolonged illness and needs rest. No one will question you. Inform the servants. I must get back to the workshop."

He went out, slamming the door behind him. He didn't go to the workshop but locked himself in his studio and didn't come out for days, leaving Stefano to run the workshop.

Any hope he'd harbored of a stable life with Isabella was dead, but he had to go on living. Pouring himself into his art was the only answer. He picked up his brushes with a ferocity he hadn't felt in years and finished his latest commission in record time. His patrons and peers touted it as his best work, but he gleaned only small satisfaction from their praise before an intense sense of doom overtook him. He refused the commissions Francesca sought for him and laid on the cot Celeste had occupied for a brief time, immersing himself in a world of what might have been.

CHAPTER TWELVE

*I*sabella's labor began seven months after Celeste's note arrived. Luciano somehow managed to go on with his life in the intervening months, but all the joy had drained from him. He'd lost Isabella. He'd lost Celeste. He cared for nothing else, but people depended on him, so he woke each morning, put his feet on the floor, and laced his boots. Daylight hours were nothing but a miserable haze until he could retreat to his studio sanctuary. Francesca tried several times to draw him out but finally admitted defeat.

She came to Luciano's studio that afternoon and pounded on the door. "Let me in, Luci. We need you. Isabella's time has come, and the midwife says she's hemorrhaging. She might save the baby but holds out little hope for my Bella. Please, Luci, help us. Go to her. Seeing you will give her strength."

Luciano unlocked the door and reluctantly followed Francesca to Isabella's chamber. The pile of bloody rags strewn across the floor sickened him. He skirted them and went to his wife. She was as white as the sheets behind her head. When he sat on the bed and took her hand, she stared at him with vacant eyes.

"I'm here, Bella," he said tenderly. "You need to be the strong, fiery young woman I married. I won't leave you. You must summon the strength to survive for your baby. It needs you."

Isabella squeezed her eyes shut and screamed as another pain overtook her. Luciano clung to her hand, alarmed to see her in such a state. Despite their estrangement, he wished he could fill her with his strength.

"One more push, Bella, and your baby will be here. The pain will be over, and you can rest," the midwife said.

Luciano glanced at Francesca, who was on her knees on the other side of the bed. She met his gaze, and he saw her surety that Isabella wouldn't survive. Isabella's screams were followed an instant later by the baby's cry. Isabella dropped onto the pillows and closed her eyes.

"You have a son," the midwife announced. "He's a big healthy boy."

Luciano couldn't tear his eyes from his wife to look at the child. Her breaths became weak, and her hand went limp in his as she faded.

"Sir, you to take your baby," the midwife said. "Signora, come help me pack your daughter with these cloths. We must staunch the blood." She held out the small bundle wrapped in a bloody towel for Luciano. When he hesitated to take him, the midwife said, "We only have moments. Take your son."

Luciano held out his arms in confusion until he realized that Isabella had never told the midwife he was not the baby's father. He gazed at the wriggling infant and felt nothing.

He shook Isabella's shoulder and said, "Open your eyes, Bella. Look at your beautiful boy."

Bella opened her eyes halfway and reached for the baby but didn't have the strength. Her arm slumped onto the bed, and she let out a shuddering sigh. Luciano shook her again, but she lay still. He laid the baby on her chest, hoping the feel of his warmth would rouse her, but it was too late. Bella was gone. He put the baby in his cradle and shivered. Francesca screamed and threw herself across her dead daughter.

The midwife bustled about, cleaning up the gore. Luciano grabbed her arm and pointed to the screaming baby. "Take that to the wet nurse. Clean this mess later."

The midwife tossed the armful of bloody cloths into a corner and curtsied before picking up the baby and scurrying out of the room. Luciano lifted Francesca off the bed and led her to a chair. He pulled a clean blanket from the cassone at the end of the bed and covered Isabella.

"She can't be gone. Get her back, Luci," Francesca whispered. "I need to tell her I love her. I've been so cruel these past months. She's been so alone, and now she's gone, not knowing she was my life. Get her back, Luci."

Luciano watched her tears drip onto the blanket and spread in varied patterns across the threads. He was too numb to comfort Francesca. Isabella had always been so strong and vivacious. He didn't recognize the lifeless shell on the bed. He didn't know how long he stood staring at his dead wife, but in time, the midwife returned to finish cleaning.

She shook Luciano's arm and said, "Sir, I know you are grief-stricken, but I must clean her, and you must notify the family and make the arrangements. Mistress Niccolo needs her daughters and sisters, and you need to summon the priest."

Luciano nodded dumbly and left the women alone. Teresa and Marsilia rushed past him and into the room as he stepped into the hall. He heard their screams and cries an instant later. The sound roused him from his stupor. Grieving would have to wait. He only had a day to arrange Isabella's viewing, processional, requiem, and burial. Her funeral would have to be an event fitting the status of the Vicente and Visconti families. After cleaning up and changing, Luciano left the palazzo, knowing his life would never be the same.

Two days later, Luciano waited in the sala with the wet nurse for Marcello to arrive. When he was more than an hour late, Luciano was about to go find him and drag him to the palazzo by his cloak, but the footman stepped into the room and announced he had arrived. Marcello pushed the footman out of his way and swept into the room as if he owned it. He dropped into a chair opposite Luciano and eyed him arrogantly.

"I offer my condolences for your recent loss. To what do I owe the pleasure of this invitation?"

Luciano stared at him stone-faced, holding back from spitting on him.

"You know why you're here." Luciano gestured to the wet nurse. She rose and held the baby out to Marcello. "I'd like to introduce you to your son."

Marcello's mask slipped only for an instant, but it was long enough for Luciano to see his reaction to the baby. "What are you saying, Vicente? Everyone knows the child is yours,"

"Isabella admitted she was your mistress and that the boy is yours. She died giving birth to your son. There's no doubt of his paternity," Luciano said, taking care to keep his voice even.

Marcello sat forward and glared at Luciano. "Were there witnesses to this confession?"

"Isabella's mother and her lady's maid."

"How convenient that you would confront me when she's not here to tell me with her own lips."

Luciano stood and clenched his fits. "Do you call me a liar?"

Marcello recoiled slightly. "I'm saying that all I have is your word and that of your household. They will say whatever you tell them they must. From what I know of your wife's reputation, the father could have been any number of men."

Luciano grabbed Marcello's collar and lifted him to his feet. "How dare you? First, you seduce and disgrace my wife, and now you denigrate our family's honor. Admit that you are this child's father, or I will announce it to the world for you."

Marcello's face turned blue, and he gasped. Luciano released him and stepped back.

Marcello rubbed his neck and cleared his throat. "I'm also from an honored and respected family. Who would believe you?"

Luciano stepped toward him again, and Marcello flinched. "From what I hear of your reputation, everyone. If you're so honorable, take responsibility for your actions. Claim this child."

Marcello stood and leaned his face within inches of Luciano's. "Never. That bastard isn't mine. Do what you want with it. Drown it for all I care."

He stormed out, leaving Luciano too stunned to go after him. The baby squealed, and Luciano turned to find the wet nurse staring at him in horror.

"Take him to the nursery," he whispered to reassure her. "Don't worry, I promise not to drown him."

She hurried out, leaving Luciano alone. He hadn't expected Marcello to accept responsibility for the baby, but the force of his refusal shocked him. Isabella had her faults, but she'd been a kind-hearted person. Luciano couldn't imagine what she'd seen in that vile creature.

He took a moment to compose himself before going to give Francesca the news. Her heart would be broken, but he desperately hoped that she could find a family member to look after her and the baby.

The steward came in before Luciano made it out of the sala. He hoped that Marcello had come to his senses, but that hope was quickly dashed.

"A messenger has arrived from Florence, Signore. He wishes to speak with you."

Luciano gestured for him to bring the messenger to him. Dropping back into his chair, he thought, what now?

The messenger knelt, and without looking up, said, "Signore Vicente, I offer condolences for the loss of your wife. I'm grieved to tell you I bring more tragic news. Your father instructed me to come for you five days ago, but he died before I set off. You are my new master. We must return to Florence as soon as you're prepared, sir."

Luciano covered his face with his hands and groaned. He had received word shortly before Isabella's death that his father was ill, but he'd rallied so many times that Luciano gave it little attention. After Isabella died, all thoughts of his father faded. Even though he and his father had never been close and rarely agreed on anything, he had loved him and hoped to see him once more. Now that chance was lost forever. His death couldn't have come at a worse time, and Luciano wondered how much grief one man could take.

"Show him to the servant's quarters," he told his steward. "Feed him and find a place for him to rest." Turning to the messenger, he said, "What's your name?"

"Filippo, sir," he said, still on knees.

Luciano gestured for him to stand. "Go with Ponzio here, Filippo. Once you're rested, begin preparations for our journey. Ponzio will help you. We leave in three days."

They rushed out to fulfill their new Duca's wishes. Luciano dragged himself to Francesca's room to give her the news. He recounted Marcello's reaction and told her about his father's death. She was devastated and sobbed into her shawl. Luciano didn't have the heart to tell her to leave with the baby. He made a hasty decision that would one day affect his legacy, but he was too overwhelmed to conceive any other option.

"There's one ray of hope in this pit of darkness," he said. "We'll baptize the baby on the morning I leave. I'll give him my name. You stay and live here with him and your daughters to run my household. You are my mother from this day forward. I'll close the workshop but take some of my apprentices with me. I'll find apprenticeships for the rest here in Venice. Ponzio will manage the rest of my holdings."

Francesca fell at his feet and wrapped her arms around his legs. "How can I thank you, my lord?" she cried.

"You can start by getting off the floor. You're my mother, remember? No mother of mine grovels."

He helped her up and smiled. She hugged him and kissed his cheeks.

"You are a good man and an honorable son. You've saved all of us today. I don't deserve your kindness."

"You've been my faithful ally and friend. You deserve this and more. I don't know when I'll return to Venice, but I'll come as soon as possible. If you ever need anything, don't hesitate to send word."

"I will, son. I promise."

~

LUCIANO LEFT Francesca and went in search of peace in his studio. He locked the door, then dropped onto the cot and tried to calm his chaos of emotions. He'd only just surfaced from the trauma of Isabella's death when he was struck with the news of his father. Aside from his grief, he felt unprepared to leave Venice to take up his title and manage his father's vast estates. All he'd ever aspired to be was the maestro of his Venice workshop, but he'd made a promise to his father and was honor-bound to keep it.

He was reluctant to quit Venice for a deeper reason, one whose existence he'd struggled to bury. He sat up and gazed at Celeste's painting of the canal hanging above the fireplace. He recalled the look in her eyes on the day she'd shown him that painting, so full of hope and longing. He could no longer deny that she'd owned his heart from that moment. How could he forsake the only ray of sunlight in his life?

He collected the few other of her paintings he'd saved, then lined them up on the mantlepiece. He imagined her standing before an easel in that very room, lost in her world of creation. The image was more breathtaking than any masterpiece he'd ever seen.

With Isabella gone, he was free, but though he and Celeste were only separated by a fifteen-minute gondola ride, they existed in different worlds. Was it expecting too much to ask her to leave her country and ascend from servant to Duchessa overnight? Would his family and the patricians of Florence ever accept her as a member of their society?

The idea was absurd, but he saw no point to life without her. No woman had filled his world as she had. There was her talent to consider, as well. Could he allow one of the greatest artists of their age to go unseen by the world? If she became his wife, no one could stop him from becoming her maestro.

He sighed and gave her paintings one last look before tucking them behind a stack of discarded frames. He could dream and scheme all he wished, but it brought him no closer to a life with the woman he loved. He had too many responsibilities and obligations to consider before his own happiness. With his world tearing apart at the seams, the last thing he needed was to add more pressure. He took her painting from its place of honor, wrapped it in his cloak, and then left his studio, locking the door behind him.

CELESTE'S MIND wandered as she rhythmically threaded the needle through the linen and tugged on the embroidery floss. Over two weeks had passed since she'd heard of Isabella's funeral, and though death in childbirth was a common occurrence, gossip about her death hadn't cooled. No one understood why the family had kept her pregnancy a secret when it should have been a joyous time. Isabella's mother said it was because she'd had a difficult pregnancy, but Celeste was one of four people in Venice who knew the truth.

She hadn't seen or heard from Luciano since sending him the note, but she knew it was behind the reason that Isabella stopped visiting Signora Viari and Marcello. Celeste had no doubt of Isabella's baby's paternity. Even so, she was heartbroken at what Luciano and Signora Niccolo must be suffering.

Tessa came to tell her the mistress wanted her in the sala. Celeste followed her out and tried to chat with her as they walked, but she was unusually tight-lipped. The first person Celeste saw on entering the sala was Aunt Portia. Celeste ran to her and took her hands before she realized anyone else was in the room.

"I'm so glad to see you, Aunt, but what are you doing here?"

Portia kissed her cheeks and embraced her before nodding to someone standing near the doorway. Celeste turned to find Luciano and three unfamiliar men standing next to Signora Viari. She dropped into a curtsy and waited with her head bowed for Luciano to speak.

He stepped closer and said, "Get up, Celeste. That's the last time you ever bow to me."

She glanced at Portia in confusion, but her aunt nodded to encourage her. Celeste stood and faced Luciano but couldn't bring herself to meet his eye in the presence of her mistress and the other men.

"Please give us a moment alone," Luciano said.

Signora Viari left without a word, followed by the three men. Luciano gestured for Celeste and Portia to sit, then he took a chair facing them.

"You're aware of my wife's passing?" he asked.

"I am, sir, and I'm deeply saddened by your loss," Celeste said, hoping he knew she was sincere.

"Thank you. It's been a terrible time. We baptized Isabella's child this morning. I've given him my name, though he's not my son, which I believe you know." Celeste nodded and looked away, shocked by his honesty. "What you do not know is that I just received word my father also passed away last week."

Celeste was even more stunned by this new revelation and searched for the right words to console him.

"How terrible, Maestro. What can I do to ease your suffering?"

Luciano and Portia exchanged a look filled with meaning that Celeste didn't understand.

"There is something you can do," Luciano said. "I'm leaving for Florence today, and I have little time to explain. Your aunt is here to take you to my country estate in Tuscany. She will groom and prepare you to enter Florentine society where I hope, after a proper period of mourning, you will consent to be my wife."

Celeste got to her feet, too stunned to speak. Portia tugged on her hand to get her to sit, but Celeste ignored her.

"What is he saying, Aunt? He must be overcome with grief,"

"It's true, my dear."

"But why, sir? Why would you do this?" Celeste asked, desperate to understand. "Is it out of pity or obligation? You owe me nothing."

Luciano stood and took her hands. "I do this because you are the most remarkable woman I've ever known, and I love you. I've wanted to make you a part of my life from the moment I saw you on that bench outside my studio, but insurmountable obstacles prevented it. I'm grief-stricken by Isabella's death, but God has taken her home for reasons of his own. Now, those obstacles are gone. I've nearly talked myself out of this a dozen times in the past three days. I can recite a long list of logical reasons this makes no sense, but one fact overrides them all. I have no desire to go on living without you by my side."

"But how can this be? I am nothing and have no one to speak for me. I have no dowry."

Portia stood and put her hands on her hips. "Don't you dare let me hear you say you're a nothing ever again, Celeste. You are a Gabriele."

Celeste absorbed Portia's words and understood their significance for the first time since she was a child. After years of being treated as little more than a beast in the field, it had been easy to forget who she was. The seed of her long-buried Gabriele pride sprouted, and a change grew within her. She stood taller and raised her chin.

"Luciano met with your father and your uncle Cesare yesterday and professed his intentions," Portia continued. "You are to become Cesare's adopted daughter. Giovanni no longer has a claim to you. Your father demanded a preposterous sum of money in exchange for his consent." She frowned and shook her head. "Luciano asks for no dowry, only you. It's all arranged, and the contracts are negotiated, except for Luciano's signature. All that remains is for you to give your consent."

"You'll be my wife, my confidant, my pupil, one of the greatest artists of our age, and the love of my life. Please, Celeste, honor me by accepting my proposal and making my life worth living once more."

Celeste gazed into his face but couldn't see him through her tears. When she whispered yes, Luciano kissed her cheeks and bowed.

"Thank you for giving me joy in my time of deepest sorrow. I must leave after signing the contracts and won't see you for some time, but I will write often. Portia will know when you're ready to come to Florence, then we'll marry as soon as we can."

He called Signora Viari and the men back into the room. He introduced the notary and two witnesses and made sure Celeste watched as he signed. When it was over, he kissed her hand and went out without looking back. Signora Viari hugged her and said goodbye before she left with the other men. The strength went out of Celeste's legs, so she grabbed her aunt's arm to keep from collapsing. Portia led her back to the chair.

"Is this real? Will I wake up to see that it was only a wonderful dream?"

"You're awake, my dear, and this is more than your mother, and I ever dared hope for you. If I had married a man like Luciano, my life would have been perfect. He is a rare and honorable man. But enough with daydreaming. We have work to do."

"What will happen to Lapa without me to help care for the children?"

"I've promised Sofia to find a replacement for you. Gather your belongings. We need to go."

Celeste took a few steps, then froze. "And what will become of Marco? He has nowhere to go. We can't force him to return to Papa. I mean Giovanni."

"Luciano is taking Marco to Florence. He's explained everything to your brother."

Celeste covered her mouth and giggled. "I would have loved to have seen Marco's face when he told him."

Portia clapped her hands. "Time to get going, girl. We must visit the seamstress today. You need a new wardrobe for the journey. We can't have you traveling in that dress."

Celeste dragged Portia to the nursery and told her to wait while she said her goodbyes. She merely told Lapa she was returning to live with her family.

Lapa eyed Portia in confusion. "She's your aunt?" she whispered to Celeste.

"Yes, Lapa. It's a long story, but I didn't want to go without seeing you. My aunt is going to help your mistress find someone to replace me," Celeste said.

"No one can replace you. I've known no one like you in my life."

Celeste laughed at her words. "At least you won't have to be rescuing me from lecherous houseguests." Celeste avoided Portia's eyes when she said it but could feel her scowling. "I must go. Take care of my sweethearts."

"I promise, Celeste. I'll miss you, friend."

"And I you."

"Promise to visit me someday."

"I'll do my best," Celeste said and meant it.

PORTIA SHUFFLED Celeste out the door, just as she had the day when she took Celeste to work for Maria Foscari three years earlier. She and Portia chatted happily about what awaited them as the gondola carried them on the first step of their new adventure, but Celeste grew quiet when the Gabriele palazzo came into view. She shivered as memories of her last time there flooded over her.

She grasped Portia's hand for strength and said, "Did you know I was here a year ago? The servants refused to let me see you and slammed the door in my face."

"I had no idea. Why were you here?"

Celeste told her of that horrible day Maria Foscari tossed her onto the street and all that happened since. Portia hugged her when she finished.

"If I had known, I would have killed Giovanni. Point out the servants that treated you so disgracefully. I'll deal with them."

"No, Aunt," Celeste said and squeezed her arm. "They were just protecting you. I could have been lying about being your niece for all they knew."

Portia leaned into the pillows and was silent for several minutes. "Maria Foscari told me she'd dismissed you, but I thought you went directly to work for Sofia. Thank goodness for Luciano and Francesca, or I hate to think what would have happened. I'll thank Francesca before we leave for Lucca."

Celeste gave a little wave. "It's in the past and forgotten. Giovanni can't hurt me ever again, and I've been content with Signora Viari.

They're good people, better than Signora Foscari. It worked out in the end."

"You're far more forgiving than I would be."

"Let's forget this and speak of the future. As overjoyed as I am, I'm frightened, too. I don't know how to be a Duchessa. I fear I'll embarrass or disappoint Luciano."

Portia patted her arm. "I've traveled to foreign lands, but I've lived nowhere else but Venice. This will be new for me, too, but we'll have each other. I'll teach you all you need to know. There's much you can teach me, too. Luciano told me about your lessons. Cesare doesn't let me read or go out in society except for family occasions or my charitable work. I think he's punishing me for not remarrying, but I've never gone against his wishes since he's been so kind. You must have incredible courage to have defied everyone to become Luciano's apprentice."

"Or no common sense," Celeste said and laughed, but her lightheartedness evaporated when the gondolier reached to help from the boat. "I can't do this, Aunt. I shouldn't be here. The family and servants will reject me. Can't we go directly to Lucca?"

"Nonsense. You're Cesare Gabriele's daughter now. No one would dare treat you poorly and risk facing his wrath. You're a future Duchessa, and you need to think of yourself as such. Remind yourself that Luciano chose you out of all the women in Venice and Florence."

Celeste nodded and squared her shoulders, but it still terrified her to enter the palazzo. She followed Portia to her temporary chambers, trying to act as if she belonged there. Portia ordered her lady's maid to find suitable clothes and told another maid to prepare a hot bath.

"Once you're bathed and dressed, I'll take you to Cesare."

"I have to face him so soon. Can't it wait until tomorrow?"

"He ordered me to bring you straight to him tonight. Courage, my dear."

Celeste nodded and did as her aunt commanded, but her anxiety mounted as the maids dressed and groomed her. She remembered when she was young and wouldn't have given their attention a second thought, but all she felt that night was awkwardness. Her hands trembled uncontrollably by the time they went to greet Cesare.

Celeste's uncle was in his antechamber, seated at a small desk covered with papers. He stood when the women entered and curtsied. His eyes widened when he got a good look at Celeste.

"You've grown into a lovely young woman, my daughter. No wonder Luciano wants you for a wife. Come, let me embrace you."

Celeste obeyed but hid her offense at her uncle's comment. He would think Luciano only wanted her for her beauty.

Uncle Cesare motioned to someone in the corner that Celeste hadn't noticed. A young woman close to Celeste's age stepped forward and dipped her head. "Do you remember me, cousin?" she asked.

Celeste smiled as recognition dawned. Her cousin, Alessandra, had the Gabriele straight black hair and coal-colored eyes, which Celeste had always envied. She had fond memories of playing with Alessandra as a child.

"How I've missed you," Celeste said and embraced her. "I wish there was more time for us to get reacquainted."

"Maybe Papa will let me visit you in Florence," her cousin said and looked to her father with hopeful eyes.

"We'll see," Uncle Cesare mumbled.

Celeste knew the visit would never happen and wondered how long it would be before Cesare married Alessandra off to someone he felt deserving of his daughter.

"You have more important things to think of, especially Luciano Vicente. You're fortunate to be betrothed to such a man." Alessandra glanced at her father.

"The wedding is far in the future. Come stay with Aunt Portia and me in Lucca before then," Celeste said. "Where's your mother? I'd love to see Aunt Teresa."

A cloud passed over Alessandra's eyes, and she lowered her head.

"My wife is unwell but longs to see you," Cesare said. "I'll take you to her in the morning. For now, our evening meal is waiting."

Celeste exchanged a look with Portia and wondered why she hadn't mentioned Aunt Teresa's illness. No one spoke of her during the meal and chatted as if nothing was wrong. Celeste relaxed and enjoyed being back in her childhood home but wondered what other secrets the palazzo held.

~

TO CELESTE'S RELIEF, the family and household staff welcomed her as if she'd only been away on a long journey, probably on Cesare's orders. After Celeste dressed and had breakfast, Portia came in with the kitchen boy and housekeeper who'd treated Celeste so terribly when she'd gone to the palazzo seeking help. The housekeeper prostrated herself before Celeste, and the boy gave a deep bow.

"My deepest apologies, Signorina. I wasn't aware of who you were," she said without rising.

Portia gave her a harmless kick. "You would have known if you'd come to me. My niece nearly died that night. That would have been on your head."

The boy glanced at Celeste in horror, looking like he wanted nothing more than to escape. Celeste bit her tongue to keep from laughing.

She reached down to the housekeeper and raised her to her feet. "The fault was my former father's. They are loyal to you, Aunt, and were trying to protect you."

"It won't happen again, madam," the housekeeper said to Portia.

"See that it doesn't," she said and gestured with her head for them to go.

They left so quickly that Celeste didn't hide her laugh. "Don't be too hard on them. I know what it's like to be in their position. Now, please tell me about Aunt Teresa before I visit her."

Portia slowly sat and straightened her skirts to stall. "My sister-in-law's health has been deteriorating for many months. The physician says she doesn't have long to live and blames it on her age, but I believe there's another cause."

"What do you mean? No secrets. I've had enough of them."

Portia looked her directly in the eye. "Your uncle contracted an illness from visiting particular women."

Celeste cringed. "You mean courtesans? Like Papa?"

Portia nodded. "Sometimes, I forget how much you know of the world for one so young. Yes, like your father. Cesare recovered but passed the illness on to your aunt. I've thought about confronting Cesare, but I'm here by his good graces, and a confession wouldn't save his wife."

Portia's words saddened Celeste deeply. Her aunt was yet another woman suffering from the behavior of a thoughtless man. She hoped her marriage with Luciano would be different. She knew so little of his private life, though probably more than most women knew of the men they married.

"We'll keep your aunt company and comfortable while we're here, though it's little consolation," Portia said.

Celeste stood and nodded. "Please, take me to her."

"Be prepared. Teresa has her good days and bad, but her mind has grown weak. She may not recognize you."

"She hasn't seen me for many years. I'd be surprised if she did."

Celeste was glad to see Teresa sitting in a chair when they got to her room, but her appearance was shocking. She looked several years older than Portia, though they were only a few years apart in age. She was stick-thin, and the veins showed through her translucent skin between the pustules covering her face. Her eyes were sunken in their sockets and rimmed with black circles.

Celeste knelt by the chair and took her hands. "Hello, Aunt Teresa. It's Celeste, Angela's daughter. It's wonderful to see you."

Teresa slowly turned toward Celeste. "Yes, I know you, Niece. I'm happy to see you after so long. What a beautiful girl you are."

Celeste smiled. "Thank you. Your Alessandra is lovely, too. You must be very proud of her."

Teresa's face remained expressionless, but tears dripped onto her cheeks. "I wish I could have lived to see her married."

"You will, Aunt. Be strong and recover so you can be there for her blessed day."

She patted Celeste's arm with her other claw-like hand but didn't speak.

"My mistress needs to rest," Teresa's nurse said.

Celeste didn't dare kiss her aunt's cheek, but she squeezed her hand as she straightened. "We'll come again tomorrow."

She barely made it into the hall before breaking into tears. Portia pulled Celeste into her arms, and she rested her cheek on Portia's shoulder.

"I want to hate Uncle Cesare for doing this to her, but how can I after what he's doing for me?" Celeste said. "Why doesn't God save her? It's not her fault."

"Who understands God's ways? Put this from your mind. We have preparations to make for our journey," Portia said and took Celeste's hand to lead her back to her chambers on the far side of the palazzo.

CHAPTER THIRTEEN

ime passed in a breathless rush until the day arrived to leave for Lucca. Celeste and Portia paid Teresa one last visit before departing. She was too weak to rise from her bed and could barely open her eyes. It broke Celeste's heart, knowing it was the last time she'd see her aunt alive. Her heart broke for Alessandra, as well. Celeste understood the pain of losing a mother.

Their last act before leaving was to pay respects to Cesare. Celeste curtsied and said, "I thank you for making me worthy of the Gabriele name once more. I can reenter patrician society with dignity and not be ashamed to marry Luciano. I'd have remained a nanny for the rest of my life without your kindness."

"It's been my honor to return you to your Gabriele roots. I hated being forced to ostracize your family after your father's betrayal, and I'm pleased to make up for that in my way. I look forward to passing you on to a man as worthy as Luciano. I only hope to find someone as suitable for Alessandra."

Celeste kissed his cheeks and waved goodbye to her uncle, who could be thoughtless, almost to the point of cruelty, but also kindhearted. She learned more each day that life was as complicated as the array of colors she once brushed across her canvases.

RIDING in a carriage was a novel experience for Celeste, and as the wheels crunched along on the dusty, pockmarked road, she reflected on how little she still knew of the world outside Venice. She was grateful she'd have time to prepare to be the wife Luciano deserved.

During their tiring week-long journey to Lucca, Portia talked nonstop about expectations for Celeste as Duchessa. Celeste was too distracted watching the passing scenery to hear much of what her aunt said. Celeste felt out of balance on the rolling hills with their terraced farms rising toward the sky as they crossed the mainland. She was used to crowded streets and canals with the fishmongers crying their wares and maids rushing about fetching water and food for their masters. The countryside was too quiet.

Determined to adjust to her new life, she found things to admire in the scenery. Seeing the men laboring in the fields alongside older children and women with babies strapped to their backs fascinated her. She thought of her brothers and sisters and wondered how they were faring on their country farm. She hoped to have the chance to help them once she settled in Lucca.

On the sixth day of their journey, Celeste was watching a shepherd corral his sheep while grape pickers filled their baskets amongst the rows of vines lining the hills when Portia tapped her arm and said, "Quit gawking and pay attention."

"Look at all those vineyards. Are these the grapes that make our wine?"

"Yes, Celeste, but that doesn't concern you. We're running out of time before we arrive in Lucca. You must listen."

Celeste nodded but continued to either ignore her aunt or ask questions that had nothing to do with aristocratic society. When she'd pushed Portia's patience as far as she dared, the carriage rolled up to Luciano's picturesque estate nestled on a hillside overlooking Lucca.

Celeste scrambled out and ran to the edge of the garden, twirling to take in the view. "I want to live here forever."

"It is lovely, but Luciano has obligations that will keep him in

Florence. Maybe he'll bring you here for holidays," Portia said, as she took Celeste's hand to drag her through the intricately carved wooden door.

The staff waited to greet them just inside the entrance. Celeste was still uneasy about having people bow and curtsy to her, but she obeyed Portia and didn't ask them to stop. Luciano had arranged for a pretty girl with a cheerful face named Gemma to serve as her lady's maid. Celeste was exhausted from her journey and gladly accepted the girl's help to get settled.

"I hope you'll acquaint me with Lucca. I'm feeling very far from home," Celeste said when Gemma brought her a tray of cheese and bread.

"Yes, mistress. I was born in Lucca and have never been anywhere else. I'd be honored to introduce you to my home."

Gemma curtsied and left Celeste alone to eat and rest. First, she surveyed her new room. After living in hovels, closets, and nurseries, her chamber felt palatial. The manor was much smaller than Luciano's palazzo in Venice but grand enough for Celeste. She had a four-post bed covered with a delicately embroidered spread. Cheerful tapestries lined the walls. Her window afforded a panoramic view of the hillsides and valley. She was going to love Lucca.

"I'M GOING to see my brothers and sisters," Celeste told Portia one morning after they'd been in Lucca for a month. "I had Gemma ask around to find out where they are. The tenant farmer they live with is within walking distance. I'll visit in the morning."

"What put this silly notion into your head?" Portia asked.

"I've wanted to check on their welfare since Luciano told me I was coming to Lucca. They're so close. To not pay them a visit would be rude."

"Going to see them will just disrupt their lives, Celeste. Let them be."

Celeste put her hands on her hips. "I'll go if I want to go. I don't need your permission. I'm mistress here, not you."

Portia gave her a half-grin. "So, you're the mistress? You're the one making sure the household runs smoothly and that we have food to eat? From what I've seen, you're the one who locks herself away with brushes and paints for hours on end."

Celeste lowered her hands to her side, defeated at being unable to argue Portia's point. Luciano had sent Celeste a letter along with the materials she needed for painting. She'd added the bundle he'd sent her in Venice and resumed work on her painting of the Blessed Virgin. As always happened, her obsession soon took hold. It was often almost painful to pull herself away to eat and sleep. She had little idea of what Portia did while she shut herself in the small room she'd converted into a studio.

She lowered her eyes and said, "I'm sorry. I'm grateful for all you do and for all you've taught me. I just meant that I have control over where I go and what I do for the first time in my life. I don't have someone else dictating every instant of my day. I am going to see them, Aunt. I'm even considering writing to Luciano and asking if I can bring them here to live with us. Why should I get this luxurious life when they're slaving away on that farm?"

"You will do no such thing!" Portia said and stamped her foot. "If Luciano wanted them here, he'd have arranged it. They're too young to remember their lives before your father's downfall. The farm is the only life they know. It would be cruel to tear them away from it and heartless to take them from the couple who already lost their own children. They're a family now."

More excellent points, Celeste thought in frustration. "I won't write to Luciano until I've seen the children, but I'm not giving up on having them live with me."

"And what do you plan to do with them when you leave for Florence to marry Luciano? Take them with you? Take them to live with you and your new Duca husband?"

Celeste scowled at Portia. "Certainly not. They'll stay here. There are plenty of people to care for them, and I'd get to see them whenever we visit."

Portia tenderly cupped Celeste's chin in her hand and smiled. "For all your experience, you still know so little of the world. You're always so determined to break down barriers, but sometimes it's best to let them be. Maybe you need to spend less time in your studio and more time listening to me."

Celeste shook her chin free with a smile. "Maybe so, but you're stuck in your old ways and can't envision new possibilities. I'll visit the children tomorrow and would love for you to accompany me."

"If you're so determined, you can go alone."

Celeste was disappointed Portia wouldn't join her, but it was time she stood on her own feet. She was no longer a child and would soon be mistress of Luciano's estates. She wouldn't always be able to rely on Portia.

CELESTE RAN to the window when she woke and frowned at the sight of the damp, muddy ground. It had rained all night, and puddles covered the road leading from the house. She refused to let that stop her from visiting her brothers and sisters. When Gemma came in, Celeste asked her to lie out appropriate clothing.

"Maybe it would be prudent to wait until tomorrow, Signorina," Gemma said. "The roads can be impassable after a storm."

"It's just mud. I'll find sturdy boots to wear," Celeste said and started digging through a chest in the corner.

"There's nothing suitable in that chest. I'll bring something from the servant's quarters."

"Thank you," Celeste said as Gemma hurried out in search of boots.

Celeste loved everything about her life except being treated like a fragile doll. She'd worked harder in her life than most of the people on her staff, and she refused to turn into a lazy princess who never lifted a finger. A vigorous walk through the mud would be beneficial for her health.

Gemma chose a simple gown for Celeste and helped her into the heavy leather boots she'd found in a kitchen storage closet. They were loose on Celeste's feet, but she preferred that to them being too small. After dressing, she ate a hearty vegetable and cheese omelet with half a pork pie left from their evening meal. She washed the food down with heated lemon water before grabbing her cloak for the journey.

Portia came rushing down the steps as Celeste was about to leave.

"I refuse to let you go wandering off alone," she said. "Berto and Ricco are going with you."

"I wasn't going alone. Gemma is coming," Celeste said.

"Two defenseless young women out roaming the countryside? What were you thinking?"

Celeste sighed. "We won't be roaming the countryside. The farm is only two miles off, and Gemma knows the way. Besides, who's going to see us? There's no one around."

"Berto and Ricco are going with you," Portia said and stomped her foot.

"Stop that, Aunt Portia. I'm not a child. They can join us if you insist."

She kissed her aunt's cheeks before marching down the hillside with her little band following behind. She had no idea where they were headed, but she didn't ask Gemma for directions until they were out of sight of the house. Gemma giggled and pointed the way. The terrain was rough and uneven, but Celeste managed to keep up with the others. By the time they saw the farmer's house, she was huffing and perspiring, so she decided to incorporate brisk walks into her daily routine.

She went directly to the door and knocked when they reached the farmhouse. A woman answered and studied Celeste in confusion. Just as she was about to explain who she was, a voice said, "Celeste?"

Jacopo ran to her and threw his arms around her. "What are you doing here? Are you coming to live with us?"

Celeste held him at arm's length to get a good look. He'd become a young man since she last saw him in Venice. She wouldn't have recognized him if he hadn't been a mirror image of Marco. He was almost fifteen, the age Marco was when he entered Luciano's workshop. That meant Veronica was eleven, Bianca seven, and Sandro five, no longer a baby. It was hard to believe so much time had passed since she left home to work for Maria Foscari.

Jacopo took Celeste's hand and led her inside. "Come meet our parents. This is my oldest sister, Mamma. Celeste, this is Masina, our new mother."

Masina stared at Celeste with wide eyes before dropping into a curtsy. "It's an honor, Signorina."

"Don't curtsy to her, Mamma. She's just my sister," Jacopo said.

"He's right. Don't curtsy to me. How can I thank you for taking my brothers and sisters into your family? They wouldn't have survived without you."

"These children have brought me such happiness. They're a joy," Masina said.

"Even Jacopo?" Celeste said and winked at him. "Where are the others?"

"I'll get them."

Masina leaned through the front door and called to the other children. They ran in moments later but stopped when they saw Celeste and the others.

Veronica hesitated only for an instant before rushing to Celeste. "Where have you been? I thought you were dead."

Celeste pulled away from her sister. "Why would you think that? I'm perfectly alive, as you can see."

Veronica's eyes widened. "And look at your clothes. Where did you get such a beautiful gown?"

Celeste ignored her question and turned her gaze to Bianca and Sandro, who was peeking at her from behind Masina's skirts.

"It's me, Celeste," she said to Bianca. "Don't be shy."

Bianca stayed where she was. "Are you here to take me back to the bad place? The place where Papa lives? I won't go."

Celeste smiled to reassure her. "No, Bianca. You never have to go there again. I just came to visit you. I've missed you more than you know."

Bianca ran to Celeste and buried her face in Celeste's gown. "Are you going to live with us now?"

"No, but I live nearby. You can visit whenever you'd like."

Celeste moved Bianca aside and stepped toward Sandro. He moved further behind Masina and squeezed her legs.

"Hello, Sandro. You're such a big boy. Can I have a hug?" When Sandro shook his head, Celeste didn't pressure him. "That's fine. There will be time for hugs later."

"Tell us why you're here," Jacopo said.

Masina brought Celeste a chair, and Gemma led Berto and Ricco outside. Celeste sat and pulled Bianca onto her lap.

"I wanted to make sure you were doing well. I see that you are. I arrived in Lucca a month ago with Aunt Portia. It took time to find you."

"Aunt Portia? Why are you with her? Where do you live?" Jacopo asked.

"We live in that house on the hillside," Celeste said and pointed through the open door.

"In the big house? I don't understand. Are you a maid?" Veronica asked.

"Your sister is Mistress of the big house," Masina said.

It shocked Celeste that Masina knew who she was. Jacopo looked even more shocked.

"Your mamma is almost right. I'll be mistress in time. I'm to wed Signore Luciano Vicente next year. He lives in Florence but owns these lands. He's the one who arranged for you to live here with Masina and her husband. He's the one who rescued you."

Jacopo dropped into a chair with his mouth gaping. The other children didn't seem to understand.

"You mean Maestro Vicente? Marco's maestro? He lives in Venice," Jacopo said.

"Signore Vicente returned to Florence when his father died. Marco is there with him, so we'll all be near each other soon. I'll bring him when I can. I'm sure he'll want to see you as much as I did."

Jacopo stood and stepped toward Celeste, clenching his fists. "You've been living as Mistress on the hill for over a month, and you're just coming to see us now? Why haven't you brought us to live with you? You see how we live. Is that why you're here?"

Celeste glanced at Masina, unsure how to answer. She couldn't invite them to live with her without Luciano's permission, and she didn't miss the look of concern on Masina's face. These were her children. How could Celeste steal them away when she'd known so much grief? But how could she not? She wished she'd listened to Portia and had stayed home.

"I can't take you with me now. I need to speak with Signore Vicente and Masina first."

Bianca jumped off Celeste's lap and ran to Masina. With her arm around her new mother's waist, she said, "You are here to take us away from our mamma. I won't go."

"I'm not taking you anywhere, Bianca. I'm just here to visit," Celeste said. "I promise you can stay if you want to."

"Will I have gowns like yours if I go?" Veronica asked. She touched Celeste's hair and said, "Will I have beautiful, clean hair like yours? Will we eat meat?"

"You would leave me for fancy clothes and meat, Veronica?" Masina said. "Don't you love us? Haven't we loved you and treated you like a daughter?"

Celeste stood and knocked over her chair. "I'm sorry. I shouldn't have come."

Jacopo crossed his arms and stepped in front of her. "Yes, you should have. Why should you get to live like a queen while we labor in the fields? I'm a Gabriele, too. Will Marco live with you in Florence?"

Celeste laid her hand on his arm. "I don't know, brother. I truly don't. I'll write to Signore Vicente today and bring answers as soon as I can." She turned to Masina. "Forgive me. I meant no harm. I'll send some meat."

She hugged Jacopo and headed for the door. A man came in as she rushed out. "Who was that?" she heard him ask. "Signorina Gabriele," Masina answered. Celeste turned and saw the man leaning through the doorway. A cloud passed over his face before she turned to head up the hill.

"What have I done?" she whispered.

~

CELESTE HID IN HER ROOM, too embarrassed to face Portia, and asked Gemma to bring her a dinner tray. She'd hoped to sleep well after the unaccustomed exertion but was awake all night, unable to get Jacopo's accusing and Veronica's pleading eyes out of her mind. She'd been selfish to go to them before writing to Luciano. What would the consequences of her visit be for Masina and her husband?

She dozed off around dawn and woke to the sound of someone pounding on the door when the sunlight was bright in her room. Portia burst in before she could answer.

"I've been looking all over for you. Why are you still in bed? Are you ill? You shouldn't have exerted yourself in the foul weather yesterday."

Celeste sat up and pulled a blanket over her shoulders. She considered telling Portia she was ill but feared her aunt would summon every physician in town before the end of the day.

"I'm not ill, just tired. I'm not used to walking so much. I need to exercise more," Celeste said while keeping her eyes lowered.

"How did your visit go?" Celeste fell onto the pillows and covered her face with the blanket. "That well? I tried to get the story out of Gemma, but she just frowned and ran off. That girl is loyal to you."

Celeste sat up and swung her legs over the edge of the bed. "You were right, Aunt. It was a disaster." She recounted the visit and said, "I've upended their simple, peaceful lives. I don't know how I can write to Luciano now, but I promised Jacopo I would."

"You'd better figure it out." Portia waved the letter she carried in Celeste's face. "This just came. Luciano will be here tomorrow. Pull yourself together and summon your courage."

Celeste stood and smiled. "Luciano's coming?" As much as she dreaded admitting to him what she'd done, it thrilled her to know she'd see him after so many weeks. Her painting was almost finished, and she was eager to show him. "That's wonderful. I have so much to do to get ready. Where's Gemma?"

Portia went out laughing and left Celeste to her preparations.

CELESTE TOOK her time getting out of bed the next morning since she wouldn't see Luciano until evening. She'd been awake long past midnight, imagining herself in his arms. Their wedding felt years away instead of months. When she finally fell asleep, her dreams were filled with Luciano in front of his easel, running his paint-stained fingers through his curls as he had when she'd first fallen in love with him.

When she finally dragged herself out of bed, Gemma helped her dress and brought her lamb with fruit and bread. Celeste ate quickly and went to her studio, excited to start her next project. With the disruptions and turmoil in her life, her painting of the Virgin had taken years. She hoped to have her newest work finished before the wedding as a gift for Luciano.

She was painting their view of Lucca from the terrace and hoped he would be pleased. She had enjoyed doing human figures but wasn't ready to do another religious theme.

She worked well into the afternoon until Portia came to tell her it was time to dress for dinner. She pulled off her dirty smock and went to her room to change, but Gemma wasn't there to assist her. Celeste had removed her dress and washed her face and hands before Gemma rushed in and curtsied. She apologized for being late but was evasive when Celeste questioned where she'd been. Celeste shrugged it off and asked for her emerald gown, which highlighted her coloring. Gemma complemented Celeste and curtsied again before rushing off to her other chores.

Celeste was the first to arrive in the sala, so she danced around the room, practicing the steps that Portia was teaching her. She was so absorbed that she didn't notice Luciano standing in the doorway watching.

"Would you like a partner?" he asked. Celeste whirled around and curtsied to hide her embarrassment. "Don't stop on my account," he said.

"I've never been to a ball," Celeste said. "I'm years behind in learning the steps. I don't want to embarrass you at our wedding."

"You could never embarrass me, my love. Come, I'll show you," Luciano said and extended his hand.

Celeste timidly stepped up to him and took his hand. She made a few missteps as they moved about the room, but he was patient with her, showing her how to make the moves correctly. Soon, they were dancing in perfect harmony.

"I see you're mastering color combinations. That gown is stunning on you," Luciano whispered.

Celeste blushed and lowered her eyes. "It's my favorite. I'm pleased you like it." Luciano turned her to face him and put his arms around her waist. "What step is this?" she asked.

"One of my own creations. Do you like it?"

Before she could answer, Luciano's steward stepped into the doorway and cleared his throat.

Luciano sighed and said, "What is it, Santi?"

Santi bowed and inched into the room. "Forgive the interruption, sir, but there's a tenant here demanding to see you. She says it's urgent and that you'll want to hear what she has to say. I tried to get it out of her, but she insists on telling you."

Portia came in and said, "What's this then? I'll handle it."

"She asks to see the master, madam," Santi said and bowed to Portia.

"Take me to her," Luciano said and strode out with Portia and Celeste following.

Santi led them to the entryway where Masina was waiting. She curtsied and began crying when she saw them.

Celeste went to her and put an arm around her shoulder. "What is it, Masina? Not the children, I hope."

Masina glanced at Celeste but spoke to Luciano. "Pardon me, sir, but Jacopo is missing. When he wasn't in his bed this morning, I thought he'd gone to the fields early, but Adamo says he hasn't seen the boy all day. When he didn't come in for the evening meal, I knew something was wrong. We've been searching for hours but haven't found him."

"Why bother the master with this?" Santi asked. "I'll get my men to help you search."

"No, Santi, it's fine. Jacopo is Signorina Gabriele's brother. Masina was right to come here," Luciano said.

Santi looked at Celeste in confusion, but she just shook her head.

"This is my doing, Masina," Celeste said. "We'll find him. Where could he have gone?"

"He's been troubled since your visit the other day," Masina told Celeste. "He's angry and says you've abandoned him. I've tried to explain, but he won't listen."

"That boy has always been a challenge. All will be well. You'll see," Celeste said. "Let me get my cloak. I'll help look for him."

"You'll do no such thing," Portia said. "There are plenty of people to look for Jacopo. Come get your dinner and let them handle this."

Celeste protested, but Luciano stopped her. "Your aunt is right. Let's eat, and maybe they'll find him by the time we're finished."

Celeste wanted to protest but didn't dare do it in front of the servants. "Very well, but if my brother isn't back by then, I'm going to look for him myself."

Luciano gave Santi instructions, then escorted Celeste and Portia back to the sala. Celeste was too agitated to eat. She paced the room as they waited for news and was grateful that Portia and Luciano didn't stop her.

"I caused this. I should have listened to you, Aunt Portia. Why did I have to be so impetuous?"

"That boy is too much like his father. I was afraid he'd cause trouble someday. You shouldn't have gone to visit, but this isn't your fault. He was silly to run off. He probably just needed to let off steam, but he'll go home when he's hungry enough," Portia said.

"No, he won't. You should have seen him. He was angry and had a right to be. What right do I have to be here when he has to live in a farmhouse? It isn't fair."

Luciano had been quiet during the meal, and Celeste worried he regretted his proposal. He had a right to. She didn't belong with a man like him.

"There I was dancing in the elegant sala before sitting down to my sumptuous meal while my brother was missing." She stopped pacing and faced Luciano. "What am I doing here? I belong in the farmhouse with the children, not as a future Duchessa in a grand palazzo. I can't do this. I have to go to them."

She started to leave, but Luciano caught her wrist, and Portia blocked her path.

"Why must I always remind you you're a Gabriele?" Portia said. "You have as much right to be here as Luciano or I do. Would you have been questioning this match if not for your father's ruin?"

Celeste pulled free of Luciano and crossed her arms. "Jacopo is also of Gabriele blood, is he not?"

There was a commotion in the hall before Portia could answer. The groom came in, dragging Jacopo by the ear. He pushed the boy to the floor and said, "I found this cowering in the stable. What do you want me to do to him, master?"

"Leave him, Puccio," Luciano said. "Tell Adamo that Jacopo is safe. They can stop searching."

The groom raised an eyebrow but bowed and left without another word.

Jacopo shivered and prostrated himself before Luciano. "Forgive me, master," he whimpered.

Luciano stared down at the boy but said nothing. Celeste went to her brother and put her arms around his shoulders.

"Get up, Jacopo," she said softly. He slowly stood but kept his eyes lowered. "What were you doing in the stable? Masina and Adamo have been frantic with worry."

"Yes, explain your disgraceful behavior, boy," Portia demanded. "I'm ashamed of you."

Luciano raised his hand to silence her. "Hush. Let him speak."

Jacopo glanced at Luciano but immediately lowered his eyes. "I was curious after Celeste came to visit. I wanted to see how she lived. I went to the front door, but they wouldn't let me in, so I've been hiding in the stable to wait for dark. I was going to sneak in through the garden. I knew Celeste would let me stay if I made it that far. I didn't know you were here, Master."

"Look at me," Luciano said.

Jacopo slowly raised his eyes. The movement looked almost painful to Celeste. She remembered the first time Luciano ordered her to look him in the eyes.

Luciano stared at Jacopo for several seconds before returning to his chair. "You look very much like Marco. Now that you're here say your piece."

"Master?"

Celeste had expected Luciano to order a lashing for the boy before sending him back to the farmhouse and wondered if that would have been the best thing for him.

"What was your plan once you got here? Or did you only come for a tour of the grounds?" Luciano asked with a smirk.

Jacopo stood straighter and said, "I was going to make sure Celeste wrote to you asking if we could live here with her. Now, she can ask you in person. Has she?"

"Impertinent boy!" Portia said and gave him a small slap. "Do you know whom you are addressing? How dare you ask such a question?"

Celeste looked to Luciano, trying to make sense of what was happening. He was clearly enjoying himself. Celeste wasn't sure if she should be amused or annoyed.

"Sit, Portia, and not another word. I don't need your help," Luciano said while still glaring at Jacopo.

Portia dropped into her chair and crossed her arms. Luciano winked at Celeste. She had to bite her lip to keep from laughing. He was toying with them. She'd forgotten his delightful sense of humor. Celeste sat and crossed her arms too.

"Yes, your sister mentioned something about you," Luciano said. "I see that you're as impetuous as she is. You may look like Marco, but you have nothing of his calm temperament." Luciano rubbed his chin and continued to watch Jacopo, making the boy fidget. "So, you want to live here and maybe be master of my estate one day? Is that your scheme?"

Jacopo dropped to his knees. "No, sir, I had no scheme. I could work for you. Adamo will tell you what a hard worker I am. I'll do whatever you ask."

"Whatever I ask? Are you unhappy with Adamo and Masina? Don't they treat you well?"

"Yes, my parents are kind and generous. I just don't want to be a farmer. I miss Venice and being in the city," Jacopo said and wrung his hands.

"How would you like to go to Florence and be my apprentice with Marco? Would that satisfy you?"

Jacopo's face lit up, and Celeste smiled. Luciano was brilliant. It was the perfect solution.

"I'd love to go with you, Maestro. When do we leave?"

Luciano stood and said, "In three days. Do you give me your word that you'll do whatever you're told?"

"Yes, Maestro. I promise. Anything you ask."

Luciano turned to Celeste and Portia with a grin. "You're my witnesses." When the women nodded, he turned to Jacopo. "Being an apprentice is hard work, but I'm a fair maestro. Marco can help train you. Listen to whatever he says, and you'll do well by me. Now, please get off your knees. I'm not the emperor." Jacopo glanced at Celeste before climbing to his feet. "I think it will be good to have this one where I can keep an eye on him. Get home. Tell Adamo I'll speak to him in the morning."

Jacopo gave Celeste a quick hug, then ran out of the room. Luciano laughed as he watched him go.

"I hope you know what you're doing, Luciano," Portia said. "That boy isn't Marco."

"He's full of spirit and is the kind of boy I need in my workshop. Reminds me of myself at that age."

160

Celeste forgot herself and threw her arms around Luciano. He hugged her and winked at Portia.

"You are the kindest man I've ever known," Celeste said when she pulled away. "What have we done to deserve you?"

"You deserve this and much more. Portia, give us a moment alone, please. I have something else I need to discuss with Celeste. I promise to behave myself."

Portia raised an eyebrow but nodded and left them alone. Luciano gestured for Celeste to sit across from him. Her anxiety rose as she waited for him to speak. It reminded her of the early days of her training during Federigo's lessons, but she was no longer a frightened young nanny. She took a breath and held his gaze.

"I'm glad we have a solution for Jacopo that pleases both of us. I'd been considering taking Jacopo to Florence even before he ran away. I would have rather talked to Adamo first, but many boys younger than Jacopo become apprentices. He'll be sorry to lose the boy, but I believe this is for the best."

"I agree, Luciano. He wouldn't have been content as a farmer."

"You need to know that I have no intention of including your other siblings in our family circle. They are to remain with Masina and Adamo. I'll make that clear to them, but I expect you to support me in this. I don't want you to visit them or have any contact with them. You're right that they are also of Gabriele blood, but they don't remember that life. This may seem harsh, but it's for their own welfare, as well as yours. You said the other children are content. Let's keep them that way."

Celeste wiped a tear from her cheek. "I agree, Luciano, and give you my word that I'll have no further contact with them. It breaks my heart, but I know it's best. Now that I've seen them content and well cared for, I can let them go."

"I appreciate that. It's difficult but will be worth it."

Luciano stood and turned his back to her. She went to him and tenderly rested her hand on his arm. "What is it, my love?"

"It's what you said before Puccio found Jacopo. Do you honestly believe you don't belong here? Have you changed your mind about becoming my wife? I want to marry you more than I need to draw breath, but I won't force you. I was forced to marry my poor Isabella. That was a disaster. I refuse to do the same to you." He reached for her hands and drew her close. "Celeste, you have a say in this. If you wish, I'll allow you and Portia to remain here, and I'll live my life alone in Florence."

He ran a hand through his curls, just as he had in her dream. The familiar gesture melted Celeste's heart. She hated that she'd made him to believe she didn't want to be his wife.

"Forgive my thoughtlessness. I was distraught about Jacopo. What I said had nothing to do with my feelings for you. My fears are for my own feelings of inadequacy. Our upcoming marriage is my reason for being. My love has nothing to do with titles, clothes, jewels, or a grand palazzo. We could live out our days in a hut, and I'd be content as long as I was with you. I love you, Luciano, and I could never leave you."

Luciano pulled her close and kissed the top of her head. "Being my wife comes with great responsibility, but I wouldn't have asked for your hand if I didn't believe you were equal to the task. I will be proud to call you my Duchessa."

"And it will be my honor to stand at your side."

He leaned down and tenderly brushed his lips against hers, then whispered, "I love you, Celeste."

She laced her hands in his curls and gave him a passionate kiss. "And I love you, Maestro, with my whole soul."

Nine Months Later

Luciano pressed his horse to make the trip from Florence to Lucca in two days instead of three. He'd forced himself to keep his distance from Celeste, but the long months of separation had been torture. His muscles were stiff when he dismounted, but the discomfort was worth it to be with his love.

After handing the reins to the groom, Luciano bounded up the front steps, calling for Celeste. He stopped inside the sala doorway and frowned in disappointment to find the room dark and empty except for a painting resting on an easel in the center of the room. Even in the darkness, he recognized the work as Celeste's Blessed Virgin.

He took an oil lamp from the hallway and carried it for a closer look. His breath caught at what he saw. The painting was breathtaking.

"When did you get here, Luciano?" he heard Celeste say from behind him. "I see you found my gift. I wanted to present it to you in Florence." Luciano turned and took her hands. Her brows furrowed when she saw his tears. "What's wrong?"

"Nothing but my reaction to your masterpiece, my love. It's one of the most exquisite paintings I've ever seen."

Celeste gave a small wave. "Don't exaggerate."

"No, Celeste, I mean it. You truly are one of the greatest artists of our age. Your abilities have far surpassed mine."

"That's not true, Luciano. I'm years away from matching your skill. I'm only as good as I am because of my excellent maestro."

Luciano forgot the painting and turned his gaze to Celeste. "That painting isn't the only exquisite thing in this room. You're radiant, my love."

"Because you're here."

He kissed her tenderly and had to restrain himself from sweeping her up and taking her to his bed that very instant.

Portia hurried into the room, and Luciano reluctantly stepped away from Celeste.

"Am I interrupting?" Portia said with half a grin.

Luciano took her hands. "Yes. You are looking as young and lovely as ever, Portia," he said and kissed her cheeks.

"Flatterer," she said and gave him a playful tap. "I'm glad you've arrived safely. Our meal is waiting. Let's go in before it gets cold."

The three of them chatted comfortably while they ate, but it was a chore for Luciano to keep his eyes off Celeste. He was pleased to see her so confident and at ease. She had come a long way from the cowering shadow she once was.

"It's a pleasant night," Portia said, once they'd finished their meal. "Let's take our wine to the terrace." They picked up their glasses to go, but the housekeeper stopped Portia with a question. "You two go ahead. I'll meet you in a moment."

Luciano watched Portia go and chuckled. "I'm surprised she left us alone."

Celeste smiled. "She has her spies."

As they walked to the terrace, he said, "Does she regret her decision to leave Venice? Does she get lonely?"

"Never. She told me this morning she feels more at home here than anywhere else in her life. I feel the same. When we first arrived, I told Portia I wanted to live here instead of going to Florence. I don't believe I've ever been as content anywhere, not even my childhood home."

He swept his gaze over the idyllic view. "This was always my favorite place as a child. I spent as much time here as my father would allow. It became my sanctuary. We'll visit as often as I can manage it."

She leaned her head against his shoulder and closed her eyes. "I'm relieved to hear that."

"Tell me about Portia's past. All I know is that she's a widow. Why hasn't she remarried? She would have made a fine match."

"I knew little of her story myself until she told me during our journey here. My grandfather died before Portia was marriageable age, so my father arranged her match when she was fifteen. Portia became the third wife of a wealthy but much older merchant with a reputation for having a violent temper. Many questioned the circumstances of his second wife's death. His first wife and child died during childbirth."

Luciano stroked his beard and watched her, remembering Isabella's tragic death. He shook the thought away and said, "Why did your father let Portia marry him, then?"

"He just wanted to rid himself of responsibility for her. The man beat Portia cruelly and never let her leave the house or have visitors. She was saved two years after their marriage when he slumped over dead at dinner one night. It was a blessing there were no children. Uncle Cesare took her back into his home, and she eventually talked him out of forcing her to remarry. She believes he only agreed because she returned with her large dowry, but she says he always resented having to support her."

"I already respected her, but now more so. Has she ever regretted her decision? She'll never have children."

"Not that she's said, but she's become like a mother to me, so that gives her consolation. She's content to be free of Uncle Cesare."

"Then, I'm glad to help another member of your family, although she also did me a favor by coming here with you. Cesare wouldn't allow you to come alone, and he seemed relieved when I asked if Portia could be your chaperon. We all benefitted from the arrangement."

"None more than me," Celeste whispered.

Luciano watched the moonlight highlight the warm color of her hair and longed to bury his face in the glistening strands. He gently wrapped his arm around her slender waist and lifted her onto his lap. He gave her a hungry kiss, and Celeste responded for a moment before breathlessly pulling away.

"We mustn't, Luciano. Portia will see us."

"I love the way you say my name," he said in a husky whisper before moving her back to her chair. "This will be my last visit before you come to Florence in two months. I'm finding it too difficult to resist you."

"I feel the same. I'll miss you, but it's better than succumbing to a temptation we'll regret."

He gave her a last tender kiss as he heard Portia's footsteps on the walkway behind him. "Continue to paint, my love. It will help pass the time until we're together."

"You don't have to tell her to paint. It's all she ever wants to do," Portia said as she lowered herself into a chair.

Celeste smiled and squeezed his hand. "I'm working on a wedding present for you."

He lifted his hand to her lips. "You're all the gift I need."

"Enough of that," Portia said. "Off to bed with you, Celeste. I have estate business to discuss with Luciano."

He watched longingly as Celeste stood and kissed Portia's cheeks before heading into the house. "That girl is my treasure. How am I so blessed?"

"We've all been blessed, but if you want my advice, don't stay long on this visit and let it be the last one until we join you in Florence."

"Wise advice, which I plan to heed. Too much temptation here."

Portia gave him a knowing look before picking up her wineglass. "Trust me, you'll survive until your wedding night."

CHAPTER FOURTEEN

*C*eleste clasped her trembling hands in her lap as the carriage neared the outskirts of Florence. As overjoyed as she was to see Luciano and prepare for their wedding, she was also afraid to make her debut into Florentine society. Adapting to her change in status had been challenging enough in Lucca but doing it in an enormous foreign city would be even worse. Portia assured Celeste that she was fully prepared to take up her new role. Celeste was grateful for her aunt's encouragement but didn't feel she'd ever be worthy to stand at Luciano's side.

Her betrothal to Luciano was still a secret that they wouldn't announce until she had been in Florence for an acceptable amount of time, so gaining acceptance in Florence was entirely up to her. Even in Florence, the Gabriele name was familiar, but she had to convince many influential people she deserved to be there. She worried about convincing Luciano's family most of all. He wrote that they were excited to meet her, but she doubted the truth of his words.

As the towers and domes of Florence loomed closer, she put her anxieties aside and craned her neck to get a better view of the city Luciano adored. She recalled the way his face glowed when he'd spoken of his birthplace during her lessons. He had called it the crown of the modern world. She couldn't have imagined any city surpassing Venice, but as the carriage passed the grand and imposing buildings lining the cobblestone streets, she understood his admiration.

Luciano had rented a small villa for them on the outskirts of the city. Celeste was glad they'd live removed from the curious eyes of the Florentines. It would give her time to adjust to the new surroundings at her own pace. They were only twenty minutes by carriage from Luciano's estate, so visits would still be convenient. Celeste found the villa charming from her first glimpse as the coach entered the gates. The staff was there to greet them and get them settled. Though Celeste had grown accustomed to others bowing and curtsying to her, it still made her uneasy, but she did her best to be as kind as possible without acting too familiar.

Celeste's most delightful discovery upon arriving in Florence was to find Livia waiting at the door of her chambers. Luciano had written for her to leave Gemma in Lucca because he had a lady's maid for her in Florence. Celeste had dreaded getting used to a new servant, so it thrilled her to see a familiar face. She forgot her elevated station and hugged Livia.

"How long have you been here?" she asked, as Livia helped remove her cloak.

"The master sent for three other servants and me a few months after he left Venice. Signora Niccolo was sad to see me go, but the master arranged for a new lady's maid to attend her before I left. It gave me time to train her on my mistress' likes and dislikes." She lowered her head and curtsied. "I beg your pardon, madam. You're my mistress now."

Celeste was tempted to laugh, but she raised her chin instead. "That's correct, but you're forgiven. Please unpack my trunks as soon as possible. I need to freshen up before we meet Signore Vicente for dinner."

Livia curtsied and glanced at Celeste long enough to catch her wink before she scurried off to comply with her new mistress' wishes. Celeste took the time to explore the villa. It had terraced gardens and a stairway to the roof where they could sit in the evenings and enjoy the view. Celeste liked it so much that she wished she and Luciano could live there after their wedding. She pictured his palazzo as some cold and colossal edifice, but she'd have to accept it as her new home. She would do anything to please him and was comforted with the hope of making frequent trips to Lucca.

Once Livia finished helping her dress, Celeste glanced at herself in the glass and nodded in satisfaction. She'd never considered herself beautiful but hoped her appearance would satisfy Luciano.

"You are exquisite," Portia said from the doorway. "Every man in Florence will want to meet this new Venetian beauty. Luciano had better lay claim to you as soon as possible."

"Please, aunt, I'm nervous enough. Don't make it worse, or I won't be able to leave this room."

"Just remember who's waiting at the other end of that carriage ride," Portia said, as she took her arm and led her to the courtyard.

LUCIANO FLINCHED with each crunch of a carriage wheel on the cobblestone drive. He hadn't seen Celeste since his visit to Lucca and wasn't sure he'd survive the separation a moment longer. Managing his inherited estate consumed his time and setting up his new workshop in Florence left little time to dwell on Celeste. It wasn't until he'd gotten acquainted with his peers and established himself as a leader in the community that he could focus on his impending marriage.

He'd decided that two months after she arrived in Florence would be long enough to wait before the wedding. Unlike the spectacle with Isabella, he wanted a quiet affair but knew he'd have little say with Portia in charge. He planned to take Celeste to Lucca for a month after the ceremony to get acquainted without being subjected to curiosity and gossip.

When the valet announced that Celeste and her aunt had arrived, Luciano checked himself in the glass and went to greet his future bride. The transformation in her was astounding. She no longer tried to be invisible but stood tall and moved with confidence and grace. Her jewel-studded hair fell freely on her back and shoulders instead of being hidden under a cap. The desire to bury his face in her gleaming curls overwhelmed him as it had his last night in Lucca. He cleared his throat and greeted Portia first, as was proper. When she presented Celeste, he took her outstretched hand and kissed her cheeks.

"Welcome, Signorina Gabriele. You look exquisite this evening."

Celeste looked into Luciano's eyes and said, "Thank you, Signore Vicente, as do you."

It delighted him to see the young woman he'd fallen in love with peeking out from her glistening eyes. He offered an arm to each woman and escorted them to the sala to introduce them to his guests.

He started with Elisabetta, the eldest of his sisters, and her new husband, Giulio. Elisabetta was several years his junior but acted more like his mother. Her reception of Celeste was formal and tepid. Luciano wanted to pinch his sister's arm and tell her to be nice like he had when they were children. The way Giulio eyed Celeste irritated Luciano even more, but he wasn't the only man in the room to take notice of the new young beauty in their midst. Luciano was instantly jealous of their attention to her.

He introduced Celeste to his two younger sisters, Angelica, and Diana, then escorted her to the table. He watched with pride as she conversed gracefully with his cousins seated on either side of her.

The instant they could escape unnoticed after the meal, he pulled Celeste aside to speak in private.

"Thank you, Luciano," she said as he led her to a corner away from the crowd. "I don't think I could have kept my composure for one more moment. Pretending I belong here is exhausting."

Luciano put his hands on her shoulders and said, "What do you mean pretending? You have as much right to be here as anyone else."

"I'm not sure your sisters agree. They seemed less than pleased to meet me."

"It's because you're Venetian, and they're protective of me. Ignore them. They'll love you once they get to know you. You've comported yourself like you were born to this." He took her hand and watched her intently for several moments. "I don't want to postpone our wedding any longer. I'm going to announce our betrothal tonight. There's no reason to wait."

Celeste pulled her hand free. "No, please don't. I've just arrived in Florence. No one knows me here. What will they think if you announce our betrothal the instant I arrive?"

Luciano moved closer and lowered his voice. "I don't care what anyone thinks. I've never been one to follow social conventions, as you know. I'm nobility here. No one would dare question my actions. We've been betrothed for over a year. That should satisfy the most pious naysayers. I've hated being separated from you, and I won't force you, but please end my suffering and tell me we don't have to wait."

He searched her face for a sign of hope and wanted to dance for joy when the corners of her mouth curved into a smile.

"How can I refuse you? Yes, Luciano, we can marry as soon as you wish."

The feel of her warmth against his body when he pulled her into his arms was almost more than he could bear. He backed away and kissed her cheeks.

"Will two weeks be enough time? I just want a small, intimate wedding."

"For me, yes," she whispered, "but Portia has been planning the wedding since we arrived in Tuscany. I'm not sure we can count on simple and intimate with her in charge."

A shadow crossed Celeste's face. "What is it, my love? Am I rushing you into this?"

"No, Luciano, it's not that. Who will give me away? I have no family but Portia and Marco here."

"I've sent word to Cesare. He's agreed to come. He takes his responsibility seriously, I assure you."

Celeste smiled. "You think of everything. Then, let's share our news."

Luciano took her arm, escorted her back to the other guests, and clapped loudly to get their attention.

"You have all met Signorina Gabriele tonight, but what you don't know is that we have been betrothed this past year. I'm honored and pleased to announce that we will wed in two weeks."

He expected cheers and congratulations, but the crowd froze and stared at them in stunned silence. Portia broke the tension by coming forward and kissing their cheeks, but even she couldn't hide her shock.

"I'm so happy for you both, though you didn't give me much warning. We have much to do to prepare."

A few of Luciano's other guests followed her example and came forward to offer half-hearted congratulations. Celeste was doing her best to be gracious, but Luciano could see her fighting back the tears. He whispered for Portia to make their excuses and get her back to the villa.

"I'll come in the morning," he said. "Do your best to reassure Celeste until then. I'll put out fires here."

Portia nodded and did as Luciano asked. He embraced Celeste once more at the door.

"Ignore these fools. Soon, we'll be joined in marriage, and nothing else will matter."

She nodded and kissed his cheeks. "I'll see you in the morning."

He lingered at the door until she was safely in the carriage and on her way before turning to face his inconsiderate guests. It took all of his strength to keep from tossing them out the door, but he needed their support for what was to come. He followed Celeste's example and did his best to be gracious, but it was a relief to close the door behind the last of them, especially his sisters.

"THIS ISN'T the reaction I expected," Portia said as she helped Celeste to bed that night.

Celeste smiled and patted the bed for Portia to sit and wrapped her arms around her knees. "What do you mean? Didn't you think I'd be overjoyed? In two weeks, I become Luciano's wife. The long wait is nearly over."

Portia brushed a curl from Celeste's forehead. "I'm thrilled to see you so happy, but I was speaking of his family and guests. They weren't very enthusiastic about the announcement."

"As Luciano said, who cares for their opinions? I'm tired of worrying about what the rest of the world thinks of me. Don't I deserve to have the desires of my heart after all I've suffered?"

"You do, and it's about time you realized that. I've been trying to convince you for the past year. Put the invisible serving girl to rest and become the woman you were meant to be."

Celeste laid back on the pillows with her hands behind her head. "Remember the day you took me to meet Maria Foscari? That terrified girl seems like a ghost from a different life. I can't wait until Maria learns the identity of Luciano's bride. I hope she comes to the wedding so I can see the look on her face."

Celeste giggled, but her aunt scowled. "Watch what you wish for, girl. There will be battles ahead when Luciano's Venetian relatives get word of your nuptials. Your marriage will widen the gulf between Maria and Luciano. She won't take that lightly. This is how feuds get started."

"Maria must know about Uncle Cesare adopting me and Luciano bringing us here. Either way, I don't care. She's nothing to me now, and I'm done playing the groveling peasant. I'm meant for a greater life. I'm marrying Luciano Vicente in two weeks, and I will become a prominent artist of our day. I have nothing to fear from anyone."

Portia feigned shock. "Is this the same frightened girl who I had to coax from this room only hours ago?"

"No, I am the woman who will conquer Florence. You'll see."

CELESTE'S CONFIDENCE had cooled by morning. The memory of the guest's shocked faces when Luciano announced their wedding had plagued her during the night. She pulled the blankets to her chin and frowned when Livia brought her breakfast tray. As lovely as it was to be mistress of the house and not the maid, seeing Livia reminded

Celeste of the place she'd occupied not long ago. A part of her longed to run back to Venice and the life she knew and forget that she'd ever met Luciano or held a paintbrush.

"Your aunt wishes me to say that after breakfast, you are to dress and prepare to meet Signore Vicente. He sent word that he will arrive shortly," Livia said.

Celeste noticed Livia's flat tone. "What's the matter with you?" She was in no mood for Livia's opinions that morning.

"Forgive me, madam, but everyone is talking about what happened at Signore Vicente's dinner last night. Is it true? Will you marry him in two weeks?"

"I would appreciate you not engaging gossip about me, Livia, but yes, it's true. Do you disapprove, as well?" She sat up and glared at Livia, daring her to speak her mind.

"No, madam. I'm happy for you, but I'm wondering what will become of me. Will the master abandon me in this strange country? Will he send me back to Venice?"

Livia looked so forlorn that Celeste burst out laughing. It was the last thing she had expected Livia to say. She'd made a patrician-like assumption that Livia would have cared more about Celeste's fate than her own.

"Stop worrying. You'll be my lady's maid and come with me wherever I go. I could never abandon you. I know your life. I've lived it." Livia let out her breath, and Celeste smiled. "Pick a suitable gown for me to greet my betrothed."

While Celeste ate, Livia chatted and prepared Celeste's wardrobe for the day. As she watched Livia, Celeste realized that her maid would make for a happy company though they could not be friends. She'd be grateful to have Livia's cheerful face greet her each morning, just as Gemma had. Celeste dressed as quickly as she could and went in search of Portia. The housekeeper directed her to the terrace.

"It's such a lovely day. I thought we should wait for Luciano here," Portia said as Celeste came toward her. "You're lovely today, too."

Celeste spun around before joining her at the table. "Will Luciano be pleased?"

"If not, he's blind. I'm encouraged to see you're still in high spirits."

"I wasn't at first, but Livia cheered me up and taught me a valuable lesson."

"Livia? You seem fond of the girl. How do you know her?"

Celeste recounted how Livia had tended her in her closet room off Luciano's studio.

"He must have sensed that I would need a familiar face here. He's very insightful."

"It was a thoughtful gesture, but you have me. Isn't that enough?"

Celeste raised her eyebrows. "Are you planning to stay in Florence? I thought you'd return to Venice after the wedding."

"I have no life in Venice, and I'm in no hurry to return. This past year has been the happiest of my long, pointless life. If you and Luciano agree, I'd love to stay. Who else will look after all your children?"

Celeste hugged her aunt in delight. "Nothing would make me happier, and I'm sure Luciano won't object."

"Won't object to what?" Luciano asked as he strode up the stairs to the terrace. "Are you already making promises for me, Celeste?"

Celeste's breath caught when she saw him. It was still a pleasant shock to see him so elegantly dressed and groomed instead of covered in paint. That morning he wore a scarlet cloak over a gold tunic, breeches, and leggings.

Portia stood and curtsied. "My niece asks that I may stay in Florence, with your approval, of course."

Luciano kissed their cheeks and motioned for them to sit. He sat next to Celeste and held her hand under the table. The feel of his skin on hers sent fire up her arm. She did her best to maintain her composure but worried that Portia could read her thoughts.

"You may stay for as long as you wish, but I planned to ask you to take over the management of my Lucca household. You've done a phenomenal job of running it this past year. Your woman's touch has been a significant improvement."

Portia gasped and put her hand to her mouth. "Nothing would

175

make me happier, as long as you promise to bring my niece to visit often."

"I promise we'll come so often that you'll tire of us," Luciano said and squeezed Celeste's hand. "Celeste and I will stay in Lucca for a month after the wedding. You may stay here until the last week. Then join us and remain after we leave. For now, I must steal your niece for another surprise. I'll send a carriage for you this evening for dinner. Until then, you can continue with the wedding plans."

"You're taking her with no chaperone? Scandalous. I'll join you," Portia said and stood.

Luciano helped Celeste to her feet. She agreed with Portia and knew she should protest but was still reeling from Luciano's news about Lucca.

"There is no need for concern, Portia," Luciano said. "I'm taking Celeste to my workshop. There will be plenty of curious eyes there. I'll draw the curtains in the carriage. No one will see that we're unchaperoned. Will that suffice?"

Portia gave a slight nod but continued to scowl. Luciano kissed Portia's cheek and took Celeste by the arm to escort her to the carriage. Celeste gazed back at Portia and gave a look she hoped would reassure her.

"You're quiet today. Have I upset you? Did you want Portia to join us?" Luciano asked as they walked.

"No, I'm just overwhelmed by your offer to her. She loves Lucca and has no desire to return to Venice. It'll be a comfort to have family nearby."

"Don't I count as family?" he asked and grinned.

His face was breathtaking when he smiled. Celeste vowed to make him smile every day for the rest of his life.

"Yes, but I need more family since yours is less than eager to welcome me into the Vicente clan."

"I spent the morning smoothing feathers, but they will come to love you in time."

"I will have to trust you on that," Celeste said and squeezed his arm.

LUCIANO LIFTED Celeste's hand to his lips once they were behind the closed curtains in the carriage. It took all his strength to resist taking her right there, and he wondered if he should have heeded Portia's objections. Luciano rested their clasped hands on his knee, and they rode in silence for the rest of the journey.

When they arrived at his estate, he didn't take her to the workshop but to a large studio that overlooked the grounds instead. It had large windows along two sides and was situated to let in a favorable light for most of the day. The stone walls glittered in the morning sunlight, giving the room a lustrous hue. Shelves filled with jars and tools lined the walls, and two sturdy worktables rested in the center of the room.

"Your studio is magnificent," Celeste said as she flitted across the floor in excitement. "It's far superior to the one in Venice."

He came up behind her and put his hand on her shoulder. "It's not my studio, my love. It's yours."

Celeste swung around to face him. "Mine? But this must rival the best studios in Florence. Maybe even in Rome. You should take it for yourself. I'm nothing but an apprentice. I haven't yet earned such a space. A studio this grand is meant for a great artist like you."

"I've grown fond of my studio in the workshop and don't want to leave it. I made this for you when I first returned to Florence. You may be an apprentice now, but you won't be for long. Soon you will be one of the greatest artists of our day and will deserve this studio to match. As you once told me, I can't put you in the workshop with the apprentices. Maybe I'll come to work here beside you occasionally."

Celeste took his hands and looked up at him with glistening eyes. "I'll never understand how I came to deserve you. I just hope I won't disappoint you."

He pulled her to his chest and kissed the top of her head as he loved to do. "That's impossible. I'm blessed to spend my life with a beautiful, intelligent, and talented woman that I love. I don't know of any other man in possession of such a priceless gift."

He cupped her face in his hands, and tenderly pressed his lips to hers. She responded hungrily and tightened her arms around him. The sweetness of her breath nearly drove him mad. He gently pushed her away and grasped her hands.

Without opening her eyes, she whispered, "I love you, Luciano."

He shuddered and took a breath. "And I love you, but I think it's best we don't see each other until the wedding. It will be a torment to separate from you, but we have the rest of this day, and I have another surprise for you."

"Between your offer to Portia, this studio, and you, there's nothing more I could desire in the world."

He smiled and offered her his arm. "You'll be pleased, trust me."

CELESTE FELT like she was floating as she walked along, clutching Luciano's arm. His kiss had left her giddy, and she hoped she'd be able to compose herself before they reached wherever he was leading her. It seemed impossible that just a year earlier, she had been a Venetian nanny with no hope of love or marriage or the chance of becoming an artist. Now she was on the eve of her wedding with a strikingly handsome artist and nobleman. She remembered her surly mood from earlier and smiled at the thought of leaving Luciano and running home to Venice.

They left the studio and strolled through the gardens to his workshop. While they walked, Luciano explained that when he had returned to Florence a year earlier, he worried that the competing Florentine Guilds and artisans would reject his plan to open a workshop. Most artisans were from the merchant class and were not aristocrats, but his father had been revered, if not feared, in the region, so that gave him the respect he needed.

Luciano brought a favorable reputation of his own, so they had welcomed him with open arms, along with his generous contributions. It didn't take long to establish his workshop and garner commissions. After a short time, he and his apprentices were as busy as they had been in Venice.

Luciano opened the workshop door for her, and the apprentices stopped working and stared when they noticed the two of them standing in the doorway. Stefano came forward and bowed. She didn't know that Luciano had brought him to Florence and was glad to see another familiar face.

"Welcome, Signorina Gabriele. What do you think of our new workshop?"

She took a moment to look around and nodded in satisfaction. The workshop was more than twice the size of the one in Venice and was stocked with many more materials and supplies. There were fewer apprentices, but she knew that would change with time.

"It's incredible, Stefano. What do you think of Florence?" she asked.

"Celeste," she heard a voice call out before Stefano could answer.

She turned to see Marco pushing boys out of the way to get to her. He grabbed her up and swung her around. Celeste stepped back to get a better look at him. He'd grown several inches since she'd last seen him, and his shoulders had broadened. A neatly trimmed beard graced his chin. Even though their father had once been a handsome man, it disturbed Celeste that Marco had grown in the exact image of him. She had to be grateful he had only inherited Papa's looks and not his temperament.

"Here's your final surprise for the day," Luciano said.

Celeste put her hands on his shoulders. "I was wondering when I'd get to see you. I hardly recognize this strapping young man. Are you happy in Florence, Marco?"

"Very happy, sister, especially now that you've arrived. You've changed more than a little yourself. Could you have imagined when we were children that we'd end up with Maestro Vicente in Florence?"

She felt tears prick her eyes and shook her head. Even if she couldn't rescue the rest of her family, at least she had helped Marco and Jacopo. It did her heart good to see him so content.

"No, brother, I couldn't have imagined what our lives would become, and we owe it all to Luciano."

"Enough of that," Luciano said and gave a backhanded wave.

"Celeste!" Jacopo called out and came up behind Marco. He'd grown as tall as his brother but wasn't yet a man. It surprised Celeste how alike they were.

"Did you get the outfit of clothes I had made for you two?" Luciano asked. When Marco nodded, he said, "Good. Wear them to join us for dinner tonight."

Marco took a step back. "No, Maestro, I couldn't. I'm meant for the workshop, not your dining table. I wouldn't know how to act."

"Then it's time you learn," Luciano said.

Jacopo pounded Marco on the shoulder. "It'll be an adventure, brother. We'll share it together."

Celeste took Marco's hand. "Please come. Aunt Portia and I will be there. We'll show you what to do." Seeing his face contort while he struggled to decide made Celeste laugh. "Don't look so pained. We're not going to eat you for dinner."

Marco grinned, and Luciano said, "It will just be family. There's no need to worry."

"Family?" Marco said. His eyes widened, and he cocked his thumb at Jacopo. "Maestro, you'll be our brother-in-law."

"You've just realized that? You still have to call me maestro in the workshop, though," Luciano said and winked.

"Yes, Maestro," Marco said, and even the apprentices laughed.

"Think how strange I'll feel to call him husband," Celeste said. She kissed her brothers' cheeks and gave them each a hug. "I'll see you at dinner. Don't be late and clean that paint off your fingernails."

She followed Luciano out and took his arm. "Thank you for including my brothers. It wasn't necessary, but I appreciate it."

"They need to get used to being in our world if they're going to spend time with us. Marco and Jacopo are smart young men. I consider Marco my second man, after Stefano. He's never disappointed me. Jacopo is more of a challenge, but he's young."

"I've worried about Jacopo."

"Don't. He knows how to take care of himself. I have some matters to attend to before dinner. Stay and get acquainted with your studio before Portia arrives."

Celeste nodded and flashed him a brilliant smile. They returned to the studio, and once they were inside, Luciano took her to a corner hidden from the windows and kissed her passionately. Just as she grew hungry for more, he pulled away.

"I must go," he said in a husky whisper. "I love you, Celeste."

He rushed out, leaving her staring after him. She grabbed the back of a chair to steady herself as the strength drained from her legs. Two weeks! How would she survive for two weeks without her Luciano?

CHAPTER FIFTEEN

*C*eleste toyed with a tassel on her gown while she and Portia waited in the foyer for Luciano and her brothers to arrive. Portia had wanted to go into the dining room without them, but Celeste refused to go until Luciano arrived.

Portia tapped Celeste's arm. "Be still, or you're going to work that tassel loose."

Celeste ignored Portia and continued to pace the foyer. "But where is Luciano? Where are my brothers? They should have been here ages ago."

"Luciano must have given the boys some task, and he is an important, busy man. He can't drop everything for family dinner," Portia said. She pulled a chair closer to hers. "Come, sit with me."

Celeste obeyed her aunt but continued to fidget. "This is no ordinary dinner, and you know it. His sisters must see me as some nameless social climber. They're going to hate me."

Portia stood and put her hands on her hips. "Then they will have to deal with me. Nameless? We are Gabrieles! We may not be noble, but we are their equals."

"What's all this commotion?" Luciano asked as he came into the foyer, followed by Marco and Jacopo.

Celeste forgot her nerves when she saw her brothers. At least they looked like nobles dressed in the elegant livery Luciano had provided.

Celeste took each of their hands. "Are these my brothers? How *debonair* you are."

Jacopo stood taller and raised his chin. Marco looked as if he wanted to crawl under a table.

"We're nothing more than boars in robes," Marco said.

Jacopo laughed and patted Marco's back. "Speak for yourself, brother. I belong in these clothes. Thank you for this gift, Maestro," he said and bowed with a flourish.

"I'm your brother-in-law here. Remember to call me Luciano."

"Yes, Maes...," Jacopo said.

Even Portia laughed at his mistake.

"Shall we go in?" Luciano said and offered Portia his arm.

Celeste was about to take the other, but her brothers stepped forward and held out their elbows.

"Allow us," Jacopo said.

Celeste took their arms and smiled. As they ascended the stairs to the sala, she marveled at the change in their lives in only a few short years and recalled the day she'd stood before their decaying front door fingering the coins in her dress. She wondered where they all would have ended up if Portia hadn't appeared when she did.

Portia's words about being Gabrieles had touched her. Celeste was no longer the poverty-stricken girl living in the slums. She straightened her shoulders and walked into the dining room with her head high. Elisabetta was the first to greet them. She took Celeste's hands and kissed her cheeks, but her manner was still restrained.

"I didn't have the chance to welcome you to the family last night. I've never seen Luci so happy. It's a blessing he's found a suitable wife after Bella's tragic death," she said.

Luciano stepped forward and said, "Thank you, and you're right. I have never been so happy."

Elisabetta kissed Luciano's cheek and said, "You're late, brother. You should know better than to keep me waiting."

"I had Guild business. Should I shirk my responsibilities to leave early for dinner with my sister?"

Elisabetta glanced at Celeste. "I assumed you were otherwise occupied. Diana saw you on the grounds earlier."

"Yes, brother, and you didn't bother to stop in to greet us. Welcome, Celeste. I look forward to getting acquainted," Diana said and offered Celeste her hand.

Celeste took Diana's hand and kissed her cheeks. "Thank you, Diana, and I look forward to having three new sisters."

"Let me introduce Celeste's brothers, Marco and Jacopo," Luciano said. "These are my sisters, Elisabetta, Diana, and Angelica."

Celeste stepped aside to make way for her brothers. Jacopo acted as if he met nobles every day, but Marco was pale and reserved. She had to bite her tongue to keep from laughing. Marco managed to survive the curtsies, bows, and cheek kissing and looked relieved when Portia came forward.

"Such lovely young women," Portia said. "Luciano didn't tell us he had such beautiful sisters. It's a pleasure to see you again."

She made an elegant curtsy and took Elisabetta's arm. "Your brother tells me we should expect joyful news in the fall."

Elisabetta nodded and began talking excitedly about her forthcoming motherhood. Luciano took his other two sisters' arms, and Celeste's brothers escorted her to the table. She was almost as relieved as Marco to have survived the introductions.

She had hoped to sit with Luciano, but Angelica directed her to the opposite end of the table next to a cousin. Celeste didn't recognize him from the previous night, but from the way he and Diana eyed each other, there had to be a connection between them. Celeste wondered if Diana had seated her next to him so he could interrogate her, but it only took moments to realize that he had no interest in anyone but Diana.

Jacopo was on her other side talking to Elisabetta's husband, Giulio, who she clearly remembered from the previous night. The way he leered at her reminded her of Marcello and left her uneasy. Since he was married to her sister-in-law, she'd have to see him often. She would speak to Luciano about her concerns after their wedding. Jacopo seemed taken with Giulio. Celeste leaned closer to hear their conversation.

"Have you come from Venice?" Giulio asked Jacopo.

"I was born in Venice, but I was living in Lucca until nine months ago. I've been in Florence since then," Jacopo said.

"Why have we not seen you before tonight if your sister and Luciano have been betrothed for a year?"

Celeste interrupted before Jacopo could answer. "Luciano didn't want to announce our betrothal until we arrived in Florence. My aunt and I only arrived yesterday."

Giulio studied her face and grinned. "I can see why Luciano kept you a secret. Where have you been hiding?"

It may as well have been Marcello speaking the words. Celeste stifled a shudder. "Not hiding. I've also been living in Lucca. Congratulations on your wondrous news," she said to change the subject.

The grin slid from his face. "Yes, wondrous news," he said flatly.

His reaction baffled Celeste. The prospect of an heir thrilled most men.

"What news?" Jacopo asked.

"Giulio is to become a father," Celeste said.

"Oh," Jacopo said and frowned. "Giulio doesn't want to talk about that."

"Clearly not," Celeste said and looked at Giulio.

The maid brought a fresh jug of wine and set it on the table in front of Jacopo. He filled his goblet and took a gulp. Celeste grabbed it from him and set it out of his reach.

"Enough wine. Isn't it time for you and Marco to go? You have to be up at dawn," Celeste said.

"It's early yet," Jacopo said and reached around Celeste for his goblet.

Celeste didn't want to make a scene, so she let Jacopo keep it but slid the jug away from him. He raised his eyebrows at her and took another gulp.

185

"Why do you have to be up at dawn?" Giulio asked.

"To be in the workshop. Marco and I are apprentices. Our maestro is a hard taskmaster," he said and laughed.

"Jacopo, remember where we are," Celeste whispered to her brother.

"How can I forget?" he said and glared at her.

Celeste wanted Jacopo to leave before he caused trouble but knew he wouldn't listen to her. He had never listened. She looked to Luciano for help, but he was deep in conversation with a man that Celeste didn't recognize. As she tried to figure out what to do, Marco came up behind her and tapped her shoulder.

"It's time we go, sister. Come, Jacopo," Marco said.

Jacopo stared at Marco but didn't move. "I'm not ready to go, brother. The evening is just getting started."

"Jacopo, go with Marco," Luciano's voice boomed from across the room.

Jacopo jumped to his feet and bowed with a flourish. He still held his goblet and dripped wine on Giulio's tunic. "Yes, Maestro," he said with a half-grin. "As you command."

Celeste grabbed his goblet, and Marco pulled him away by the arm. The rest of the group watched them leave in silence. Giulio scowled and took a corner of the tablecloth to wipe his tunic. Celeste clasped her hands and stared at the floor, too ashamed to meet Luciano's eye.

"Reminds me of myself at that age," Luciano said and laughed.

Celeste dared raise her eyes as the rest of the guests laughed, too, and went back to their conversations, except for Elisabetta. She watched Celeste without expression for several moments before turning to answer a question from the maid. Luciano came and put his hand on her shoulder.

"He's just a boy, Celeste. No harm done. See, it's already forgotten," he said and gestured toward the chatting guests.

"I don't believe your sister has forgotten, and don't forget that Jacopo is my father's son," she said without raising her eyes.

"He is, but so is Marco, and you're his daughter. He truly reminds me of myself at that age. It was just too much wine and being in new surroundings. I'll speak to him in the morning and remind him of his place. You don't have to shoulder this. Let me handle Jacopo."

Celeste raised her eyes to his. "It would be a relief not to worry about him, and he'll respond better to you. Thank you, Luciano."

"Thank me by smiling and enjoying yourself. My sisters are eager to hear the wedding plans. Here's Portia. Go speak of gowns and music and flowers. Smile, my love. This is a joyous time."

Celeste grinned at him and allowed Portia to take her arm to lead her to Luciano's sisters. The women spoke excitedly about the wedding, but Celeste couldn't put aside the incident with Jacopo as easily as the others had done. She had seen that drunken behavior from her father too many times to forget. She only hoped that Luciano could keep him in line and guide him into the young man he had the potential to become.

"THAT WAS HARDLY the impression I'd hoped to make," Celeste told Portia as they rode back to the villa after dinner. "I could have strangled Jacopo. What would I have done if Luciano hadn't stepped in to rescue me?"

"I would have strangled the boy myself, but you're fretting too much. Trust me when I say this isn't the worst Luciano's sisters have witnessed at a family dinner. They know Jacopo is young and had too much wine. It's forgotten by now, and we're all focused on our own concerns. You should do the same," Portia said and squeezed Celeste's arm.

"Perhaps you're right, but I saw too much of Papa in Jacopo tonight. I'll put my worries aside for now and ask what you think of Luciano's family."

The carriage went over a bump, and Portia adjusted herself on the seat. "I miss traveling by gondola. It's much easier on my old bones. I found Diana and Angelica delightful to answer your question, but Luciano had better keep an eye on Diana. Did you see her with the cousin? There's trouble brewing."

Celeste giggled. "I noticed. I tried to engage him in conversation, but he couldn't tear his eyes from Diana. Surely Luciano noticed. What did you think of Elisabetta?"

Portia huffed. "Too haughty, but that's not surprising. She fancies herself mistress of the palazzo, although I suppose she was until her marriage. There may be trouble for you with her, but Luciano keeps Elisabetta in her place. Her husband is another story. Give him a wide berth. There's little affection between the two of them, and his eyes wander, mostly to you."

Celeste nodded. "I noticed that, too."

"I've seen men like him. Fortunately, Luciano was aware of his attention. I don't believe even Giulio would dare cross him. Otherwise, I see no reason for you to fret. They're a typical patrician family, and the family will accept you in no time. Everyone who knows you loves you as I do. It won't be the same in Lucca without you."

"And I'll be lost without you." Celeste leaned against the cushions and closed her eyes. "I want to be a Gabriele and make you proud, Aunt. At times, I feel I can conquer the world. At others, I'm afraid of failing and disappointing you or Luciano, and I wonder what I'm doing here. When I woke this morning, I wanted nothing more than to run home to Venice, though there's nothing there for me now. How are you so strong all the time? I lack your strength and courage."

Portia laughed softly. "You'll understand when you're my age. I wasn't born strong. I was an anxious, shy girl. My brothers had no patience for me, and my mamma was a cold and distant woman who I rarely saw. I used to wish for someone to hold and care for me like my nanny had when I was young, but there was no one to do so. I was left to protect myself."

"Sounds like your childhood was unhappier than mine."

"It was just lonely. When my husband died, and that horror ended, I moved in with Cesare, and your aunt Teresa became my dearest friend. I wouldn't have survived without her. She was the only confidant I had until you. The news of Teresa's death broke my heart. I miss her terribly."

They rode in silence for several minutes. "Will you be lonely in Lucca?" Celeste finally asked.

"Not at all. You know me. I can't keep my nose out of everyone's business. I'll be running Lucca before long," she said and laughed. "I'll have visits from you and Luciano to look forward to, and in time, your little ones too. They'll need a grandmother since they have none." Celeste frowned and studied her hands resting in her lap. "Have I said something wrong?"

"I'm afraid to have children after what happened to Mamma, Luciano's mother, and even Isabella. I don't want to die, but Luciano will expect an heir," Celeste said.

"Nonsense. Some women die bearing children, but most don't. Your mother bore six children before God took her. Women have died choking on a fishbone, but you haven't stopped eating fish. You can't fear what might happen. You can only face what is happening."

Celeste kissed Portia's cheek. "That's wise advice. I must give it more thought."

"It doesn't matter much if you're afraid to have children, my dear. From what I've seen of the way Luciano looks at you, I won't have to wait long to become a grandmother."

Celeste was glad it was dark, so Portia couldn't see her blush. She couldn't wait to give herself to Luciano, but she was aware of the consequences. Luciano wanted children, and she hoped to grant his desire. She prayed God would allow her to survive childbirth and left it in His hands.

CHAPTER SIXTEEN

 eleste slept little the night before the wedding and was like a
fidgety bird while Portia and Livia dressed her for the
ceremony, but once they had finished, she hardly recognized the
woman staring back at her from the glass. Luciano had given her the
wedding gown as a gift, along with a single strand of pearls. The pale
blue fabric favored her coloring and reminded her of the serving dress
Maria Foscari had given her for the gala. That was the night she met
with Luciano in the garden and learned he had feelings for her. She
wondered if he'd selected the color for that reason.

Portia tried to force Celeste to eat before they left to meet
Luciano's family's women for the processional to the church, but she
was too nervous to swallow a bite. Portia finally relented and led her
to the carriage. Celeste would have fainted before they reached their
destination without Portia reminding her to breathe.

Celeste pulled the carriage curtains aside and spotted the crowd of
women waiting to greet her for the processional. Luciano had
promised a small, quiet wedding, but at least forty women waited
outside Elisabetta's house. They lined up to kiss and hug her as she
exited the carriage. Their faces blended into an indistinguishable blur.
Celeste clung to Portia's hand until her aunt begged her to loosen her

grip before she crushed her fingers. She relaxed slightly once the procession began moving since walking provided an outlet for her nervous energy.

Uncle Cesare was there to greet her at the church door. She'd never been so happy to see anyone in all her life and clung to him until it was time to go inside and join her groom. All doubts and worries vanished the moment she saw Luciano standing before the altar. He was resplendent in an indigo cloak covering his silver-trimmed white tunic and leggings. The combination was breathtaking against his dark coloring and reminded her of the hours she had spent crushing paint pigments with him in the Venice studio. The dark blue was the perfect accent to her gown, no doubt by design.

She was too overwhelmed to grasp much of the Matrimonial Mass and only remembered her satisfaction at seeing Maria Foscari's disgruntled face as they left the church. Soon after, they were at Luciano's estate for the wedding feast. There were at least 200 people in attendance. Celeste made a note to talk to Portia about what a small, intimate affair meant.

She enjoyed the dancing and was grateful to Portia for forcing her to practice in Lucca when she would rather have been painting. She was ravenous by the time they sat down for dinner but was careful to watch her wine intake.

Sometime around midnight, Luciano took her hand and led her up the back stairs to his chambers. Her night-dress and other personal items lay neatly on the bed.

"You can change there," he said and pointed to the changing screen from his Venice studio propped against the wall.

"You think of everything, " she said and hugged him.

"Do you need help to undress? I can call Livia."

"She's here?" Celeste asked in surprise.

"Of course. Livia's your lady's maid, and you live here now, don't you? We'll take her with us to Lucca if you'd like, although you'll have Gemma there. Livia insisted on being allowed to view the ceremony. I don't know why I tolerate her impertinence."

Celeste laughed and went behind the screen to change. She heard sounds of Luciano changing, too, and was glad that he hadn't called his valet to help so they could be alone. It took time to work out of her layers of clothing, but she was proud of herself for managing it on her own. She put on her satin nightdress and stepped from behind the screen to greet her husband without fear. He stood next to the bed in nothing but pale linen breeches. As he pulled her into his arms, she felt the warmth of his hands through the cloth.

He gave her a lingering kiss before sliding his lips down her neck. "Are you nervous?" he asked in a whisper.

She shuddered and said, "No, my love. I've dreamed of this night for years."

He tenderly lifted her onto the bed and kissed her with renewed hunger. She groaned in delight at his touch. Portia had warned that the first time would be painful, but Celeste only felt exquisite pleasure. Luciano took his time and loved her with a building passion that left her euphoric. When they finished, he shifted onto the mattress and turned onto his side, facing her.

Brushing the hair from her face, and said, "Did I hurt you? I tried holding back until you were ready. It wasn't easy."

"You didn't hurt me. I had no idea such ecstasy existed. How long before we can try again?"

Luciano rolled onto his back and let out a hearty laugh. "I should have known my Celeste would be the one woman to beg for more."

Celeste leaned over him and kissed his chest. "Because this is how it feels when you're with the person you truly love."

"Our bodies were created for each other. A perfect fit."

He wove his hands through her hair and pulled her lips to his. They talked and laughed and made love twice more before dropping into a satisfied sleep. Their union had been more than she could have imagined.

CELESTE WOKE before Luciano the morning after the wedding and smiled at the feel of him beside her. Not wanting to wake him, she quietly climbed out of bed and settled onto a cushion in the window seat. As she watched the dawn light spread over the golden domes of Florence, she sighed in contentment.

"Running away from me already?" Luciano asked from the bed. Celeste moved to go to him, but he said, "Stay where you are, framed in the sunlight. I think I'll paint you sitting there one day."

She giggled and said, "You can't paint me in my nightdress. It would be scandalous."

"It would only be for my eyes."

He went to her at the window and brushed the hair from her shoulders to kiss her neck. She closed her eyes and said, "I like that."

"I would love to stay here doing this all day, but it's time to prepare for our trip to Lucca."

She jumped up and threw her arms around him. "Where I get you to myself for an entire month? Can I see the gifts before we go?"

Luciano laughed again and kissed her. It was a sound Celeste hoped to hear every day for the rest of her life.

THEIR FIRST MONTH in Lucca passed in such a blissful rush that Celeste begged Luciano to stay longer. He had estate affairs to manage, so he agreed to an additional month. When that time too had passed, Celeste was sad to leave their idyllic sanctuary, but Luciano couldn't delay his return to Florence any longer.

The night before returning to Florence, they took their evening meal on the terrace. Portia had gone inside to arrange for their breakfast and make sure their packing was in order. Luciano was rambling on about how grateful he was to Portia for her excellent management of the estate. Celeste heard little of what he said.

ng Lucca wasn't the only concern weighing on Celeste as she
he sun slip below the horizon.

ned close to kiss her, but she moved away, so he angled
faced him. "What's wrong, my love? You've grown

pensive. Is it because we're leaving? We'll return as soon as my schedule allows."

She shook her head. "It's not that. I am sad to go, but I understand you have responsibilities in Florence." She paused and toyed with the lace on her sleeve. Without looking at him, she said, "I was going to tell you when we went to bed, but since you ask, I believe I'm carrying a child. I'm frightened, Luciano. I want to give you children, but I don't want to die."

Luciano tenderly lifted her onto his lap and kissed her cheek. "But this is wonderful news. There's no need to be afraid. Women have babies every day."

"And some die, as you know better than most."

He stroked her hair and stared out at the hills. "True. Isabella's death was tragic, but most women survive childbirth, and you're young and healthy. We'll fill the nursery with many children."

Celeste looked into his eyes. "But you can't know. Even healthy women die, like Mamma and your own wife and mother."

"Listen to me. I can't promise that nothing will go wrong. No one can, but if you are with child, being plagued by worry for months won't help either of you. You need to look at this as the joyous blessing it is and leave it in God's hands."

They heard Portia returning before Celeste could answer, so Luciano lifted her back to her chair.

"What secrets were you two whispering about out here?" Portia asked as Luciano stood and pulled out a chair for her.

"You, Aunt," Celeste said. "Luciano was telling me how grateful he is to you."

He grinned at Portia. "It's true. My hope of marrying Celeste would have failed from the start without you."

"It's been a tremendous blessing. Celeste is like a daughter now, and I'm content in Lucca. I dreaded the thought of returning to Venice after the wedding."

"You're running the estate much better than any steward," Luciano said. "I'm pleased you're content."

"More than content. I'm happier than I've been in my life." Portia shifted her gaze to Celeste. "What are you hiding from me, girl?"

Luciano squeezed Celeste's hand. "We have news to add to your happiness. There will soon be an addition to our family."

Portia jumped up and squeezed Celeste's cheeks between her hands. "That's wonderful news! Congratulations to you both."

Celeste freed herself from Portia's hands and tried, but failed, to duck out of the way before she planted a kiss on each cheek. She sat back with her arms folded and felt Portia eying her.

Luciano put his hand on her shoulder. "She's concerned about the danger."

Celeste looked up to see Portia wave off Luciano's comment. "What silliness is this? As strong as you are, you'll have a passel of babies in the nursery before you know it."

Celeste shifted her gaze to Portia, desperate to believe her. "Luciano said the same. You genuinely believe that?"

"Yes, my sweet girl, I do. Calm your mind and focus on taking care of yourself and that little one. That's your primary responsibility. Luciano, I'll trust you to make sure she doesn't work too hard. She has the rest of her life for painting. That baby is her priority now."

THE RETURN TRIP to Florence was miserable. The rocking movement of the carriage made Celeste's stomach churn. She couldn't keep the smallest morsel of food down and wanted nothing more than to climb into her bed. Luciano fussed over her, desperate to ease her agony, but all he did was make matters worse. The moment they arrived home, he ordered Livia to have Elisabetta send for her midwife. Celeste tried to convince him it could wait a day. All she needed was quiet, but he wouldn't listen.

The moment Celeste nestled against her pillows, Livia burst into the room with the midwife on her heels. She was tempted to order them out but knew Luciano would scold her if she did.

The midwife reminded her of Pia with her plump frame and rosy cheeks, but she had a kinder face. She pulled back the blankets and lifted Celeste's dressing gown as she said, "My name is Tessa, madam. I'm told Baby is making it difficult for you to keep food down. I have remedies for that." She put her hands on her hips and studied Celeste's exposed abdomen. "You're too thin. We'll remedy that, too. Baby needs you to have meat on your bones."

She gently ran her hands over Celeste, mumbling unintelligible words. Celeste was too mesmerized to resist. When Tessa completed her examination, she replaced the covers and hummed a lullaby while she poured warm wine into a goblet. She sprinkled herbs over the wine before handing it to Celeste.

"For your nausea, and it will help you sleep. Drink that down, and after you rest, we'll try bread and cheese."

Celeste nodded numbly and did as she was told. The warm liquid tasted good. She soon felt her queasiness receding.

"Thank you, Tessa," she whispered. "I have many questions, but I need to rest after my tiring journey. Will you come tomorrow?"

"I'll come whenever you wish, madam. I've assisted hundreds of women in bringing new life into this world. It is my honor to help you, as well. Rest now. I'll return in the morning."

Celeste felt the wine taking effect as she watched Tessa bustle out of the room. Livia opened a trunk to finish unpacking, but Celeste told her to leave it.

"You may go. Finish that up in the morning. I need to sleep. Please tell Signore Vicente I wish to speak with him."

Livia curtsied and left to find Luciano. Celeste struggled to keep her eyes open and was relieved when Luciano came in moments later. She reached her hand out to him as he stepped up to the bed. He wrapped his fingers in hers and kissed the back of her hand.

"Thank you for sending for Tessa. I'm feeling much better. I'm sorry for being so stubborn."

He sat next to her and brushed the hair from her face. "You had me so worried. You must promise to take care of yourself and let others help. We all love you and want what's best for you and the baby."

"I know, my love, and I count myself blessed."

"Tessa left me with strict instructions to fatten you up and make sure you get enough rest. I'll sleep in my old chambers tonight, so I won't disturb you. Send Livia to fetch me if you need anything." He stood and kissed her forehead. "It's good to be home. Goodnight, my love."

She gave him a weak smile and closed her eyes, thinking that home was what they'd left in Lucca.

LUCIANO ENTERED their darkened chambers four weeks later and searched the room for Celeste. All he found was Livia embroidering by the fire.

"Where's your mistress?" he asked.

Livia set her embroidery aside and curtsied. "I haven't seen her since the afternoon, sir, but I believe she's in her studio."

Luciano went out, slamming the door behind him. He'd begged Celeste to stay out of her studio that day and was furious that she'd ignored him. Every day since they'd returned from Lucca had been a battle of wills. He'd known she was stubborn before marrying her, but he'd learned just how much in those first months of their marriage. She seemed incapable of sitting still for one moment. He considered tying her to the bed to force her to be still.

He threw the studio door open and stood in the entrance with his arms crossed, but she wasn't at her easel or worktable. He scanned the room and spun around when he heard a muffled cry from the corner.

"I'm here, Luciano," Celeste whispered.

She lay in a heap with her head resting on a wooden box. Luciano rushed to her and lifted her off the floor.

"What's happened? What were you doing there?"

"I got overheated and dizzy. Please put me down," Celeste said as Luciano carried her to their chamber. "I feel like enough of a fool."

He ignored her protests as he hurried down the hallway. When he reached their chamber, he tenderly laid her on the bed and ordered Livia to send for Tessa.

"I just need fresh water and air," Celeste said. "I'm feeling better."

"Your face is gray. I told you to rest today. Don't you care about yourself and our baby?"

Celeste looked away and rubbed her belly. "Of course, I do, my love, but painting isn't strenuous. Women in Lucca worked in the fields until they gave birth."

"But you haven't been well. You still can't keep food down, and Tessa ordered you not to leave this bed."

"I'm sorry, but I promised myself I'd never become one of those pampered noblewomen who spend their pregnancies lounging in bed. It's just a warm day. I got overheated. Please bring me some water and bread. I'll be fine."

Luciano shook his head as he left to do his wife's bidding.

The midwife was there when he returned with bread and wine. He poured a goblet and handed it to her. "Drink this. No arguments."

Celeste glared at him but took the goblet and sipped.

"How is she?" Luciano asked Tessa.

"Weak. I sent Livia for the doctor. We need to get food and liquid into her. You must keep her cool, and she needs rest, as I told you both." She shook her finger at Celeste before opening a pouch hanging from her waist. She retrieved some herbs and sprinkled them into Celeste's goblet. "This is a new remedy for your nausea. Dip that bread into the wine and eat."

Celeste did as she was told, but Luciano could see her struggling to swallow. "Tell me how I can help her. I feel so useless."

Tessa wrung out a cloth that had been soaking in a bowl. "Put this on her forehead."

As Luciano wiped Celeste's brow with the cool cloth, horrible visions of Isabella's death washed over him.

"I'll return in the morning, madam. You're not to leave this bed until then."

Celeste nodded. "Yes, Tessa, I promise. I'm sorry, Luciano. I was only thinking of myself. I'll rest and get my strength back. Stay with me?"

Livia came in with the doctor before Luciano could answer. "I passed Tessa in the hall," the doctor said. "She says you've been a disobedient patient."

"I was, but now I'm reformed. I promise to eat and rest," she said and took a nibble of bread.

"Can you stay tonight?" Luciano asked the physician. "I want you nearby. I'll have a maid make up a room for you."

"Yes, I think that's best. Let me send word to my wife."

As the doctor followed Livia out, Luciano said. "I know it's a sacrifice to put your artwork aside, but it's only until you're stronger. Remember what Tessa said. Most women feel wonderful after the third month. I'll have Filippo bring my dinner here so you won't be alone. Finish your bread and wine. It'll help you sleep."

Celeste did as Luciano asked for once, then fell into a deep sleep, but he was awake long after midnight. Nothing had ever frightened him as much as seeing Celeste so ill, not even Isabella's death. Since their marriage, she had become as much a part of him as his brain or heart. He would do whatever it took to ensure she survived. He pulled her to his chest and closed his eyes before finally drifting off to sleep.

After what seemed like only moments, a shriek invaded his dreams. When he opened his eyes, Celeste was sitting up, staring at her blood-covered hand.

"Get the doctor!" she screamed as she doubled over.

When Livia ran into their chamber, Luciano ordered her to call the physician. Celeste was standing when he turned around. He shivered when he saw her nightdress stained with blood and a puddle spreading at her feet.

"What's happening? Help me," she cried as her legs gave way.

Luciano caught her just before she hit the floor. He lifted her onto the bed and paced frantically as he waited for the physician.

"Move aside," the doctor said as he rushed in and pulled back the blankets to examine Celeste. "You, girl, bring warm water and towels," he said to Livia. "Then, send someone for the midwife."

Livia's eyes were wide with fright as she ran out without a word. She'd looked the same on the night of Isabella's tragic delivery.

Luciano prayed it wasn't an ill omen and went to Celeste's side and grasped her hand.

"I won't leave you, my love. You're going to be fine. Focus on me."

"I'm sorry, madam, but you've lost the baby. The bleeding has stopped, thank God. You'll recover in one or two weeks."

Celeste grabbed Luciano and sobbed against his chest. "I'll never be fine. I killed my baby. I did this."

Luciano swallowed his own anguish. "It's not your fault. This happens to many women. Don't blame yourself."

"He's right, mistress," Tessa said as she followed Livia into the room. "Most often, there's nothing to prevent this. There will be other babies for such a healthy, young woman like you. You must rest for at least two weeks. I'll check in every day." Turning to Livia, she said, "Help me clean her. Please excuse us, sirs," she said to Luciano and the doctor.

The men went into the hall, and Luciano grabbed the doctor's arm. "Are you certain she'll survive? All that blood."

"Physically, yes, but some women take these losses harder than others. Keep her surrounded by female family and friends. That's what she needs. We men are useless in these times."

"Thank you," Luciano said as he watched the doctor go.

Celeste had little family and few friends in Florence, but she had Portia. Luciano woke the page and groom to send them to Lucca. It would take more than a week for Portia to arrive. He and his sisters would have to suffice until then.

Celeste was clean and crying quietly into her pillow when Luciano returned. He laid next to her and stroked her hair, lacking words of comfort to give. Celeste drifted off at dawn, but Luciano stayed awake, wondering how he'd ever sleep again.

CHAPTER SEVENTEEN

*C*eleste didn't hear Luciano come into their chamber and flinched when he said, "Portia will be here soon. She's prepared to stay as long as you need."

"Forever?" Celeste asked.

"Do you want her to live with us? I can arrange for someone else to manage the Lucca estate if that's what you wish."

Celeste turned toward Luciano and took his hand. "I couldn't do that to her. Lucca has become her life. Your sisters have been truly kind, but it will be a comfort to have Portia here for as long as she is able to stay. I won't stop her from leaving when she's ready. It was thoughtful of you to send for her, my love."

"I'll do whatever it takes to help you heal," he said and kissed the top of her head. "Nothing else matters."

"Nothing but God will cure this sickness, my love. No matter what you say, I caused this, and I'll pay the price for the rest of my life. I promise if God sees fit to bless us with another baby, I'll rest and take better care of myself."

Luciano pulled her to him and stroked her hair. "I'll never blame you for this, but I trust you. We'll have children one day."

"I hope they take after their father," Celeste said with half a grin.

"Heaven forbid," he said and laughed. "Careful what you wish for."

Livia ran in and said, "She's here. She wants to see you now."

Portia burst in two-seconds later and nearly knocked Livia over to get to Celeste. She squeezed her so tightly that Celeste was afraid she'd faint.

She struggled free and took Portia's hands. "How I've missed you, Aunt. Thank you for coming."

"No one could keep me away from my darling girl. I was on my way an hour after Luciano's men arrived." She grasped Celeste's chin and turned her head from side to side. "You are pale, but don't worry. I'll soon nurse you back to perfect health."

"That's what we've hoped," Luciano said.

Portia pulled him into a hug as she had Celeste. After letting go, she said, "Poor man. What grief you've suffered, but you'll be a father soon enough. Now, I must wash off the dust of the road and rest. I expect to see you dressed and at the table for dinner, Celeste."

Luciano shook his head. "She's not up for that, Portia."

"Nonsense. It's just what she needs. Enough of this dark and stuffy room. It's a lovely evening. We'll sit on the terrace after we eat."

Portia rushed out before he could protest.

"Maybe she's right. The terrace sounds nice, Luciano."

"Is that wise? You're still weak."

Celeste climbed off the bed and held the bedpost to steady herself. "That feels good. I'm tired of this bed. Livia, help me dress, please, and open the curtains."

"I'll leave you then and check on the workshop." He kissed Celeste's cheek. "It's nice to see you on your feet. I'll see you at dinner."

CELESTE RELAXED into her chair as she watched the moonlight glinting off the domes of Florence. She'd come to love the city in her short time there. She missed Lucca, and no place would ever replace Venice in her heart, but she was content to call Florence home.

Portia disturbed the peaceful moment when she said, "I'm sorry to tell you I have other unhappy news, Luciano. It concerns you, too, Celeste. Adamo Massaro, the farmer who took Celeste's siblings in, has taken ill with a fever in his chest. He was gravely ill when I left and may have passed by now. If so, I need to speak with you about what I hope we can do to help Masina and the children. I'd like to find work for her and Veronica in the big house."

Celeste jumped to her feet and said, "You can take Masina in, but I want to bring Veronica and Bianca here. Or why can't the girls and Sandro live with you as your nieces and nephew, as I did?"

Luciano tugged on Celeste's arm to get her to sit. "Calm down, my love," he said. "We'll talk about our options and decide what's fair together."

Portia shook her finger at Celeste. "Masina may have just lost her husband. Do you want to take her children away as well? And I thought you understood why the children can't live with me. It's not the life they know."

Celeste took a breath and lowered herself into the chair. "They're young. They'll adjust like I did. I won't have them abandoned to the street like urchins. They're my responsibility. I promised Mamma!" she said and pounded on the arm of the chair.

Portia took Celeste's hand. "I know, dear. No one is considering abandoning them. We'll make sure they're cared for. Maybe Bianca can go to the convent. Bianca and Veronica probably would have ended up there even if your mother had lived."

Celeste ignored Portia and said, "Luciano, can't you hire a girl to tend to the children while Masina works? It would only be until they're old enough to work. I don't want to tear my family apart more than it is. Those children have been through too much."

"Any girls old enough to care for the children will already have work or are already in the convent," Luciano said.

"There are always girls in need of work. Remember Lorena, Aunt Portia?"

"Yes, and do you remember how that turned out?"

"That was because she had an evil character, and Papa wouldn't keep his hands off her. I'll find the right girl with a good heart," Celeste said.

Luciano rubbed his forehead. "Let me send a rider to check on Adamo. If he's dead, I'll have to find someone to take over his land. In the meantime, let me think this through. We'll figure it out, Celeste. Trust me. The last thing we need is you making yourself sick with worry."

Celeste studied Luciano's face. She did trust him. He had done so much for her family, but no one loved them as she did. How could she not worry? She nodded and said, "I'm tired. Portia, will you help me to bed?"

Celeste kissed Luciano and let Portia take her arm. Once again, she had to surrender to the Fates, and all because of Papa.

Luciano lay awake, staring into the blackness that night. It comforted him to hear Celeste's deep, even breaths. She'd been so agitated on the terrace he was afraid she'd be as sleepless as he was, and she needed her rest.

Her violent reaction to Portia's news had disturbed him. After so much time, she still expected her brothers and sisters to live as equals to her. Housing, clothing, and training her brothers were expensive. Luciano knew Celeste appreciated it, but she couldn't expect him to support her entire family.

He hoped her reaction was from her emotional state at the loss of the baby. If not, he feared the welfare of her siblings might come between them.

"Are you awake?" she asked softly.

"Yes, my dear, but don't worry. I'll sleep soon."

She snuggled closer to him. He lifted his arm so she could put her head in the crook of his shoulder in the way he loved.

"You're worried about the children. I am, too. I know you don't understand my strong attachment to them. You've never known hunger, abandonment, or want. Your future has never been uncertain.

Mine has, but now because of you, I have nothing to fear. I want my siblings to have that same kind of security. You've been so generous to provide that for Marco and Jacopo. It's asking much to provide for the others, but I must ask. They're victims of my father's betrayal, as I once was. If Adamo is dead, what will become of them?"

"Portia and I will never let them become destitute. We'll find a way to assure their futures, but don't close your mind to Bianca going to a convent. She'll learn skills that can prepare her for a better life, and she may even like the cloistered life and want to take orders. I'll find a family to take care of Sandro until he's old enough to work. Then, he can work on Adamo's farm and take over when he's grown, which is what would have happened if Adamo had lived. Those are excellent prospects."

Luciano felt Celeste nod. "Yes, but there is another possibility, however unlikely. I could write to Uncle Cesare. He was willing to adopt me. Maybe he'll take the children."

Luciano hated to tell her not to bother writing to her uncle. He knew Cesare only adopted Celeste because of the marriage proposal. Cesare would never take in his nieces and nephew with no prospect for their future. Otherwise, he would have taken them in from the beginning.

"Don't send your letter yet. Wait until we have word back from Lucca. Then we'll see what the future holds."

Luciano felt Celeste's muscles tighten. She wasn't happy with his answer. The last thing he wanted to do was disappoint her, but there was no choice.

"At least this took my mind off the baby. Maybe it's time I returned to my studio," she said.

Visions of the night she miscarried flashed into his mind, and the anguish became real. "It's too soon. You need to wait at least two more weeks."

"Staying in bed is making me weaker. I'm not used to idleness. Having a distraction will be good for me."

"If that's your wish but promise to start slowly. There's no rush."

"Yes, my love," she said and yawned.

Luciano held her while she drifted back to sleep. Once again, knowing there would be no sleep for him.

CELESTE WAS ENGROSSED in painting when there was a tap at the studio door. "Enter," she said without turning, thinking it must be Livia. Luciano had tasked the maid with making sure Celeste didn't work too hard. The door opened and closed. Celeste said, "I'm not finished, Livia. Go tell your master I'm fine for another hour." When she didn't hear the door, she turned and ask, "What is it?"

Portia stood in the doorway instead of Livia. Her aunt had never set foot in her Florence studio. Portia disapproved of Celeste being an artist but knew it was pointless to dissuade her. She wanted Celeste to play the meek and dutiful wife, as expected.

Celeste put her brush down and took Portia's hands. "I never thought I'd see your feet grace this threshold," she said and smiled.

"I bring news," Portia said, without emotion. "Adamo is dead. Luciano is leaving for Lucca to find someone to take over the farm and make arrangements for the family. He's taking Jacopo, and I'm going with him."

Celeste removed her smock and dropped it on a bench. "Poor Masina. Poor children. Is there no end to their suffering? Who will comfort them?"

"That's why I must go, and Luciano will need me."

"But I need you. I thought I'd have you here to lean on for months, not weeks."

"You don't need me. You spend all day in your studio and hardly know I'm here."

Celeste put her hands on Portia's shoulders. "That's not true. I'm always aware of you when I'm working, even if we're not in the same room. If you and Luciano are leaving, I'm going with you."

Portia put her hand on her hips. "No, you're not. That's why Luciano sent me. He was afraid he wouldn't be able to refuse you, but

I can. Being well enough to paint doesn't mean you're strong enough for the trip to Lucca."

Portia was right, but Celeste felt useless for not coming to her family's aid. "Please reconsider letting the children come to live with you," she said. "You can teach them. They need a family. As you once told me, they shouldn't forget that they're Gabrieles."

"Their situation is worlds different. Be reasonable, Celeste, and trust me to decide what's best for them."

Celeste lowered herself onto the bench. "I have no choice but to trust you. Swear that you'll honor my promise to Mamma as you act in my place."

"You have my word." Portia kissed her cheeks. "I'll miss you, my dear. Come as soon as you're well."

Profound sadness enveloped Celeste as she watched her aunt and confidant go. The thought of being without Luciano and Portia frightened her. Her only solace was her art. She put her smock on, picked up her brush, and went back to work.

CELESTE HARDLY NOTICED the passage of time while Luciano was in Lucca. She rose each dawn after a fitful sleep and spent the day in her studio until exhaustion overtook her. She ignored Livia's pleas that she rest and eat more. The need to paint drove her like a madness.

One day while she was putting the last feverish touches on her latest wood panel, she heard a gasp from the studio doorway. She turned to find her beloved staring wide-eyed at her painting of a shepherd girl guiding sheep up a hillside in Lucca. It was the first landscape she'd done since painting the canal in Venice.

She dropped her brush and threw herself into his arms. "Oh, my love, how I've missed you! This past month has been a bottomless void without you."

Luciano held her at arm's length and studied her, the worry evident on his face. "I came back to you as quickly as I could. You're so pale and thin. You're overworking." He kissed her cheek before turning toward the shepherdess painting. "This work is remarkable. When I think your abilities have reached their peak, you climb higher. As I've known since I saw your first works, there's no limit to what you'll achieve. What a cruel fate that we have to pass your work off as Stefano's."

Celeste bowed with a flourish. "Thank you, Maestro, but is your impression skewed by your love for me? Will others see it as you do?"

"I'll answer that when I see your patron's reaction," Luciano said and smiled.

Celeste clapped and twirled around to face him. "My patron? When did this happen? Who is it?"

"Save that for later. First, I have another surprise for you. Come with me."

Celeste tossed her smock over an easel and followed Luciano to the sala. It was her turn to gasp when she saw Veronica seated on a bench near the window. Veronica squealed in delight and ran to Celeste.

"Why didn't you tell me you were bringing my sister to me?" she asked Luciano. "Is she to stay?"

"I didn't know she was coming until I was about to leave Lucca. Arrange quarters for her. I'll explain once we're alone."

Celeste didn't like Luciano's cryptic tone, but she called for Livia to have one of the other maids make up a room for Veronica. Livia stared at Celeste with wide eyes before leaving to fulfill her mistress' wishes.

Veronica's eyes were as big as platters as Celeste walked her to her room. "Do all of these beautiful things belong to you?" she asked.

"It belongs to my husband's estate, but I have a few of my own treasures. I'll take you on a tour of the palazzo tomorrow."

Once Celeste got reacquainted with Veronica, she left her with a maid named Helena and went to find Luciano. He was stretched out on their bed, still wearing his boots. Celeste lovingly removed them and laid down next to him.

"What happened in Lucca? Where are Bianca and Sandro?"

Luciano rolled on his side to face her and said, "Masina arranged for Veronica to work in the kitchens of the main house with her and live in the servant's quarters. It was generous of Portia to agree to her idea. A tenant farmer and his wife took Bianca and Sandro. When Masina told Veronica about the children going away and working in the kitchens, she became hysterical and begged me to bring her to you. I couldn't resist her pleadings. Curse my weakness," he said and shook his head. "Portia was livid, but I was more afraid of Veronica than Portia, so here she is. Sandro seems content with the farmer, but Bianca is devastated at Adamo's death and losing another mother and her sisters. Masina promised to check on her as often as she can. I still favor bringing Bianca to a convent in Florence so you'd be near her, but she's fine where she is for now."

Celeste wiped the tears dripping down her cheeks. As happy as she was to have Veronica in Florence, her heart broke to hear of Bianca's pain. She wished Luciano had been willing to bring her, too, but she didn't dare ask after all he had done.

"Veronica will stay with us. She's a beautiful girl, much like her older sister." Luciano kissed Celeste's nose. "She has her sister's stubbornness too, but I may find a husband to take her. Maybe a widower."

"You are the most generous and kind-hearted man on earth," Celeste said. "I'm sorry for the trouble Veronica caused. I feel guilty for thrusting my family troubles on you, but having my sister here is a great comfort."

"This may not be permanent. There won't be much for her dowries, especially if Bianca goes to the convent. I'll write to Cesare to see if he's willing to contribute, but I expect little from him. Veronica's much older than most girls with a nanny, but I want you to engage one, anyway. She needs training for her new life, but I don't want you taking time from your work to do it."

"I'll start my search tomorrow. Maybe your sisters can make suggestions."

Luciano rolled onto his back and rubbed his forehead. "Oh, my sisters. They will not like this, and they'll make sure I know of their displeasure."

Celeste laid her hand on his chest. "I'll tell them myself and take full responsibility. Angelica and Diana understand a sister's bond, even if Elisabetta does not."

"Don't expect a happy reception for your news. They'll see this as more money going to your family and less to theirs." He sat up and threw his legs over the edge of the bed. "I need to clean up and rest. Go to Veronica. All the upheaval must be overwhelming for her."

Celeste grabbed his wrist to keep him from going. "First, tell me about the patron."

Luciano's face glowed with excitement. "His name is Agostini Benedetto. He's a fierce rival of Lorenzo de' Medici and highly motivated for his collection to outshine de' Medici's. This benefits us. I showed him your Blessed Virgin, and he was genuinely impressed. He offered to buy it, but I'll never part with it. Instead, he's commissioned a *cassone*, a *Desco da parto*, and a wood panel similar to your Blessed Virgin. This is a monumental victory and the first step on your journey to greatness."

"I'm humbled, Luciano. This is your doing, not mine. I'm ready to begin my work in earnest, and I won't disappoint you," Celeste said and kissed him.

"Of that, I have no doubt."

VERONICA LOOKED anything but overwhelmed when Celeste got back to her room. She was lying on the bed, smiling with her tresses spread out on the pillow like a halo.

"I love it here, Celeste. Do I really get to stay?"

Celeste sat next to her and smiled. "Yes, you can stay. Did you thank Luciano for bringing you?" When Veronica nodded, Celeste said, "It was wrong of you to behave the way you did. As happy as I am that you're here, you've created problems for Luciano and me."

Tears welled up in Veronica's eyes. "Aunt Portia was so angry with me. She yelled at me for an entire day. I was afraid of living with strangers in the servants' quarters, and even though I helped Masina, I just wanted to be safe with you."

"Come here," Celeste said. Veronica sat up, and Celeste pulled her close. "You're here now. I'll look after you for the next few days, but then you'll have a nanny. I have many responsibilities during the day, but we'll have time together in the evenings. I want you to listen to your nanny and work hard. You have much to learn."

PART III

VENICE AND FLORENCE 1480-1483

CHAPTER EIGHTEEN

EIGHTEEN MONTHS LATER

*L*uciano froze in the doorway of Celeste's studio when he saw the chaos of black and red paint splashed across her canvas.

"I've been searching for you. What is this?" he asked, gesturing toward the painting.

Celeste continued to stare into the blackness from where she sat curled up on the window seat. "It's nothing. Ignore it."

"What are you doing here so late?"

"You told me this morning to go to my studio to work, so where else would I be?"

Luciano went to her and gently rested his hands on her shoulders. She winced at his touch, but he didn't move.

"That was hours ago. It's too dark to work now. Eat something and come to bed."

She pointed to the easel. "Why? That's all I see when I close my eyes."

He sat next to her and took her hands. "It's been two months since you lost the last baby. I thought sending you to Portia for a month in Lucca would revive you, but you're getting worse. What can I do to ease your suffering?"

"Bring my babies back to me," she said and slumped against

Luciano with a sob. "I never wanted children, was afraid to bear them, but now three are gone. A part of me has died with each one."

"But you are alive, my love, and I'm here with you. You have much to live for."

He stroked her hair and remembered that Isabella once told him Francesca had suffered three miscarriages before she was born. He wondered if Francesca could help lift Celeste out of the darkness she had descended into after losing her third pregnancy.

He turned her to face him and caressed her cheek. "I have to go to Venice to check on my holdings there. Come with me, Celeste. The change of scenery would be good. We'll take Marco with us."

Celeste raised her head, and Luciano saw the flicker of light in her dark-rimmed eyes.

"Jacopo, too? It wouldn't be wise to leave him alone for so long. And Veronica?"

"Jacopo can come, and I'll send word to see if Portia wants to join us. Veronica needs to stay here with the nanny. She's too young to come and having Jacopo along will be enough of a challenge. Ask Livia to have your trunks ready in the morning."

He extended his hand to help Celeste to her feet. She started for the door but hesitated after a few steps. "What about our commissions? You said my patron is getting impatient."

"I'll tell him Stefano was called home on urgent family business. He won't question that."

Luciano took her arm. It felt like a twig. He longed for the vibrant young bride he'd married two years earlier. Celeste's miscarriages had devastated him, and he wondered if he'd ever father a child, but the trauma was destroying Celeste. He'd thrown himself into his work to cope with the loss, but she needed more. He hoped the answer awaited them in Venice.

THE DISTANCE between Tuscany and Venice seemed to have doubled in the years since Celeste last traveled it. She savored resting with the sun on her face during their stops but riding in the jolting carriage became unbearable by the time they neared the ferry.

When they reached the shore, Celeste stepped out of the carriage and drew a breath of sea air. The familiar aroma aroused her senses and gave her new life. Sea fowl dipped and darted over the water as waves lapped at the sand. Luciano had been right to bring her to Venice. When he climbed out of the carriage behind her, she kissed his cheek and smiled.

He returned the smile and said, "Welcome back."

"I lost my way in a dark place, Luciano. Venice is the light guiding me home. It may take time, but I have hope for the first time in months. You've rescued me yet again, my love."

"I feared our Celeste was gone forever," Portia said from behind them. "Venice was the tonic she needed."

Luciano bowed and offered the women his arms. Celeste glanced at her brothers as they walked to the ferry and saw the same joy of homecoming radiating from their faces. They were home.

AS THRILLED as Celeste was to be gliding along her beloved canals in a gondola, her gut tightened as they neared the landing to Luciano's palazzo. She hadn't stepped through the main entrance in the six years since she was Federigo's nanny. She was uneasy about sleeping in the bed Luciano had shared with Isabella and was anxious about how Francesca would receive her.

Luciano once told her that Francesca had voiced her objections to his marrying Celeste but let the matter drop when Luciano reminded her he had claimed Isabella's son as his own. Still, Celeste hoped enough time had passed for Francesca to have accepted their marriage.

Marco took Jacopo to show him the deserted workshop as soon as they climbed out of the gondola. Even though Marco was adjusting to his status in life, he still preferred apprentices to patricians.

Luciano laughed as he watched them go. "He asked if he could sleep in the workshop instead of the house. I offered him the studio cot, but he wanted his old bunk. Francesca had to have it cleaned, and the fire lit before we got here. Jacopo refuses to sleep there, so hopefully, Marco will change his mind after a night alone in the dark and silent workshop."

"Not likely," Celeste said. "I've been trying for a year to persuade him to sleep in our house in Florence."

"I'm glad you didn't insist on sleeping in the workshop," Luciano said.

"I was used to sleeping in grand houses before we married, just not in the master's chamber," she said and squeezed his arm.

Luciano winked at her. "I'm glad to hear that."

"She's still reluctant to order the servants around," Portia said. "She treats Livia like an equal. It's disgraceful."

"Livia's more my friend than a servant," Celeste said. "I owe her a great deal."

"Mark my words. That's trouble in the making," Portia said and laughed.

Celeste was grateful for the light-hearted exchange as they climbed the stairs. It distracted her from what was waiting at the top.

Luciano threw open the sala doors and ushered the little party inside. He surveyed the room and nodded in satisfaction. "I've missed Venice, too. I was not much more than a boy when I came here to apprentice, not much younger than Jacopo. Of course, I slept in my master's workshop then, not here. That didn't happen until I married Isabella."

They all grew quiet at the mention of his first wife's name.

"I have fond memories of those days," Francesca said as she entered the sala through the far door. "You were nothing more than a snip of a boy."

Luciano turned to face her. "Just what I was saying." He hugged her and kissed her cheeks. "You look well, Mother."

Celeste dropped into a curtsy out of reflex.

"Get up, girl. You're the mistress of this house now. You curtsy to no one," Francesca said. She eyed Celeste as she slowly rose to face her. "Have you been ill, child? You're a wisp of your former self."

Celeste tried to explain, but the words wouldn't come. Portia came to her rescue. She hugged and kissed Francesca, then said, "It's good to see you, old friend. She and Luciano recently lost another child. She's here to recover."

Francesca looked at Celeste with a sadness in her eyes that spoke empathy for Celeste's anguish.

"You've known this kind of grief?" Celeste asked her.

"Three times. One baby was born fully grown but never took a breath. I lost the other two early on."

"This is our third loss as well," Luciano said.

Francesca took Celeste's hands. "Do not fret, child. Your time will come, a hearty girl like you. My lovely daughters came with time. Be patient."

Celeste gave a slow nod. "Yes, madam."

Francesca took her arm and patted her hand as they walked. "If you call me madam again, I shall make you sleep in your little closet. Call me Mamma if you wish, but Francesca will do. Come, dinner is waiting. We need to fatten you up. Where are your brothers?"

"In the workshop," Luciano said. "I'll send someone to fetch them."

Marco came in, bowing and scraping several minutes later. He shuffled to his seat without raising his eyes.

"I see it runs in the family," Francesca said and laughed. "Look at me, boy. You're part of this family, not some urchin off the street. How do you like Florence?"

Marco gave an inaudible answer.

"I can't hear you. Speak up. I'm not a young woman."

He looked her in the eye and said, "I enjoy Florence, but it's good to be in Venice. I feel at home here."

He said it so loudly that Celeste was sure they heard him on the canal. She had to bite her cheek to keep from laughing but reminded herself that she had behaved the same way when she arrived. Francesca's comment that she was the mistress of the house caught her off guard. It hadn't occurred to her until that moment. While Francesca still deserved her respect, Celeste promised herself to act her role as Duchessa while they were in Venice.

Jacopo came in like the master of the palazzo and took Francesca's hand. "I've looked forward to meeting you. Thank you for welcoming us so generously."

"I like this one. You can learn from him," Francesca said to Marco.

Celeste came to Marco's rescue and said, "How is the workshop? Has it changed?"

Marco sat up straighter, and his shoulders relaxed. Her brother loved nothing more than talking about the workshop.

"It's quiet and empty but looks and smells the same. It seems much smaller than I remember."

"You've grown, boy," Francesca said. "I remember the night you helped move Celeste from the studio to her room. You're a head taller now."

"I didn't know you even noticed me," Marco said.

"She notices everything," Luciano said. "It's best to keep that in mind."

Francesca glared at him, and they all laughed. With the ice broken, they went on with their meal. They chatted about their journey and what they were looking forward to doing in Venice.

"Will you be staying with Cesare Gabriele or us?" Francesca asked Portia.

"I'm hoping to stay here if it's not too much of an inconvenience. My brother doesn't know I'm here yet. I'd like to keep it that way for as long as possible."

Celeste had forgotten Cesare and wondered how her uncle would take the news that Portia had returned to Venice.

"You're welcome to stay, my friend. I had a room made up for you just in case," Francesca said.

"Now that your daughters are married, what do you do to occupy your time?" Portia asked as they were finishing the meal.

"Mateo keeps me busy. I hope you'll come to the nursery to meet him after dinner," she said to Luciano. "You're all welcomed to join us."

A shadow passed over Luciano's face, but he nodded. He and Celeste had never discussed his adopted child, but she knew that Francesca sent frequent reports. Even though he wasn't Luciano's flesh and blood, Celeste had almost suggested they send for Mateo to join them in Florence after losing the first baby. She thought it might distract them from their grief and give Luciano the chance to be a father, but she never summoned the courage to mention it. After she lost the third baby, it required all of her strength just to survive. She wondered if Luciano planned to take the boy with them when they returned to Florence.

"It would be lovely to meet him," Celeste said.

Francesca nodded to her with the hint of a smile, but Luciano avoided her gaze, and Portia studied her plate.

"Thank you, dear," Francesca said.

Celeste stood, and the rest followed. Marco thanked Francesca for dinner and hurried out to the workshop. He'd tried to persuade Jacopo to join him but had no luck. Portia made her excuses and headed to her chamber to rest. Celeste felt Luciano tense beside her as they walked to the nursery. He'd shared the ordeal of Mateo's birth and Isabella's death with Celeste soon after they married. His grief and guilt had left a permanent wound that had resurfaced after her miscarriages. Facing the living reminder of that trauma wouldn't be easy for him.

Mateo was playing at the feet of the nanny near the fire. He turned toward the commotion when they came in, and Celeste gasped when she saw a miniature of Marcello with his blond curls and oval face. There could be no question of his parentage. Mateo squealed in delight when Francesca swept him up and playfully nibbled his cheek. Luciano stood near the door like a statue. Francesca went to him and held Mateo out to him.

When Luciano hesitated, she said, "It's not his fault, Luciano. He's a cheerful, easy mannered child. It's time for him to know his Papa."

Celeste put her hand on Luciano's arm to encourage him. Luciano reluctantly took the boy, and Mateo stared at Luciano for a moment, then broke into a slobbery grin.

"Aren't you adorable," Celeste said and took his hand. He rewarded her with another smile, and she felt Luciano's muscles relax.

Mateo leaned his head on Luciano's chest for a moment, then

wiggled to get down. Luciano carefully put him on the floor, and he ran to Francesca. She took him to the other chair by the fire and handed him a box of wooden blocks. She watched him lovingly while he played.

"See, he's harmless. I'm determined to make sure he always knows that he is wanted and loved. That responsibility will fall to you someday. Will you promise to honor my wishes?"

Luciano watched them for several moments without answering. When Francesca looked at him, Celeste said, "We will make sure he is always loved. You have our promise."

Francesca looked at her in gratitude when Luciano nodded his agreement.

"Very well. I can grow old in peace, knowing that my grandson is cared for and loved." She handed Mateo to the nanny and stood. "I'm off to bed. Let Livia know if you need anything. She knows her way around here better than most."

When Celeste and Luciano were alone in their chamber a short time later, Celeste said, "I hope you aren't angry with me for speaking on your behalf to Francesca. It's clear how much the boy means to her. Mateo is all that remains of Isabella. I wanted to ease her burden."

Luciano held her to his chest. "I'm not angry. I'm so happy to see you returning to your old self that nothing you say or do could upset me. I couldn't imagine a few days ago that I'd ever see you smile again or laugh. I know the pain is still fresh, but now we can begin to heal. Getting to know Mateo will help."

"I'm relieved to hear you say that." She grew quiet as she searched for a way to ask her next question. In the end, she decided on a direct approach. "Is this the room you shared with Isabella? Is this where she died?"

Luciano stepped back and lifted her chin with his finger. "No, my love. I haven't set foot in her chamber since that night. This is the room I occupied for most of our marriage. We led separate lives in the years before her death." He gave Celeste a tender kiss. "I spent many nights in this room dreaming of you. There are no ghosts here but my own. You will help me vanquish them."

"How? Like this?" she asked and kissed him again.

His breath quickened, and he pulled her closer. "How much longer before we can be together again? I've missed the feel of you."

"Three or four more weeks, at least. I long to be with you, too, but the physician said we must wait. Until today, I thought it would take months for me to be ready, if ever. Now, having to wait so long is a struggle."

"Would you prefer I sleep in my studio?" he asked half-heartedly.

"No, my love. There's no reason we can't sleep in each other's arms, as long as you promise to behave yourself."

"What did I do to deserve you?" he asked and lifted her onto the bed.

She snuggled against him and closed her eyes. She had missed the feel of being near his warm, muscular body. She drifted off quickly and enjoyed her first dreamless sleep in weeks.

CHAPTER NINETEEN

*C*eleste woke to sounds rising from the busy canal below. She smiled and reached for Luciano, but his side of the bed was empty. She called Livia to see if she knew where he was. She came in, carrying a tray of food.

"Wonderful, I'm starving. Where's my husband?"

"Signore Vicente wishes me to tell you he had business to attend to this morning. Signoras Gabriele and Niccolo are waiting for you in the garden."

Celeste climbed out of bed and gave Livia orders through bites of food.

"Find something comfortable for me to wear today, please."

Livia curtsied. "Yes, madam."

"How does it feel being in Venice? Are you getting reacquainted with friends?" Celeste asked.

"The maids I knew are no longer here. Signora Niccolo doesn't need as much help now that her daughters are married. The housekeeper is still here, but we never got along. I think she was jealous of my closeness to the signora, even though she had the run of the household."

Celeste loved that Livia wasn't afraid to speak her mind. Portia warned her of impending doom if she didn't keep Livia in line, but Celeste knew her maid was harmless.

"Let me know if she gives you trouble," Celeste said.

She went to the garden after dressing and found Portia and Francesca getting caught up on gossip. Celeste held her chin high as she approached their table, reminding herself that she was mistress in Luciano's home. Portia kissed Celeste's cheek and offered her a chair. Celeste smiled as she took a deep breath of Venetian air.

"You look rested. We were wondering if you were ever going to join us," Portia said.

"I feel wonderful. I'm looking forward to getting into the studio."

Francesca raised her eyebrows. "The studio? You're not still holding on to that artist nonsense, are you?"

Celeste started to rise from her chair, but Portia put a hand on her arm to hold her down.

"It's not nonsense. I have a wealthy patron, and I'm gaining acclaim in Florence."

"You mean Stefano is gaining acclaim," Portia said. "When is Luciano planning to reveal the real artist of your works?"

"That's not possible yet. It may take years."

"What's this?" Francesca asked. "Are you passing your work off as someone else's? I can't believe Luciano would agree to this. It's disgraceful, and Stefano should have refused. It will be disastrous if your patron or the Guild discovers your deception. Did you seduce Luciano into this?"

Celeste's fingers curled into fists, but she took a deep breath to calm her temper. "It was Luciano's idea. I was against it, but I trust his judgment. He's cautious, and he'll know when the public is ready for my unveiling."

"My son doesn't always use the best judgment when it comes to art and other matters. You two are playing a dangerous game. You could destroy everything he's worked to achieve, and for what?"

"For the advancement of the greatest artist of our age," Luciano said as he came up behind Francesca. "How dare you question and accuse my wife this way? Do not speak of this matter again."

Francesca lowered her head. "Forgive me, Luci. I'm just concerned for your welfare. I know how hard you've worked to build your reputation."

"I know what I'm doing, and it's none of your business. Come, Celeste. The studio is ready for you."

"Excuse us," Celeste said as she stood to follow Luciano. She gave Francesca a triumphant look as she passed her and grinned at Portia. "I'll see you this afternoon, Aunt."

Portia stared at her with wide eyes before giving a slight nod. Celeste strode away, basking in her first victory over Francesca.

CELESTE FORGOT Francesca and let the warm embrace of homecoming wash over her as she stepped into Luciano's studio. The smells and sights awakened her longing to cradle a brush in her hand. She ran her fingers across the little table where Luciano had first persuaded her to paint for him. That first attempt rested on a ledge at the back of the room. She picked it up and hugged it to her chest.

"This is the room where I was reborn. Maybe it will guide me back to the world of the living." She turned to Luciano, who watched silently from the doorway. "How can I thank you for bringing me here? You're a genius."

He threw his head back and laughed. "Bringing you to Venice was a whim and feeble hope but seeing the flame in your eyes is thanks enough."

Celeste went to her latest work, which was waiting on the easel in the center of the studio. It was of a young shepherdess done in oil on a poplar wood panel. Celeste had learned much from Luciano over the years, but her confidence had waned after arriving in Florence. Being surrounded by such rare and masterful pieces had made her doubt the odds of ever attaining such skill. Luciano helped by reminding her that all artists started out as novices. She just needed experience. So, instead of becoming intimidated by the masters, she became inspired by them.

Her work improved rapidly but also made her weaknesses glaringly obvious, and her walks in darkness after the loss of her babies had set her back. Her lack of inspiration was reflected in her latest painting. Feeling a renewed surge of creativity, she was eager to get back on course.

"This is terrible. I'm starting over," she announced.

A corner of Luciano's mouth curved into a grin. "I was hoping to hear those words. I'll leave you to work. I don't want to distract you."

She crossed her arms and frowned. "You won't stay and work with me? I need my maestro."

"You will soon outpace your maestro, I'm afraid. I need to meet with my steward and go over the accounts. I'll join you in a few hours." He hugged her and kissed the top of her head. "I dreamed many times of you standing in this very spot without fear of getting caught. I never thought it would come to pass. It's a miracle."

"It is. A miracle mixed with bits of luck and daring."

Luciano kissed her goodbye and left her to work. She grabbed a sheet of paper and charcoal and began sketching her new idea. The image flowed from her mind and onto the paper without effort. She hadn't drawn so quickly since her days as Federigo's nanny. She worked without distraction until Portia glided into the studio hours after Luciano had gone.

"Francesca sent me to find you. She insists that you take a break and eat with us."

Celeste stared at Portia for a few moments before recognizing her. She looked out of place in Luciano's studio, and Celeste had been so absorbed in her work that she forgot where she was. Her stomach growled at the mention of food. She hadn't eaten since breakfast and was ravenous. She set the charcoal on the table and wiped her hands on her smock.

Portia shook her head. "You have black smudges on your face, my dear. Clean up before you join us."

Celeste laughed and followed her aunt up the stairs. "Good idea. Is Francesca still upset?"

"I calmed her down, but I'm not afraid to say that I agree with her. What you and Luciano are doing is reckless."

"We're aware of the risks, but Luciano says they're worth it."

Portia turned to face her. "This is about more than a loss of your place in society. The Florentines are serious about their art. Is being an artist worth putting your life at risk?"

Celeste wanted to say yes but knew Portia would never understand. "You're overacting. My life isn't in any danger. Luciano understands Florence much better than we ever will. I trust him."

Portia turned and continued up the stairs. "Then, I will have to trust you both."

CELESTE WAS DISAPPOINTED when Marco chose not to join them for dinner. Luciano had arranged for him to apprentice in a friend's workshop while they were in Venice, and Marco had already moved his belongings.

"That was quick. He didn't even bother to say goodbye," Celeste said.

"It's for the best. Marco will be more at home there, and it's not healthy for him to be idle while we're in Venice," Luciano said. "He needs to keep his skills sharp."

"I can understand that, but he could have worked in the studio with me," Celeste said.

"He needs to be around other young men, not his married sister. His new maestro will give him more instruction than I have time to offer. It's a valuable experience to work with a different maestro."

Celeste nodded and took a bite of fish. Luciano's point made sense, but she would have enjoyed working alongside her brother. She saw little of him in Florence.

"What about Jacopo? Where is he tonight?"

"I'm keeping him by my side and finding tasks for him. I'm not comfortable letting him loose with a new maestro here. I'll make sure he stays busy," Luciano said and rubbed his chin. "I sent him for supplies."

Francesca turned to Luciano and said, "I'm planning to stay with Teresa for a time and leave you in peace. I've been cooped up here for too long with Mateo. Time away will be good for us. Portia can manage the household while I'm gone if Celeste's too busy in the studio to bother with such matters."

Celeste caught the subtle insult, but she relished having the run of Luciano's palazzo, so she held her tongue. She was fond of Francesca, but she didn't have the strength for a constant battle of wills.

"It's unnecessary, Mother, but if you feel you must, then fine. The door is open whenever you wish to return," Luciano said. "This is your home for the rest of your life. I made that commitment to you."

"But I'm no longer the mistress. I've never truly been mistress, even if I have become accustomed to having free rein these past three years."

"I understand, and I'd be honored to manage the household in your absence," Portia said. "I'm used to being occupied and don't want to become idle any more than Marco does."

"It's settled then. I'll leave in the morning." She stood and curtsied to Luciano. "I'm going to kiss my grandson goodnight and go to bed." She went only a few steps before turning to face the others. "I forgot to mention that Maria has invited us to dine on Saturday. I made excuses and told her of your recent sadness. She understood and says to come when you're ready."

Luciano tossed the chunk of cheese he was holding onto his plate. "And how does Maria know we're here?"

"Everyone knows, Son. It's the talk of Venice. Was it supposed to be a secret?"

"No, but that seems terribly fast, even for Venice," he said.

"You should have asked us before declining the invitation. It's not your place to speak for us," Celeste said.

The others turned and stared at her in shock.

"My apologies, child. What you say is true, but after what Maria did to you, I assumed you'd never want to set foot in her house," Francesca said.

"I've long dreamed of seeing Maria Foscari's face at having to curtsy to me. It's time that hateful woman was put in her place."

"You should walk in on the arm of Cesare," Portia said, with a grin. "Even Maria wouldn't dare stand up to the might of the Gabriele family."

"Or the Vicentes," Luciano said with a smile. "Are you serious about this, Celeste? If we're already the center of gossip, there's no need to stoke the flames. We're here for you to rest and recover."

"I am serious, and I've always wanted to thank Pia for her kindness to me on that terrible night. I shouldn't have been so sharp, Francesca. You were right to refuse, even though you should have spoken with us first. I'm not strong enough to take Maria on yet. I'll let you know when I am so you can be a witness," Celeste said and grinned.

Francesca nodded to Celeste and kissed her cheeks. "You have earned the right to be mistress here."

"I'm going to follow Francesca's example and go to bed. I'm still worn out from the journey," Portia said.

Luciano and Celeste wished her goodnight and went to walk in the garden.

"I've never strolled in this garden with such a beautiful woman," Luciano said.

Celeste glanced up at him. "Isabella was a beautiful woman."

"We never did things like this. Our marriage was unhappy from the start, like most marriages amongst our class."

"It's unfortunate that most people will never know what we have. Most couples from my former class married for romantic and not financial reasons sometimes, but not all were happy either."

Luciano gave her a tender kiss. "I often envied those free to choose their marriage partners before I met you. I didn't imagine it could happen to me."

"I didn't imagine I would ever marry or have the chance for children. I hope that blessing will come one day," Celeste said and leaned on his shoulder.

"It will. As Francesca said, we need patience. We have our art in the meantime."

They walked in silence for several minutes until Luciano led Celeste to a stone seat in an alcove. "You handled Francesca well tonight. I'm proud of you."

"I've lived at the whim of others for most of my life, even yours for a time, Luciano. I'm ready to take my place at your side and fulfill my potential. From today forward, I control my destiny."

"Your spirit is what I love most about you," Luciano said.

"You fired that spirit, my love. I owe you everything, even my life. Remind me of that if I ever forget."

"There won't be a need. I owe you far more than you know. I meant it when I said you gave me a reason to go on living after Isabella's death. Our debts to each other cancel themselves out. Now we walk as equals."

Celeste kissed him and said, "No, Luciano, now we soar together."

CHAPTER TWENTY

*L*ivia jerked on the sleeve of Celeste's gown, then stitched it tighter around her and frowned. "Why didn't you order a new gown for Signora Foscari's dinner like the master wanted?"

Celeste had insisted on the blue gown she'd worn to dinner at Luciano's her first night in Florence, but as Livia tugged and pulled, she began to regret her choice. She'd regained some weight during her first weeks in Venice, but the gown still hung on her slender frame. Luciano begged her to eat and sleep more and spend less time in the studio, but it was hard to tear herself away from her work. She would have spent every minute in the studio, if possible. Her skills had reached new heights, and she didn't want any distractions to hinder her progress.

"It's an unnecessary expense. No one in Venice has seen this gown, and I don't need new clothes every time I step out of the door," Celeste said. She swayed from side to side in front of the mirror and nodded in satisfaction. "And I have you to make me look presentable. This will be fine."

Livia went away, mumbling, to fetch her mistress' cloak from the wardrobe. Celeste understood why Luciano wanted her to make a good impression, but she could do that without extravagant new clothes. She was what mattered, not layers of fabric and lace. When she was ready, she joined Luciano and Portia in the foyer.

"You are stunning as always, my love," Luciano said and offered her his arm to escort her to the gondola. "Are you nervous?"

Celeste pondered his question. When they had talked about confronting Maria with Francesca a month earlier, it had seemed important, but she could no longer recall why. She cared little for what Maria or anyone else thought of her. All that mattered was the quality of her art.

"I'm looking forward to thanking Pia, and I have a healthy appetite. Maria always sets a sumptuous table."

"That's refreshing news," Luciano said.

"I'm anxious, even if you're not," Portia said. "I've been avoiding Cesare and the rest of the family since we arrived in Venice, but my brother wrote to insist my place is here and not in Lucca. He says it's my duty to the family to come home."

"Just tell him no. You're no longer a defenseless widow," Francesca said.

"Yes, you're the mistress of a Tuscan estate," Celeste reminded her.

"That won't sway Cesare. He doesn't share your enlightened views, and he's fiercely loyal to the family. That always comes first in his eyes."

"I have a good rapport with your brother. I'll come to your rescue if he causes trouble," Luciano said and winked.

Portia glared at him as he helped the women into the gondola and climbed in beside them. Celeste grew nostalgic as the boat carried them closer to her former employer's palazzo. Memories of peaceful nights with Luciano in the studio flooded over her. No treasure on earth could tempt her to trade her new life for the old, but that time held a precious place in her heart.

"Why haven't you been to the studio this week?" she asked Luciano. "What's so important to keep you from me?" He glanced at her before turning to look over the canal. Celeste noticed Portia staring at her hands, clasped in her lap. "What are you not telling me?"

Luciano looked directly at her. "I've been painting in the workshop. I want you to have the studio to yourself."

Celeste frowned. "I don't need the studio to myself. There's room for both of us. Working next to you inspires me."

"No, it doesn't. You're oblivious to all else in the world while you work. It disturbs me and distracts me from my work. I'm more comfortable in the workshop."

His words stung, even though she was sure he hadn't meant them to.

Celeste turned to Portia. "You knew about this?"

"Yes, my dear. Don't overreact. You two don't have to spend every hour of the day together. It isn't meant as an affront."

Luciano took her hand. "No, it isn't. It's merely an arrangement that suits both our needs."

"You're right. Forgive me," Celeste said and gave him a weak smile.

"No more talk of art," Francesca said with a smile. "Let's enjoy ourselves tonight as you exact your vengeance on Maria Foscari."

Celeste let the matter drop, but the hurt remained. Even if what Luciano had said was true, she still felt his presence when he wasn't with her. She had avoided admitting how the force of her passion was sometimes disturbing, even to her. At times, it grew into an insatiable appetite that she feared would consume her.

She had hoped that with painting as long and as often as she wished, the intensity would subside, but it only increased. She wondered if other artists struggled the same way but had no one to ask, fearing even Luciano wouldn't understand. He didn't seem to suffer from an obsession to create.

"Here we are," he said, interrupting her thoughts. "Are you ready?"

Celeste painted on her brightest smile. "Yes, my love. It's going to be a lovely evening."

CELESTE'S REUNION with Maria Foscari was anticlimactic. Celeste had hoped to put the woman who had caused her so much anguish in her place, but Maria was cordial and respectful and led Celeste through the sala, introducing her as if she were a cherished cousin. Celeste soon saw Maria as no different from the countless women she'd mingled with in Florence. They had nothing else to do but spend their days in needlepoint and endless gossip.

There was a time when Celeste would have given anything to stand as an equal with Maria or Francesca and other patrician women. Now she pitied them. They would never know the satisfaction of having a purpose in life other than producing children.

"Where's Pia?" Celeste asked as Maria led her to the table.

"Sadly, we lost Pia to a fever last year," Maria said and lowered her eyes. "I've missed her greatly. She was my trusted servant for many years. She had almost become like a part of the family."

Celeste was heartbroken at the news. "Pia was once most kind to me at a desperate time," she said, taking a subtle stab at Maria. "I'd hoped to thank her."

"I'm sure she was aware of your gratitude," Maria said. "Here's your cousin Alessandra." She handed Celeste off and scurried away to greet her other guests.

Celeste was glad to see Alessandra on the arm of her handsome new husband. Celeste guessed him to be in his early thirties, and he seemed attentive and obliging with her.

"This is Bertolo Donato," Alessandra said and blushed. "We married shortly before you arrived. This is my cousin, Celeste Gabriele."

Celeste curtsied, and Bertolo kissed her cheeks.

"Welcome home. Alessandra speaks highly of you," Bertolo said. "Where's your illustrious husband?"

Celeste turned to search for Luciano and found herself face to face with Marcello Viari. She stepped away and bumped into Alessandra.

"Signore Viari, let me introduce my cousin, Signora Gabriele. She's recently returned from Florence," Alessandra said.

"Have we met? I wouldn't forget your face," Marcello said.

"How could you know her?" Alessandra asked. "She lives in Florence. Did you meet her there?"

Marcello rubbed his chin and squinted at Celeste. "You're the nanny. Celeste, isn't it?"

Luciano came up behind Marcello and said, "She's my wife and Signora Gabriele to you."

Marcello swung around to face him. "The nanny, your wife? But how?"

"And she's my daughter," Cesare Gabriele said from behind Celeste. "Is there anything else you wish to say, Marcello?"

Marcello bowed to Celeste with a flourish. "A thousand pardons, Signora. I mistook you for someone I once knew. You look very much like her."

Luciano opened his mouth to respond, but Celeste put her hand on his arm to silence him.

"I'm not ashamed of my past," she said, squaring her shoulders. "I was the nanny for your sister's children and for Maria Foscari, but only because my family had fallen on difficulties. I am a Gabriele."

Luciano and Cesare stepped to either side of her.

"Again, my apologies. I meant no disrespect," Marcello said.

"You're forgiven, this time," Cesare said.

"Is your wife with you?" Alessandra asked.

Celeste was grateful to her for diffusing the tension. Alessandra acknowledged Celeste's discreet nod with a smile.

"She's in her confinement. Our third child," Marcello said without emotion. "She has yet to produce a son. May God grant our desire this time."

You have a son, Celeste thought but kept it to herself. "Your third? So soon?" she asked. Marcello grinned at her suggestively and nodded. "And your sister? Is she here?"

"Also in her confinement with her fifth child," Marcello said. "And you? Is your nursery filling up?"

Celeste took a step towards him, but Luciano squeezed her arm as she had done with him.

"We haven't been so blessed yet," Luciano said.

"I'm sure you'll have another son soon," Marcello said before bowing and rushing back to his family.

"Arrogant upstart," Uncle Cesare said. "He'll never be half the man his father was."

"No, he won't," Luciano said.

Luciano was still holding Celeste's arm, and she felt his grip relax once Marcello left. She let out her breath, wondering if they'd ever be free of that cretin.

"Shall we go to the courtyard for some air?" she asked Luciano.

He nodded and pulled her toward the steps to the courtyard. She nearly had to run to keep up with him. Luciano steered her through the crowd to the far corner of the garden where he had asked her to become his apprentice years earlier. He motioned for Celeste to sit on the bench where she had come upon him sleeping. He sat next to her and pulled her into his arms. Celeste could hear his shallow, quick breaths.

She kissed his cheek and said, "Forget Marcello. He's nothing." She pulled away and stared out into the garden. "This is one of my favorite places. After the night of our secret meeting, I used to sneak here and sit on this very bench, imagining myself in your arms, as I am now. I never expected my fantasy to become real."

"Yet, here we are," he said and gave her a tender kiss. "That night with you here is one of my fondest memories. My life changed when I discovered you loved me as I did you. I'd tried to ignore my feelings out of respect for Isabella, but it was impossible after that night. I saw no future for us, but I could at least be close to you during our lessons. After you went to Sofia Viari, my life was empty. It was a dark time."

When he grew quiet, Celeste said, "All I wanted was to be with you, but you were out of reach. Seeing you at Sofia's dinner with Isabella was torture."

"Now, nothing can come between us. I love you, Celeste."

She responded urgently to his kiss. "Take me home, Luciano," she whispered between gasps. "Take me to your bed."

He stood and offered her his hand without a word. They ran to the sala and searched for Portia. She was speaking with a handsome man who looked to be about her age that Celeste didn't recognize.

"Paolo," Luciano said and pulled the man into a hug. "How are you, old friend?"

"Luci? Is that you? Do I see a ghost? When did you get back to Venice?"

"A month ago." Luciano turned and gestured for Celeste to come closer. "Let me introduce my wife, Celeste Gabriele. This is Paolo Fonte. I've known him since my early days in Venice. He was an evil influence on me. My aunts commanded me to stay away from him, but I didn't listen," Luciano said and laughed.

After Celeste curtsied, Paolo took her hand and kissed it. "Another Gabriele? How many of you are there? You're a lovely girl. What are you doing with this wretch?"

Celeste smiled when Luciano laughed. "I see you know my Aunt Portia," she said.

Paolo turned and winked at Portia. Celeste glanced at her aunt and saw her cheeks flush.

"I was Portia's suitor, but I lost out to the scoundrel that Giovanni Gabriele married her off to. By the time her husband died, I had married my first wife. She died giving birth to our first child. I lost my second wife two years ago to a fever. I was just telling Portia that my daughters look after me, but it's a lonely life."

He grinned at Portia. Celeste giggled when her aunt looked away and frantically fanned herself.

"Dine with us tomorrow," Luciano said and pounded Paolo on the back. "Bring your daughters."

"Will you be there?" he asked Portia. When she nodded, he said, "Then we'd be delighted to accept."

Luciano turned to Portia. "I'm sorry to cut your evening short, but Celeste is fatigued and ready to leave. Have you seen my mother?" He turned and searched the room. "There she is," he said and rushed off toward Francesca.

Portia looked so disappointed that Celeste almost giggled again. "I'm sorry, Aunt. I'm just not used to being back in society yet."

"My daughters and I would be honored to escort your aunt home," Paolo said, just as Luciano came back with Francesca.

"Are you sure you can't stay longer, dear? The evening is just getting interesting," Francesca said.

"Paolo has just offered to escort my aunt home. Can Francesca join you?" Celeste asked.

Paolo kissed Francesca's cheek and bowed. "Delighted," he said.

Francesca tapped Paolo with her fan and smiled. "You old fool."

"Splendid," Luciano said. "Thank you, Paolo. We'll see you tomorrow." He kissed Portia and Francesca's cheeks. "Until the morning, ladies."

Celeste waved goodbye as Luciano pulled her towards the door. She did her best to keep pace, as eager to get home as her husband was.

"Do you think you can go any slower?" Celeste said and glared at Livia as she helped her undress.

"What's the rush, mistress? It's early yet," Livia said.

Celeste slapped Livia's hands when she struggled with a knot on her bodice. "Let me do that," Celeste said.

"Yes, madam." Livia crossed her arms and grinned at Celeste while she worked at the knot.

Celeste didn't have much better luck. "I'm sorry, Livia. It's warm tonight. Why do we have to wear so many layers of clothes? Please, just help me into my nightdress, then you're dismissed for the rest of the night."

She was quiet while Livia finished removing her layers of clothing but smiled when Livia slid the nightdress over her head.

"Have a pleasant sleep, madam," Livia said with a grin as she went out and closed the door.

Luciano came in from his antechamber moments later and swept Celeste onto the bed.

As he covered her with kisses, she stopped him and climbed off the bed, then held her hand out to him. "Not here, my love. Come with me."

Luciano frowned but took her hand. She led him down the hall to the stairs leading to the studio. When he realized where they were going, he picked Celeste up and carried her the rest of the way.

When he put her down, she said, "Where's the cot?"

Without a word, Luciano went to a dark corner and started rummaging through piles of wood scraps. After several moments, he said, "Good, it's still here."

While he set up the cot, Celeste went to a cupboard and shook out a few rumpled blankets. She spread them on their makeshift bed. "Now, I'm ready," she said and held her arms out to Luciano.

The cot creaked when Luciano laid next to her. "Will this hold our weight?"

"I don't care," Celeste said and covered his mouth with hers.

The first time was frantic and breathless, but Celeste craved more. Luciano kindled her desire slowly the second time until her passion crested again and again, but still, she wasn't satisfied. It was like the same obsession that overtook Celeste when she painted, and she felt she'd never get enough of him. She pleaded for more until Luciano rolled onto the cot in exhaustion as dawn crept into the room. Celeste nestled against his shoulder and tenderly sketched on his chest with her finger.

"You made up for our time apart, my love. You're a different woman tonight."

Celeste leaned on her elbow and gazed down at him. "Does this new woman please you?"

Luciano covered her hand with his. "Please me? Oh, my love. It was extraordinary. You're extraordinary. Where has she been hiding?"

"I struggle to subdue my passion when I paint. I'm powerless against it. The same happened tonight. I couldn't tame my hunger for you. I was afraid you'd think me shameless or immodest, but I want you to know all of me."

Luciano cradled her face in his hands. "Immodest? Celeste, you're my wife. You've done nothing more than express your love for me."

Celeste wrapped herself in a blanket and went to the window. As she looked out over the canal, she said, "But Aunt Portia said women shouldn't enjoy the act of love. She said we must submit to our husbands out of obligation, but my desire to be with you is no obligation. Why am I not like other women? Tonight in the gondola, you said you've seen how I become consumed while I paint. What's wrong with me, Luciano? What is this thirst I can't quench?"

Luciano chuckled. "Portia is hardly an expert on the matter. Ignore her. Your spirited nature delights me. It's the mark of a true artist, and it's what I love most about you." Luciano went to her and wrapped his arms around her waist. "You're a unique and remarkable woman, a gift to the world, most especially to me. One day you'll see it. There will be no holding you back from your potential then."

Celeste rested her head on his chest and closed her eyes. "I want to believe that, to feel it as you do, but I'm plagued with doubts. I'm afraid of failure and disappointing you."

"That is impossible."

Celeste sighed and turned to face him. "I'm tired. Let's go upstairs before the servants awaken. I don't want to have to explain to Livia."

Luciano nodded and retrieved Celeste's nightdress from the floor. She lifted it over her head and let the soft fabric slide down her body. Once they dressed, Luciano took her hand, and they tiptoed to their chamber. Celeste curled up to Luciano and fell into a deep and satisfying sleep.

NOONDAY SUNLIGHT STREAMED into their bedchamber by the time Luciano opened his eyes. He gave a satisfied sigh and reached for Celeste, but her side of the bed was empty. His stomach growled, and he realized that he hadn't eaten since Maria's dinner. The valet helped him wash and dress quickly before he headed downstairs. Celeste was in the dining room with Francesca and Portia. He smiled to see Celeste's plate piled high with food. He greeted the women and kissed Celeste's cheek before filling his own plate with food.

"Good afternoon," Portia said and grinned at him. "I trust you had a satisfying sleep."

Francesca covered her mouth and chuckled.

"They've been teasing me all morning," Celeste said and rolled her eyes. "I had to hear it from Livia while I dressed. Last night wasn't our wedding night. We've been married for more than two years."

"True," Francesca said. "It's just that with your recent sadness..." Her words trailed off, and she shrugged.

"Well, I'm recovered and ravenous," Celeste said and stuffed a piece of fish into her mouth.

"That is a sight I like to see," Luciano said as he carried his plate to the table. "You'll regain your strength in no time. Are we ready to entertain Paolo and his daughters tonight?"

Celeste giggled when Portia blushed, but Francesca huffed.

"I like the man," Portia said.

"He's a jovial fellow," Francesca said, "but he'll have you in his spell if you're not on your guard. We'll be ready, Luci."

"Are you painting today?" Portia asked Celeste. When she nodded, Portia said, "Don't be late for dinner. I know how you forget the time."

Celeste grinned at her. "Don't worry, Aunt. I won't be late for this dinner."

"Me either," Luciano said. He took a bite of food and washed it down with a gulp of wine. "I'm sending Marco and Jacopo back to Florence. Marco is eager to go, and I need him to check on the workshop. Jacopo wants to stay, but I'm running out of ways to keep him occupied. He needs to get back to work in the shop."

"You're not sending them alone? Is that safe between the soldiers and the bandits on the road?" Portia asked.

"A friend has business in Florence and has agreed to let the boys join his caravan. They'll be safe, and they'll be a help to him on the journey."

"When are they leaving?" Celeste asked. "Will I get to say goodbye?"

"Day after tomorrow," Luciano said. "I've told them to join us for dinner tonight, and I'll make sure you can see them off, but I'm planning on us following in a month. My business here is almost concluded, and I have obligations in Florence to return to."

"That soon?" Portia and Celeste said at the same time.

"We've already stayed longer than I planned. We can't delay forever. We're Florentines, remember." Luciano stood and picked up his plate. "I'm going to finish my meal in the workshop. I'm behind schedule." He kissed the top of Celeste's head and bowed to the women. "Until tonight."

He was glad to have the workshop to himself. He missed his studio, but he was glad not to have his apprentices pestering him since he had to use the workshop. He had sent Jacopo to his supplier to purchase raw materials for pigments and fetch wood for panels from the lumber mill. He wouldn't return until it was time for dinner. That would give Luciano enough time for several hours of work.

When he finished eating, he took out plans for a fresco he'd been commissioned to paint when he returned to Florence. He sketched and made notes until it was time to dress for dinner. He reluctantly put away his materials as he waited for Jacopo to return. When another half hour passed, and the boy hadn't shown, Luciano went in search of him. He wasn't in his room or in the empty sala, and Luciano was glad to see that Paolo hadn't arrived.

He went next to the workshop of Marco's maestro. Marco hadn't seen his brother in days and didn't know where he might have gone. He enlisted Marco's help to search for Jacopo. Luciano tried his various suppliers and the lumber mill, but no one had seen Jacopo for hours.

"There's one more place we might look," Marco said when they'd exhausted all their ideas. "Jacopo takes after my father. We should try the public houses."

Luciano turned toward the public houses near the wharf. They found Jacopo on the third try. He was seated, holding a mug with a woman straddling his lap. Luciano pushed her off and grabbed Jacopo by the neck of his tunic to drag him out to the street. Jacopo tried to fight him, but Marco helped Luciano wrestle him to the ground.

Once they had him pinned, Luciano said, "What did you do with the money I gave you? Where are the supplies?"

Jacopo cocked his head toward the door. "Inside, in a corner."

"Please go retrieve the materials," Luciano told Marco. Once he was inside, Luciano grasped the front of Jacopo's tunic and pulled his face close. "This is how you repay me? Stealing from me? You'll work off every Florin. How much other money have you taken?"

"None, maestro, I swear it. This was the first time. They gave me a good bargain at the mill. There was money left over, so I came here. I've heard rumors about what happens in these places. I was curious."

Luciano loosened his grip and leaned Jacopo against the stone wall. He was slurring his words and had trouble staying upright. Luciano spat in disgust. Jacopo stumbled forward a few steps and vomited onto his boots. When Marco returned with Luciano's supplies, he laid them on the ground and slapped the back of Jacopo's head.

"You're no better than Papa. If I catch you at this again, I'll toss you into the canal myself."

Luciano was proud of Marco and nodded at him. "That punishment is a bit severe, but we will find a way to keep him in line. Help me get him home."

Luciano dumped Jacopo onto his bed an hour later. "Stay with him," he told Marco. "I'll send word to your maestro explaining where you are."

Marco nodded and dragged a chair next to the bed. Luciano left the boys alone and went to his chamber to change. While he dressed, he wondered what Celeste's life had been like before working for Maria. She rarely spoke of her father, saying she wanted to forget that time of her life. Luciano hoped he could help Jacopo avoid the same fate as Giovanni Gabriele.

Finding his friend entertaining the women when he finally made it to the sala was a relief. Celeste raised her eyebrows but didn't ask where he'd been.

"A thousand apologies," Luciano said and bowed. "An urgent situation arose, but it's been managed. What have I missed?"

Luciano did his best to enjoy entertaining Paolo and his family, but images of Jacopo kept forcing their way into his thoughts. Luciano admitted that he'd been no saint at Jacopo's age, but he never would have done anything so brazen. He remembered how Jacopo drank too much during their first dinner in Venice and Celeste's concern for Jacopo. Luciano felt she had overreacted that night, but he wondered if her worries were justified and hoped he wouldn't fail the boy.

As soon as he and Celeste were in their chamber that night, she faced him with her hands on her hips and said, "What are you keeping from me? Why were you late for dinner?"

He told her the truth about Jacopo. "This day started so well, and you had such a lovely evening. I'm sorry to spoil it with such news."

Celeste went to him and took his hands. "I should apologize to you for forcing Jacopo on you. He's been a handful since he was a child. I've always feared he'd grow to be like Papa. What are you going to do? Is it too late to set him on the right course?"

"He's still a boy, Celeste. He has plenty of time. Let's put this aside and discuss it when we're rested. Tell me about Paolo. He seems to be under Portia's spell, not the other way around. I've never seen him so taken with any woman."

Celeste hesitated for only an instant before smiling. "She was like a young maiden with him and seems to share his feelings. It's refreshing to see at their age. Will anything come of it, do you think? He was her suitor when they were young."

"It's probably a harmless flirtation, and Paolo knows Portia is leaving the country with us soon. That doesn't mean I'd be sorry to see him make an offer to Cesare for her hand. They could both use the companionship."

"I think he wants more than companionship," Celeste said and giggled.

Luciano pulled her into his arms and said, "I wouldn't mind a little more companionship if you have the strength."

"I think I can manage it," she said, "but don't expect a repeat of last night."

"I'm not sure I have the strength for that." He lifted her onto the bed and nuzzled her neck. "But I'm willing to try."

～

CELESTE ROSE EARLY and hurried to Jacopo's room. Marco was snoring in a chair by the bed, where Jacopo was buried in a jumble of blankets. Celeste took a cup of water from the bedside table and splashed it in his face. He snorted and tried to sit up but fell back onto the bed with a groan. Marco heard the commotion and sat forward, rubbing his eyes.

"How dare you shame our family this way?" Celeste said. "I told Luciano to throw you out, but he's more patient than I. As it is, he's decided to send you to work in the stone quarries to earn back every bit of money you stole. You'll return to Florence with Marco, and he and Stefano will keep you under their boots until we return. Then it's off to the quarry for you. This is your last chance, brother. Any more trouble and you'll be on the street."

"The quarry?" Marco said. "The hard work would be good for Jacopo, but I've heard the conditions there are dangerous. Men die in the quarries."

"Good morning, Marco," Celeste said and kissed his cheek. "Thank you for helping Luciano last night and for staying with Jacopo."

"He's my brother and my responsibility, sister."

"No, he is not, but I appreciate it all the same. On the other matter, Luciano is the Maestro, and it is his decision. He assures me it's the best cure for Jacopo's rebellious nature. We're counting on you to keep Jacopo in line until we return to Florence."

Marco yawned and stretched. "You can rely on me. I'll get him dressed and bring him to you before I go to the workshop."

Celeste thanked him and returned to her chamber to find Luciano's valet dressing him for the day. She waved the valet off and said, "You may go, Filippo. I'll finish dressing the master."

When Filippo left them alone, Luciano wrapped an arm around her waist and drew her close. "I'd rather you undress me."

She gave him a playful slap and wiggled free. "Haven't you had enough? And my brothers will be here shortly."

As she laced his tunic, he said, "How is our prisoner this morning?"

"Paying for his crimes with a pounding head."

"Excellent. That will make him think twice before he enters a public house."

"It never stopped Papa." She finished her work and straightened to face him. "I want to ask a favor before my brothers get here."

"If you're going to ask me to drown Jacopo in the canal, Marco already thought of that. The punishment is a touch harsh considering his crime," Luciano said with a grin.

"As much as he deserves a good dunking, the favor has nothing to do with Jacopo. I'd like to visit my friend, Lapa, the wet nurse for Sofia Viari. I'm hoping Francesca can arrange a visit, and I'll stop into the nursery while we're there. Can you find an escort? Unless you'd like to join us."

"I have to meet with my steward and banker, but Jacopo can accompany you. What's your interest in this wet nurse?"

"She was a dear friend and confidant during my time as the nanny for Sofia. I want to check on her welfare."

Luciano kissed the top of her head. "You have such a caring nature. Few others in your position would care about the welfare of a servant."

"I too was a servant, remember, my love? I understand that life. There were hardships, but I'm grateful for the perspective I gained during that time. It has instilled a desire in me to ease the burdens of others. And if not for my time amongst the serving class, we would never have met, and I wouldn't have discovered the glorious world of art."

She was about to say more, but Marco tapped on the door before coming in with a very humbled and hungover Jacopo. Celeste stood and stepped in front of them with her arms crossed.

"What do you have to say to Luciano?"

Jacopo dropped to his knees with his head bowed. "Forgive me, Maestro. I have learned my lesson. I'll work to earn back every florin."

"Get up, Jacopo," Luciano said. Jacopo did as ordered but kept his head lowered. "I'll count this as a youthful indiscretion, but you must learn to control your impulses and abstain from alcohol. Time in the quarries will help. Now, clean yourself up and sleep it off. You'll escort your sister and aunt on a visit this afternoon. I expect to see you in time for dinner."

"Yes, Maestro," Jacopo mumbled as he shuffled out of the room.

Luciano let out a hearty laugh as soon as the boy was out of earshot. Celeste had seen her father in that condition too many times to find humor in the situation.

"I need to get back to my maestro," Marco said. "I have work to complete before Jacopo, and I leave for Florence in the morning."

Celeste took his hands and kissed both cheeks. "I'll miss you, but we won't be too far behind you. Getting back to Florence will be good for both of you."

"I'm eager to see Stefano and return to work." He gave Luciano a quick bow. "I'll try to join you for dinner."

Celeste frowned as she watched him go. Luciano studied her for a moment, then said, "They're good boys, and you'll only be separated for a month or two. I must go. My steward will be waiting."

Celeste smiled, then gave him a tender kiss. "Will I see you before dinner?"

"I'll do my best. Enjoy your outing to Sofia's."

CHAPTER TWENTY-ONE

*C*eleste sat slightly removed from Francesca, Portia, and Sofia as they went on endlessly about the impending birth of Sofia's fifth child. It looked as if the child would burst out of her swollen belly at any moment. Each time Sofia lovingly rubbed the enormous bump was a stab at Celeste's heart. When she could take no more, she slipped out of the room without the older women noticing and went to find Lapa.

As she walked the familiar halls of the Rosselli palazzo, her feelings fluctuated between contentment and sadness. She had known her most peaceful days before marrying Luciano in that home, but she also had the memories of Marcello and the uneasiness he had caused her. In a small, twisted way that she rarely allowed herself to admit, she had reason to be grateful to him. If he hadn't impregnated Isabella, Celeste never could have married Luciano. She'd still be nanny to Sofia's growing brood of babies.

Lost in her thoughts, she rounded a corner and, to her horror, found Marcello blocking her path.

Leering at her, he said, "If it isn't the nanny turned Duchessa. What brings you to grace us with your presence?"

Celeste crossed her arms and eyed him. "I am a Duchessa, so

249

watch how you address me. I'm no longer a defenseless servant. Let me pass."

He stepped closer and reached for her arm, but she backed away before he touched her. "Why do you always refuse me? Am I not young and handsome? I could give you more pleasure than that dried up old husband of yours, as I did for Isabella? She often came begging for more. Or do you deny Luciano, too? Is that why there are no children?"

"I warn you. If you lay a hand on me, you'll see what my 'dried up old husband' is capable of, as well as my father, Cesare Gabriele. With your reputation, who do you think they'll believe if I cry out?"

He grabbed her shoulders before she could duck out of the way. "Where are they now? I see no one here to defend you."

As Celeste opened her mouth to scream, she heard Aunt Portia's voice behind her.

"Remove your hands from my niece, or I'll have your brother-in-law's guard on you before you reach the end of the hall."

Marcello let go of Celeste with a smile and gave Portia the same exaggerated bow. "Just getting reacquainted with an old friend. No reason to call the guard." He brushed past them with a laugh. "Afternoon, ladies."

Once he was gone, Portia turned to Celeste and took her hands. "Do you feel faint? Are you hurt?"

Celeste gently pushed Portia's hands away and crossed her arms. "I'm perfectly fine and didn't need you rushing to my rescue. Why does everyone think I'm a helpless butterfly? I've escaped Marcello's groping hands more than once."

"I sometimes forget how strong you are, but you were lucky in the past. It won't always be so. Trust me, I know from painful experience."

Celeste often forgot what her aunt endured at the hands of her husband. She smiled and squeezed Portia's hand. "Then, I thank you for protecting me."

"That brute Marcello must be stopped. I'll ask Francesca to speak to Sofia. She has more of a right than any to want Marcello put in his place. He caused Isabella's death."

Celeste wasn't in a mood to talk about Marcello or Isabella, so she said, "What are you doing here? Is it time to leave?"

Portia shook her head. "I saw you sneak out and sensed why you left. I couldn't listen to Sofia complain about her swollen ankles or aching back for one more moment, either."

Celeste rolled her eyes. "She acts as if she's the first woman to ever carry a child, but Sofia's complaining wasn't the only reason I left." She linked her arm in Portia's. "I'm on my way to visit Lapa in the nursery."

She raised her eyebrows. "Lapa?"

"The wet nurse. She was my friend when I served here."

"I remember. You insisted on saying goodbye the day you left service here. Lapa seems like a sweet girl. Do you mind if I join you?"

Celeste took her aunt's hand to lead her to the nursery. When she opened the door, she was pleased to see that nothing had changed, except Lapa wasn't here. Rosalia sat at a small table near the fireplace. Her eyes widened when she recognized Celeste and ran to her with her arms outstretched. Celeste swept her up and swung her around, kissing her cheeks.

"My little angel. I'm so happy you remember me. How old are you now? Seven?"

Rosalia bobbed her blond curly head. "Where have you been? Why did you go away?"

Celeste put her down and rubbed her silky locks, feeling the nanny's eyes on her. "That's a story for another day. Where is Lapa?"

"Mamma sent her away, too. Villana is nanny now. Bettina is here to feed the new baby when it comes."

Villana stood and curtsied, while another woman Celeste hadn't noticed in the corner came forward. She held a child who looked to be a year old. Celeste wondered if Sofia would make her send him away when her own child arrived. Images of Lapa's sad eyes came into her mind. She pushed them aside and smiled at the women.

"I'm Signora Gabriele, a friend of your mistress. Do either of you know Lapa?"

Villana shook her head. "No, madam. She was gone before we

arrived. There was a lapse of time between our mistress' babies, and I'm told Lapa's milk dried, so there was no use for her here."

So, Sofia tossed her out like an old rag, Celeste thought. "Do you know where I can find her?"

Villana just shrugged. Portia cleared her throat. Celeste had forgotten she was there. She seemed so out of place in the nursery and in Celeste's memories of her time there.

"Your questions are answered. It's time to go."

Celeste hugged Rosalia. "I'll try to visit again before I go to my home far away. Kiss Benito for me."

Celeste's heart warmed to see Rosalia's eyes glisten as she turned to go. She would not want to return to her old existence, but she was pleased to see she'd made a difference in one little life.

"WHERE DID you two get off to?" Francesca asked when they walked into the sala.

"I went looking for Lapa," Celeste said.

"She's been gone for ages. It's a shame," Sofia said. "I was hoping she'd be here to feed this new addition. She was such a good milk producer, but too much time passed after Angelica was weaned, and she went dry."

Sofia's comment made Celeste ill. She spoke of Lapa like a cow. She swallowed her disgust and said, "Do you know where I can find her?"

Sofia raised her eyebrows. "Why would you want to find her?"

Celeste took a breath to calm her rising anger. "She was my friend. I wanted to check after her welfare."

Sofia stared at her for several moments before shaking her head. She groaned and tried to stand but couldn't raise her belly out of the chair. Francesca helped her to her feet.

"I'm afraid I'm going to have to cut our visit short. I've been out of bed too long already."

Francesca and Portia wished her well and promised to come as soon as they got word of the baby's arrival. Celeste hurried down the main stairs, determined to never again set foot in that palazzo. As she hurried toward the gondola, she heard someone call out to her and turned to see a page running toward her. He bowed and asked permission to speak.

"Yes, what is it?" she asked, impatient to get into the gondola.

The page straightened, and Celeste recognized him as the one named Salvi, who she'd trusted to take the note informing Luciano of Isabella's infidelity. He'd grown a foot since she last saw him, but she recognized his face.

"Pardon me, madam, but I overheard you asking about Lapa. I can take you to her. I escorted her home the day Signora Viari dismissed her."

Celeste opened her mouth to respond, but Portia stepped between them before she could.

"I can read your thoughts, niece. I will not allow you to traipse all over Venice, trying to find this wet nurse. You tried. She is gone. Accept that."

Celeste glared at her. "Allow me? I'm no longer a child, and I don't need your permission."

"You may not need my permission but see sense. It's too dangerous in that part of the city for our kind. Aside from the thieves and marauders, bands of *condottieri* roam the streets. They could capture you, and we'd never know what became of you."

"What could the *condottieri* possibly want with me? I'm unknown here and not a member of the battling, ruling political families. No one will even notice me."

Portia caught her arm as she turned toward the canal. "Don't do this, Celeste. Lapa's not worth the danger. Remember who you are."

She squared her shoulders and raised her chin. "Yes, I am Duchessa Celeste Maria Gabriele, but have you forgotten that I lived on those streets as a child? After Mamma died, I often wandered alone in search of food and wood for the fire. Tell me, Aunt, where was your concern then? I could have been murdered, and my body dumped in the canal for all you cared."

Portia gasped, and Celeste saw the blush of shame rise in her cheeks, making her regret her harsh words. Her aunt had become a loving mother to her and didn't deserve such treatment.

She covered Portia's hand with hers and said, "Forgive me, Aunt. That was unkind. I know you only care for my safety, but I am going. The gondolier will take you and Francesca home before Jacopo and I go in search of Lapa."

She brushed past Portia and told Salvi to inform his master of their errand before joining them, then climbed into the gondola, kicking the snoring Jacopo out of her way. Francesca and Portia exchanged a glance before climbing in beside her. She turned away and gazed over the canal to hide her smile of victory.

AFTER DEPOSITING Portia and Francesca at the palazzo, Celeste set off with the gondolier, the page, Salvi, and a reluctant Jacopo, who had no desire to travel into the old quarter with her. Celeste wasn't much happier about it, but she felt driven to find Lapa. The courage she'd shown Portia faded as they approached their former neighborhood, but she hid her feelings from Jacopo so as not to encourage his grumbling. When Salvi directed the gondolier to a landing, and they disembarked onto the dusty walkway, she became the young, frightened girl trying to ensure her family's survival in an unforgiving world.

Salvi guided them through the shabby and bustling streets to Lapa's dwelling. As they moved along, the crowd often parted to let them pass. Many bowed or curtsied to Celeste, and she eyed them in wonder. She had been one of them a few years earlier, yet all it took was a change of attire to gain their respect. She smiled kindly and held her head higher, though she felt unworthy of their reverence.

She sighed in relief when Salvi stopped before a large and noisy building containing small apartments filled to bursting with families. He asked after Lapa, but no one seemed to know her or weren't willing to expose her whereabouts. After several tries, Celeste asked Salvi if he was sure they had the right building.

"I'm certain, madam. This is where I brought her. She even pointed out where her husband worked in the fish market across the way. Maybe we can find her there."

Celeste nodded and followed him across the square to the market. She ignored the filth of the fish market, staining her skirts as they searched the stalls for Lapa. She received the same reaction as on the street. No one would speak to her or look her in the eyes. Instead of finding it humbling, she became increasingly frustrated. The day was wearing on, and she needed to return home before Luciano, but she refused to leave without finding Lapa.

Jacopo had walked quietly beside her, eating up the adulation that followed in her wake, but he also soon tired of the game. He nudged Celeste and said, "Loosen the strings of your coin purse. That'll open their mouths."

She agreed and was irritated with herself for not thinking of it sooner. Offering to pay for information delivered quick results. The wrinkled old wife of a fishmonger recognized Lapa's name and was eager to share what she knew.

"She's gone, Mistress. Her husband was taken by a fever many months ago. Lapa returned to her father's home."

Celeste gasped at the terrible news. She'd hoped that Lapa had returned to her husband and been blessed with a healthy baby of her own. Instead, she'd suffered another tragedy. The fishwife gave Salvi directions to Lapa's family and held out her hand for the coins. After paying her, she again followed the page through the crowded, winding streets. He found the dilapidated house and pounded on the door. A rail-thin man of about her papa's age came to the door, and his eyes widened at the sight of Salvi's livery.

"What do you want here, boy?"

Celeste stepped in front of Salvi and glared at the man. He dropped into a deep bow.

"Apologies, madam. I did not see you there. How can I be of service?"

Celeste suppressed a grin and said, "I am looking for Lapa. I've just heard of her husband's tragic death. Is she here?"

He straightened but kept his head bowed. "No, madam. My daughter came here ages ago looking for food and shelter, but I can't support another mouth to feed. I sent her out to make her own way. We haven't had a word from her in months."

Celeste grudgingly pressed a coin into his palm, wondering how he could have been so callous as to send his own daughter out into the street. Then, she remembered her own papa, who had done much worse. She gave him a quick nod and turned away, saddened by her failure to find her friend. She started for the gondola, but Salvi stopped her.

"Madam, please, let me look a little longer. Someone will know where to find her."

She struggled with how to answer. She wanted to keep searching but knew it would upset Luciano if she was late for dinner. Finally, she said, "Just a little longer, then we must go."

"Stay here with your brother. I can move faster through the crowds alone."

He disappeared into the throng before she could object. Jacopo found a bench for them to wait.

They sat in silence for several minutes, lost in their private thoughts, until Jacopo said, "Why are you doing this, sister? She's just one poor servant out of thousands."

"How can you ask that? Have you forgotten the pain of hunger and hopelessness? What would have happened to us without Portia's kindness or Luciano's? Would you deny someone else the same in their time of need? If so, I'm ashamed to call you brother."

Jacopo stared at his hands. "It was a thoughtless question," he mumbled. "I haven't forgotten. Being here has brought out unpleasant memories and made me more grateful for having escaped. But there are so many like we were. You can't save them all."

"True, as much as wish I could. Luciano often reminds me of the same thing, but today, I'm only here to save one. If Salvi doesn't find a clue to her whereabouts soon, we'll go home."

As she said it, Salvi burst through the crowd and waved for them to come with him.

As they walked, he said, "I've found her working as a serving wench in a public house. Please wait at a safe distance while I speak to her."

Jacopo found another bench within view of the public house. He waited for her to sit but remained standing. "I'm going with him," he said and started to cross the street.

Celeste grabbed his sleeve. "No, Jacopo, I don't trust you in that place after last night."

"I'm only going to convince her to come to speak to you. It might help if she knows I'm your brother."

He made a good point, but she still felt uneasy letting him, leaving her alone. "Fine, but please hurry. Portia was right to be concerned for my safety here."

"You were never afraid to walk alone on these streets but don't worry. No one would dare harm you dressed like that."

Another excellent point. She waved him off and sat with her head held high to wait. It didn't take long to see that Jacopo had been right. Most gave her a wide berth or bowed and hurried off. Each passing moment gave more proof of how much power she wielded.

She'd been reluctant to exploit her social status the way other patricians did, but the reaction of the throng taught her that her position could be used to lift others instead of pressing them into submission. Even if they failed to find Lapa, the day would have taught her a valuable lesson. She'd return home with much to ponder.

As she lifted her eyes to watch the stream of humanity flowing by, Jacopo and Salvi burst through the crowd, followed by a thin woman with all but her eyes covered by a shawl. It only took an instant for Celeste to recognize the eyes as Lapa's. She ran to her and embraced her arms, saddened to feel her ribs through the fabric of her gown. The crowd formed a circle around them and gawked.

"Not here," Lapa whispered. "I know a place where we can talk."

She took Celeste's hand and led her to a nearby alley. Once they were out of sight of curious eyes, Lapa lowered the shawl and stared at Celeste.

"What are you doing in Venice? How did you find me? You shouldn't have come. I'm ashamed for you to see how far I've fallen."

"I'm just Celeste, your friend, and you have no reason to be ashamed. I'm here to take you home with me. Get your belongings. We're going."

Lapa backed away in shock. "How can I go with you? Look what I've become. I'm just one rung above a woman of the streets. Leave here and forget me."

"Stop talking nonsense. I see nothing but a woman doing what is necessary to survive." Celeste took her hands and smiled reassuringly. "You know my history. This is something I understand, but we'll talk later. Now we really must go. Where are your things?"

"I have nothing but what you see."

"It's settled, then." She called to Salvi, standing guard with Jacopo at the end of the alley. "Please, lead us to the gondola."

Salvi bowed with a grin. "With pleasure, madam."

LUCIANO RACED up the stairs to the sala, eager to see Celeste. Fond memories of their lovemaking had distracted him all day, and he was hoping the coming night would bring more of the same. He changed for dinner, then went in search of his wife.

He entered the dining room to find Paolo, Francesca, and Portia, but no Celeste. He caught the furtive glance between the two women as they stood and curtsied. He sensed he would not enjoy what they had to tell him.

He greeted Paolo, then dropped into a chair and stroked his beard. "Dare I ask? Where is she?"

Francesca lowered herself into her chair, avoiding his eyes, but Portia stepped closer with her hands on her hips.

"We tried to stop Celeste, but she wouldn't listen. You know how headstrong she is. She's gone to the old quarter with Jacopo and

Rosselli's page to search for Lapa. They've been gone all afternoon without sending word."

Luciano let out a weary sigh. As magnificent as his dear wife was, she was also stubborn and impetuous. An afternoon with Sofia was one thing. Running off to the old quarter and putting herself in danger was another. He would have to put a stop to such behavior.

He slapped his palm on the table and said, "Then, send to the kitchen for them to serve my dinner. I'm starving."

Francesca raised her eyebrows. "You're not going after her? You never allowed Isabella to behave in such a way."

"Celeste has made her choice, and she's with Jacopo. That boy knows his way around the streets, and he wouldn't dare let anything happen to his sister." When Portia frowned at him, he glared back. "You should have tried harder to stop her. They'll return soon, and all will be well. Now, bring my dinner."

LUCIANO PACED THE SALA, growing more concerned by the moment. Two hours had passed since dinner, but Celeste and Jacopo still hadn't returned or sent word. His annoyance had turned to anger, then to concern. He was considering calling for his gondolier when Portia marched into the sala, followed by the ever-amused Paolo.

Portia stepped into his path and stomped her foot. "This is enough. It's time to go retrieve your wayward wife. She won't be hard to find in that part of the city, standing out like a jewel on the garbage heap."

Paolo chuckled. "Nice image. Luci, this happens when you give women too long a leash. Wives belong in sitting rooms with their stitching and children at their feet."

Portia turned and glared. "Hush, Paolo." His smile faded, and he slumped in his chair to pout.

For all Portia's bluster, Luciano read the fear in her eyes. "Calm yourself, Aunt. I was about to fetch Carlo."

There was a commotion in the foyer as he started for the stairs. He hesitated on the top step as Celeste climbed up to greet him as if nothing had happened. Jacopo stopped on the bottom step and bowed. Luciano accepted Celeste's kiss in silence, then waved for Jacopo to join them. He slowly ascended the stairs with his eyes lowered, then followed them into the sala.

"Forgive my tardiness, Maestro," he said.

"I don't blame you. Get a plate of food, then go to your room to pack for your journey. You leave at dawn."

"Yes, Maestro," he whispered as he hurried from the room.

Celeste smiled and shook her head. "For all his mischief, he was cooperative and helpful today. I will miss him. Thank you for not punishing him, Luciano. This was my doing."

Though Luciano was overwhelmed with relief at her safe return, her unapologetic attitude infuriated him. He'd expected her to beg his forgiveness, as Jacopo had done.

"Paolo, Portia, please leave us," he said, with a backhanded wave. "I wish a private word with my wife."

Portia left without meeting Celeste's eyes, no doubt aware of the scolding that was coming.

Paolo patted Luciano's shoulder as he passed. "Until tomorrow, friend."

Celeste laid her hand on Luciano's arm. "What's wrong? Is there bad news?"

Luciano turned away and dropped into a chair. "No, all is well, except that you seem oblivious to the trouble and embarrassment you've caused me today."

Celeste took the seat next to him. "What trouble, my love? Because I was late?"

"That and running off with no thought to how your actions affected the rest of the family or me. You are hours late, yet I get no word of apology. I was about to go searching for you."

"Don't speak to me as if I'm your disobedient child. I informed Aunt Portia and Francesca exactly where I was going. Jacopo and Salvi never left my side, and I'm familiar with the old city, having lived there, in case you've forgotten. I was never in danger."

He hadn't expected resistance, and his anger escalated. It was a sensation he hadn't felt since the days before Isabella's death.

"How was I to know? You never bothered to send word. You're no longer an impoverished servant who can come and go as she pleases. This behavior is unacceptable and irresponsible for a Duchessa, and I won't tolerate it. You're no better than Jacopo."

Celeste gasped, then squared her shoulders and raised her chin. "Is that what you truly believe, that my going to rescue a friend in dire circumstances is the same as Jacopo stealing from you and getting drunk in a public house?" She lowered into a deep curtsy. "Have no worry, my lord. I did nothing to shame you today, nor would I ever. I am not Isabella."

Her rebuke stung, but he held his ground. "Watch your tongue, wife, and yes, your actions were just as irresponsible. Can you not see that, or are you being deliberately ignorant?"

"Oh, yes, I understand. Will you send me to the quarries, too?"

He took a breath to keep from grabbing her shoulders and shaking sense into her. Instead, he changed tactics.

"This is not a joke, Celeste. Not sending word was reckless. The condottiere could have attacked or taken you, or worse. I was sick with worry."

She let out her breath and relaxed her shoulders. "You're right. I am sorry for frightening you. By the time we found Lapa and persuaded her to come with us, it was too late to send word."

Luciano sprang to his feet. "You brought Lapa here? Without asking my permission?"

"There was no time. I had to get her away from that terrible place. She wouldn't have survived much longer."

Luciano stood stone still with his fists clenched. "I won't allow her to stay. Carlo will take her back after getting your brothers on their way in the morning, and I forbid you to bring any more strays into my home. We're full to bursting with them."

Celeste faced him with tears pooling in her eyes. "You mean strays like me, or Jacopo, Marco, or Veronica? Was I any different from Lapa when I stumbled into your studio the night Papa beat me? Am I not also a stray?"

"You know full well, there's a world of difference between Lapa and you. She springs from the lowest class. You are the daughter of a Gabriele and have the potential to become a master painter."

"I see. And if I hadn't been a Gabriele or talented artist? Would you have thrown me out to die in the street?"

He turned and began to pace, unable to face her accusing eyes. Her questions had twisted his thoughts into a knot of confusion. He'd prided himself on being above the callous ways of other patricians, but had he been fooling himself? Was he no better than Sofia or his cousin Maria? No matter the answer, he knew in his bones Celeste had been wrong to bring Lapa into their home without asking him.

With his back to her, he said, "That question is no better than accusing me of comparing you to Isabella. How can you, after all I have done for you and your family?"

"And how can you compare me to Jacopo?" She tenderly placed her hand on his arm. "Please, look at me." He hesitated for a moment before turning to face her. "I am sorry, Luciano. I owe you my life. You are my life. And while that is all true, I insist you allow Lapa to stay. I couldn't live with myself if you sent her away and something terrible happened. She's skilled at sewing and embroidery. She can assist the seamstress with the mending when we return to Florence. Until then, she'll help Mona in the nursery with Mateo. Pay her with the earnings from the sale of my paintings if you wish."

"You're planning to take her to Florence? She's Venetian. This is the only life she's ever known."

"She's eager to leave Venice and her sad memories behind. Without me to protect her, she'd end up back in the gutters. Please, let me take her to Florence. You'll soon forget her among your throng of servants."

He would never forget. Lapa would be a constant reminder of Celeste's defiance and recklessness. A wave of weariness washed over him at once again, having to choose between doing what he knew was right and pleasing Celeste. If he held his ground, the hairline crack opening between them could become a chasm. If he relented, Celeste would never learn to respect societal boundaries or his authority over her.

In the end, his relief, and his desire to reignite her brilliant smile won the day. Indulging her was his greatest pleasure and his curse.

"Lapa may stay, but only with your word that you'll never run off like you did today and that you'll stop dragging in strays."

Celeste clapped and twirled in delight. "Thank you, my love. You have my solemn promise. No more strays." Putting her arms around his waist, she said, "Let me get Lapa settled, then I'll bring my dinner to our chambers."

Though he was glad to see her mood brighten, their argument had left him uneasy and remained unresolved. His fond memories of the previous night had vanished, and he wanted to be alone.

"I'm tired, Celeste. I'm going to have my man make up the spare room for tonight."

"No, you won't. I know I've upset you, but we are husband and wife. We must pull together in times of trouble, not drift apart." She gave him a sensual kiss. "We'll share our bed tonight and every night, for as long as we live."

He was powerless against her, and his heart softened. "Sometimes, the power you have over me is frightening."

"Good," she said as she moved toward the stairs. "I expect to find you waiting in our chamber when I return."

He gave a slight bow. "Eagerly, my love."

CELESTE LISTENED to the rhythmic rise and fall of Luciano's breathing as he slept, wishing she could do the same. Their lovemaking had lacked the passion of the previous nights, and their argument had been unsettling. As much as he had tried to mask it, Luciano's displeasure was obvious. She was sure he wanted her to admit she was wrong but as sad as she was to have disappointed and worried him, she didn't regret her actions. Ensuring Lapa's survival meant far more than giving Luciano his way.

She understood why he'd feared for her safety, but his forceful objection to her bringing Lapa home was baffling. Lapa's wages would be a trifle, and Luciano was generous with his other servants. Celeste had always viewed him as sensitive to the plight of the lower classes, but she wondered if his actions stemmed from nothing more than a desire to please her. If that were true, he was not the man she had come to love and revere.

Even more unsettling was him comparing her actions to Jacopo's. In her heart, she assumed he'd said it out of anger and concern, but she couldn't be sure. Saying she had embarrassed him had stung when she'd hoped he'd be proud of her. She wasn't the first noblewoman to venture into the lower city. Patrician women often went among the poor to offer alms or to hire servants and laborers. How was what she'd done any different?

Her adventure had succeeded without incident and without her bringing down the Vicente family or all of Venetian society. She had helped save a life, and she was grateful, but she'd seen a side of Luciano that left her questioning the man she thought she knew.

She pushed her thoughts aside as she closed her eyes to try for a few hours' sleep before it was time to bid her brothers farewell. All she could do was wait for dawn to learn what the new day would bring.

CHAPTER TWENTY-TWO

The weeks after Celeste's tearful goodbye to Marco and Jacopo settled into a peaceful routine. The rift with Luciano faded, and their relationship went on as if that night never happened. Celeste spent her days in the studio and evenings with Luciano entertaining Paolo and Portia or traveling to their many social engagements. She enjoyed being part of Venetian aristocracy but always took care to treat servants with respect and kindness.

The incident with Lapa had heightened her awareness of the delicate divide between the classes. Most patricians were oblivious to how precarious their positions in society were. The slightest shift in power or the smallest insult could strip them of all they held most dear. She wondered how long any of them would survive without legions of servants slaving after them.

Lapa adjusted to the nursery with ease, and Celeste was pleased to see her putting on weight and regaining the color in her cheeks. She shuddered to think what would have happened to her friend if she hadn't rescued her and insisted that Luciano allow her to stay. It was just one more proof of how precarious life was.

One morning, three weeks after her brothers had gone, Celeste slept late, and when she climbed out of bed to dress for the day, a wave of nausea washed over her. She fell back onto the pillows and called for Livia. Through her tears, she asked for bread and wine with herbs.

Livia beamed at her. "Why the tears, mistress? This is joyous news?"

Celeste answered her with a groan. "Is it? This condition has brought me nothing but pain and heartache."

"I predict this time will bring a strong and healthy son."

"Who needs your predictions? Just fetch the bread and wine, and not a word about this to anyone. Tell my aunt I overindulged last night, and I'll take breakfast in my chambers."

She fought back her tears as Livia skipped off to do her bidding. She found no joy in her condition, only dread, and the fear of dying in childbirth if the pregnancy survived still hung over her head. As desperately as she wanted to become a mother, the foreboding of what may lay ahead increased her anxiety.

Being with child didn't surprise her after the way she and Luciano had carried on the past few weeks. But she had hoped it wouldn't happen until they returned to Florence. Since her hope was dashed, all she could do was hide her condition from Luciano and the rest of the family for as long as possible. That would be no simple task if she were plagued by nausea as she'd been the three previous times.

One thing was sure, they'd have to leave for Florence as soon as possible. The longer they waited, the more unbearable the journey would be. Her first chore would be to convince Luciano that it was time to go without making him suspicious. It would not be a simple task.

～

CELESTE WAS PROPPED up on pillows, trying to keep her midday meal down, when Portia burst into her room. Celeste stifled a groan and pasted on a smile.

Portia stopped next to the bed with her hands on her hips. "What's this? Still in bed in the afternoon? What's wrong with you?"

Celeste swallowed and widened her smile. "Nothing, Aunt. I've just been working too hard and thought I'd rest today."

"Nonsense." Portia sat on the edge of the bed and gestured for Celeste to move over and make room. Celeste grunted and did as her aunt wanted. "I went to the studio to speak with you, and when I didn't find you there, I had to threaten to horsewhip Livia to get her to tell me you were here. Then, I find you lounging like a queen. You never rest when you work too hard."

"You're constantly scolding me for working too hard and not resting enough. When I take your advice, you chastise me. There's no pleasing you."

"In all the time we've been together, you've never listened to my advice. The only time you take to your bed is when..."

Her eyes widened, and a smile crept up her face. To confirm her notion, Celeste leaned over the bed and vomited into the wash bucket. Portia handed her a cloth to wipe her mouth and brushed the hair from her face.

"This is happy news, my dear. Congratulations!" She stopped and squinted at her. "You told Livia before me?"

Celeste shook her head. "She guessed, as you did. I don't want anyone else to know, not even Luciano. Please, Aunt, promise to keep my confidence."

Portia squeezed Celeste's hands. "You have my word, though I don't think it will be long before the rest figure it out if the past is any proof."

"That's my worry, too, but I've learned to manage it better. Old Tessa's bread and wine with herbs helps, as does eating small, frequent meals. I just overate the cheese and fish at lunch. I'll take more care now." She grew quiet and picked at a stray thread on her blanket. "I'm frightened at what will happen if the baby doesn't survive, and what will happen if it does."

"I understand, but since it's in God's hands, imagine the joy when this new little one arrives. It's what you and Luciano have longed for. God will bless you this time."

"God's will," she whispered, wondering what God had against her being a mother the other times. Why will this time be different? She pushed the thought away with a sigh, then looked at Portia. "Why did you go to speak with me in the studio? It must be important since you dislike my studio so much."

Portia's face brightened. "Possibly more joyous news. Paolo has declared his wish to marry me. He wants to ask Cesare for my hand, but I asked him to wait until I've spoken with you and Luciano. I trust your opinion."

Celeste hugged her. "How wonderful, Aunt, but why do you need my opinion? Don't you want to marry Paolo?"

Portia blushed and gave a shy grin. "Yes, but what I want is irrelevant. Is it unseemly at my age? I'm ancient. What will people think?"

"Forty is hardly ancient, but people will think you are two lovely and lonely people who desire companionship. But forget what others think. If you want to marry Paolo, marry him. I believe your bigger concern is convincing Cesare. He won't be so willing to part with your dowry after all these years."

"Paolo says he doesn't need or want the dowry."

"Regardless, it is your dowry, and Cesare has no right to it. Let's speak with Luciano. I'm sure he'll be glad to be present when they negotiate the contracts. Have you seen him?"

"I was hoping you'd say that. I haven't seen Luciano since breakfast."

"Oh yes, he said he had business that would keep him occupied all day. We'll speak to him at dinner. The matter will need to be resolved quickly as Luciano and I need to leave for Florence as soon as possible, given my condition."

Portia put her hands to her face. "I hadn't thought of that, but you must stay for the wedding. We want a simple, quiet affair."

Celeste laughed. "I hope you don't mean simple and quiet like my wedding."

"No, Paolo and I had all the pomp and circumstance with our first marriages. We only want immediate family and close friends and to wed as soon as possible."

Celeste took Portia's hands. "I just realized that your marrying Paolo would mean staying in Venice. How will I survive without my adopted mother and friend just two days' ride away? Venice is too far. I'll need you close when the baby comes, and Luciano will need to hire someone else to manage the Lucca estate. He'll never find someone that can do it as expertly as you."

"No need to worry, my dear. Paolo is going to move to Lucca. He'll miss his daughters and grandchildren, but we can always visit Venice a few times a year. He says he's ready for a change of scenery. He has traveled to Lucca and is enchanted with it."

"Then, I have no objections to your marriage. I'm certain Luciano will agree."

~

LUCIANO STROKED his beard as he stared at Cesare. "Be reasonable, man. Doesn't your sister deserve happiness? Why would you deny her?"

Paolo leaned forward and said, "I agree. I thought you'd be thrilled for me to take over her support. If your objection is the dowry, I don't want it, as I told you."

Cesare frowned. "I haven't been supporting her. Luciano has, and I must hand over the dowry. How would it look if I denied you? That's just not done. My objection isn't about her support or the dowry. It's propriety. She's too old for such foolishness. It's disgusting."

Paolo sprang to his feet. "You insult her and me with such language. There is no impropriety. You are a powerful man, Cesare, and we're old friends, but I have my allies. I won't be denied. Portia will be my wife."

Cesare stood and moved within inches of Paolo. "You dare threaten me in my own home? I don't fear your allies, and I can ruin you with a snap of my fingers."

Luciano stepped between them and pushed them apart. "I'm more powerful than both of you, and I have the Doge's ear, so sit down." The men stared at him for a moment before returning to their seats.

"No need to start a war over Portia. This is ridiculous, Cesare. Is it just a matter of wounded pride for some unknown reason? You know Paolo is a good man who will care for your sister. We'll have a small, private ceremony in your family chapel, then the happy couple will leave for Lucca. The prying eyes of Venice will never know nor care."

Cesare slumped in his chair and rubbed his forehead. "It is a matter of pride, but not in the way you think, Luciano. I spent Portia's dowry many years ago cleaning up Giovani's debts. When she kept refusing to remarry, I thought the need for her dowry had passed. When she stayed in Lucca, I put the matter from my mind, thinking her past the marriage age. Now here you are asking for her hand, Paolo, and I have no marriage funds to give. I'm ashamed to admit that after paying Alessandra's dowry, the coffers are bare."

Luciano put his hand on Cesare's shoulder. "Are you in financial difficulty? I thought your shipping empire was flourishing."

"It is, but the profit is tied up in ways that prevent me from using it for such a purpose. After Giovanni nearly ruined us, we put strict regulations in place. I wouldn't be able to transfer the funds without the other signatories' knowledge. I'd be humiliated."

"I said I don't care about the dowry if that's your only objection," Paolo said. "Denying me Portia's hand is pointless."

Luciano leaned against the fireplace mantle and crossed his arms. "There's a simple solution. I'll pay the dowry."

Cesare glared at him. "I won't take your charity."

"This is not charity. Need I remind you I'm your adopted son-in-law? I'm family, and Portia has been managing my Lucca estate. I can't pay her a wage, but I can give her earnings to you. The money would be yours to do with as you wish."

Cesare sat up straighter. "That's acceptable. Transfer the funds to me, then I will pass them to Paolo as part of the marriage contracts. That will deflect any questions or suspicions."

Paolo stood and extended his hand to Cesare. "Is it done then?"

Cesare ignored his hand and stood to hug him. "Done. Forgive me, old friend. You know I have a way of letting my pride get the best of me."

Paolo stepped away and bowed. "It's forgotten. A toast to celebrate."

Luciano patted their backs. "But just one. I'm sure your bride is eager for news."

Cesare laughed. "Odd. Portia, a bride after all this time. Who would have imagined?"

~

CELESTE SAT with Francesca and Portia in the sala, confronting the wave of nausea threatening to overwhelm her. She wanted to be alone in her studio, but Portia had asked her to wait for news from Paolo. Since she would have felt just as ill in the studio, she had agreed to stay with Portia.

Francesca was regaling them with her opinion of why a marriage between Portia and Paolo was absurd. Celeste closed her eyes and willed her to stop talking.

"Marriage is for the young, for producing an heir or uniting families," she said. "Since you're past the age of childbearing and Paolo certainly doesn't need your dowry, what plausible reason could he have for asking for your hand? I hope Cesare has the sense to put a stop to it. Don't you agree, Celeste?"

Celeste swallowed and took a breath to calm the volcano in her gut. She disagreed with Francesca but felt it unwise to answer.

When she didn't respond, Francesca said, "What's wrong with you? Are you listening, or is your head off in the clouds as usual?"

Portia came to her rescue and said, "Leave her be. Can you blame her for ignoring your incessant rambling? And you insult me by saying Paolo has no need for marriage. We have affection for each other, and both long for companionship. What's so wrong with that?"

Francesca ignored her question and walked to Celeste's chair. Celeste could feel her leaning over her, studying her face.

She opened her eyes a slit and mumbled, "What is it, Francesca?"

She straightened and put her hand to her mouth. "You're with child. Why didn't you tell us?"

"I knew," Portia said gleefully.

Celeste leaned forward and wrapped her arms around her abdomen. "Portia guessed, as you did. I was trying to conceal the news until I was sure the baby would survive, but it's getting too hard to keep my secret. I'm in absolute agony, and I'm afraid. I couldn't survive it if I lost this baby. I can't go through that again." She turned to Livia, who was sitting quietly near the fire. "Please, fetch my bucket."

Francesca placed her hand on Celeste's shoulder as Livia ran off to do her bidding.

"Stop fretting. This baby will be born healthy and resilient, like his mother."

She shook her head. "You can't know. None of you can. This pregnancy is starting just like the others. How can you be sure it will end differently?"

"Poor child. I understand your fears but trust me, you and the child are going to be fine. You don't have to suffer this alone. This news will thrill Luciano. You should tell him immediately."

Livia returned and handed her the bucket, which she used to deposit her meal. Livia gave her a cloth to wipe her mouth, then left to dump the bucket.

"I'll tell him tonight when we're alone, but this is a time to celebrate Portia." She covered Francesca's hand with her own. "Paolo has every right to marry her. Doesn't she deserve happiness after what she's suffered?"

When Francesca returned to her chair with a huff, Portia said, "You act as if we're the first couple our age to marry, but it happens every day."

"For men, but not women. You must admit, my friend, that men rarely seek women past their prime like us unless they need a title or wealth."

Portia fluffed the lace at her collar. "Speak for yourself. I'm not past my prime. You're just jealous that Paolo chose me and not you."

"Nonsense. What would I want with that old fool?"

Celeste giggled. Her nausea had subsided, and her head was

clearing. It cheered her to hear their playful banter. Francesca would miss Portia when she left for Lucca.

To Celeste, Francesca said, "If Cesare takes leave of his senses and approves this match, will you be able to stay for the wedding? You must return to Florence soon due to your delicate condition."

Before she could answer, the men came in, making a cheerful commotion in the front hall.

"Sounds like good news," Celeste said and laughed when she saw Portia's face, looking like a nervous young maiden.

Paolo burst into the sala, followed by Luciano and Cesare. When the women stood and curtsied, Paolo grabbed Portia around the waist and swung her. Portia gave his shoulder a playful slap and told him to put her down.

Luciano laughed. "Your bride is ordering you about already."

"Bride?" Portia said and turned her wide eyes on Cesare. "You approved?"

Cesare puffed out his chest. "I signed the contracts, though what you want with this oaf, I'll never know."

Portia kissed his cheeks. "Thank you, brother. You've made me very happy."

After hugs of congratulations, Luciano said, "You must stay to dine and celebrate. Celeste, order us up a feast!"

He winked at her but grew serious when he saw her pale face. She lowered her head and rushed off to find the housekeeper, but Luciano followed her out. He caught her arm in the hallway and spun her to face him.

"Are you ill? Your face is as white as your collar."

"I'm just excited for Portia. It's wonderful news."

He gently cupped her chin in his hand. "Tell me the truth, Celeste."

"Not here. Let me speak with the housekeeper. Wait for me in our chambers."

Francesca joined them in the hallway. "I'll arrange for dinner."

Celeste nodded and took his hand to lead him up the stairs to their rooms. She lowered herself onto the bed and patted the blankets for him to join her. He sat close to her, and she rested her head on his shoulder.

"I'm sure you've guessed that I'm going to have a baby. I planned to tell you tonight."

"I recognized that pallor. This is wonderful news. Why do you sound like you're announcing a funeral?"

She sat up and looked into his eyes. "You must know why. I'm so frightened, Luciano."

"You need not fear. This child will survive, and we'll be blessed with a beautiful son."

The more they all declared her child would be born healthy, the more cursed she felt.

"Please don't say that. You're tempting fate." She stood and stepped in front of the fire with her back to him. "If I lose this baby, there won't be another. Do you understand what I'm saying?"

He came to her and wrapped his arms around her waist. "Let's just get this little one here, then we'll decide the future. I love you, Celeste, and I'll do whatever I must to keep you safe."

She leaned back into him, savoring his warmth and strength. "Thank you, my love. I don't deserve you."

He kissed the top of her head. "You deserve infinitely more. Let's go celebrate with Portia and Paolo. We'll make our announcement of the blessed event after the wedding."

She was lost in her thoughts as they strolled to the sala. Life would be easier without having to hide her secret from Luciano, but his assurances had done nothing to calm her fears. All she could do was go on as before and wait for the inevitable. She would have Portia's wedding preparations to distract her, but for the first time since they arrived in Venice, all she wanted was to go home.

PORTIA AND PAOLO'S wedding would be just an intimate affair with only a fraction of Gabrieles attendance. Portia had insisted on an elaborate violet gown for the occasion, and as Celeste helped lace the ribbons, she remembered the dress Portia had worn when she came to whisk her off to Maria Foscari's palazzo. Celeste had been little more than a child who expected nothing more for her future than the life of a servant. She couldn't have envisioned the life she was living.

She looked fondly at Portia as she admired herself in the mirror. She had been a stranger to Celeste on that fateful day but had since become a second mother to her. Celeste placed her hand on her stomach and smiled. God willing, she'd soon be a mother herself. She smiled, and for the first time, she looked to the event with eager anticipation.

"That smile is something I haven't seen for some time," Portia said, "but I don't believe it was for me."

"It was for you and for me. I was reminiscing about the day you came to my rescue so long ago. It's hard to believe we're the same women."

Portia hugged her before taking her hand and leading her to a pair of chairs near the fire. Once they were seated, she said, "We're not the same, which is as it should be. We've been greatly blessed. I don't tell you enough what a treasured daughter you've become to me."

Celeste reached over and patted her hand. "And you, a loving mother to me. I'm thrilled you'll be living in Lucca. I don't know what I would have done without you, especially when the baby comes."

Portia studied her face for a moment. "So now you believe this little one might, in fact, arrive?"

Celeste blushed and grinned at her. "I do. There has been a subtle change I can't explain. I have more strength. The nausea has subsided, and I woke hungry for breakfast this morning."

"This is welcome news. Feeling well will help on the journey back to Florence. Are you ready to go?"

"Livia has the trunks packed. We depart first thing tomorrow, but this day isn't about me. You are the bride."

"Being called a bride seems silly for such an old woman, but I am eager to start my life with Paolo. He has an infectious humor and a cheerful manner. He'll keep me young."

Celeste stood and helped Portia out of the chair. "I couldn't be happier for you, Mamma. Let's get you to your waiting groom before he changes his mind."

As the carriage bumped along, Celeste watched Venice receding in the distance. She would miss her beloved city but was content to be heading for the place she now called home. The wedding ceremony had been touching, and she smiled at the memory of Portia's glowing face.

Portia and Paolo would follow a few days behind to have time to tie up his business affairs and bid farewell to his family. They planned to travel to Florence as the time for the baby's arrival drew closer. Celeste would miss her until then, but she would have much to keep her busy as she worked on finishing her latest commission before the birth.

Luciano's Venice studio held a special place in her heart, but she longed to return to her magnificent Florence studio with its gleaming marble and perfect lighting. She'd left home under a black cloud but was returning with bright hope. The trip to Venice has been a healing balm, and she was ready to bask in the sunlight once more.

CHAPTER TWENTY-THREE

*A*fter washing off the dust of their journey, Luciano stretched out on the bed to rest before dinner.

Celeste came in and leaned down to kiss him. "You look content," she said.

"I'm glad to be back in Florence. Venice is no longer my home, and the endless pomp and revelry there were becoming tiresome. Florence is in my blood. I belong here."

Celeste sat next to him on the edge of the bed. "I never thought I'd be happy to leave Venice, but I missed Florence. I can't wait to return to my studio and feel the brush in my hand."

Luciano frowned. He was pleased Celeste's strength had returned, but her returning to the studio worried him. He feared her obsession with painting would jeopardize the baby's health.

He propped up on his elbow and said, "Is it wise to continue painting? That hasn't gone well during your past pregnancies."

She patted his cheek. "No need to worry, my love. I promise to be sensible. I have a healthy appetite, and I haven't suffered from nausea since before Portia's wedding. I have time to finish the altarpiece for Signore Renzo's chapel long before the baby comes."

"Give me your word that you'll listen if I say you're working too hard and need to stop."

"I promise to behave. I don't wish to endanger our child any more than you do." She stood and stretched. "I must wash and dress for dinner."

Luciano watched her with a smile as she walked across the room to call for Livia. He was much relieved that her strength and good humor had returned and wondered if he dared hope to become a father after so many disappointments. He tucked his hands under his head, savoring the rare moment of peace. God knew they came seldom enough.

Just as he closed his eyes, the page came in, and cleared his throat. He opened one eye and said, "What do you want, Berto?"

Berto bowed and said, "Messer Stefano wishes to speak with you, sir. He's waiting in the sala."

"I just got home. Can't this wait until morning?"

"The boy doesn't know, Luciano," Celeste said. "It must be important for him to bother you so soon after your arrival. Berto, please tell Stefano that your master will join him in a moment."

When Berto rushed out, Luciano grunted and got to his feet. "You'd better come with me, Celeste. This might concern you, too."

Luciano's contentment faded with each step toward the sala. Stefano rarely came to the house and never in the evening, especially when Luciano had just returned from a long journey. He feared Jacopo had gotten into trouble, although if that were the case, Marco would be the messenger, not Stefano.

Stefano bowed and offered Luciano his hand as they entered the sala. They gripped forearms, and Luciano patted him on the back.

"It's good to see you, Stefano. Thank you for running the workshop so well in my absence." He guided Celeste to a chair and took the one next to her. "Are you only here to welcome me home? You could have done that in the morning."

Stefano gave Celeste a quick glance, then said, "I am glad to see you back safely, Maestro, but I have a serious matter to discuss with you."

Luciano rubbed his forehead. "Is it Jacopo?"

Stefano eyed him in confusion. "No, sir. Jacopo has been a model apprentice since he returned. This concerns me."

Luciano gestured for Stefano to sit. "Why do I have the feeling I won't want to hear your news?"

Stefano avoided Luciano's eyes as he lowered himself into the chair and hesitated before saying, "I'm leaving for Venice once Signora Gabriele completes her latest commission."

Luciano let out his breath and rubbed his temples. He'd known this day would come but hoped it would be years in the future. Losing Stefano meant not only that he'd have to replace him in the workshop but that he'd also have to find someone he trusted to pose as the painter of Celeste's works. Stefano's moving to Venice would help deflect suspicion and questions, but it left Luciano in a difficult position.

"How can I convince you to stay? If it's a higher percentage of the commissions you need, we can negotiate that."

"You are generous as always, Maestro, but this isn't about the money. I no longer wish to take part in our arrangement. If we were discovered, it would destroy my future as an artist. The risk is too great, and it's time I return home to build my own career." He turned to Celeste and said, "Forgive me, madam, but I want to sell my own paintings, not take credit for yours."

"Do not apologize," Celeste said. "Trust me, I understand."

Luciano didn't mistake the weight of the meaning behind her words. "I appreciate your willingness to stay until Signore Renzo's commission is completed. It will give me time to figure out who will replace you."

Celeste stood, and both men joined her. "Thank you for putting your reputation at stake on my behalf for so long. We're deeply indebted to you."

Stefano bowed. "It has been my honor. I only wish I possessed half your talent."

"I'll see you in the workshop early tomorrow," Luciano said and dismissed Stefano with a wave. As he turned, Luciano heard a sound in the hallway outside the sala. He ran to see what it was, but the hallway was empty.

"What are you doing?" Celeste asked as he strode back in, shaking his head.

"You didn't hear a noise just now?"

"No, but it was probably just a servant. Stefano, please ask Berto to make a quick search of the area, just in case."

"I'll do it myself," he said and hurried out.

Celeste folded her arms and turned to face Luciano. "This is just your guilt, making you suspicious."

Luciano ran a hand through his hair. "I feel no guilt. I'm certain I heard something in the hallway."

"Then, Stefano will find him." He grabbed her hand without a word and hurried her toward their chambers. "Where are you taking me?" she asked between breaths.

He shooed Livia and Filippo out. "I want to talk about Stefano's departure away from curious ears." Celeste nodded and began unlacing her gown to change into the dress Livia had laid out, but Luciano caught her hand to stop her. "That can wait. We must deal with this disaster first."

Celeste let go of the laces and sat on the edge of the bed. "Stefano leaving is a concern but hardly a disaster. There's a simple solution staring us in the face."

Luciano eyed her for a moment, then said, "I've told you, Celeste, applying for entrance into the Guild is out of the question."

"Why are you so unwilling to even consider it? Times are changing. The guilds admit women on rare occasions now, and we wouldn't have to submit my application until I return to painting after the baby comes."

"The guilds only admit women for spiritual or charity work. Florence will never accept a female painter."

She stood and stepped closer to him. "What do you mean never? Are you saying you have no intention of ever presenting me as an artist or allowing me to take credit for my work?"

He put his hands on her shoulders. "Calm down, Celeste. I misspoke. I should have said we must wait until the proper time. With tensions high between Rome and Lorenzo de' Medici, we have to tread carefully. He has his eye on all aspects of Florence."

"Lorenzo is a powerful man, but he is also the greatest supporter of the arts the world has ever known. If you can gain his favor, he may agree to be my patron once he sees my paintings."

"That doesn't mean he would look favorably on a female painter. Be patient a while longer. I'll know when the time is right."

He reached to pull her into his arms, but she backed away and started unlacing her gown with an angry tug.

"You always have excuses. When I consented to become your protégé, you told me your dream was to transform me into the greatest painter of our day. I wonder if you ever intended to allow me to be an artist in my own right, or has this all been about bringing you glory?"

"How dare you accuse me after all I've done for you? I've supported and tolerated your brothers and sisters, despite my better judgment. I rescued you from the gutter and made you a Duchessa, who has yet to give me an heir, for the love of God. Show your gratitude for once and know your place."

She backed away in shock at his words. He wished on his life for the power to unspeak them.

"Am I nothing more than a tool to fill your coffers with coins and your nursery with babies?"

It was a question he'd asked himself more than once, but the answer was always an emphatic no. While Celeste's innate talent as an artist had drawn him to her, he could never deny the depth of his love for her.

"I beg you, please forgive me, my love. That was cruel and untrue. I love you with my whole soul and have from the moment I noticed you on your bench outside my studio. If you never again lift a brush, if you never give me a son, I will continue to love you to my dying breath."

She trembled as she stood, ignoring the tears running down her cheeks. He hadn't meant to hurt her but had only spoken out of fear and frustration.

"We have time to resolve the problem of how to sell my paintings," she whispered. "Tell Livia I'll take dinner in the sitting room. Have Filippo make up the guest room for you tonight. I'll sleep alone."

"No, Celeste. You told me in Venice that we would share a bed for the rest of our lives, and so we shall. I deserve your anger. What I said was hateful, but you know it is not true. I love you, and I will sleep by your side tonight and every night."

Celeste's lip quivered before she collapsed onto the bed, sobbing. Luciano sat next to her, stroking her hair, and whispering comforting words while she had her cry. His evening had gone from peace and contentment to sadness, regret, and uncertainty. Celeste was the most precious thing in his life, and he had wounded her. Beyond knowing if she would ever forgive him, he wondered how he could ever forgive himself.

CELESTE YAWNED as she waited for Livia to bring her breakfast. Luciano snored beside her after they had talked long into the night. He had refused to sleep until he'd convinced her he'd lashed out from fatigue and frustration at Stefano's news. The incident had still left her feeling uneasy as she had in Venice the morning after arguing over Lapa.

Though she'd wrung a promise from Luciano that he would never speak to her in anger again, she wondered if he was capable of living up to his word. He was an even-tempered man, but she'd seen his rare flashes of temper, usually directed at his apprentices, and feared they might become more frequent as he aged. She hoped the painful consequence of his actions that night had imprinted on his mind, and he wouldn't soon forget.

He stirred and looked up at her with bloodshot eyes. "Glad to find you're still in my bed," he said in a raspy whisper. "I had a nightmare that you were floating away from me into a mist. The faster I ran to catch you, the further you drifted out of reach."

"I'm not going anywhere, my love. I could never leave my most excellent studio." When he gave her a playful slap, she said, "You brought the nightmare on yourself by being so wretched to me, then drinking too much wine with your heavy dinner."

"True. I deserve this." He sat up and leaned against the headboard. "What I don't deserve is your forgiveness. Allow me to tell you again how sorry I am."

"I appreciate that, but let's put this behind us. We have other matters of concern to discuss."

He rubbed his face with a cloth Filippo had left, then said, "Such as how to sell your paintings? Is it wise to bring up such a sensitive topic?"

She ignored his question. "We have another option."

"Marco?"

"Yes, Marco. His style is comparable to mine, even if not as brilliant, if I may say so. He's already aware of the arrangement we had with Stefano. We can trust him to keep our confidence."

"I agree, but I'm afraid he'll object on moral grounds. He's a fine and pious man of strong character. I'd loathe having to force him."

"I despise this arrangement as much as he does, but apparently it's the only recourse if I want to continue sharing my work with the world."

"Yes, for now, it is."

"Marco wouldn't dare refuse. He's too indebted to you."

"Why do I suddenly feel like a heartless tyrant?"

"If I'm a willing participant in this, what does that make me?"

"Not so willing last night if I recall. I'm forcing you into this arrangement as much as Marco. Trust me, my love. If there were another way, I would take it."

Livia came in with her tray, so she left the matter there. Despite what Luciano said, he wasn't forcing her to participate. She was no more ready to give up painting than he was to let her. She would just have to bide her time until Florence was prepared to accept her for who she was.

～

AFTER SUBMITTING herself to an examination by the physician, Livia helped her dress for the second time that morning. As she was about to hurry to the studio, the housekeeper came in to announce that Luciano's sisters were waiting in the sala.

"This day just keeps getting better," she whispered as she pasted on a smile and headed off to greet them. Elisabetta and Angelica curtsied as she entered, then came forward to kiss her cheeks.

"Welcome home," Elisabetta said, doing her best to look pleased to see Celeste. "Congratulations on your joyous news. Luciano just told us. This time will bring a healthy son."

Celeste smiled and instinctively placed her hand on her stomach. "Thank you, Elisabetta. I hope God wills it. I'm feeling much better this time."

Angelica hugged her and flashed a genuine smile. "How I've missed you," she said, as she led Celeste to a chair.

Though Elisabetta was arrogant and judgmental, Angelica was sweet and kind and reminded Celeste of her mother. She had treated Celeste as a sister and friend from the beginning, for which she was grateful.

"I've missed all of you as well. It's good to be home. How is Diana?"

Elisabetta frowned. Though she loved her youngest sister, she told anyone who would listen that she disapproved of her marriage to their cousin, Umberto Donato. She didn't deem him elevated enough for a Vicente bride. She had urged Luciano to prevent the union, but he ignored her. He'd confided in Celeste that he was glad of the match because it pleased Diana, and Umberto had requested such a small dowry.

"Diana is in her confinement and sends her greetings," Angelica said.

"That's wonderful news. I'll visit as soon as I'm settled."

Veronica came in and curtsied to her sisters-in-law. Celeste caught the glance that passed between the women and wondered what was behind it. Veronica took the chair on the other side of Celeste and rested her hands on the arms in a way that reminded her of Maria Foscari. Veronica was dressed in an azure gown. It was striking against the Gabriele olive skin and brown eyes Celeste had always envied. It was still a daily surprise to see what a beauty her sister had become. If only she had the temperament to match, she thought.

"And how are my nephews and niece?" Celeste asked.

Elisabetta beamed at the question. Nothing pleased her more than rambling on about her three children. She didn't accept Mateo as Luciano's rightful heir, and since Luciano had yet to produce a son, Elisabetta expected her son, Giuliano, to be the heir. Celeste was determined to do all in her power to prevent that. She touched her stomach again and prayed for God to give her a son.

They visited for another hour before Celeste feigned a yawn and stood to signal that it was time for them to go. Veronica bid them goodbye and hurried off to her room.

As Celeste walked them to the door, Elisabetta stopped her and said, "I'm glad your sister left us time to speak privately. There was an incident while you were away. I want you to hear of it from family instead of from town gossip."

Angelica put a hand on her arm. "No one is gossiping, sister."

Celeste looked at her in confusion. "An incident with Veronica? How is that possible? She never leaves the palazzo."

"Three weeks ago, we invited your sister to join us in handing out food to the poor, believing it good for her to see us performing acts of charity. When we were in the piazza near San Lorenzo's, she slipped away from us, and we found her shamelessly conversing with Octavio Barbaro's sons in the market. It was disgraceful, but by the grace of God, we found her and whisked her home before more damage was done."

Though Celeste felt Elisabetta was overreacting, Veronica's behavior was inexcusable.

"My apologies for having to suffer through that," she said, in thinly veiled sarcasm. "I'll speak with my sister and help her understand why her actions were inappropriate."

"I made it perfectly clear to her on the ride home what she had done wrong, but she hardly seemed to listen. That girl will end up wild if you don't correct her ways. I've informed my brother of the shameful incident."

Celeste gave a silent groan. "You told Luciano without coming to me first?"

"I felt it my duty. Veronica is at a marriageable age. It's time my brother finds a husband for her. He becomes distracted with his workshop and rarely considers such matters. If his search for a husband fails, I recommend the convent. Veronica should be there now, learning from the nuns. Clearly, her nanny and others have not taught her what is acceptable."

Celeste ignored the insult. It wouldn't help to lose her temper with Elisabetta, but under no circumstance would she allow Luciano to send Veronica to the convent.

She swallowed her annoyance and did her best to smile. "You are right that it's time to find Veronica a husband. I'll discuss it with Luciano tonight." She linked her arm in Angelica's and nudged her toward the door. "Thank you for bringing this to my attention and for being so kind as to visit and welcome me home. We'll have you to dinner as soon as we're settled."

It was a relief when Elisabetta took the hint and followed to the door. She kissed their cheeks and sighed in relief when the door closed behind them. She and Luciano had enough trouble without adding Veronica to the mix. She should have gone to speak with Veronica immediately, but the studio beckoned. She made a mental note to have a word with her before dinner and hurried off to the sanctuary of her studio.

~

AFTER WHAT SEEMED like mere minutes, Livia came to the studio and cleared her throat to get Celeste's attention.

Without turning away from her easel, she said, "What is it now, Livia?"

"The master sent me to fetch you for dinner. He and your sister have been waiting for nearly half an hour."

"Dinner already?"

She put her brush down and glanced toward the window in time to see the sun slip below the horizon. The studio torches were burning. She hadn't even noticed anyone come in to light them. She pulled off her smock and wiped her hands on it.

"Tell them I'm on my way, then come help me dress. From now on, alert me earlier when it's time to change for dinner. I promised Luciano I won't work too hard. I need you to help me keep that promise."

"Yes, madam," she said and rolled her eyes as they hurried out of the studio.

Celeste changed and made it to the dining room in record time. Luciano gave her half a grin, but his displeasure was obvious. She kissed his cheek and made her apologies.

As she took her seat, she said, "You have my word. This won't happen again. Good evening, Veronica." Her sister gave a slight nod but remained silent and lowered her eyes. Her look reminded Celeste that she had planned to speak with her before dinner and feared Luciano had beaten her to it.

She took a spoonful of soup and said, "Your sisters mentioned that they spoke with you this morning."

"Yes, Veronica and I were just discussing what they had to tell me. I imagine they informed you as well?"

"They did. I was planning to speak with my sister after dinner."

Luciano's smile faded. "No need. I've taken care of that for you."

"I didn't see it as urgent since the incident happened three weeks ago, Luciano. Veronica, what happened when you went to San Lorenzo's with Elisabetta and Angelica?"

Veronica sat straighter and looked Celeste in the eye. "You're the first to ask for my version of the story. I did nothing wrong. After we left San Lorenzo's, I walked toward the market. Two boys stopped me and asked me who I was, so I told them. They pointed out their father, who was watching nearby. Then Elisabetta ran up and dragged me away moments later. Nothing else happened."

Elisabetta had overreacted, but Veronica did need to learn she couldn't wander the streets alone.

"I know what you did seems innocent enough, but it was wrong to wander off with no chaperone. I understand that you often did that in Venice when you were young, but you're a young woman of social standing now, and you were supposed to be distributing food to the poor. Have you forgotten what it is to be hungry?"

Veronica looked away to avoid Celeste's eyes. "No, sister, I haven't forgotten, but I was only curious. I've learned my lesson, and I'm sorry."

"I'm glad to hear that," Luciano said and turned to Celeste. "I was just explaining to Veronica that it's time she prepares for marriage. Elisabetta suggested I send her to the convent school, but I don't think such a drastic step is necessary, and I know your feelings against it. I'm going to look for a tutor and companion for her instead. She's outgrown the nanny."

Veronica's eyes brightened. "Will she teach me to dance?"

Celeste laughed. "Among other more important things like sewing, keeping the household accounts, and managing the servants. I'll take a more active role in her training, as well, Luciano. I've neglected her for too long."

"Good, as long as it doesn't interfere with your work. Portia can help, too, when she comes for the birth. She did an excellent job with your education."

Veronica frowned. "Aunt Portia's still angry at me for refusing to work in the kitchens with Masina."

"I'm sure she's forgiven you by now, but I'll ask her not to be too hard on you. Would you like it if we hire a dancing tutor? If you work hard and behave yourself, we'll hold a ball when you're ready."

Veronica jumped up and threw her arms around Celeste's neck. "A ball? Thank you. I promise to be an obedient and attentive student." She let go of Celeste and twirled in delight.

Luciano gave a backhanded wave to dismiss her. "Leave us now so I can speak to your sister alone."

Veronica kissed his cheeks on her way out, which she had never done before. Luciano blushed and cleared his throat. "You Gabriele girls will be the death of me. Why do I feel we've just rewarded her for misbehaving?"

"What she did was an innocent mistake. She still knows so little about the world."

"She's been with us for almost two years. Hasn't she learned anything?"

"She's hardly left the palazzo during that time. Her childhood has been a difficult one through no fault of hers. She's a bright girl. With the right training, she'll become a young woman who will make you proud."

"She's fortunate that Cesare agreed to help with her support, or I would have had no choice but to send her to the convent. I hope she appreciates that."

"I'll make sure she does." She carried her plate to the sideboard and piled it with food, relieved that her appetite had returned. "What are her chances for a husband?"

"I have prospects in mind. Her dowry won't fetch a Duca like her sister, but she'll have a comfortable life." He chewed a bite of fish, then said, "Speaking of your siblings, I spoke with Marco today."

Celeste froze with her knife stabbing a piece of chicken. "So soon? I thought you would wait until I was ready to return to painting after having the baby. That gives us more than a year."

"I must train him to take Stefano's place in the workshop before he goes. I thought it was best to be honest with him about our other expectations."

She dropped her knife and stared at him. "How did he take it?"

"Much as we thought he would. I feared he was going to be sick. He's frightened, Celeste but says he'll cooperate. He was bold enough to ask why we don't present you to the Guild. I explained why that's not possible."

She disagreed that it was impossible but held her tongue to avoid another argument. She hoped that by the time she was ready to show her paintings, the climate would be more favorable for her to apply to the Guilds.

"I'll speak to Marco and calm his fears. We've passed my work off as Stefano's without suspicion all this time. It will be the same with Marco."

"He said he'll visit your studio tomorrow."

"Good, then we can put this matter to rest."

He watched her eat for a moment and smiled when she looked up at him. "You look well tonight. There's color in your cheeks."

"Surprising after so little sleep last night. I'm going to climb into bed as soon as I finish my meal."

"I'll join you. It's been a trying few days."

"It can only get better from here, God willing."

A GOOD NIGHT'S sleep and hearty breakfast had done wonders for Celeste. She'd made it to the studio early and had a pleasant morning of work. She had just finished cleaning her brushes to go for lunch when Marco tapped on her door. She waved him in and opened her arms for a hug.

"It's wonderful to see you, brother. I've missed you these past months."

Marco stepped away and leaned against the worktable. "Good to see you, too. It hasn't been the same here without you and Luciano. Congratulations on your news."

"Thank you. I have hope that all will go well this time." She stepped aside and showed him her latest project. It was of the Virgin and Child seated on a green hillside based on one of Celeste's favorite vistas in Lucca. "What do you think?"

He studied the painting for several moments. Without turning, he said, "It's awe-inspiring. You truly are one of the most talented painters of our time. I'll never have a fraction of your talent."

His praise touched her. Sharing her love of art with Marco was a blessing. Jacopo had a budding talent, but not the passion they did.

"Luciano told me he talked to you," she said softly.

She saw Marco's muscles stiffen before he slowly turned to face her. "I don't like this, sister, but how can I refuse Luciano? I wasn't able to sleep last night thinking about it. Can't you persuade him to change his mind and speak to the Guild?"

"I tried, and we had a terrible argument. For now, this is the only way to continue selling my paintings."

He began to pace, chewing his thumb as he used to when he was a child. She was reminded of how young he was and hated being the source of his anxiety.

"This scheme is dangerous and could destroy all of our careers or worse. Luciano is a powerful man, and you have his protection, but what of me? They'll throw me to the lions."

"Luciano would never let that happen, but don't give up hope. It will be more than a year before I'll have another painting ready to sell. We must pray that conditions become more favorable by then. Who knows what the future holds?"

"I hold out little hope that Luciano will change his mind. He's determined to go forward with this."

"I'm sorry to force you into this deception, but there is no other choice."

He turned to face her. "You're wrong, sister. There is another choice."

"You mean I stop painting until I can apply to the Guild?" He gave a slight nod. "You would ask that of me? To abandon my work and dreams?"

"I'd never ask but hoped you'd do it on your own."

She prayed for the strength to do that for her dear brother. She could rationalize that her art brought light and beauty to the world but forcing him to lie was just an act of selfishness. Was she prepared to destroy those she loved in pursuit of her own ambitions? Was the sacrifice too great?

"I'll consider what you've said, but we don't have to decide now. I appreciate your willingness to help me. I recognize what your sacrifice means."

Marco started to nod but froze and stared at something behind her. She turned to look in the same direction but saw nothing there. "What is it, Marco?"

Instead of answering, he rushed out of the studio and searched the hallway before coming back to join her.

"I saw a flash of color in the doorway and was afraid someone was listening. I must have imagined it."

She remembered Luciano's suspicions the night they spoke with Stefano and wondered if someone had been eavesdropping. There was only one person she could think of who would dare do such a thing in Luciano's house.

"Where's Jacopo?"

"Jacopo? Why?"

"Just answer me."

He looked at her in confusion. "Luciano sent him to the apothecary for supplies. It's too soon for him to have returned. Do you suspect him of spying on us?"

She lowered herself into a chair and rubbed her temples. "I'm letting my imagination get the best of me. Luciano heard sounds when Stefano told us he was leaving but didn't find anyone. I'm sure it's nothing. Speaking of Jacopo, has he given you any trouble?"

"None. He's been cooperative and hardworking. Luciano's threat of sending him to the quarries must have worked. He told Jacopo today that he's forgiven and doesn't have to go away, but he still expects him to work off the debt. I've never seen anyone more humble or relieved."

"I share his relief. Maybe there's hope for Jacopo yet. I was just going for lunch. Will you join me?"

He shook his head. "I have workshop business to attend to. I'll walk you down and join you later for dinner."

She stood and linked her arm in his. When they reached the dining room, he kissed her cheek and left without a word. She watched him go, knowing the day would soon come when she'd have to choose between loyalty to family and pursuing her dreams. She prayed for strength to follow her conscience and make the right choice.

CHAPTER TWENTY-FOUR

SIX MONTHS LATER

Celeste groaned in the darkness as the baby performed its nightly acrobatics, robbing her of sleep. Not wanting to disturb Luciano, she heaved herself off the bed and lumbered to her small sitting room. She pulled her shawl tighter as she walked the freezing hallway. It was the coldest January she could remember, but as she passed a window looking out to her favorite part of the garden, she smiled in delight to see a light snow falling. She was glad she'd asked Livia to have the houseboys keep the sitting room fires burning during the night.

Snowstorms were rare in Florence. She hoped it wouldn't hinder Portia and Paolo on their journey. They were due to arrive any day, and Celeste didn't want them to be late if the baby made an early appearance. Tessa estimated that it would arrive within four weeks. Celeste was so miserable that she prayed Tessa's calculations were wrong, and the baby would come once Portia arrived. The nursery was prepared. All that remained was to wait, but patience had never been her strongest virtue.

She had set aside her brushes three weeks earlier after completing Signore Renzo's painting, and the days now dragged by with little to occupy her mind. Luciano had begged her to rest in bed, but she had too much energy to idle away her days and had insisted on continuing her daily walks despite the cold weather. The fresh air rejuvenated her and gave her an hour of distraction. Finding other ways to keep busy wasn't as easy.

The empty hours did allow her to spend more time with Veronica. Her education was coming along well, and her sister had blossomed into a graceful and accomplished young woman. Celeste smiled at the memory of practicing dance steps with her after dinner the previous night under Luciano's disapproving eye, though even he had to laugh at seeing her maneuver her enormous belly around the sala.

Celeste carefully lowered herself into a chair and picked up the blanket she was embroidering for the baby. She'd designed a pastoral scene of shepherds guarding their flock on a hillside above Lucca. She often longed for her beloved countryside villa, which she hadn't visited for more than a year. She couldn't wait to return once the baby was old enough to travel.

She tugged the embroidery floss through the cloth, but as she pressed the needle for another pass, a twisting pain started low in her back and spread forward to her abdomen. She shifted in her chair and panted until it passed. She'd experienced less intense spasms in the past few days, but Tessa said they were nothing more than false labor to help her body prepare for the birth. This had been far more powerful than the others and left her breathless.

When the spasm faded as quickly as it came, she shrugged and went back to stitching and watching the snowflakes float past the window. A quarter of an hour passed before she had another pain, more intense than the last. She clutched her swollen belly and closed her eyes while she waited for it to subside. When it was over, she struggled to her feet and headed for her chamber, wondering if she should send for Tessa. With the snow, it might take longer to travel to the palazzo.

She climbed into bed, deciding it was best to make sure the pains weren't just false labor before alerting Tessa. When the third pain struck moments later, she shook Luciano awake.

He grunted and rubbed his eyes, then squinted at her in the dark. "What's the matter, my love?"

"The baby is coming," she gasped. "Send for Tessa."

He flew out of bed and pushed the door open to Livia's adjoining room. "Make yourself useful, girl, and tell the page to fetch Tessa and the physician. The baby is coming."

Livia mumbled something Celeste couldn't hear, then ran out while pulling her cloak on an instant later. Luciano bellowed for his valet to come and help him dress. While he waited, he knelt next to the bed and took Celeste's hand.

"I'm sure Tessa will chase me out of the room, but I'll just be down the hall if you need me." He brushed her hair aside and kissed her forehead. "I love you more than life, and I can't wait to meet our child."

She smiled up at him as her pain faded. "I love you, Luciano. God is with me, and I promise to be right here with our baby when you return."

The valet came in and bowed, then followed Luciano to his dressing room. She was calm and felt no fear as she watched him go. Taking that as a good omen, she propped herself higher on the pillows, ready to get to work.

THE SNOW STOPPED during the night, and dawn sunlight flooded the room. Celeste felt like days had passed since her first pain, but Tessa insisted it had only been six hours. The spasms came and went in a blinding blur of agony. She glared at the doctor when he said she was progressing nicely. He didn't have the slightest inkling of her suffering.

When she reached the point of utter exhaustion and begged God for relief, she heard a commotion in the hallway before Portia burst into the room and shoved Tessa out of the way. Portia leaned over the bed and grasped Celeste's hand.

"I'm here, my darling girl, and we're going to get you through this together. Now, stop playing games and push that baby out into this world."

As if by her command, Celeste felt an overwhelming urge to push. She gritted her teeth and pushed with all her might. When the feeling passed, she fell back onto the pillows, gasping for air.

"I see the baby's head," Tessa said. "A few more pushes like that, and your work will be done."

"Here comes another one," she cried and heaved with all her strength.

"The baby is coming," the doctor said. "Push once more."

She did as he ordered, determined not to stop until that child was out of her body. She squeezed Portia's hand and let out a deafening scream, then felt a whoosh, and the pain vanished. Seconds later, she heard her baby's cry and broke into tears.

"You did it," Portia said, wiping her cheeks. She peeked around the end of the bed to where the doctor was cleaning the baby. "She is a beautiful, healthy girl and looks just like you when you were born."

"She's absolutely lovely," Tessa said. "Now, get ready to deliver the afterbirth."

As the words left her mouth, another urge to push overtook her. She drew a deep breath and tensed her muscles as hard as she could.

Just as she thought it was over, Tessa said, "Stop pushing, Signora. Doctor, come here, please."

The doctor handed the swaddled baby to Portia and moved to Tessa's side. After examining Celeste for several moments, he said, "Your work isn't finished after all. I see ten little toes. When the next pain comes, you have to push this little one out all at once. Don't stop until I tell you. Once the legs are delivered, it will try to breathe. We can't let that happen."

Celeste didn't have time to absorb the fact that she would have two babies before another urge to push overwhelmed her. She gathered her remaining thimbleful of strength and pushed as hard as she could. As the room started to spin and go dark, the baby slipped out, and she heard another cry.

"Another beautiful girl, exactly like the other," Tessa said, dabbing her eyes. "It's a miracle."

Celeste immediately felt another spasm. "Here comes another one," she gasped.

The doctor checked her, then shook his head. "No, my dear, that's the afterbirth. Rest now. Now you are finished, madam."

She fell onto the pillows and struggled to catch her breath.

Portia wiped Celeste's forehead with a cloth and said, "Would you like to meet your first daughter?"

Celeste held out her arms, and Portia gently handed her the little bundle. She stared at the perfect face as tears dripped onto her blanket. The baby was a miracle. After all the loss and heartache, she had become a mother of not just one but two little angels. The doctor handed her the second baby, an identical copy of the first. She kissed their soft heads, overcome with a joy that she couldn't have imagined existed.

She heard the door bang open as Luciano barged into the room. Portia glared at Paolo, who had stopped in the doorway.

"I told you to keep him away until I came to get him," she said.

Paolo shrugged. "I tried. He overpowered me."

Luciano stared at his wife and daughters in stunned silence.

"Two girls, I'm afraid. I hope you aren't disappointed," Celeste said, laughing. "Aren't they the most exquisite jewels you've ever seen?"

He reached down and scooped them into his arms. "Twins? I have two daughters?" He gazed at them in awe. "Oh, Celeste, they look just like you, thank the Lord. I love them already. Look, Portia, I'm a father."

"This is all very touching, but you need to give me those little darlings and go," Tessa said. "We're not ready for you yet, but it won't be long."

Luciano reluctantly handed over his daughters, and Tessa shooed him and Paolo from the room.

Tessa laid the babies in their cradle, then Portia helped her clean and change Celeste.

Before bringing Luciano back into the room, Portia took Celeste's hand and said, "I have news of my own. I'm going to become a mother in late spring."

Celeste stared at her in shock. "How can that be? Aren't you too old to bear a child?"

"According to my physician, women as old as fifty have borne children, so forty-three isn't too old. It is more of a risk, but he says I'm healthy enough. I had a bit of a scare because I thought it was a tumor before he confirmed that I'm with child."

Celeste squeezed her hand. "This is joyous news. Are you frightened?"

"I'm not. I never expected to have love in my life, but I found Paolo. Now, God has blessed me with this child for reasons of his own. I believe it is part of a plan, and my child will grow up with your daughters. Who could have imagined?"

"I couldn't be happier." The babies began to wail in unison, and she said, "Now, please hand me my daughters so I can feed them and get Luciano in here before he breaks down the door."

CELESTE TOOK A WELL-DESERVED nap after the babies were fed and quiet five hours later. Luciano sat in a chair next to the cradle and watched his sleeping daughters, unable to take his eyes off them. After Isabella's tragic death and Celeste's miscarriages, he had resigned himself to never becoming a father. It was almost more than he could comprehend that now he had two perfect angels to spoil and love.

He glanced at Portia, who sat next to Paolo by the fire, fiercely stitching away on a blanket. He'd been as shocked as Celeste by her news. He only hoped it would end in as much joy for them.

"Are you ever going to stop admiring them?" Portia asked. "I've never seen a man so besotted with two daughters. You realize that means twice the dowry?"

Without taking his gaze from the cradle, he said, "I'd pay ten times the dowry for them. You'll understand when your baby comes."

"He's right," Paolo said. "I'm proud to have a son and heir, but I love my daughters just as much as Piero. All I hope is for baby and mother to be healthy this time."

Portia put aside her sewing and went to stand behind Luciano. "What are you going to name them?"

"Celeste wants to name them after our mothers, Angela and Cristina."

Veronica ran into the room and squealed in delight. She knelt next to the cradle and said, "Let me see my nieces. My teacher wouldn't let me come until I finished my lessons."

"Hush, girl," Portia said. "You'll wake them and your sister. She's going to need all the sleep she can get."

Veronica rolled the babies onto their backs and brushed their cheeks with the back of her hand. "They're magnificent. I thought they would be dark like us, Luciano, but they have Celeste's light coloring."

Portia stepped closer. "That will change as they get older."

One of them squirmed and made a squeak, then opened her eyes. She watched Veronica for a moment and smiled. "Did you see her smile? She likes me already."

"Just gas," Portia said. "I still think it's a mistake for Celeste to refuse a wet nurse. It would have been difficult enough with one baby. How will she keep up with two?"

"Thousands of peasant women nurse their own children every day, even twins. I can manage my daughters," Celeste murmured from the bed.

Luciano sat next to her and said, "Sorry, my love, did we wake you?"

"I'm too excited to sleep. Bring my babies to me." Veronica picked up the one who was awake and rocked her for a moment before handing her to Celeste. "The other one, too."

"Haven't you heard, never wake a sleeping baby, Celeste?" Portia said. "There will be plenty of time to hold them."

"We can all sleep tomorrow. I don't want to waste a moment with them."

Luciano handed her the other baby. "How will we tell them apart?"

"I can tell the difference," Celeste said.

"You're their mother. The rest of us will need a hint." Paolo said.

"One will wear a coral necklace and the other pearls," Luciano said.

Celeste smiled. "When they're older, perhaps, but for now, ribbons will do. Angela is the oldest. She'll wear rose, and Cristina will wear green, like the colors of the family crest."

Veronica ran out of the room and returned moments later with two lengths of satin ribbon. "Which one is Angela?" When Celeste pointed, she freed the baby's arm from the swaddling and tied the rose ribbon on her wrist, then did the same of Cristina. "Now, they have names and are ready for baptism."

Luciano jumped to his feet. "I forgot about baptism. I need to see the priest and make arrangements. Elisabetta and Giulio have agreed to be godparents, but now we can have two sets. Paolo and Portia, would you do us the honor of being Cristina's godparents?"

Paolo stood and bowed, "Gladly."

"It is settled, then. Paolo come with me to the church. We'll stop for Giulio on the way." He kissed his daughters and Celeste. "I'll share our news with Elisabetta. I'm sure she'll be here by morning."

Celeste frowned. "If not sooner."

"Patience, Celeste. She loves you in her way and is happy for us. She'll be even happier when she hears you produced two girls and not a son."

Veronica giggled. "She acts like her Giuliano will be king one day instead of Duca."

"He won't be either if I can help it," Celeste mumbled.

Portia snickered. "Planning another baby so soon? These two haven't yet been alive for a day."

Luciano laughed as he went out with Paolo. Producing an heir would solve matters with Elisabetta, but if Celeste never bore him another child, he would be content.

❦

AFTER WHAT FELT like only moments of sleep, a baby's cry startled Celeste awake. The room was still dark, but Luciano's side of the bed was empty.

Lapa came in carrying the wailing infant and said, "I'm sorry, madam, but Cristina wishes to eat."

Celeste sighed and propped herself on pillows. "Didn't I just feed her?"

"That was Angela, and it was more than an hour ago. Cristina hasn't eaten for three hours."

She took her unhappy daughter and put her to her breast, then leaned her head against the headboard and closed her eyes. She hadn't had more than an hour's sleep in the two weeks since the girls were born. Portia had pestered her daily to change her mind about hiring a wet nurse. Celeste wished she had listened. Even with Lapa, Livia, and Portia pampering her like a queen, she was more exhausted than she'd ever been.

"Where is my husband?" she asked Lapa, who was sitting by the fire, trying to keep her eyes open.

"He left to sleep in his quarters after you fed Angela. He said he has a long day ahead and needs to sleep."

She imagined how wonderful it would be to hide and sleep for several uninterrupted hours. I chose this, she thought, as she handed Cristina to Lapa for burping.

Lapa turned the baby over and patted her back to get her to bring up a bubble. "I know it's not my place to say so, madam, but twins are difficult for any woman to manage. There's no shame in asking for help."

"Has Portia gotten to you too?"

"No, I can just see how tired you are. The circles under your eyes get bigger every day, and your face is drawn. I'm concerned about your well-being. Your girls have hearty appetites."

Cristina let out a man-sized belch, so Lapa handed her back to Celeste to finish nursing. She cuddled her daughter and said, "It seems no matter how often I feed them, they're never satisfied."

"I hear your sister-in-law's wet nurse has finished weaning her youngest. Maybe you could speak with her."

"It surprises me to hear you say this after the way Sofia Viari treated you. Would you wish that on someone else?"

Lapa gave her a warm smile. "You would never treat anyone as Signora Viari treated me, and Signora Vicente's wet nurse cares for the baby in her home, so she can spend time with her own children."

"Yes, Angelica told me. I would not agree to that arrangement. My darlings aren't going anywhere." Cristina finished nursing and drifted off to sleep. Celeste carefully handed her to Lapa. "I'll consider what you've said. Maybe between a wet nurse and me, my girls would get enough to eat, and it would lighten the work for you and Livia."

"I think that would be wise."

Lapa gave a quick curtsy before heading back to the nursery. Celeste had given up trying to get her to stop curtsying and calling her madam, even if just when they were alone, but she refused, saying it wasn't proper. Livia piped up once and said she'd have no problem calling her Celeste, but she just scowled at her, knowing it wouldn't be wise to give Livia too much latitude.

Celeste scooted down into the warm blankets and was about to close her eyes when she heard another cry. She groaned and sat up, waiting for Livia to bring Angela, but instead of Livia, it was Portia who came in carrying the squealing bundle. She handed her to Celeste and pulled a chair close to the bed. Celeste smiled to see the little bump forming under her skirts.

Portia dropped into the chair and said, "I passed Lapa on her way to the nursery. This has got to stop. I'm going to start looking for a wet nurse today."

"Stop lecturing, Aunt. I agree with you. Speak with Angelica and see if her wet nurse is willing to live here. She can bring her children if she wishes."

"Is that wise? What if she has ten?"

"I'll ask Luciano to find quarters on the estate. She can bring her entire family. We won't even know they're here."

"That's reasonable, but she will need to sleep in the nursery until the twins are older. There won't be time to send a houseboy for her every time they're hungry."

Celeste gazed down at Angela. "They're always hungry."

Portia studied her for a moment. "Why are you so cooperative this morning after resisting the past two weeks?"

"I was trying to prove a point. I'm too tired to remember what it was."

Angela burped and smiled up at Celeste with milk dribbling down her chin. "Such a proper little lady," Portia said and laughed.

Celeste wiped Angela's chin and moved her to the other side. "It will be a relief to have help. I can't keep this up much longer."

"You've done a remarkable job, and I'm proud of you. I didn't think you'd last this long."

"Go back to bed and send Livia to get the baby. You need your rest more than you can imagine. Take advantage of this time."

Portia stood and stretched. "Especially for such an old woman. I'll visit Angelica today and arrange for the wet nurse. If she can't come right away, I'll find one to fill in until she can."

"I still want to nurse the girls too, but I look forward to having more than an hour of sleep at a time."

Portia kissed their foreheads before going to find Livia. Celeste was glad to have a moment alone with her daughter. People traipsed in and out of her room day and night, never giving her a moment's peace.

She removed Angela's cap and smoothed her silky auburn hair. It was a daily wonder to her that her daughters were little replicas of her. She had expected Luciano's dark coloring. When she was young, everyone said her hair and complexion were signs of sinfulness. She didn't believe them, but the accusations hurt, nonetheless.

Those characteristics were part of what made her different. She viewed it as a blessing that her daughters were just as unique. She planned to spend every day of their lives reminding them they were special and loved and protecting them from anyone who dared say otherwise.

CHAPTER TWENTY-FIVE

ONE YEAR LATER

*L*uciano threw the door open and stormed up the staircase, shouting for Celeste. When she didn't answer, he went to her studio but found it empty. He started for the nursery but stopped when he caught sight of her with Angela and Cristina in the garden. He raced down the stairs and jogged across the lawn, calling her name. Livia and Lapa jumped to their feet and curtsied when they saw him coming.

Celeste was on the grass, holding Cristina's hands, trying to get her to take a step. She turned toward him and smiled.

"You missed it. Angela took her first steps today. I'm coaxing Cristina to do it, but she's not ready yet."

"Sorry I missed that," he said before scooping his daughters up and nuzzling their necks to make them giggle. "Here, Lapa, Livia, take these two little pixies inside. I need to speak with their mother."

The women gathered up the blankets, trinkets, and toys, then hurried inside with the babies.

Celeste lovingly watched them go. "I can't get enough of my angels. It's almost painful to be separated from them for a moment."

Luciano put out his hand to help her to her feet. She took it and gazed at him in confusion.

"I've noticed," he said brusquely. "Come with me."

It took great restraint not to throw her over his shoulder and carry her like a sack of wheat. When they reached the studio, he dropped her hand and began pacing.

"What has gotten into you? Has something happened?"

"I just spent the last half hour having my ear chewed off by my sisters because you were supposed to join them at San Lorenzo's today but never arrived. Elisabetta is beside herself. This is the third time, Celeste, and you haven't accompanied me in public for a single event since the christening for Portia's son. That was six months ago. You have responsibilities."

Celeste crossed her arms and stared at the floor. "I'm sorry, Luciano, but why do I have to be at Elisabetta's beck and call? She should cater to my wishes."

"I heard you agree to go with them three nights ago at dinner. No one forced you."

"What choice did I have? She doesn't accept no from anyone."

"That doesn't excuse breaking your commitment. What else did you have to do other than spend every moment in the nursery? I love our daughters as much as you do, but they're nearly a year old. Lapa and Marissa are capable of caring for them without you."

"I'm proud to be a devoted mother. Most patrician mothers forget they have children. I refuse to do that."

"There's a vast middle ground between neglect and spending every waking moment with your daughters. I need you at my side and at work in this studio. You promised to start painting two months ago."

Celeste slowly looked around the room. "This used to be my favorite place in the world. It was my sanctuary and haven, but now, standing here, I feel nothing. It's just a beautiful marble room."

"Are you saying you're abandoning your art and the promises you made to me? You once told me you would rather give up breathing than stop painting."

"Did I?" She walked to her box of brushes and drew one from the pile. He watched as she ran her fingers through the bristles. "That fiery young girl is gone. I'm a mother now, content, and more mature. The canvas has gone silent and no longer cries out to me as it did."

Luciano slammed his palm on the worktable, and she flinched. "I refuse to accept that. Why is it always everything or nothing with you? How can you be certain until you have given it a chance?"

She dropped the brush into the box and looked at him without emotion. "I just know."

He took a breath to cool his temper. He'd learned through hard experience that the more he pushed Celeste, the harder she resisted. A soft, sensitive touch was what she needed. He went to her and put his arms around her waist, then kissed her forehead. The feel of her sent a thrill through him. She had agreed to share his bed since giving birth but, fearing another pregnancy, had refused to share her body. He decided she had denied long enough.

"Forgive me for losing my temper. You are an excellent mother, and I respect that you take your responsibility seriously."

"I appreciate you telling me. I wondered if you had noticed."

He brushed his lips along her neck and whispered, "I won't force you to return to work. Painting used to give you so much joy and pleasure. I thought you might miss it, but if you aren't ready, please take the time you need." He gave her a lingering kiss. "Have you missed that?"

She responded by pressing her body against his and untying his cloak. She let it drop to the floor and said, "Yes, this I have missed."

He loosened her gown and slid it off her shoulders. "Remember that night in my Venice studio? Too bad there's no cot here."

She pulled away from him and slid her work materials to the end of the table. "Who needs a cot?"

By the time he locked the door, she had removed her clothing and faced him in her bare, exquisite beauty. He spread his cloak on the table and tenderly laid her on it before climbing up to join her.

"I haven't felt whole or alive without you, my love. You are my heart and my life."

She wove her hands through his hair and lowered his mouth to hers. She kissed him with a fervor he hadn't seen since Venice. He responded with a passion equaling hers.

When their lovemaking was over, Celeste pulled the cloak around her body and leaned over him. "I'd forgotten how much I need the feel of you. I'm sorry for pushing you away for so long."

He brushed his thumb along her cheek. "It's forgotten. All I want is your happiness."

She climbed off the table and began to dress. "I believe we need a cot in here."

"I'll arrange it today."

CELESTE WAITED for Luciano to leave for his workshop before sneaking to her studio the following morning. Their night of lovemaking had made her wonder if she might rekindle her passion for painting, too. When she entered the studio, morning sunlight illuminated the clean canvas resting on the easel. She ran her fingertips over the surface and pictured an image forming there. The familiar spark of creativity ignited within her, and she rushed to the worktable for paper and charcoal to begin her sketch.

The next thing she knew, Livia was coming to tell her Luciano's sisters had arrived for lunch. She had invited them to apologize and smooth Elisabetta's ruffled feathers. She swallowed her pride and charmed them until all was well once more. They chatted about their children, and Elisabetta insisted on going to the nursery to visit Angela and Cristina. Celeste finally ushered them out the door two hours later with a promise to accompany them the next time they went to distribute food to the poor.

Once the door closed behind them, she hurried to her studio and worked until Luciano came in carrying a cot as the sun was setting.

"Livia told me you were here. This is a welcomed surprise."

She kissed him and stepped to where her sketches lay spread on the worktable. "Don't think I didn't notice the clever way you manipulated me yesterday, but I'm not offended. I'm grateful."

Luciano put the cot down and smiled. "You're too clever for my schemes."

"True, but you were right that my hunger to paint had not died. It only lay dormant. But in the future, Luciano, please remember that I'm not one of your apprentices. I needed that time with our daughters. A man will never know what it is to be torn between such worthy pursuits as parenthood and following his passion. You must be patient as I learn to walk this unfamiliar ground."

Luciano came up behind her and put his arms around her waist. "I will do my best to be patient, but this is unfamiliar territory for me as well. You have changed, my love. There's a new depth to you." He released her and leaned over the table. "Show me your sketches."

"This reminds me of the day I showed you my drawings for the first time in Venice. I was frightened and in awe of you. I was afraid of disappointing you."

"You could never do that. When I saw your sketches, I felt in my bones you were destined for greatness. For an untrained servant girl to possess such innate abilities was remarkable. I refused to let you slip through my fingers, but who could have imagined you would end up as my wife and mother of my children?"

"I dreamed of that every day but thought it impossible. There are still moments when I can't believe it's real. I'm deeply grateful."

She watched as he studied her work and felt transported back to that day in Luciano's Venice studio. She held her breath and waited for him to speak.

"These are extraordinary. Your skills have far surpassed mine. This is only the beginning of the heights you will reach." He looked into her eyes and said, "I going to show your work to Lorenzo de' Medici, but not one painting at a time. I'll arrange an exhibition and gala. We'll hold it in one year during Carnevale. I'll invite Lorenzo and other Florentine patricians and artists. It will be the event of the season."

"You want to show my work to Lorenzo? Isn't the risk too great? If he discovers our deception, we'll be ruined. What would become of

Marco? Please reconsider presenting me to the Guild. Now is a perfect time."

"Attitudes in Florence have not changed. If we apply to the Guild and they reject you, all hope will be lost."

"We could reapply when there's a change in power. I'm willing to wait."

He dropped her sketch on the table. "I'm not. That could take years."

"Marco only agrees to go along because he's afraid to challenge you. It makes me sick to force him into this. If you tell him you're going to present him to Lorenzo de' Medici, he might refuse. Will you cast him out of your workshop if he does?"

"I'm not a heartless brute, Celeste. It saddens me you think me capable of that. He has the choice to refuse. It won't affect his place in the workshop."

"Does he know that? What will you do if he refuses?"

He turned away and ran his hand through his hair. "There's no need to argue this now. We'll decide when your paintings are ready."

His refusal to present her to the Guild was disheartening. Female painters were rare but not unheard of as they once were. She had hoped Luciano would see reason and take the honorable path but arguing was pointless.

"You're right, my love. There is time to decide. For now, let's visit our darlings before I change for dinner."

"Nothing would please me more," he said and took her arm.

They were no closer to a resolution than they had been eighteen months earlier, but she was learning time could be her friend. Her task would be to focus on the present, set thoughts of the future aside, and let the answers come.

CELESTE LAID her brush on a cloth and rubbed her aching neck. She'd worked since dawn with only a brief pause for lunch. The sun had set, yet Livia hadn't come to let her know it was time to dress for dinner. She didn't have long to wonder when Portia strolled the studio with a swish of her skirts.

"I bring my beautiful son to visit, expecting you to spoil and fawn over him, but you ignore us and spend your time here, seducing that canvas. I should be offended, but I know you too well for that."

Celeste removed her smock and tossed it over a chair. "You know I love Tomaso. He's an adorable boy, but I must finish my work. Luciano needs my portfolio completed in time for the exhibition."

"He pushes you too hard. You are a mother before you are a painter. How long has it been since you spent time in the nursery with your daughters?"

She crossed her arms and glared at Portia. "Are you accusing me of neglecting my children? I spend far more time with them than Sofia Viari ever did with her children when I was their nanny. Many patrician women ignore their babies entirely. I'll have you know I was with Angela and Cristina for an hour this morning before coming to the studio."

"Forgive me for accusing you falsely, but there's also the matter of Veronica. She says she only sees you at dinner. You've had no hand in her training. I'm concerned about that girl. She enjoys her wine too much, and I've caught her flirting with the house boys more than once. Her eyes wander whenever she leaves the palazzo. It's a good thing I'm here with a firm hand to keep her in line."

"Why is it my responsibility to manage everyone in this family? Take Veronica to Lucca and throw her into the kitchens, then. That will put her in her place."

"My, you are sensitive this evening. Dare I mention my concerns about Jacopo?"

Celeste dropped into a chair and covered her face with her hands. "I feel torn in a thousand directions with everyone demanding so much of me. I only have so much time in a day." She lowered her hands and looked up at Portia. "To answer your question, Luciano assures me he can handle Jacopo and that he's no different from other spirited boys his age, but I'm not convinced. I see too much of Papa in him."

"He is so much like Giovanni was at that age. Maybe he's the one I should take to Lucca. I'd toss him out to work the fields. Then he'd learn his place in a hurry."

"Laboring in the fields would be better than the quarries, I suppose."

"Give Luciano more time to tame Jacopo, but Lucca will always be there as an option." She pulled a chair closer and sat facing Celeste. "Why don't you tell Luciano you want to stop painting? He would never force you."

"I'm not so sure of that, but I don't want to stop, Aunt. I know you don't understand my life in the studio, but nothing is more fulfilling except motherhood. In some ways, finishing one of my pieces is akin to giving birth and brings immense satisfaction. I just need to manage the competing areas of my life better."

"I've never heard you speak this way, but it helps me understand, especially now that I'm a mother. How can we describe the profound joy of becoming a mother to one who hasn't experienced it? If painting is the same for you, I'll do my part to support you and lighten your burden while I'm in Florence."

Celeste patted her hand. "Coming to my rescue once again. I am grateful, and my work won't be so demanding once the art show is over, especially if Lorenzo de' Medici agrees to sponsor us."

Portia shook her head. "You're treading a dangerous path with your hopes for Lorenzo. The Guilds pronounce severe judgments in fraud and deception cases, and Lorenzo is one of the most powerful men in Europe. I asked Paolo to talk Luciano out of this scheme, but he's determined to go forward."

"I've done my best to convince him, but I owe it to Marco and myself to keep trying. Pray that I succeed."

"I shall. Then, we can put it from our minds and leave it up to God." She leaned back and smiled. "I came here for a happier reason than to discuss such weighty matters. Getting back to Veronica, she's been pestering me about having the ball you promised to host eighteen months ago. I've relented and spoken to Luciano. He's given permission as long as I agree not to involve you in the preparations."

Celeste groaned and rubbed her face. "So close to the showing? I just told you how overburdened I am."

"Leave it to me. I can enlist Luciano's sisters to help, and I'll ask Veronica to assist me. It will keep her busy and out of trouble. We'll have it in four weeks, before Paolo and I leave for Lucca."

"It's not fair to put it all on your shoulders."

"Nonsense. Arranging a ball is a trifle compared to managing the Lucca estate. All you have to do is get fitted for a new gown."

"That's not necessary. I have wardrobes filled with gowns."

"I insist, so don't bother to argue. I'll schedule it with the seamstress."

Celeste sighed and got to her feet. "Luciano and I aren't the only stubborn ones. Very well, I agree on a new gown, and I welcome the idea of a ball, especially since I don't have to arrange it."

"It's settled then. I'll inform Veronica at dinner. She'll be beside herself."

Celeste helped Portia to her feet. "Speaking of dinner, it's time I go change. I'm sure they've started without us."

Portia held Celeste's arm and guided her toward the door. "I told Luciano we'd be late and to wait, so you needn't worry."

"Where would I be without you?"

"With an irritated husband, so we'd best hurry. He won't wait forever."

PORTIA HAD BEEN true to her word and arranged the ball without a whisper to Celeste. She was only aware of the preparations from their lively conversations at dinner. Veronica's excitement was infectious, and Celeste got caught up in it as the day grew closer. She even relented and let the seamstress design a far more elaborate gown than her usual.

The only cloud dampening her enthusiasm was concern for her brothers. Jacopo was a dutiful apprentice in the workshop, but the minute he was set free in the evenings, he found no end of ways to get into trouble. Luciano had even caught him trying to sneak a young servant girl into the stables after dark. Instead of blaming or punishing Jacopo, he was going to dismiss the poor girl until Celeste intervened. She reprimanded her but insisted that Luciano punish Jacopo as well. Luciano made him muck the stables for a week, but that wasn't nearly enough to satisfy her.

She was anxious about how Jacopo would behave at the ball. She would have her hands full keeping track of Veronica and couldn't assure they were both behaving themselves. Luciano promised to keep Jacopo in his sights throughout the night. She accused him of not taking her concerns seriously, so he enlisted Paolo to help pacify her. She hoped with the two of them minding Jacopo, they could avoid any unpleasant incidents.

Her bigger worry was for Marco. As the day of the exhibition drew closer, he became more withdrawn and anxious. He avoided her when she sought him out to help calm his fears. He resented that she hadn't done more to stop Luciano from going forth with his scheme and felt she was going along out of her own pride and self-interest. It was painful to concede he was closer to the truth than she liked to admit.

Marco agreed to attend the ball out of obligation, but she knew it was the last place he wished to be. When she voiced her concern to Luciano, he said it was time Marco started thinking of marriage and suggested introducing him to a lovely young maiden at the ball. She doubted that would do much to lighten Marco's heart since he was so shy and awkward. All she could do was hope they made it through the night unscathed.

WHEN THE DAY of the ball arrived, Celeste shook off her cares and put away her brushes. She'd worked so hard the past several months and felt she deserved a night of lighthearted merriment. When she emerged from their chambers to meet Luciano, he bowed and pulled her into his arms.

"You are more exquisite than on our wedding day. I hadn't thought it possible."

She tapped him with her fan and said, "You're exaggerating as usual, but the seamstress did a remarkable job, even if it is too extravagant."

"Think of it as a priceless work of art, which is what you are." He wrapped his fingers around her arm and guided her toward the stairs. "Shall we go down and greet our guests? Portia has been waiting for half an hour."

"I'm ready," she said, as she glided toward the stairs by his side. "Are Veronica and the boys with her?"

"They are. Just wait until you see them."

She tugged on his arm to hurry him and had to restrain herself from dancing down the stairs. Her breath caught when they stepped into the gardens. Festive torches glowed over their resplendent guests, who danced or mingled in the fragrant air. Cloth-covered tables laden with golden platters of meat and fruit lined the lawn, and colorful bouquets and greenery adorned the columns and statues. Celeste felt transported into one of Sandro Botticelli's paintings.

As she took in the enchanting scene, Veronica came up with Portia and spun her around. Celeste stepped back to get a look at her. She was stunning in her delicately embroidered rose and gold gown. Her lush brown hair was braided elegantly and woven with beads and gems. Celeste was reassured that Luciano would have no trouble finding a match for her.

"Isn't it magical, sister? Thank you for this," Veronica said.

Luciano laughed and said, "Don't I deserve some credit?"

Veronica curtsied and said, "Yes, brother. I'm incredibly grateful."

Portia kissed Celeste's cheeks and said, "I'm relieved to see you. I was afraid you were in the studio, making love to your canvas, and had forgotten about the ball."

"How could I forget? I have a view of the gardens from my studio window, but I wouldn't have missed this, Aunt. What you've achieved is breathtaking. We need to do this every time you visit."

Portia dabbed her brow. "Maybe not every time. This one was nearly the death of me."

"I can vouch for that," Paolo said with a smile. "She always overdoes with these events."

Luciano gave an exaggerated bow. "Thank you again, Portia, for arranging this without Celeste's help." He then took Veronica's arm and led her away, saying, "Come, I have someone I wish you to meet."

As they walked off, Jacopo and Marco came up to greet them. Tears glistened in Celeste's eyes to see her handsome brothers in their fine, deep-blue velvet doublets and capes. It gave her joy to know she was instrumental in raising them from poverty to such heights. While it was Luciano who had supplied the financial support, but without her help, their futures would have been bleak at best if they survived at all.

After each hugged her, she said, "You are the most handsome men here. I'm so proud to call you my brothers."

Jacopo beamed at her. "I never could have dreamed I'd attend an event such as this. Thank you for inviting us."

"Of course, we invited you," Portia said. "You are family."

He winked at her. "You look lovely tonight, Aunt."

She smiled and gave him a little slap. "You run off and give some of these poor young ladies a partner."

He bowed with a flourish and said, "With pleasure," before dashing off.

Celeste noted that Marco had been quiet during their exchange. Hoping to put him at ease, she said, "Aren't the gardens lovely? Aunt Portia did a magnificent job planning the ball."

"Yes, Aunt, everything is perfect," he mumbled.

Knowing it was pointless to engage him in conversation, Celeste said, "Go find Luciano. He'll introduce you around, and do me a favor, keep your eye on Jacopo. Make sure he doesn't overindulge with the wine."

Marco nodded and walked away without another word.

"He'd better be more cordial than that at the exhibition, or it will be a disaster," Portia said.

Celeste was thinking the same thing, but she said, "No talk of that tonight. I intend to make the most of this beautiful occasion. Paolo, shall we dance?"

~

LUCIANO COULDN'T REMEMBER a time when he had enjoyed himself more. He hadn't been one for dances and festivals since he was young but wondered what he and Celeste may have missed. Though they attended events when required, they didn't go out of their way to participate in Florentine social life. Maybe it's time for a change, he thought as he sipped his wine.

Long after midnight, he decided it was time to find his wife. He'd been discussing art and politics with his colleagues from the Guild and had lost sight of her. He climbed a wall to get a better view of the grounds and sighted her having a heated conversation with Veronica near the terrace steps. He didn't need to read their lips to know the subject of their argument.

He'd introduced Veronica to the man he hoped would become her husband, but she was less than pleased with his choice. He'd seen her flirting more than once with a much younger man of low ranking in the community. He'd asked Celeste to stop her behavior before people gossiped but didn't envy her the task.

He was about to climb off the wall when he spotted a commotion on the opposite side of the gardens. Shouts reached his ears an instant later, and he saw someone shove Jacopo to the ground. He jumped down and raced across the lawn as quickly as he could through the teeming throng. As he ran, he recalled his promise to Celeste that he would keep Jacopo under his wing, which he had failed to keep.

By the time he reached Jacopo, he was standing over a young man lying unconscious on the ground with a bloodied nose. It took only moments to recognize him as the son of Signore Daniello Fiorino, a long-time family friend from a neighboring Ducato.

He parted the crowd and knelt next to the boy, patting his face to wake him. After giving him a handkerchief to wipe his nose, he stood and grabbed the drunken Jacopo by the collar to drag him back to the workshop. Once they were inside, he pushed him down onto a bench and took several breaths to calm his temper.

It incensed Luciano that Jacopo would dare shame the Vicente name before the elite families of Florence. Celeste's concern had been justified.

"Look at me, boy," he hissed. Jacopo slowly raised his bloodshot eyes. "Do you know who that boy was? He's the son of my old friend and powerful Florentine Duca. What are you? You're nothing. I rescued you from the streets, brought you into my workshop, and gave you a vocation. I clothed you and fed you the bread from my table. I tried to teach you honor and responsibility. Yet you repeatedly disrespected me and threw it back in my face, but this time you've gone too far."

Jacopo sat up straighter and glared. "I'm grateful for what you've done for me, and I own my mistakes, but how can you speak to me of respect and honor? I heard you speaking to Stefano before he left. I know of your conspiracy to pass Celeste's paintings off as Marco's. I may have trouble controlling my youthful impulses as you call them, but what you're doing flies in the face of everything the Guilds and this city stand for, and you've dragged my brother and sister down with you."

Luciano raised the back of his hand to strike, but when Jacopo didn't flinch or back down, he closed his fist and lowered his arm. He was sick with himself for contemplating such violence. Jacopo had spoken the truth. His anger was directed more at himself than the boy.

He rubbed his face, then said, "Why did you strike that boy?"

Jacopo shook his head and lowered his eyes. "He called me a drunken Venetian gutter rat dressed in velvet threads. He said I dirty the Vicente name and asked how you could stand to allow me into your palazzo. Unlike you, Maestro, I understand honor, and I was defending mine."

Luciano felt like he'd punched him in the gut. He couldn't fathom where Daniello's son could have heard such talk, but regardless, insulting Jacopo meant insulting Celeste.

"Did you provoke him, Jacopo?"

"No, sir. A group of us were joking about the physical attributes of a certain serving girl. It was all good-natured play until Fiorino came along and began spitting insults at me. The others laughed with him, so I put him in his place."

Luciano was at a loss for what to do. He might have done the same at Jacopo's age, but that didn't make it right.

"Despite what Franco said, you were wrong to strike him. There are better ways to defend the family honor. I'll arrange a meeting with Signore Fiorino and Franco. You will apologize for what you've done."

Jacopo stood and clenched his fists. "I won't until Franco apologizes to me."

"You will do as I say or leave my home. Go to your room for the rest of the night. We'll speak more in the morning."

He left Jacopo staring after him and went to find Celeste, sure she'd heard of the incident by then. She came running toward him as he reached the wall of the gardens.

"Where's Jacopo, Luciano?" she cried. "What did you do to him?"

He put his hands on her shoulders and did his best to smile. "I sent him to bed. He's fine other than having drunk too much wine."

"Andriana Fiorino is fuming. She said Jacopo struck Franco and that his nose is broken. Is it true?"

"It is, but it was just an altercation between two young hotheads. I'm taking Jacopo to apologize in the morning. Don't fret, my love. I'll smooth it over with Daniello. Let's return to our guests and reassure them."

Celeste didn't look convinced but got into step beside him. "I warned you, Luciano. You were worried about Veronica, but this is far worse."

Luciano agreed, but not for the reasons she believed. "All will be well. Trust me."

◆

319

LUCIANO WOKE late with a sick stomach and a pounding head. After the encounter with Jacopo, he had consumed several goblets of wine, hoping to calm his troubled mind. As he got up and asked Filippo to bring him a bowl of cold water, Celeste came in and glared at him with her hands on her hips.

"It's about time you're awake. Paolo and Portia are waiting to leave but wanted to say goodbye. Hurry and dress. We'll see them off and spend time with the girls before you take Jacopo to Daniello."

She turned and hurried out before he could respond, which was probably best since he had nothing worth saying.

Just as Filippo was helping him with his tunic, Marco pounded on the door. Luciano told him to come in, dreading what he had to say.

"Jacopo is gone. I went to check on him and make sure he'd recovered from last night, but he's not there. His belongings are gone, too. We've searched the grounds. He's not here."

It was worse than Luciano feared. Jacopo knew their secret and could use it against them. "Don't worry, Marco, we'll find him. How far could he have gotten?" He patted Marco's shoulder. "Let's see your aunt and uncle off, then we'll widen our search. He'll be back home before dinner."

Marco nodded and followed him to the sala. Celeste was there waiting with Portia, Paolo, and Veronica.

When he told them about Jacopo, Celeste said, "Why would he go? You told me everything was fine when you sent him to bed."

Luciano decided the best course was to tell them the truth. He'd held back to avoid hurting Celeste, but she had to know before she found out through local gossip.

He recounted his conversation with Jacopo, then said, "He's just angry and letting off steam. He has little money and can't get far. I'll enlist my apprentices to help in the search. I won't stop until I find him, Celeste."

"Should we stay?" Paolo asked. "You might need another set of eyes and ears."

"Thank you for the offer, but you need to get your family home, and you aren't as familiar with Florence. My boys know all the cracks and crevices in the city. We'll send word as soon as he's found."

They said a hurried and tearful goodbye, then Luciano and Marco went to the workshop to rally the search party. Once they were on the way, he returned to Celeste and found her pacing in the sala.

"Why didn't you tell me the truth last night?" she asked as soon as he was through the door.

"I wanted to spare your feelings and didn't want to spoil your night. Clearly, I made the wrong choice. You could have gone to him if I'd told you and persuaded him not to leave. I shouldn't have insisted on making him apologize. That Franco Fiorino is an arrogant bully."

"You thought you were doing right. I don't blame you." She hesitated for a moment before saying, "Do you think others feel the same as Franco? Do they see my family as gutter rats in velvet?"

"Don't be ridiculous. Everyone who knows you cares for you and respects you. Franco is a child. Like I said, he's a bully."

She laid her hand on his arm and looked into his eyes. The fear he saw broke his heart. "You're not just trying to protect me again, are you?"

"I'm not. You've convinced Elisabetta, and she's the toughest nut in town. Florence loves you, as I do."

She let out a sigh and said, "I want to help in the search. We need to find my brother before he causes real trouble."

"No, Celeste. You need to be in the studio. The showing is four weeks away, and you have no time to waste. Focus on your work. I'll take care of Jacopo. He's my responsibility, and I'll return him to you by dinnertime."

"I have your word. Don't fail me, my love."

CHAPTER TWENTY-SIX

*L*uciano didn't find Jacopo that day or any of the immediate days that followed. He and his men searched and made inquiries, but Jacopo seemed to have vanished. Celeste was frantic with worry. Jacopo knew little of the world outside of Florence, and Venice was too far for him to travel the distance alone. Her last hope was that he was hiding out with a friend and licking his wounds.

Unfortunately, Jacopo wasn't Celeste's only cause of concern. Veronica had been sullen and uncooperative since the night of the ball, and Luciano's failure to find Jacopo had made him as irritable as Veronica. They argued daily over her refusal to consider the man he'd chosen as her husband. She confessed her love for Duccio Zani, the young man she'd met at the ball, but Luciano demanded she abandon her foolish notion of marrying him. Though Duccio was heir to a title, his family had no financial holdings, and she'd soon regret giving up her luxurious, pampered lifestyle.

Celeste did her best to remain neutral in their quarrels, but it was becoming increasingly difficult. Luciano had once promised Celeste and Portia that he'd never force Veronica to marry against her wishes, but her obstinance was wearing on his patience. He had even threatened to send her to the convent.

As the exhibition drew closer, Celeste became more convinced that they needed to postpone. All she needed was the courage to tell Luciano. With their ongoing family troubles, no one would question the delay. It was just an art show. They could reschedule once their storms had passed.

Celeste stood before her easel one morning, struggling to complete the exhibition's final piece, but her heart and mind were locked. Jacopo had been missing for over two weeks, and her work, which had seemed so vital before he disappeared, now felt trivial and self-indulgent. After two fruitless hours, she put down her brushes and went to walk alone in the gardens. It was a lovely spring day with the flowers just starting to bloom. She breathed in the rich fragrance, wishing she were in Lucca and free of her troubles.

She had just sat on a bench in her favorite spot when Livia came running toward her across the lawn.

"You must come to the house," she said between gasps. "Veronica has gone off to meet Duccio Zani."

Celeste stood to follow her inside and said, "What do you mean, gone to meet him?"

"Her maid, Helena, told me in secret before Veronica left. They are meeting behind the candlemaker's shop."

Celeste touched her arm to stop her. "Does your master know?"

"No, madam. I came straight to you."

Celeste pulled off the slippers she wore for working in the studio and handed them to Livia. "Let's keep this between us for now. Fetch my cloak and a pair of shoes while I get Marco. Get Helena and meet us at the west garden gate. We'll find Veronica ourselves."

As she ran to the workshop, she prayed that Luciano was still meeting with the Signoria and hadn't yet returned. She felt like the young pupil, sneaking off to her lessons with Luciano, but the consequences in this situation were far more severe. She forced herself to slow her step as she reached the workshop. When she opened the door, it relieved her to see Luciano hadn't returned. Marco was instructing an apprentice. When he noticed her in the doorway, she motioned for him to follow her outside.

Once they were alone, he said, "What is it, sister? Has Jacopo been found?"

"No, I have more bad news." She told him about Veronica in a rush and said, "Are you able to get away to help search for her?"

"Of course. I'll do whatever it takes to find my sister. We can't have her ending up like Jacopo. I'll tell my assistant I have to visit the apothecary for pigments and ask him to take over for me. He won't question that, and it should allay Luciano's suspicions. Just give me a moment." He glanced at her feet before he turned to go. "Where are your shoes?"

She shook her head and shooed him off with a wave. There would be time to explain later.

As the four of them rounded the corner to the apothecary shop, Veronica and Duccio were just heading off in the opposite direction. When Marco called out to them, Veronica turned and stared in shock.

"What are you doing here? How in heaven's name did you find us?" She noticed Helena and stabbed a finger at her. "You did this. How could you? I took you into my confidence."

Duccio spun around and ran off through an alley. Marco took off after him, leaving the women alone. Veronica started to follow, but Celeste took hold of her arm.

"No, you don't. You're coming with me." Veronica began to cry and struggled to pull her arm free. "Livia, take her other arm. Let's get her off the street away from curious eyes."

Realizing she was no match for them, Veronica stopped resisting and resigned herself to her fate. Celeste's heart broke to hear her whimpering as they walked her home, but she knew she had to protect her sister from herself. When they reached Veronica's rooms, she thanked Livia and Helena and dismissed them.

When they were alone, Celeste said, "Where were you going with Messer Zani?"

Veronica threw herself onto the bed and sobbed into her pillows. Celeste dropped into a chair and let her have her cry.

When she finally quieted, she rolled to face Celeste and said, "He was just escorting me on a stroll along the river. We're in love, sister. Why can't you believe that? How is what I did any different from you running off for secret lessons with Luciano? At least we wouldn't have been alone."

Celeste sat next to her and put an arm around her shoulder. "I do believe you, but what you did is nothing like my lessons with Luciano. I have my doubts that Messer Zani's only intention was to take you for a walk. Otherwise, he would have asked permission from Luciano. Why is he courting you in secret if his intentions are honorable?"

Veronica sat up and looked her in the eye. "He wanted to, but I told him Luciano opposes our match. Your husband is a powerful man, Celeste. Duccio fears him."

"That's nonsense. Luciano may be powerful, but he's no tyrant. If he were, you'd be in a convent by now."

"He is so set on me marrying that arrogant and ancient Signore da Leze."

"He may be arrogant, but thirty-five is not exactly ancient. Duccio Zani is only seven years younger." When Veronica scowled at her, she said, "Give me another chance to talk to Luciano. He may seem insensitive, but he's only concerned for your welfare, and he's much wiser than you. Please be patient and give me time to resolve this. With Jacopo gone and the exhibition two weeks away, Luciano has much on his mind. Don't add to his worries. He's done a great deal for you."

"I suppose I can hold off a little longer, but don't take too long. Duccio won't wait forever."

"You've only known each other for two weeks. We have time."

Veronica looked down and played with a loose thread on her blanket. "Are you going to tell Luciano what I did?"

She stood and kissed her forehead. "We'll keep this between us for now, but if you run off again, you will face the consequences. Remain in your room for the rest of the day. I'll tell Luciano you have a headache. I doubt he'll miss seeing you at dinner."

She left Veronica alone and went to see if Marco had returned. He was waiting for her in the studio.

She dropped into a chair and rubbed her temples. "Did you catch Duccio?"

"Yes, easily. I just asked him to face me like a man, and he did."

"That's fortunate. What did he say?"

Marco folded his arms and leaned against the table. "He says he was going to take Veronica for a walk in the Piazza San Lorenzo and that his intentions were honorable. He's intimidated by Luciano and is aware of his opinion of him. I tried to convince Duccio that Luciano is fair and understanding, but he didn't believe me."

"Veronica told me the same. Do you believe him?"

"I do, but what does it matter if Luciano refuses to consider him as a match for Veronica?"

"He has his reasons." She made a sweep of her arm and said, "Do you think Veronica would be happy to leave all of this to live in a quaint country manor without a myriad of servants catering to her? That's what her life would be."

"Yes, if she genuinely loves him. I would be."

"Veronica is not you. Luciano doesn't think she'd last a week."

"If it's her choice, she'll have no one to blame but herself."

Celeste stood and put on her smock. "I must get back to work, and you need to get back to the workshop. I promised I'd talk to him for Veronica after the art show unless he agrees to postpone it."

Marco frowned at her. "You haven't asked him yet? We must postpone. We need time to change his mind about presenting you to the Guild. Our reputations and futures as artists all rest on this. I'm eager to begin my own career. I don't want that ruined before it begins. You must convince him."

"I'm fully aware of the stakes, brother. Luciano has been in a dark temper lately, as I'm sure you've noticed. I've been waiting for the right time."

He hesitated a moment before saying, "Then you should know the

Guild has granted me membership, and I'll soon be classified as a master artist."

Celeste felt an array of emotions at his declaration. She was proud of his success but also deeply envious. He was a skilled painter, but his achievement was based on her talents, not his. The injustice of it weighed heavily on her heart.

She took his hands and smiled. "You have my congratulations. I'll speak with Luciano about the postponement tonight at dinner."

"I will pray for your success, then."

Marco went out, shaking his head, and Celeste found herself wishing Portia wasn't on her way to Lucca. Her aunt had a way of making any problem seem like only a silly trifle. Celeste needed a good dose of her no-nonsense logic as she felt the world weighing on her.

She picked up her brush and paints, then stepped to her panel of Peter with his hands raised in question to the heavens.

"Enough of this," she said to the painting. "Unlock your secrets and show me what you desire so I may grant it. Then we may both be at peace."

Luciano hurried to the dining room, excited to share his news with Celeste, but he found the room empty. When Livia passed with a tray of food, he stopped her to ask where his wife was.

Livia curtsied and said, "My mistress is in the sitting room. She wishes to take her dinner there and would like you to join her."

"Very well. Ask Filippo to bring my dinner after you take your mistress her tray."

"Yes, sir," she said, then followed as he bounded up the stairs.

He found Celeste lost in thought by the fire in her sitting room. She slowly raised her eyes when he entered but didn't seem pleased to see him.

He kissed her, then knelt by the chair. "What is it, my love?"

"It's nothing. I was just thinking about Jacopo. Where could he be, Luciano?"

"If there's one thing I know about your brother, it's that he knows how to survive. I expect him any day with his tail between his legs." He stood and took the chair opposite her. "Why are we eating here? Where's Veronica?"

"Veronica has a headache, and I saw no point to the two of us eating in the drafty dining room." Livia came in with her tray, and Celeste waited for her to leave before saying, "Isn't this more intimate?"

He grinned and winked at her. "I have excellent news. Lorenzo has accepted our invitation to the exhibition. I'm elated. He's bringing Sandro Botticelli and some young artists from Domenico Ghirlandaio's workshop. This is better than I could have hoped."

He watched her reaction, which was far less enthusiastic than he'd expected.

"Congratulations," she mumbled. "You've worked hard for this. It's an impressive achievement."

"You don't look pleased. Isn't this what you've worked for all these years? Some of the greatest artists in the world are going to view your work."

"But it's not my work, is it, Luciano? To all the world, it will be Marco Gabriele's triumph, not mine."

"Are you so vain that you must have your name praised and applauded? Isn't it enough that the world will admire your artwork, no matter whose name is attached?"

"Imagine if they had forced you to pass your work off as Botticelli's or da Vinci's or Bellini's. What if Italy had never heard of Maestro Luciano Vicente? Would you be content to have others take credit for your masterpieces?"

Her question caught him off guard. He'd never stopped to consider how it must feel to remain in obscurity while Stefano and Marco received credit for her work. He'd always assumed it was enough to see her paintings praised and respected.

"You agreed to the arrangement knowing what the cost would be. It is the only way. Must we always argue about this?"

"I don't wish to argue, but I am going to ask you a favor. Please delay the showing. With Jacopo missing, it feels wrong to be hosting a gala and art exhibition. Delaying would also allow time for you to present me to the Guild first."

He took a breath and waited for his anger to subside before speaking. She didn't want an argument, so he wouldn't give her one.

"There will be no postponement. Messer de' Medici is a powerful and busy man who has made time to come to our exhibition. He has already invited prominent artists and guests. Half of the Florentine elite have accepted our invitation, not to mention patrons from all over Europe, who are traveling here now. The showing will take place as scheduled, but I promise to discuss presenting you to the Guild once it's over."

She stiffened and looked at him with eyes of stone. "I understand, Maestro. I won't mention it again."

"Please, Celeste, you must see why your request is unreasonable."

"I said, I understand. The topic is closed."

Filippo came in with his food, so he let the matter drop. They ate in silence for several minutes, until he said, "How long until the Peter is ready?"

"It's finished."

He looked up at her in surprise. She'd been struggling to paint since Jacopo disappeared, and he'd lost hope of her finishing the work in time for the showing.

"That's wonderful, my love. You've pulled off a phenomenal feat this past year. Take a much-deserved rest until the exhibition. Spend time with the girls."

"Yes, Luciano."

He ignored her stony reply and said, "Messer Rosso mentioned seeing you in the piazza with Veronica and Marco this afternoon. What were you doing in town?"

She eyed him for a moment before lowering her knife to her plate. "I hadn't planned to tell you this, but I don't wish to lie. I was stopping Veronica from meeting Duccio Zani. He said he wanted to take her for a stroll on the piazza. Helena alerted us in time to prevent it."

He jumped to his feet and knocked his plate to the floor. "He what?"

"Marco spoke to him. He wants to ask for her hand but knows you'll refuse. Veronica is determined to marry him."

Filippo bent down to clean up the spilled food, so Luciano moved to the fireplace and leaned on the mantle. "How much more trouble do I have to endure from your family?"

"Not just you. I'm suffering as well."

"Forgive me. I know you are. A match between Duccio and Veronica would be disastrous. His father tells me the boy is lazy and cares nothing for the family legacy. He hoped to rely on Duccio to help rebuild the family estates, but he has no interest. Alberto plans to name his second son as heir. Duccio will get nothing and be forced to make his own way."

Celeste sighed and relaxed against her chair. "I agree with you on this, but I'm at a loss for what to do. I won't let you force Veronica to marry against her will, and she believes she is in love. Should we allow her to marry this boy and live with the consequences?"

"Is that what you wish for her future?"

"Does it matter what I want?"

He turned to face her. "Of course, it does, but there is another way. We could send her to the convent until she learns to behave herself. She'll soon forget this boy."

"And you believe that would bring her happiness?"

"Eventually, yes. She's just a girl, too young to know her own heart."

"She's the age I was when we met."

"Veronica isn't you. There was a depth and maturity to you she'll never possess. She reminds me more of Isabella. That's why I'm certain that a match with Duccio will fail. The life Duccio could offer would never satisfy Veronica."

She moved her tray aside and got to her feet. "She's promised to stay away from him until after the exhibition. I've asked Livia and Helena to keep a closer eye on her. Maybe the incident today scared Duccio from his designs on Veronica. There are plenty of eligible maidens in Florence."

He took her hand and said, "I pray you're right. We just need to survive these next two weeks. Jacopo will come home, Veronica will change her mind, and life will return to normal. All will be well. Trust me."

He smiled with more optimism than he felt. They'd avoided one disaster that day, but with Veronica's childish stubbornness and Jacopo on the run, God alone knew what loomed on the horizon.

CHAPTER TWENTY-SEVEN

*T*he day of the exhibition had dawned gray and damp to match Celeste's mood. A month had passed with no sign of Jacopo, and Veronica had rarely left her room since the incident with Duccio. She had refused to cooperate with the seamstress in fittings for her gown for the gala until Celeste told her Duccio would be there. Marco was so anxious about the exhibition that he was having trouble keeping food down and spent his time hiding out in the workshop.

If that weren't trouble enough, when Celeste got up to start her day, a violent wave of nausea overcame her. Praying it was from the fish she'd eaten for dinner, she fell onto the pillows and asked an elated Livia to bring her remedy of wine and herbs. When her stomach settled enough that she could stand without being sick, she dressed and went to check on the twins.

Cristina had started with a fever three days earlier and wasn't improving. Celeste instructed Lapa to separate her from Angela, but the girls cried so much at being parted that she had to reunite them in the nursery.

Angela was coughing when Celeste had gone to her after dinner the previous night and felt feverish when Celeste picked her up that morning. She wanted nothing more than to spend the day in the nursery cuddling her precious girls but knew Luciano would never agree. He needed her at his side.

She tore herself away from her ailing daughters around noon and went to reassure Marco. He was on his bed looking gray and miserable, making her wonder if they were all suffering from the same ailment.

She dipped a cloth in cold water and placed it on his forehead. "You look as miserable as I feel. Are you ill?"

He sat up and shook his head. "It's just nerves. The only thing that will cure me is putting this day behind us."

She handed him some wine and cheese from his table. "This might help."

He took a long draught of wine but refused the cheese. "I'd rather have bread. How are my nieces this morning?"

"Cristina is slightly better, but Angela is worse. Lapa assures me it's just a childhood fever, and they'll both soon be running in the garden. I pray she's right. This is going to be a long night."

She sank onto the bed, and Marco rested his hand on her shoulder. "Here I am, only thinking of myself when you have genuine concerns. How's Luciano today? He hasn't been to the workshop."

"He's gone to supervise the preparations for the exhibition. Portia and Paolo arrived late last night and are helping Elisabetta oversee the gala. I'm going to spend the afternoon with the girls until I have to dress." She bowed her head, too ashamed to look him in the eye. "I'm sorry I didn't have the courage to keep you from getting dragged into Luciano's plan. It was never my intention. I should have refused to go along with this from the beginning."

"Please, don't apologize, and don't waste your worries on me, sister. I also had the chance to refuse. The wine and your visit were all the medicine I need. I shall get off this bed, stop feeling sorry for myself and go to work as usual." He stood and offered her his hand. "Go tend to my nieces. I'll see you tonight."

"I don't deserve your kindness, but I'm grateful. This will soon be behind us, then we can start afresh. Until tonight, brother."

CELESTE WATCHED the glorious city of Florence glide by as she rode to the exhibition with Portia, Paolo, and Veronica. She'd dreamed of this night for years. Now that it had arrived, her heart was torn between the nursery and the gallery. Cristina's health was much improved, but Angela's was worse. The physician had promised not to leave her side until Celeste returned, but Portia still had to drag her to the carriage. The physician and Lapa gave her assurances that Angela would recover fully, but Celeste was still sick with worry.

As if reading her thoughts, Portia squeezed her hand and smiled. "Angela is a hearty little lamb. She's in capable hands. She'll be skipping in the garden before you know it. Put her from your thoughts and focus on what lies ahead." She pointed to the torches lining the drive to the gallery. "Look what your husband has accomplished."

Luciano had spent the past year converting an old storage warehouse into a gallery near the Ponte Vecchio. Celeste had visited twice during the construction, but Luciano had kept her away as it neared completion. She leaned out the window and gazed in amazement at the transformation. A stone archway framed the delicately carved wooden doors, and sculptures from the palazzo decorated the beautifully landscaped grounds.

When they arrived, Luciano lifted her from the carriage and whisked her to a private corner away from the burgeoning crowd.

With a sweep of his arm, he said, "Take in your triumph, Celeste. It was your brush that created these masterpieces. This is the culmination of our years together. I remember those dark days when I thought this impossible, yet here we are. I couldn't be prouder of you."

Seeing her artwork magnificently adorning the gallery walls left her breathless, proud, and desperately yearning to claim ownership of her creations.

"It hardly seems real," she said with tears glistening in her eyes. "I have dreamed of this moment for so long." She tenderly pressed her hand to his cheek. "Though I can't claim credit for my work tonight, I know that day will come soon. Tonight is only the beginning. You're the one who has believed in me and made this possible. I owe it all to you."

He pulled her close and brushed his lips to her ear. "We achieved it together."

As he took her arm and led her toward the dais at the front of the room, she spotted Marco coming toward them dressed in a simple but elegant green tunic. He beamed as he stepped before them and bowed with a flourish.

"This is stunning, Maestro. I've never seen anything to compare. I'm so proud of you, sister."

The smell of wine was heavy on his breath, and Celeste felt a twinge of concern. Marco rarely drank to excess, and they needed him to be at his best for their plan to succeed.

She touched his arm and said, "How much have you had to drink?"

"Don't worry, Celeste. I only had enough to give me the courage to leave the workshop."

His speech wasn't slurred, and he seemed steady enough on his feet. "Very well, but no more wine until we arrive at the gala."

He winked and said, "As you command, madam."

Luciano wrapped an arm around Marco's shoulder. "Wait with Paolo and Portia until I'm ready to introduce you. I'll signal when it's time to come forward. You remember my instructions on what to say?"

"Yes, Maestro. I will not disappoint you."

"Good man. Now, go."

Marco hurried off, and Luciano escorted Celeste toward the line of guests waiting to greet them.

"So, it begins," he whispered, then bowed to a foreign nobleman with pale skin and gray eyes who Celeste had never met.

She struggled to quiet her churning emotions while they welcomed the unending stream of visitors to the exhibition. She recognized some faces, but most were strangers and foreigners. The thought of them viewing and judging her work was intimidating. She became faint and had to grip Luciano's arm to steady herself. She was about to ask for a moment to sit when Lorenzo de' Medici's retinue arrived.

Celeste had only seen the banker and ruler of Florence once from a distance. While there had been constant opposition to Medici rule through the years, the family still had many ardent supporters. Luciano had always favored Lorenzo for his passionate support for the arts and literature. He had transformed Florence into one of the most revered and envied cities in the world. If what Messer de' Medici saw that night impressed him, it could change their lives forever.

He approached with his wife, Clarice Orsini, a powerful but pious noblewoman whom Celeste greatly admired. She had traveled extensively throughout Europe and had even served as Lorenzo's ambassador on occasion. The heights she had achieved gave Celeste hope for all women.

After Luciano and Lorenzo greeted each other, Lorenzo patted Luciano's back and said, "I've been looking forward to this night, Vicente. I'm always on the lookout for promising new talent."

"Then you will be pleased tonight, sir," Luciano said. "Allow me to present my wife, Signora Celeste Gabriele."

Celeste curtsied, and Lorenzo said, "So, this is the Venetian beauty Vicente brought home to Florence. Your reputation does you credit."

"You flatter me, sir. It's my honor to meet you. My husband speaks highly of you."

"I'm grateful for his loyalty. Luciano tells me your brother is an artistic genius. I'm excited to see his work."

"We hope you won't be disappointed, Messer de' Medici."

Luciano and Lorenzo walked off ahead while Madonna Orsini took her arm, and they followed at a slower pace. Celeste was honored to have such an important woman at her side but wished she would move faster so they could hear what Lorenzo was saying.

"Your brother's paintings are quite remarkable," Clarice said. "He is as talented as your husband says."

"Thank you, madam. Are you as interested in art as your husband?"

"Art and literature are Lorenzo's passions, and I've learned a great deal from him, but I don't have the eye he does. Do you know much of art, Signora?"

Celeste turned to hide her smile. I could write volumes on what I know of art, she thought, but said, "Yes, Luciano has taught me almost from the moment we met. I can say the study of art is my passion as well, though I'm not at liberty to pursue it as I would wish."

"It can be difficult for women to follow their aspirations. I will ask Lorenzo to speak to your husband about allowing you more freedom."

"That's kind of you, Madonna, but it isn't Luciano who hinders me. It's the attitudes and restrictions placed on women by society at large. But you have overcome many of those restrictions."

Clarice nodded and gave her a knowing smile. Celeste turned her attention to Luciano and Lorenzo, who were standing on the dais talking. By the time they reached them, Luciano was calling for quiet, and Lorenzo took his seat of honor behind him.

Luciano motioned for Marco to join him on the dais. As her brother walked to the front of the audience, Celeste's heart pounded, and she again felt faint. Clarice had rejoined Lorenzo, so Celeste was left with no one to lean on for support. She searched the crowd and found Portia standing before Luciano in front of the eager crowd.

She pushed through the crush of people and stepped to where Luciano could see her. He winked and dipped his chin to acknowledge her, then said, "Honored guests, I'm sure you are all eager to meet the creator of these exceptional works of art. Please, let me present my brother-in-law, Marco Gabriele."

Tears spilled onto Celeste's cheeks when the audience cheered and applauded. She pictured herself at Luciano's side instead of Marco and again wished for the day when she would be the one receiving credit for her creations.

Marco bowed and was about to speak when someone at the back shouted, "Liar!"

Luciano's eyes widened in shock, and he said, "Jacopo?"

When the crowd turned to see who had spoken, Jacopo climbed onto a chair and raised his arm.

"My name is Jacopo Gabriele, brother to Marco, and until lately, apprentice to Maestro Vicente. I'm here to expose a fraud being perpetrated tonight."

Marco moved to the edge of the dais and cried, "Don't listen to him. Stop this now, Jacopo."

Jacopo ignored him and continued. "These paintings are not Marco's but my sister's, Celeste Gabriele. She is the actual artist. Luciano has been selling her work as that of other artists for years, first Stefano de Calvio and now my brother."

The audience erupted into an angry roar and swung around, facing Luciano. Messer de' Medici went to Luciano's side and lifted his hands to quiet the chaos. Putting a hand on Luciano's shoulder, he said, "Be honest with me, friend. Is what Jacopo says true?"

Before he could answer, Celeste climbed onto the dais and stepped between the men. She curtsied, then straightened her shoulders and raised her chin.

"It is true, Messer de' Medici. I have been Luciano's protégé almost from the moment we met." She gestured toward her artwork, gracing the walls. "These paintings are the work of my hands."

Lorenzo searched her eyes for a moment, then said, "Signora, did Marco assist you with your work in any way?"

"No, Messer. I had no assistant, no apprentices. This is my work alone."

He gave a quick nod, then eyed Luciano with disappointment before turning with a sweep of his cape and storming out of the gallery. Clarice Orsini caught Celeste's eye and gave her a look of sadness and understanding before following after her husband.

Marco leaped from the dais and dove through the clamoring crowd to get to Jacopo. He knocked him from the chair and drew his knife. The crowd parted as Celeste screamed and chased after him. She reached her brothers as Jacopo scrambled to his feet and placed his hand on his sheath.

Marco's hand trembled as he aimed the knife at Jacopo's chest. "Why have you betrayed us, brother? Do you hate us so much after all we've done for you?"

Jacopo let go of the sheath and slowly raised his hands. He loosened his tunic to bare his chest, then said, "Go ahead. Strike, Marco, but first, deny that what I've spoken is true."

Marco slowly lowered his knife and let it fall to the floor, then sank to his knees. Jacopo sneered at him in disgust before turning on his heel and walking out into the night.

Luciano shouted for his men to clear the gallery. They ushered the astonished guests out, and soon only the family remained. Celeste helped Marco to his feet, then went to join Luciano and Portia. Luciano's sisters and their husbands had formed a half-circle around them.

Elisabetta moved closer to Celeste, taking quick, shallow breaths. "This is your fault. You Gabrieles have shamed the noble Vicente name. You are nothing but filthy gutter rats." Then, in a flash, she raised her hand and struck Celeste hard across the cheek.

When she raised her arm to strike again, Luciano caught her wrist. "How dare you assault my wife? Get back," he hissed. Elisabetta obeyed in shocked silence. "This fiasco is all my doing. Celeste and Marco begged me not to do it, but I refused to listen. I forced them to go along with the conspiracy, though Celeste pleaded for me to present her to the Guild. I was too selfish and arrogant to listen. I wanted to hide from the world that my wife's talents have far surpassed mine."

"Luciano, how could you?" Elisabetta whispered. "We'll be outcasts in Florence after this."

"I don't understand," Paolo said. "Aren't you all overreacting? Luciano just told a little lie. Marco is Celeste's brother. It's all still in the family."

Luciano shook his head. "No, Paolo. What I've done is a crime. Florentines take their art seriously, and the Guilds have strict rules and harsh punishments. This violation won't be taken lightly, and punishment may be severe."

"Then, why take the risk?"

"The Guild never would have admitted Celeste, but the world needs to see her genius. Few artists in a generation come along with artistry to equal hers. Is it her fault she was born a woman?" He slowly looked around the room, then said, "It's over now. Go home, sisters, and give me time to repair the damage. This storm will pass."

Elisabetta, Angelica, and Diana turned with their husbands and silently filed out into the darkness.

Celeste put a hand to the stinging welt on her cheek, trying to ignore the greater pain twisting in her gut. "How could Jacopo betray us this way?" she whispered. "Why such anger and hatred? All we've done is love him, even when he didn't deserve it."

Luciano sighed and avoided her eyes. "Jacopo isn't the only one who betrayed us tonight."

"Who do you mean, Luciano?"

He shook his head. "Go home to our daughters, Celeste. Leave me to clean up this mess."

She watched him cross the room and order his apprentices to box up her paintings. Marco retrieved his knife and left without a word. She didn't resist when Portia put a hand on her elbow to guide her toward the door, with Veronica and Paolo following quietly behind.

She was numb as she slumped into the seat of the carriage, trying to fathom how it had all gone so horribly wrong in an instant. Jacopo was alive but had only resurfaced to ruin them. What would the cost of Jacopo's revelation be? Her paintings would be locked away, hidden from the world. The doors of Florentine society would be closed to her forever. Her hope for a future as an artist had evaporated like smoke on the breeze. Her only remaining joy was her darlings waiting at home. For the present, that would have to be enough.

CELESTE WOKE to another dreary dawn after a restless night cradling Angela in her arms. She gently pressed her palm to the child's forehead and was elated to find that her fever had broken, and her cough had quieted. It was the one bright spot in the darkness that had descended upon them. She stretched her aching arms and handed Angela to Lapa. When she stood to go, a wave of nausea washed over her, and she vomited into the basin. Lapa eyed her with a gentle smile but said nothing.

She shuffled to her chamber to wash and change and sent Livia for the wine and herb remedy. Once she was dressed, she went in search of Luciano but didn't find him in the palazzo. Not wanting to bother him in the workshop, she walked to the gardens in search of peace. Thankfully, the servants had cleared away all signs of the gala, so she didn't have to face the painful reminder of what might have been.

After settling on a bench near the pond, she watched a mother duck guide her chicks across the water. What would she have given for their simple, carefree life at that moment? She placed her hands on her stomach, remembering that soon she'd have a new little chick to love. Maybe she would give Luciano a son to make up for all they had lost.

She felt the churning again and leaned over to be sick on the shrubbery.

"I know what that means," Portia said, as she came up behind her. "How long have you known?"

Celeste wiped her mouth and dropped onto the bench. "Only since yesterday morning, but I'd hoped it was just from eating bad fish."

"Apparently not. Speaking of food, when was the last time you ate?"

"I had a bit of cheese and grapes before we left for the exhibition. I had planned to eat at the gala."

"We need to get you some breakfast. Where is that Livia when you need her?"

"She offered to bring a tray, but I told her I wanted to be alone."

"You have that growing baby to feed now, or are you unhappy with your news?"

"I've hardly had a moment to absorb it in all the chaos. What's going to happen to us, Aunt? We're ruined."

"Nonsense. So, you won't achieve fame and fortune as you'd hoped. Is that the end of the world? Leave it to Luciano to repair the damage." She put her hand under Celeste's chin. "You have much to be grateful for, my child, and soon, you'll have this new little one to love."

Celeste gave her a weak smile, wishing it were that easy, but she said, "Thank you for reminding me. Let's get that breakfast."

As they started back to the house, Helena came running toward them, clutching a piece of paper. When she reached them, she curtsied and held out a letter.

Celeste took it and broke the seal. "What is this, Helena?"

"Signorina Gabriele left it in her room. She and her belongings were missing when I went to wake her this morning,"

"What has that girl done now? Please read it to me, Celeste," Portia said.

Celeste slowly unfolded the letter, ignoring the dread growing in her gut.

My Dearest Sister,

I have gone off to marry Duccio. After the events of last night, I saw no point in staying. The almighty Luciano Vicente has been knocked from his throne and lost the right to rule my life. His choices for a suitable match will want nothing to do with this family, so I left to be with the one I love.

I pressured Marco into signing the marriage contracts in Luciano's place. Duccio's father says Luciano cannot legally withhold my dowry. He's drawing up the necessary papers. They will arrive in a matter of days.

I love you, sister, and I am grateful for all you and Luciano have done for me, but I do not expect we will see each other again in this life. I wish you the greatest happiness and hope you soon recover from what Luciano has done. You truly are an incredible artist.

With my deepest love,

Veronica

The letter fell from Celeste's hand and floated onto the damp grass before a gust of wind lifted it into the pond. Helena started after it, but Celeste motioned for her to stop. As she watched another member of her family sink away from her life, her legs gave out, and she crumpled to the ground. Portia and Helena went to her side and helped her to her feet.

"I can get the Signora to the house," Portia told Helena. "Have Livia take a tray to your mistress' chamber, then meet us there so we can decide what to do." Helena ran up the lawn to the house while Portia supported Celeste with her arm around her waist. "You'll feel better once you've eaten."

"My Veronica is gone, Aunt, just when we had become so close. Now, I will never see her again. She might as well be dead."

"So much doom and gloom, Celeste. You must snap out of this. This is just more of Veronica's theatrics. I'll write to Duccio's mother today and tell her you're expecting an invitation to the wedding. She won't care about that nonsense at the gallery when it means a chance to have a Vicente at her son's wedding."

Celeste hadn't thought of that, but she feared Luciano would never accept Veronica's marriage after what she'd done, though he was in no position to judge. Celeste would just have to insist that he allow her to attend the wedding.

As they reached the stairs to her chamber, Marco called out to her from the sala.

Portia helped lower her onto the steps and said, "Let me see to this. Stay there. I don't want you tumbling down the stairs."

Celeste gave her a weak smile. "I have no intention of going anywhere."

Portia hurried off but returned in a few moments with Marco in tow.

When he saw her bent over on the steps, he rushed to her side. "Are you ill? Is it the fever the twins have?"

"What your sister has is not infectious," Portia said. "She's with child."

Marco gave her a quick hug. "That's the only good news I've heard in days. Congratulations, sister. May you bear a strong and healthy son."

"Thank you, brother. How's your head today?"

"Pounding, but that's the least of my troubles."

"No more than you deserve. What is it you want to tell me? Is it about Veronica?"

He glanced at Portia, then shook his head. "No, but Portia told me about her letter. Luciano knows, too. He doesn't hold it against me."

"I don't blame you either. She left you no choice. It was better than her running off with Duccio and living in sin. What's your news then?"

"I'm leaving, too, sister."

Celeste reached for the handrail and pulled herself to her feet. "Leaving? And where are you off to? Somewhere to lie low until this chaos blows over?"

He shook his head. "When I became concerned about Luciano's insistence on carrying out his ruse, I made other arrangements in case they discovered our subterfuge. I applied for entrance into the Bellinis' workshop in Venice and sent some of my paintings. I received word this morning that they've accepted me. I hate to abandon you at such a time, but I'm leaving today."

Celeste clasped his hand in hers. "The Bellinis'? That's one of the most renowned workshops in the world. This is a great honor, and I'm elated for you. Do you have money for the journey? Are you going alone?"

"I'm traveling with a caravan of silk merchants returning to Venice. Luciano was generous enough to provide me with funds for the journey. Come to Venice as soon as you can, sister. This isn't goodbye."

"It won't be for some time with a baby coming, but until then, I'll listen for rumors of the promising new Venetian artist, Marco Gabriele."

"And I will look for Celeste Gabriele, the most talented artist of our day."

With a hug and a kiss on the cheek, her brother was gone like all her siblings before him.

As Portia helped her up the stairs, she said, "My family is melting away like a spent candle. Promise you'll never leave me, Aunt."

Portia clicked her tongue. "Just try to get rid of me."

CHAPTER TWENTY-EIGHT

Celeste's strength returned after a hearty lunch and a satisfying nap, but her mood hadn't improved. She hadn't seen Luciano since leaving the gallery and was desperate to speak with him. Aside from needing to tell him about the baby and discuss Marco and Veronica's departures, she needed to know what to expect in the aftermath of Jacopo's betrayal. She sent the page Berto with a message for him to meet her in the studio.

She went to her beloved sanctuary to wait. The morning clouds had lifted, and sunlight bathed the studio, but her chest was tight with a weight of sadness that threatened to crush her. Her tools lay where she had left them two days earlier. As she ran her fingers over the table, her thoughts traveled back to the first time she cradled a brush in her small room at the Benetto palazzo. It was the day she sprang to life. Now, that life was ending.

Luciano quietly stepped through the doorway but stopped on the other side of the room. A small cry escaped Celeste's lips as she ran to him, but he stiffened when she wrapped her arms around his waist. He gently pushed her away.

"What is it, my love? Do you fear I blame you for what happened?"

"Blame me? How can I be at fault when it was Jacopo's betrayal and yours that has ruined us?"

His words stunned her like a splash of icy water. She stepped back and bumped the table. The box of brushes crashed to the floor and scattered across the tile.

"I don't understand, Luciano. I've never betrayed you."

"You had the chance to save us when Lorenzo asked if Marco had assisted you. All you had to do was answer yes. With Jacopo's reputation as a drunkard and braggart, who would have believed his word against yours? But you told him the truth out of your hunger for fame and adoration. You've ruined us."

Celeste began to tremble. "How dare you accuse me? This disaster is your creation, as you admitted at the gallery. How could you have expected me to lie to Lorenzo de' Medici's face? The Guild would have investigated Jacopo's claims and uncovered the truth. Our situation would have been far worse."

"You can't know that, but there's no re-stopping the bottle. You got what you wanted."

"You believe my vanity and desire for praise moved me to reveal the truth? Perhaps those are your cravings, not mine. Marco and I tried to warn you, but you refused to listen. I did what I believed right and best for this family, with no thought to myself, as I have always done. If you can't see that, then I have nothing else to say."

Luciano glared at her with eyes hard as flint, then turned on his heel and stormed out of the studio. She stared at the spot where he'd stood, taking rapid, shallow breaths. Of all the consequences she had predicted, Luciano turning against her was not on the list. She stepped over the spilled brushes and left the studio, planning never to return.

⁓

CELESTE WENT in search of Portia and found her with Tomaso and the twins in the nursery. She gave each of her girls a kiss, then said, "When are you planning to leave?"

"We had no plans. With your new condition and the family in

346

chaos, I'm willing to stay as long as you need me."

"Is tomorrow morning too soon to leave?"

"This morning, you were begging me not to abandon you. Now, you're pushing me out the door."

She crossed her arms and looked away. "The girls and I are going with you. I can no longer stay here."

Portia patted the chair next to her. She reluctantly sat but kept her eyes lowered. "If you're leaving to hide from Elisabetta and the Florentine gossips, don't bother. What do you care about their opinion of you?"

"I care nothing. I'm not leaving for them. I'm leaving my husband." Portia opened her mouth to speak, but Celeste raised a hand to stop her. "I don't wish to speak of it yet. I'll explain on the way to Lucca. For now, find Paolo and tell him to prepare. I want to be on the road by sunup."

LUCIANO MARCHED across the lawn to his workshop and threw open the doors. "Everyone put down your materials and go. Don't return until I send for you." He tossed a leather pouch filled with coins on the table. "Marco is on his way to Venice, never to return. Antonio, distribute the wages in his place."

He strode to his office and slammed the door. How could Celeste have dared contradict him? He'd expected her to grovel and plead for forgiveness. What had happened to the young Celeste, who had once refused to sit in his presence? What kind of woman had he created?

He poured himself a goblet of wine and dropped into a chair. His life was spinning out of control, and he couldn't deny bearing some responsibility, but Celeste's constant insistence that he present her to the Guild had come from a place of ignorance. She understood nothing of the world of men. Had he been wrong to encourage her to walk a path that existed neither in her world nor his? He'd done it with the best of intentions, but the art world wasn't ready for Celeste Gabriele.

He glanced across the room to where her first work of the canals of Venice hung. He'd always kept it close to remind him of the day he discovered her genius. Putting down his wine, he walked to the painting and ran his fingers over the ridges and valleys in the strokes. An image of her looking to him with hope glistening in her eyes flashed into his mind.

He pulled the painting from its nail and clutched it to his chest as he sank to his knees. What had he done? She was his heart and his life. She'd done nothing but tell the truth. How could he have punished her so harshly? He climbed to his feet and lovingly replaced the painting. He had to get to her and repair the damage he'd done, hoping this time it wasn't eternally too late.

There was a knock at the door as he reached for the handle. He swung it open to find Berto holding a letter. He bowed and pressed it into Luciano's hand before scurrying away. Luciano glanced at the folded paper and recognized the seal. It was from the Tribunale di Mercanzia. His gut tightened, and his hands shook as he broke the seal and slowly unfolded the paper. They were summoning him to appear before the Guild tribunal in two days.

He pulled his cloak from the chair and ran out to order his driver to prepare the carriage. He had to speak with his legal counselors and had no time to lose.

LUCIANO BATTED Filippo's hand away and finished lacing his tunic. He was in a foul mood after having only two hours of sleep. He and his counselors had worked long into the night, constructing a defense that might save his workshop and reputation. He'd been sleeping in his spare room so as not to disturb Celeste and give her space until he could apologize properly. He was still anxious to beg her forgiveness for the pain he'd caused, but that would have to wait until after the tribunal. When all was ready, he descended the stairs and went to face his fate.

Luciano arrived at the Tribunale di Mercanzia and bowed to the panel of judges seated in a semicircle at the head of the room. It disappointed him to see Lorenzo de' Medici sitting at a separate table near the front and assumed they had called him as a witness. It was not unexpected, but Luciano had hoped the great man would be too busy for such an insignificant matter.

The judge seated at the center of the panel called the hearing to order and asked Luciano to step before them.

"Signore Luciano Vicente, you face grievous charges today. Before us, we have complaints from twenty parties, stating that you knowingly misrepresented the artist of certain works of art sold to them. We also have statements from guests in attendance at your art exhibition two days ago, attesting that your wife admitted to these charges. If you are found guilty, the punishments for these egregious acts include repayment of proceeds from the sale of these fraudulent works, permanent banishment from the Guilds, a prohibition on the sale of your personal works of art, and closure of your workshop. How do you answer the charges?"

Luciano bowed, then proudly faced the panel. "Honored Signores, I do not deny the charges, but I offer the following in my defense. For you to understand the rationale for my actions, I must first share the history of my association with my wife, Celeste Gabriele."

Luciano withdrew a leather-bound journal from the satchel tied at his waist and began to read the story of his journey with his beloved Celeste. He read of the moment he discovered her rare and remarkable talents, told them of taking her on as his protégé, then continued on to explain how their marriage came to be. He ended by telling them of the completion of her training. The judges listened with rapt attention to his astounding tale.

When he finished, he returned the journal to his bag and gestured for his two apprentices seated with the audience to retrieve a large cloth-covered painting and easel from a corner on the far side of the room. They carried it to the front and set it next to where Luciano stood.

"To understand my actions that followed, you must comprehend my motivations. I present one of Signora Gabriele's most recent works as evidence."

He removed the cloth to reveal what he considered her most brilliant painting. Some judges gasped, and the chief judge moved closer to inspect the painting.

He studied it in silence for several moments, then whispered, "Stunning."

The work was entitled The Serene Virgin and Child. It was oil on canvas and featured Mary seated on a flower-covered hillside near a stream. She held Jesus on her lap as angels looked down on them from above. When Luciano first viewed the painting, he felt he was staring into the soul of the Mother of God. It moved him so deeply that he'd often gone alone to Celeste's studio in the night to stare at it for hours.

"Signora Gabriele created this work without assistants or apprentices in two months. I hope you now see why I pressured my head apprentice, under threat of discrediting him and casting him out of my workshop, into posing as the artist of my wife's paintings."

He paused while the judges mumbled to each other. When they quieted, the chief judge signaled for Luciano to continue.

"When Stefano left my workshop and returned to his home country three years ago, I forced my brother-in-law to step into his place. The exhibition two nights ago was the first time I presented my wife's work under his name, against his and her vigorous objections. My wife had pleaded with me for years to present her for admittance into the Guild, but I refused, knowing her petition would be rejected."

"Rightly so," one judge mumbled.

Luciano ignored the comment and said, "My wife is a woman born before her time. God infused her with a divine talent to bless this world with art and beauty. Knowing Florence was not prepared to accept her as an artist in her own right, I took it upon myself to find another way to bring her creations to light. I carried out these actions with the best of intentions. In doing so, I have disgraced my beloved wife and her family, the Guilds, and the Vicente name."

"Your wife's extraordinary talent is not under question here today,

Signore, but your violations against Guild law are. Do you have so little disregard for the Guild's ruling body that you refused to allow them to make a wise and fair decision on your wife's worthiness for admittance?"

Luciano hesitated a moment before saying, "Despite what appears to be blatant contempt for Guild leadership, anyone acquainted with me knows I have great respect for their laws and governance. I took it upon myself to judge that they would refuse to consider my wife's application."

The chief judge sighed and clasped his hands. "Do you have any other evidence or witnesses to present to this tribunal?"

"I do not, sir."

Lorenzo de' Medici stood and raised his hand. "I ask permission to address the tribunal."

The judges stared at him in surprise, but the chief judge dipped his chin and said, "Granted, Messer de' Medici."

The only sound as Lorenzo walked to the center of the room was the faint scratching of the clerk's quill on parchment.

He bowed to the judges, then faced the audience and said, "I have known Signore Vicente for many years as an honorable and exemplary leader in this republic. While I do not condone his actions, I plead with this court to take his contributions to our community into account. Consider the fate of those in his employ before passing sentence. I ask of leniency as too harsh a judgment could have far-reaching, detrimental effects on our beloved city and the art world at large. I entreat you to pass a just and fair sentence."

He returned to his seat and gave Luciano an almost imperceptible nod.

"We're honored that you would condescend to attend this hearing and address us, Messer de' Medici. We will take your statement into consideration. I now adjourn this hearing for three hours while we decide your sentence, Signore Vicente. Please return then to receive our judgment."

The judges stood, and the audience followed in mass, then shuffled out of the room. Several of Luciano's friends and colleagues of many years avoided his gaze as they passed. He shook his head with sadness, then covered Celeste's painting with the cloth and lovingly carried it to his carriage.

He'd decided to use the time until the tribunal reconvened to meet with his steward and accountant. If the judges ordered him to refund the earnings from Celeste's paintings, it could cost him hundreds, if not thousands of florins. They needed to dig out the bills of sale and draw up the necessary bank withdrawals. It would be no easy or happy task. Though his holdings were extensive, the sentence would be a blow to his financial stability. Contrary to the accusations he'd flung at Celeste, he had no one to blame but himself.

THE HOURS FLEW by before the sands in the hourglass ran out, and it was time to return to the Tribunale di Mercanzia. His steward and accountant assured him that his situation wouldn't be as dire as he'd feared unless they forced him to close the workshop. He prayed on his way to the tribunal that the judges had heeded Lorenzo's plea.

His heart pounded as he stood before the judges, awaiting his sentence. The panel of men staring back at him would dictate the course of his future.

The chief judge stood and said, "This case is more straightforward than most that come before this tribunal, yet it has more far-reaching implications as Messer de' Medici reminded us this morning. We took this into account as we decided the sentence."

Luciano bowed. "I am grateful, sir."

The judge nodded. "Signore Vicente, we order you to return all proceeds from the sale of your wife's artwork to the current complainants and all complaints that come before this tribunal in the future. Your Guild memberships are revoked immediately, and we prohibit you from selling any artwork created by you from this day into perpetuity. On the wise advice of Messer de' Medici, we will allow your workshop to remain in operation. You may continue to instruct and support your apprentices, but you may not profit from their work, including that of Marco Gabriele."

"Marco Gabriele has left Florence, Signore, and is returning to his home country, permanently."

"We are glad to hear it. Though we cannot condone your actions, Signore Vicente, it saddens us that the world has lost a master artist today. You are a respected nobleman in this great city. We hope this experience will encourage you to continue to put your energies into guiding and supporting this city. This tribunal is adjourned."

Luciano held his head high as the crowd parted to let him pass. As he was about to step into his carriage, he felt a tap on his shoulder. He turned to find himself facing Lorenzo de' Medici. He held out his hand, and they gripped forearms.

"I offer my deepest thanks, Lorenzo. If not for your words this morning, my sentence would have been far more damaging. I am in your debt."

"I appreciate you saying so, but I did not do this for you. I did it for the sake of your current and future apprentices. I did it for this city and for the sake of art. Most of all, I did it for your innocent family, to protect them for any more suffering at your hand."

"I understand, and it is more than I deserve. I will tell my family and apprentices of your help today."

Lorenzo bowed and turned to go, then stopped and said, "I trust that it wasn't lost on you that the judges made no mention of your wife or the sale of her paintings during sentencing. Make of that what you will."

Luciano watched the great man as he walked to his carriage. The point had not been lost on him, but one question remained. Would Celeste be willing to carry on after what he had done to her? He climbed into the carriage, more concerned with facing his wife than he had been at standing before the tribunal. He prayed the damage he'd caused wasn't too great to repair but vowed to do all in his power to make it right.

~

CELESTE LEANED against the terrace railing and gazed over the tranquil hillsides and valleys of Lucca. Her days there had brought a morsel of peace, but she still felt cut loose from her moorings. She'd had no word from Luciano and refused to be the one to reach out to him. Her brothers and sisters were out of her life, and she was sure her friends in Florence had turned their backs on her. The divide between her and Luciano's sisters was too vast to bridge from a distance. Her only remaining loved ones were those surrounding her in Lucca.

Portia joined her on the terrace and sank into a chair with a sigh. "Having your nightly sulk, I see."

"Don't tease me, Aunt. I'm in no mood for it."

Portia swallowed a sip of wine before saying, "When are you in the mood these days?"

Celeste turned to face her. "What do you expect? My marriage is ending. My family has abandoned me. My career as an artist is nothing but a hopeless dream. Even the food I eat refuses to stay with me. I'd hoped after carrying the twins without trouble that my days of sickness were behind me."

"The nausea will pass soon. As for your other tragedies, Luciano can no more live without you than survive without air. He'll come riding in on his stallion at any moment, and all will be forgotten."

Celeste rolled her eyes. "If you believe that, you have a more active imagination than I do."

Portia ignored Celeste's comment and continued. "Your siblings haven't abandoned you. As I recall, you were the one who fled Florence. Jacopo may be lost to us for a time, but we'll visit Marco as soon as the baby is old enough to travel." She reached into the neckline of her dress and pulled out what looked like a letter. "I almost forgot to tell you about this."

Celeste shook her head. "Aren't you a little old to be hiding letters in your bodice, Aunt?"

Portia waved off her comment. "I received word from Duccio's mother today. She'd be honored for you to attend the wedding. It's in two weeks. She tells me Veronica will be a delightful daughter-in-law.

She can't be speaking of our Veronica. When has that girl ever been delightful?"

Celeste couldn't help but smile. Her aunt had a way of turning the end of the world into a garden party. "I suppose I should see the seamstress about a new gown, then. Mine are getting too snug."

"A good sign that your son is growing."

"As long as I'm not carrying another set of twins." She sat next to Portia and took her hand. "Thank you for your love and support these past days. I wouldn't have survived without you. Despite your optimism about Luciano, I'm terribly worried. Will this baby know his father? What if Luciano forces us to leave Lucca and packs us off to Venice?"

"Then, we'll go to Venice. Would that be the worst thing? It's our home. We have family there."

Her throat tightened, and tears stung in her eyes. "I can't survive without Luciano any more than he can without me. Even after everything, I love him with my whole soul."

"Then go to Florence and tell him."

Celeste crossed her arms and raised her chin. "No, he must come to me and apologize first."

"Then, that is what he'll do." Portia stood and tugged on Celeste's hand. "You hardly touched your dinner, and I am concerned about your health and the baby. Come have some broth and bread. You'll feel better."

CELESTE OPENED her eyes the next morning, feeling rested and ravenous. She'd slept peacefully for the first night since leaving Florence and was aching for the feel of a paintbrush in her hand. She ate a hearty breakfast of eggs, cheese, and fruit, then spent an hour playing with her daughters before heading to the studio.

Her Lucca studio was a third the size of the one in Florence, and the lighting wasn't as favorable, but working there reminded her of the pleasant year she'd spent preparing to marry Luciano. She had avoided setting foot there since returning to Lucca because she feared the memories would be too painful, but when she crossed the threshold, the room welcomed her home.

She hadn't planned to paint in Lucca but had brought along her materials if she changed her mind. They were still in the traveling case, so she lovingly unpacked them and set to work on a new project. As she stared at the blank sketching paper, clutching the charcoal in her fingers, she was only sure of one thing; this would be a work from her heart with no thought of pleasing anyone but herself. For the first time in her brief career, she'd create a painting no one else would ever see, and she was content with that.

She closed her eyes and let the image form in her mind. She blocked out all thoughts of Luciano, the child growing within her, and the upheaval from the exhibition. All that mattered was the story longing to be told by the stroke of her brush. Opening her eyes, she swept the charcoal across the paper with a renewed eagerness. She soon lost track of time, immersed in her familiar world of creation.

After what felt like mere moments, she heard a clap and someone calling out her name. She looked up to find Portia standing with a man she recognized from the exhibition. He was tall and pale with piercing gray eyes. Celeste set down her charcoal and wiped her hands on her smock as she stood to greet them.

"We've been searching the grounds for you," Portia said. "I didn't know you planned to work today."

While holding her gaze on the pale man, she said, "Neither did I."

The man smiled and bowed. Portia gestured towards him and said, "This is Count Sebastiaan van den Born from Amsterdam."

Celeste curtsied and said, "Yes, I remember you from the exhibition, sir. You're welcome to our home, but I'm sorry to disappoint you after traveling so far. My husband isn't here. He remained in Florence."

"I am not here for your husband, Signora," the count said in a thick Dutch accent. "It is you I am here to see."

Celeste wasn't sure how to respond. What could this foreign noble want with her? "Aunt Portia, please escort our guest to the sala. I'll join you in a moment."

Portia motioned for the count to follow, but he didn't move. Facing her, he said, "Madam, I wish to speak privately with your niece, if it is not too much trouble."

Portia glanced at Celeste, who gave a slight nod. "Very well, sir. I'll be in the sala if you need me, my dear."

As Portia reluctantly left her alone with him, Count van den Born walked to the worktable and shuffled through her sketches.

Without looking up, he said, "You are a most difficult person to find, madam. I went to your palazzo two days after the exhibition and was informed that you had left the city. I enquired into your whereabouts, but the doorman refused to share that information. He was quite protective of you."

"Yes, my husband's staff is very loyal. Did you ask to speak with Luciano?"

"I was told your esteemed husband was not available."

Celeste lowered herself onto a bench near the window and watched him continue to examine her sketches. "How did you find me, then?"

"Through my network of contacts in Florence. When I learned your location, I concluded my business and came here straight away. I am pleased to find you working. After the unfortunate events at the exhibition, I was unsure if you would wish to continue painting."

"As was I, but I don't paint for commissions or praise. Painting is my passion, maybe even my obsession. I apologize for what happened at the exhibition after you had traveled such a long way to attend."

"No need to apologize. As I said, I had other business to conduct in Florence." He looked up from the sketches and turned to face her. "Even with the incident at the exhibition, I do not regret attending."

Still confused by his presence, she said, "If I may ask, sir, why have you gone to so much trouble to find me?"

"For no other reason than to say that I am about to make you the most famous woman in Europe."

~

CELESTE CRADLED a bowl of broth while she contemplated whether her extraordinary encounter with Count van den Born had all been a dream. Portia had long gone to bed, but Celeste was too agitated to sleep. The path of her life had been a maze of unpredictable twists and turns, but this was one of the most unexpected and bittersweet. She took her last sip of broth, then nestled under the covers and ran her hand over Luciano's cold and empty side of the bed, fearing she was destined to continue that pathway alone.

She rolled onto her back with a sigh and stared at the ceiling. It was pointless to dwell on what had been. She needed to find her way forward. If Luciano had indeed deserted her, maybe Portia was right about returning to Venice. She would have to decide soon. If she were leaving Lucca for good, she would have to travel before her pregnancy was too far along.

She blew out the candle and breathed deeply to calm her churning emotions. As she drifted off, voices and footsteps in the hallway startled her awake. Not knowing the cause of the commotion, she arose quickly and grabbed her wrap without bothering to search for her slippers. Nothing mattered but getting to her babies.

As she reached for the door, it flew open, and Luciano's silhouette was framed in the doorway. After recovering from her shock, she was torn between running into his arms and slapping him across the face. Every fiber of her body cried out for him, but she forced herself to hold her ground.

"How dare you burst in here at this time of night without sending word you were coming? You frightened me nearly to death. I thought you were a robber, or worse."

Livia peeked around from behind him, "I tried to stop him, madam, but he pushed me aside before I could."

"Leave us," Luciano ordered.

As Livia scurried out, he swept Celeste into his arms and bathed her in kisses. She was so overjoyed that, for an instant, she forgot her hurt and anger and surrendered to him. Then, coming to her senses, she pushed against his chest and broke free of his hold.

When he started for her again, she raised her hands to stop him. "How dare you storm in here and make love to me as if nothing has happened? You caught me making plans to return to Venice permanently."

He lowered his arms and backed away. "No, my love, I understand how deeply I've hurt you. I behaved horribly in Florence and have hated myself since I spoke those cruel words. I'm here to beg your forgiveness."

Celeste stepped away from him. "I may forgive you, Luciano, but how can I ever trust you again?"

"Please, allow me to spend the rest of my days earning back your faith in me. I'll do whatever I must, my love. Life is meaningless without you."

"You can start by explaining where you've been, and how could you leave me suffering here with no word from you? We've had nothing but silence."

"The Tribunale di Mercanzia ordered me to appear three days after the exhibition. I spent long hours with my counselors in the intervening days preparing my defense. I rushed home to you once the tribunal delivered their ruling, only to find you'd left for Lucca. I wasn't aware you'd gone until that moment."

"That was nearly two weeks ago. It's only three days' travel to Lucca."

"They prohibited me from leaving Florence until I had complied with the tribunal's ruling. You'll understand once you've heard my story. I didn't write because I needed to apologize in person, but I'm sorry for not alerting you I was coming. I expected to arrive hours ago, but a storm delayed us on the road."

She took a breath to stall and gather her wits. If what Luciano had said was true, she was willing to listen, but not before sharing the news she'd desperately wanted to tell him for weeks.

"Before you say anything more, I have something to tell you."

Placing her hands on her stomach, she said, "You're going to be a father again."

Celeste didn't resist again when he pulled her into his arms. "This is more than I could have dreamed. I don't deserve such happiness after the pain I've caused." He stepped away and studied her face. "How is your health? Are you well?"

She gave a weak smile. "Better each day."

He led her to a chair by the fire, then sat facing her. "When will the child arrive?"

"Portia's midwife estimates five or six months." She grew quiet for a moment, then said, "There's more, Luciano."

"If it's about the Guild, our situation isn't as grave as we feared."

"No, it's not that. Do you remember the Dutch nobleman who attended the exhibition?"

Luciano eyed her in confusion. "You mean Count van den Born, the pale man with gray eyes."

"Yes, the very one."

"Certainly. The count is a renowned art patron and sponsor. He travels throughout Europe, buying and selling master artworks for elite clients. That's why I invited him to the exhibition."

"He was here today."

"In Lucca? Why? He could have visited me in Florence."

"He wasn't looking for you."

Celeste stood and went to her small writing table to retrieve a leather-bound roll of parchments. She handed it to Luciano and watched as he unrolled the bundle.

He studied the documents for several moments, then froze. "Celeste, this is a contract," he whispered. "Count van den Born is offering to become your patron."

"Yes, my love. He was so impressed with my work that he wishes to tour my paintings in Europe. All that matters to him is discovering exceptional art to share with the world. He believes we're moving into a new era where my work's quality will be judged above the fact that I'm a woman. He anticipates brilliant success."

Luciano sank back in the chair and stroked his beard. "This is extraordinary. After I brought this black stain on the Vicente name, I was certain I had destroyed any chance for your career as an artist. When the tribunal was over, Lorenzo de' Medici pointed out that the ruling excluded mention of you or your work. He told me to make of that what I would. I brushed his comment aside, thinking it no longer mattered."

She leaned against him and closed her eyes. "You would be wise to heed Lorenzo's advice. Luciano, will you sign the contract?"

"Only a fool would refuse an offer from Count van den Born, but this is about your road to greatness," he answered softly. "Do you see that this venture won't be without risk? Despite the count's assurances, others will oppose you. Not everyone is as enlightened as he claims. Is the world truly ready for Maestra Celeste Gabriele?"

Celeste stood and retied the bundle before placing it into Luciano's hands. "Well, my dear Maestro, there's only one way to know."

THE END

〜

The story continues...
DELICATE BRUSHSTROKES
The Master's Protégé Trilogy: **Book II**

〜

Enjoy reading **Shades of Brilliance?** Please take a moment to post a review with your favorite retailer. Much appreciated!

〜

- Follow Eleanor on BookBub
- Follow Eleanor on Goodreads

ABOUT THE AUTHOR

Eleanor Chance is a writer of award-winning suspense, thriller, and historical women's fiction. She cherishes books that influence her writing and her life. She hopes to create the same experience for readers and thrives on crafting tales of everyday superheroes. Her debut novel, Arms of Grace is a finalist in consideration for production by Wind Dancer Films, a silver medalist in the Readers' Favorite Awards, and a recipient of the B.R.A.G. Medallion. She also writes under the pen name E.A. Chance.

Eleanor has traveled the world and lived in five different countries. She currently resides in the Williamsburg, Virginia area with her husband and is the proud mother of four grown sons and Nana to one amazing grand-darling.

She loves connecting with readers! Contact here at:
www.elenorchance.com
vipclub@eleanorchance.com